USA TODAY BESTSELLING AUTHOR

Dale Mayer

SIMON SAYS... SWIM

A KATE MORGAN NOVEL

SIMON SAYS... SWIM (KATE MORGAN, BOOK 8)
Beverly Dale Mayer
Valley Publishing Ltd.

ISBN-13: 978-1-773368-06-1
Print Edition

Books in This Series

The Kate Morgan Series

Simon Says… Hide, Book 1

Simon Says… Jump, Book 2

Simon Says… Ride, Book 3

Simon Says… Scream, Book 4

Simon Says… Run, Book 5

Simon Says… Walk, Book 6

Simon Says… Forgive, Book 7

Simon Says… Swim, Book 8

Simon Says… Die, Book 9

About This Book

Detective Kate Morgan is stumped, trying to decide when a case is really a case and when it belongs on her desk or someone else's. She's homicide and this? … This is something else, right? Following up the leads doesn't help, only confuses the issue—until someone slips up or slips away *literally*.

Simon wakes, choking on water, drowning in the darkness of his night, struggling to understand what madness he is connecting to now. As usual, he has few answers, and the ones he does find make no sense. Add in a young man in desperate need of assistance—yet hiding something—has Simon caught up trying to help someone, who maybe doesn't want help in the first place.

As Kate works her way through the details of multiple cases—or *not* cases—the realization is worse than anyone had realized.

Sign up to be notified of all Dale's releases here!
https://geni.us/DaleNews

CHAPTER 1

Two Weeks Later, Second Week of November

DETECTIVE KATE MORGAN walked into the station, a bright smile on her face. She looked around at her team, who had gotten up on their feet to clap and to cheer. "What was it this time? Three days and three cases closed? We're on a roll," she crowed.

Immediately came high fives all around her. "Right, and we needed it. Damn, we needed it," Lilliana stated.

"Oh, we needed some quick successes, all right," Kate agreed. "Just so many open cases and more new ones happening all the time that it's almost impossible to feel anything but depressed."

"I know," Rodney agreed, coming up behind her, walking with the help of a cane.

She looked at him critically. "Are you back? How are you doing?"

"Oh, I'll survive," he replied, with a casual shrug, "and I'll probably walk with a limp for quite some time. That SOB got me good, and, thanks to that asshole, I'll suffer some for a time," he muttered. "Yet I'm damn glad to be alive."

It had been weeks since Kate had shot Peter while he was attacking Rodney, intent on adding yet another cop to his list of victims. That snapshot of Rodney's near-death encounter with their perp had given Kate a whole new perspective on Rodney, as he struggled to recover from the debilitating physical attack. She told him, "I'm just glad that you're doing better and that you're back. Doing without you and Andy was tough."

"I am back and better and thankful," he declared, with a smile in her direction, "and know who to thank for it."

"Oh, no, don't even go there," she said, with an eye roll. "That's the last thing I need."

"Yeah, what she said," Owen pitched in from the nearby desk, with a grin.

Rodney grinned at the joke and looked back at her, holding up a baggie. "Does that mean, if my girlfriend baked you some cookies, you'll turn them down?"

"I'll never turn down cookies," she stated, staring at him. "What do you think I am? A psycho?" And, with that, she snatched the bag from his hand and eyed it with a greedy expression on her face. Then it came to her. "These were for your lunch, weren't they?"

He burst out laughing. "Damn, I'm so busted."

She groaned and handed them back. "You can keep them." She smiled. "Besides, you're the injured person, not me."

"Ah, I'm not injured though," he added. "I just got released to return to duty."

"Sure, but you still have to go to physical therapy, right?"

He glared at her and nodded. "Why did you have to go there and ruin my day? Do you know how painful PT is?"

"Oh, I do," she noted, with a satisfied nod. "Trust me. I absolutely do, which is why you're not getting out of it." He just continued to glare at her, and she chuckled. "Not happening." She pointed at his miserable face. "You need to get that leg back." Kate turned to ask her team, "Anybody have an update on Andy returning to work?"

Just then Sergeant Colby walked in. "So …" he began.

Something about his tone of voice made Kate cringe. "What?" she asked cautiously.

He nodded at her. "We have the potential of something ugly coming up on the board—reports of a drowning up at Cultus Lake."

"That'll be up to the local law enforcement, right?" Kate asked.

"Yes, it's from a while ago, but yes."

"What do you mean, a while ago?"

"We have that case, and we have a couple other cases. Those others concern us because they probably link to that older one."

"Whoa, whoa, whoa," Kate said. "You're not making sense."

"I will, unfortunately," he replied, raising his hand to stop her onslaught. "Okay, listen up. I'll fill you all in from the top. We've had a drowning at Wreck Beach."

At that, Rodney whistled. "It certainly isn't from the weight of the bathing suits down at that new beach," he noted, with a smile.

"Maybe, but it happened early in the morning, off one of the rocks," Colby noted, with a sigh. "According to a witness, somebody out there apparently tried to help, supposedly tried to help, but the victim drowned and was carried along the shore, before being dragged to shore by the guy who had been trying to help. However, in hindsight, now our witness is not so sure."

Kate frowned at him in confusion. "I don't get it."

Lilliana snorted. "Thank you. I'm so glad you said that, though I never thought I would hear those words coming out of your mouth in one million years. And, Sarge, for the record, I sure as hell don't get it either."

"According to the eyewitness, this person trying to save our victim may have instead drowned our victim."

"So it could have been one or the other? That's hardly a solid witness account or a conclusive statement," Lilliana pointed out.

"Exactly, which is why it has ended up in our purview."

"So," Kate asked, "we don't have a body, or do we?"

Colby faced her. "As of twenty minutes ago, we have a body."

She groaned. "Okay, so we have a drowning victim. I'm still confused how that has anything to do with us."

At that moment, their analyst Reese walked in, with several files in her hand. "Because," she interjected, as she passed out copies to everyone, "we have three other victims with eyewitness accounts, making it sound as if somebody watched them drown and didn't do anything to help them— or possibly tried to help them but failed."

Kate winced, then asked cautiously. "Watched them drown or actively helped them drown and then stepped back?"

"That's what you get to find out," Colby stated, with a nod in her direction. "We're taking it in the worst way possible—that they put this person in a position to drown and then stepped back and watched them drown. Now, if that's the case"—he gave them all a stare—"it's murder, and, therefore, it's ours."

"And if that's not the case?" Kate asked cautiously.

He shrugged. "Then it has nothing to do with us." She

glared at him, and he smiled. "All I can tell you is that this case has crossed our desk, so it's up to us to take a look."

"Okay then," Kate confirmed, "but it does sound …" Then she frowned and shrugged. "It sounds a little off."

"Which means it should be a perfect case for you then," Lilliana noted, with an eye roll. "Nobody does a *little off* like Kate."

"Regardless of who does it well," Colby butted in, "this is a serious case, and, as Reese pointed out, three other cases have similarities. No conclusive link but similar in the manner of death and in the eyewitness accounts."

"Why the hell would you drown anybody with eyewitnesses around in the first place?" Kate wondered out loud.

Colby turned, looked at her, and nodded. "Exactly, so see what you can come up with and get back to me as soon as you can."

She groaned. "Will do." She turned to the others. "I suppose you all have cases to work?"

"Yep, you're the one who took time off," Owen pointed out. "So guess what? You're it."

"Seems that I'm always *it* somehow," she mumbled to herself, as she walked over to her desk with the folders, wondering how the hell she would even start on this. Eyewitness accounts were notoriously unreliable, not to mention the fact that a lot of the time these convenient witnesses had ulterior motives.

As she looked down at the files in front of her, she had to wonder just what motive anybody would have for this.

CHAPTER 2

KATE STOOD AT the edge of the water, watching as the sea reached for her boots with every roll of the tide. She was far enough back that she should be safe from getting her feet wet. It was a cloudy and dismal mid-November day, yet not as cold as it could have been. Although a very balmy fall season by anyone's standards here in Canada, the water would still be cold for swimming. Or drowning.

With various rocks along the water's edge, and logs that were obviously a favorite of many of the beachgoers, the scene looked worn and a bit worse for wear, but still it was a beauty in its own right. Wreck Beach was a local nudist beach and, for the most part, kept itself pretty much self-regulated.

As she looked around, the beach itself was empty. She smiled as the breeze washed through and lifted the hair off her face and, in a surprisingly odd twist, gave her a sense of renewal, a sense of peace and calm. Something was generously healing about Mother Nature, particularly in a beach setting, like this.

That might seem odd, considering what she was here for, but death was the other half of the constant cycle of life. It would just be nice if people would leave each other to die on their own terms. So, when they didn't, that's when Kate ended up involved. She stood here, enjoying the solitary peace of the wondrous space and the fairly isolated beach, looking out to the Vancouver harbor, which had grown to be quite famous.

Several tankers were out there in front of her, plus lots of sailboats and pleasure craft of all kinds. It was hard to imagine, but it was a day like none other in the sense that everybody knew that this season was slowly coming to an end. Fall was well into its cycle, and winter would not be far behind. Winter in Vancouver meant more rain than anything, but that was typical of coastal towns and cities all over the world.

Still, it would be a change, but she really loved living here and experiencing four distinct seasons. She couldn't imagine living someplace in the world where it was 74 degrees all year round and never changed. She absolutely loved the contrasts that each season brought in Vancouver. There was such a sense of renewal in spring, yet a special rebirth coming after a hibernation period, and fall was special with a sense of closure. A period to go inside and then return to the world, with a renewed sense of enjoyment and peace in the spring.

She knew a lot of people didn't feel that way, and unfortunately, for her, crime never ceased, no matter what the season.

She returned her attention to the terrain. Not a whole lot of rocks could be seen, as they were underwater, but a few buoys were out there. A few visible rocks were at the end of the beach around the bend. She had already spent an hour wandering back and forth on the sand, getting a feel for the location. She had a good idea where the body had been pulled from, which was farther down, and a good idea of where the eyewitness saw the woman drowning.

Shitty people were all over the world, but that still didn't mean it was murder. Yet not making an effort to assist or to contact people to render aid was also a crime, though not necessarily one easy to prosecute.

Of course, if the body had zero signs of struggle but just evidence of a simple drowning, then that made her job still harder, at least to enforce any kind of criminal activity involved. However, if the cops had several other cases, as Colby and their analyst had pointed out, then that was a different story. Was somebody deliberately doing harm, or was it a series of ugly accidents?

She didn't believe in coincidence, never had. Too many times what seemed like coincidences just raised her instincts to delve in further, or sometimes those coincidental events were—and she hated herself for even thinking this—fate intervening. She really didn't know what she believed anymore. Simon's psychic visions interacting with her black-and-white attitude had completely changed her worldview to allow for a lot of gray, getting grayer every day.

It wasn't easy to admit, but her other team members often questioned her to see if she had any contribution from Simon, her boyfriend and reluctant psychic, regarding any of the various cases that crossed their desks. Thankfully for the last little while, he'd been calm, quiet, and sleeping peaceably. So no nightmares to warn them of something coming soon.

Everybody was happy for his sake, but, for some of these cases, that still had them bothered. Most of her team much preferred that Simon wake up screaming the name of a murderer or giving them exact locations of bodies and weapons. Of course nothing in his world worked that way.

So, for him, silence was golden.

Kate looked out at the harbor, noting several pleasure craft heading toward the marinas. The day was slowly ending, and most of the daytime boaters were heading back to their safe harbors for the night. It was only 5:30 p.m., but in mid-November, an overcast day heading toward dusk had a dark gloominess to it.

She suspected boating would be right up Simon's alley, or *sailing* as the rich called it. He wasn't much for beachgoing out in the hot sunshine for very long though, but he would be out on a day like today, thoroughly enjoying the weather and the change in temperature. She glanced down at her watch and nodded. She would be here specifically on site around the time of the most recent drowning, as identified in the police report.

Not the time that the body had been discovered but the time when the female witness had supposedly seen somebody refusing to help the drowning victim or had tried to help them and had failed. Had this witness herself called it in? She supposedly had, but Kate hadn't seen a copy of the transcript yet to read exactly what she'd told the cops or how her phone call may have set all this in motion.

Stepping back, Kate got a broader, wider-angled view of the beach itself and the cliffs rising behind her. A few people walked around, all dressed, mostly because of the weather. Just because it was a nude beach, people didn't have to be nude all the time or at any time. People came with all different levels of comfort, depending on how modest they were in regard to their own bodies. For some people, nudity would never be okay because of religious or cultural upbringing, and that was okay too. This beach was relatively hidden, safe from the public eye, except for those who came to enjoy the same pastime, whether partaking in the nudity or coming to ogle it. Still, predators were possible too.

Those were the ones who Kate would prefer just stay away, but it was almost impossible to have any say in that.

She wandered back and forth for a bit at the specified time of the drowning. Not long afterward, she headed to her vehicle. Still, she stopped several times, looked down at the view, nodding, as she saw various people on the beach and what any onlooker might have seen or what they *couldn't* have seen.

Yet, at this time of day, it was quite possible that nobody had even been around. The body had also been found fully dressed, so not out for a swim, and that's the part that concerned Kate. If the body had been in a bathing suit, potentially with evidence of having gone for a swim and gotten caught in a tide, well that was a different story.

Accidental drownings happened, far too many to make anybody happy. Outside of posting lifeguards here twenty-four hours a day, it was almost impossible to regulate. British Columbia was known for hundreds of miles of beaches up and down its coast. So common sense must be used when swimming, and, if common sense were lacking, not a whole lot anybody could do about it. But still, Kate was always sad for the families, and, in this particular case, she sighed because the victim was a young woman, only twenty-three years old.

Patty was her name.

Kate had her last name, but, for some reason, only the victim's first name stuck with Kate. As she continued up to her vehicle, stopping yet again to peruse the shoreline, she saw a large boat, maybe a yacht—she wasn't even sure; she didn't do boats. That was a Simon thing. It was a boat of some sort out in the distance that looked pretty interesting.

She stared at it for a long moment, picked up her phone, and took a picture of it, wondering what it would cost to have something like that and what it would take to keep something like that maintained and on the water. Would anybody have been close enough to have seen what had happened to her drowning victim? Or, with the rocks nearby in the water, were they parked so far out that nobody could have seen the shoreline?

The one boat came in, closer and closer to the shore, and she stood here watching, wondering how shallow it was out there and how they knew about that. It stopped about one hundred yards off the beach. It could get deep around here, and the harbor itself was well-known for quite easily handling the large ships that came and went, but wouldn't boats beach easily at this location?

As she stood here, her phone rang. She looked down to see it was Simon. "Hey. Where are you?"

"I was going to ask you the same thing."

Frowning at the odd note in his voice, she replied, "I'm at Wreck Beach."

A half snort came at that. "You went without me?"

She smiled into the phone, knowing he couldn't see it, but appreciating the comment anyway. "We can always come back another time," she teased. "It's pretty-damn cold for swimming, and I, for one, am not baring my butt out here for that, not until summertime."

He chuckled. "I think I see you."

She froze. "Are you on that boat, right across from the harbor?"

"I'm right across from Wreck Beach," he clarified, "hardly a harbor." She frowned and Simon chuckled. "I know. I know. I'm not supposed to tease you about your lack of marine knowledge."

"It does feel like something I need to brush up on," she muttered.

"Lots of things you feel the need to brush up on," he noted. "I don't think you need to make this another one."

She groaned. "And somehow, just like that, you make me seem neurotic or even anal about my lack of information."

"I don't mean that at all," he stated. "I'm out for a test ride on a yacht that a friend of mine is selling."

She tried to read the name on the side of it. "I see a boat somewhat close to the shore. I don't know that it's you though, and I can't see the name on the boat."

He added, "Take another look."

And suddenly the person on the nearby boat stood up and waved both arms. She laughed into the phone. "I guess that's you."

"Yep, it sure is," he confirmed. "What do you think of it?"

"As if I can really tell. I'm on land. You're on the water," she said, then waved. "I don't know why you need a boat though."

"I don't *need* a boat," he replied, "but I've always wanted one, and I really, really love the days when I can come out here and just float. Besides this isn't just a boat it's a yacht." And he laughed in delight.

"Would you come out and just float?" she asked seriously. "The Simon who I know rarely takes time off."

"Which may be one of the reasons I should consider this," he pointed out, a note of humor in his voice. "Not to mention, you could use the same thing."

"Maybe," she muttered, looking into the distance. "It

looks pretty nice, not that I know anything about it."

"Good point, but you're right. It is pretty nice." His tone changed, and he said, "Listen. I'm taking it back to the marina. Are you coming home?"

"I'm going home," she replied, with an inflection in her voice. "You'll be at least an hour anyway, so I might go shower and get some basics like laundry done."

"Okay. You want me to stop by?"

"No, it's fine. Enjoy your time out on the water, with your test run. I've got some notes on a new case to consider. So I'll just work from home for a bit."

He suggested, "Or you can come over to my place and spend time there."

"Your place isn't really set up for me to plan or take notes or set up a whiteboard. … I guess I could sit and work at your dining room table, but that's not exactly conducive to the way I work."

"Do you need more than that right now for a new case?" he asked, surprise in his voice. "Sounds like a big case. Did I miss something on the news? I hadn't really heard of any murders."

"No, it just crossed my desk today," she shared, with a sigh. "It's kind of a strange case and was given to me because … it's a *strange* case."

A note of surprise came over the phone, and then he laughed. "You have become quite good at these odd cases."

"It's not that I'm good at them," she argued. "They just seem to be ones you also connect to."

"Ah, so you're thinking that I'm the one who's solving them?"

"Nope, good old-fashioned police work is solving them," she declared, "and thank God for that. I would hate to think the entire department could only run with the input of *Simon the psychic.*"

"No, that's definitely not the way this works," he said, with a chuckle. "Anyway I'll bring this yacht safely back into harbor. How about I pick up dinner and bring it over?" When she hesitated, he added, "Or will that not work out either?"

There was a point where he would back off, and he'd been trying very hard not to pressure her, mostly because about two weeks ago he'd pressured her to consider moving in. She'd been so flabbergasted that he'd backed off. Yet it had been put on the table, and, once on the table, it was kind of hard to ignore.

"You could do that," she agreed quite happily, "particularly if I get a chance to go home and to get a shower and to get some work done first."

"Head home by all means," he said, obviously pleased with her decision. "I'll pick up dinner and bring it by."

"You're sure you'll be okay to get that thing back in on your own?"

"Absolutely. It might take me a little longer than an hour but probably not much."

"In that case," she told him, "I'm heading home now." Then she quickly ended the call and got in her vehicle.

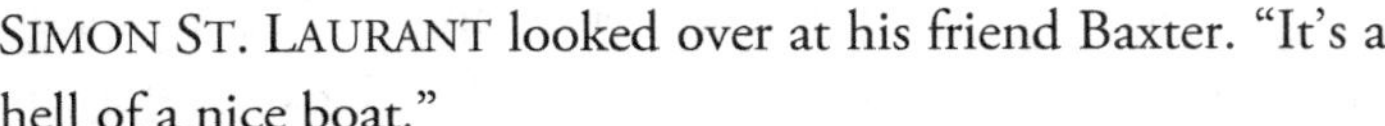

SIMON ST. LAURANT looked over at his friend Baxter. "It's a hell of a nice boat."

Baxter rolled his eyes. "You could call it a lot of things, but ... a *nice* yacht isn't one of them."

Simon flashed a grin. "Depends on what you'll take for it. If I call it a *yacht*, you'll raise the price, won't you?"

Baxter laughed uproariously. "I should raise it anyway."

"You wouldn't be selling it at all unless either you need the money or you don't need the expense."

Baxter looked at him in appreciation. "It's not exactly either of those, but it's definitely both."

Simon nodded. "At some point it's time to decrease the expenses and all the headaches in our lives and the things that we have to look after," he stated, his tone serious. Baxter was maybe sixty. "Your kids all graduated from college and moved out yet?"

"Last one just left about two months ago, so the wife and I are talking about doing some traveling."

"But not on the water?"

Baxter rolled his eyes. "She wants to go on one of those big cruises." He groaned. "Why do I want to get on a ship with six thousand other people, when I could be out here on my own yacht, enjoying life?"

"But that's not what she wants, I presume?"

"Nope, she wants the evening shows and no cooking. She doesn't want to catch a fish and then prepare it to eat, and she doesn't want to make a bed. She wants clean bedding, hot showers, and all that fancy prepared food." He just sighed. "We've had this yacht for a couple decades, and we've run it quite a bit. The kids have enjoyed it, but they aren't interested in going out anymore. None of them got licenses or learned how to sail beyond the family trips," he shared, with a shrug, yet disappointment filled his expression. "So, it's like that RV that you took the kids traveling in forever. Suddenly the kids want to be with their friends, and they don't even want to go camping anymore."

"I get it."

"I'm sure you do. It's all part of life. Times change.

Things change. People change."

"I can imagine." Simon nodded.

"You got kids yet?" Baxter asked, looking at him. "I thought I heard you had a family."

"Nope, not me." Simon shook his head, as he stepped back on the dock to look at the lovely little sloop he had taken out for the afternoon. "It might be in my future. I'm not so sure," he said, with a smile. "For the longest time I thought, hell no, I wasn't ever doing that, but lately …"

"Ha, that can only mean you have a woman in your life," Baxter noted, "and that would be good. One woman versus twenty is much better."

Simon's lips quirked. "If you say so."

"You and I both know there's nothing quite like coming home to somebody who understands who you are and what makes you tick and what your needs are. That sense of both of you ripening at the same time, staying equal, both of you heading to the proverbial rocking chairs on the front porch, holding each other's hands. Honest to God, she's the other half of me, so I understand what she says about the cruise and the maintenance and the work and living at a slightly different level. We'll try it for a while, and, after all that, if we want to come back and if I want to get back out on the water, I'll either buy myself a small sailboat and come out alone or maybe we'll go buy something that's big enough to travel around Europe and maybe stay over there for a while. At least the water's warmer."

Simon laughed. "It is, indeed. Canada's not bad, but …"

"Oh, Canada is darn cold sometimes," he interrupted. "It's not as if we're living off the Mexican coastline."

"And yet you could," Simon pointed out. "This is certainly big enough to do ocean-bearing waters."

"It is. It is." Baxter eyed his yacht with a sense of nostalgia. "You'll have to change her name of course."

"I don't know. I kind of like the wistfulness of it."

"I called it *Running Mate* because of my wife."

"I like that. I might just have a different running mate in mind."

"And that's the way it should be," Baxter replied, with a smile on his face. "My Kate's been around a long time, but, like a good wine, she's aged well over the years."

After more small talk, Simon told Baxter that he'd think about it, and he headed back to his car, checked his watch, and realized that the dinner he ordered should be ready to pick up. It was a new Indian restaurant, located about halfway between his place and Kate's. As he drove to it, he considered the fact that he and Baxter both had partners named Kate, and that the *Running Mate* had been named after one.

It was almost fitting that Simon would consider buying her, and he doubted that he would even change the name. *Running Mate* sounded pretty good to him. He got to the restaurant, quickly picked up and paid for the order, and stepped back out. He could use a hot shower himself. His face was a bit sun-dried, and his hair was stiff from being out in the wind all day. Yet he felt an exhilaration he hadn't experienced in a very long time.

He sensed a certain joy from being out on the waves, just letting the world pass on by, without any immediate need to deal with problems, phone calls, emails, or any of the other stuff that came with running your own business and with having multiple million-dollar projects underway all the time.

Simon was still dealing with Bartlett's company too, but

a good share of that had eased up, at least slightly. Eleana Mayfield Morris, Bartlett's wife, had confessed to the attempted murder of Simon, which was a good thing because it saved them all a trial on her guilt or innocence. She had been caught red-handed with the gun at the time of the shooting, and, with multiple witnesses, it would be hard for anybody to find her not guilty.

Still, she had sentencing before a court of law. When all was said and done, the judge and jury had gone relatively easy on her, after understanding her husband had committed suicide and that their businesses were all failing, but she still got eight years in jail. Simon figured, with the legal system the way it was, chances were, she'd get out in about five years. Yet those five years would make a big difference to somebody rich and spoiled and pampered like her.

She wouldn't get her $15,000 Gucci suits or anything else in prison, but she also wouldn't suffer, compared to a lot of others in prison, simply because she did have access to money. Simon couldn't be bothered to spend his energy worrying about her, not when he still had Bartlett's company to save, and that was a whole different story. Still, the process was well underway, and Simon had much less to deal with daily now on that company.

Driving to Kate's, Simon found the traffic was intense. He wasn't exactly sure what was going on, whether impacted by an accident or some parade or protest or some traffic light malfunction or whatever, but he was a little frazzled by the time he got to Kate's place. He'd barely escaped two rear-ends when he had to swerve rapidly to avoid a head-on collision, getting out of the way before another vehicle hit a median.

Walking up to Kate's apartment, swearing because she

didn't have an elevator, he stopped at her door, realizing that he couldn't just go barging in there with his own frustration spilling out everywhere.

She wouldn't take kindly to that and would probably close the door on him. Laughing at that image and appreciating how even the thought of something like that happening could make him laugh, he knocked on the door, then used his key to open it.

She looked up from her kitchen table and smiled when she saw him. "Hey." Then she frowned, as if seeing his angst under all the facade. "You don't look so good."

He chuckled. "And here I thought I was doing just fine."

With a raised brow, she added, "Maybe to other people, but not to me. What happened?"

He told her about the traffic and that he'd almost been rear-ended and still barely escaped a head-on collision.

She groaned. "It's getting worse over here, I swear to God."

"It's as if something's not quite right out there today."

Looking up from her pile of papers, she shrugged. "It is a full moon."

He slowly turned to face her.

She smiled and went back to the work before her.

"I presume that you're just trying to get my goat with that comment."

"Hey, lots of people swear by movements of the moon or Mercury in retrograde, all that good stuff," she added, now chuckling.

"Maybe," he acknowledged, "but I can't say that any of it makes me feel better."

"I didn't say it to make you feel better," she clarified, batting her eyelashes at him, as she got up, walked over, and gave him a hug.

He smiled down at her in the circle of his arms and muttered, "If nothing else, it's always nice to get a welcome."

"Absolutely," she agreed, "particularly when you're bringing food." She leaned back slightly to smile up at him. "And it smells delicious."

Laughing, he stepped back and unpacked the bag he'd brought. The smell of a wonderful Indian curry filled the room.

"Oh, wow, that smells absolutely divine."

"It's a new restaurant, kind of in-between our two places, so I figured it was worth a try."

"It's always worth a try," she declared, as she picked up one container and took off the lid. "I don't know what kind of a curry this is, but it looks fascinating."

He grinned. "I can't even pronounce the names of the dishes. I tried, but I failed." He smiled at her in delight. "I just told them to give me something that's really good and to give me enough for four people."

She frowned at him and repeated, "Four?"

"Sometimes you eat enough for two, and I definitely feel like I could eat for two tonight," he admitted, rubbing his stomach. "If nothing else, we can always have curry for breakfast." She winced at that, and he laughed. "Don't tell me that you haven't had curry for breakfast when you haven't had time to eat."

"Most of the time I just don't eat, if that's the case," she stated, frowning at him. "I'm not sure how my stomach would handle it."

He added, "You might get a chance to find out tomorrow, or you might not because I could eat it all tonight," he said, as he sniffed the food. "God, that smells really good."

"It does," she said, as she grabbed a couple plates. "Let's eat."

And that's precisely what they did. Finally she sat back and pushed away her empty plate. "Wow. I didn't think I was that hungry."

"Of course you were," he replied. "Chances are you haven't eaten all day."

She glared at him, but he raised an eyebrow, and, after a moment, she shrugged. "I had a granola bar."

He groaned. "You need to stop doing that."

"It's not a case of stopping. I'm not doing anything."

"Precisely," he declared, with an eyeroll. "You need to start *doing* something, and it's called eating properly." She just stared at him, and he sighed because he knew she wouldn't change her work habits, which impinged on her eating. This was Kate, after all. "Ignore me then. That's what you usually do."

"Ignore you?" she repeated, with a laugh. "The last thing I can do is ignore you, and, besides, … you won't tolerate it."

"Why would I?" he murmured, as he continued to eat, but a grin was on his face. He assessed the weariness in her gaze and the fatigue on her forehead. "Tough day?"

"I don't know," she replied, with a shrug. "Not tough so much as long, put it that way. I had lots of reports to file, lots of cases to catch up on."

"Of course," he noted. "Taking a holiday can often be worse than staying on the job, can't it?"

"It's just that everybody needs something, and they all need it now," she explained. "Sometimes that gets to be a little much."

He didn't say anything, just finished eating. Then he

added, "So, tell me why you were at Wreck Beach."

She shook her head. "I'm sure you would rather talk about other things, besides my latest case."

"Actually I suspect your latest case is probably pretty interesting," he replied, looking at her curiously, "particularly if you're hanging out at a nudist beach all of a sudden."

He kind of sang the *nudist beach* part, and that made her smile. "It's not so much about a *nudist* beach. However, somebody drowned there."

He nodded. "That much I heard on the news, but that doesn't usually concern your department. What's going on here?"

"Usually, no, it wouldn't concern us, unless …"

His eyebrows shot up. "Unless?"

She shrugged. "Unless there are suspicious circumstances or something like that. It's kind of an odd case really."

"So, tell me," he said, his curiosity piqued, because he did find the blend of her work and his abilities fascinating. It was something he had gradually become accustomed to, something that still needed a lot of work on his part. Still, he also felt a divine sense of accomplishing something— especially when the two of them managed to solve a case and to find closure for the families. As he had already discovered, the value in her work was almost incalculable, something he hadn't really seen or understood until he had met Kate.

She had become a ground for him, not that he would use that term out loud to her because it would probably freak her out. However, something was very special about her that kept him on the straight and narrow when it came to his abilities. If anything got scary or out of control, he could refocus on who she was, who they were, and it brought him back. An awful lot could be said for that.

He listened, as she began to explain about this new case.

"Seriously?" he asked. "So, Colby thinks, or at least your analyst seems to think, that you have multiple cases like this drowning on purpose?" He shook his head. "It's not as if Wreck Beach has the privacy to kill someone without witnesses, even by drowning, particularly since it's open to the public. Even in November, just look at what you had for a view today. Plus, the fact that it's a nudist beach should bring in all kinds of looky-loos."

She nodded. "I know, and I went there to get the lay of the land. With such a unique location, somebody must have seen what happened. We have an eyewitness, but I need more than that. Her report was already vague."

"Isn't that the whole point of why you were given the case because somebody did see?"

"Absolutely," she confirmed, "and I'm meeting with our witness tomorrow morning."

"And yet you don't seem terribly happy about it."

"It's not that I'm unhappy," she clarified, "but, as I start to get a reputation for these things, that can be daunting."

"Ah, so you're afraid that you might not get anything on this case, yet everybody expects you to figure it out?"

"I don't know what anybody's expecting, but Colby more or less gave it to me because it's one of *those* cases." She rolled her eyes, and, even if she hadn't, Simon knew that was the intent behind assigning it to Kate.

He smiled. "Of course, and you don't really want to acknowledge that you're damn good at *those* cases."

"It's not that I don't want to acknowledge it," she countered, with a half laugh, "but sometimes I suspect that it's more because of you than of me."

At that, he sat back and looked at her. "What?"

CHAPTER 3

KATE STUDIED SIMON'S surprised expression, and, seeing his genuine confusion, she added, "Surely you understand that."

"No, I don't understand anything," he admitted. "Very little of what I ever have to offer is helpful, and too damn much of it, if helpful at all, comes in way too late."

"I'll give you that," she said, with a smirk. He glared at her, and she chuckled. "But, when you do have something, sometimes it *is* helpful," she stated, with a nod. "I'm not sitting here and going over all that woo-woo stuff with you because you already know how much trouble I have with it."

He nodded. "That I do know."

She smiled. "So, with that in mind, I feel like everybody else thinks that, if I do have a woo-woo case, I can always just ask you to tap into the woo-woo-*ness*, and you will potentially find the answers for me." He sat back, frowning. "You have no clue, do you?" she asked, staring at him intently.

"No clue about what?" he asked, clearly bewildered.

"They really do appreciate whatever information you can provide."

"That's great. Yet again, … lots of times I don't get anything, or anything useable, plus you know how much I struggle with whatever I do get."

She nodded. "That's probably a good thing because they understand you can't always bring in information, but when you do? … They usually jump right on it. Sometimes I feel that they're a little too quick to believe it all."

He looked at her and then started to laugh. "Is that what bothers you?" he asked, an odd look on his face. "Do you think you're not being given these cases because of your ability to solve them but because you're connected to me?"

She frowned. "I know it sounds stupid, but is it really that stupid if you think about it?"

"It's absolutely stupid on their part, if that's the reason," he declared, "because I can't guarantee anything that I might come up with. I can't even make a bit of sense of it half the time. So I sure as hell can't guarantee anything on a regular basis. I love helping you close cases and helping the families find closure, but these cases are few and far between. Besides, you've done lots of cases since the last one that have had absolutely nothing to do with me."

"True," she noted, "and I'm kind of happy about that too."

"Of course you are, as you are so competitive, even with yourself," he noted, rolling his eyes. "I suggest you either have a talk with them or just let it go because that would be foolishness on everybody's part. And, if it bothers you that much, you probably should take it to Colby."

She smiled. "If only it were that easy."

He glared at her and replied, "It's a whole lot easier than you're thinking."

"Maybe," she muttered. "Anyway, I'll go meet the eyewitness tomorrow and see what she has to say, and then I'll bring up everything we've got on the other cases and start taking a closer look." She frowned. "It just seems so nebulous because there's a difference between drowning somebody—as in holding them under or putting cement boots on them and dropping them into the ocean—versus standing there and not rendering aid. It's still a crime, yet ..."

He nodded. "Yet very different in a sense, isn't it?"

"People can't render aid for all kinds of reasons," she noted. "One of the biggest is the fact that people often freeze and panic, not knowing quite what to do, or they're absolutely petrified of water and can't swim and, therefore, can't go in and help them. In many cases, the person who jumps in and tries to help ends up drowning, even if they do know how to swim, and a lot of people know about that. So, I can't really hold it against anybody."

"But that's not the same thing as what this is," Simon pointed out. "At least what it sounds like so far."

"No, and that's why it's such a confusing thing for me because it's a very nebulous accusation."

"It is a fascinating thought though."

"Not for me," she said, scrunching up her nose. "I think it's sad, upsetting, scary even, but something like this could play out in so many different ways that I just have to keep an open mind and then go back to the team with what I find."

He grinned at that. "You're a little more worried about that, aren't you?"

She shrugged. "I really don't want my solid police work to be obscured by the shiny glamour of your contributions." As he sat back, she caught the wince on his face. Reaching out, she added, "I'm sorry. Look. I don't mean to say that I don't appreciate all the help. It's just—"

"No," he interrupted. "Believe me. I understand. I get it. It's much more about your own abilities, and, for you, it's a huge part of who you are. So for somebody to discount all your hard work, of course that would sting."

She sat back, frowning and nodding. "And that just makes me feel even shittier."

He burst out laughing. "You need to get over it, and fast." He held her hand, but, for sure, wouldn't bring up his latest weird dreams. Not good timing. Besides, he couldn't make heads or tails of them. No true visions. No words. Just feelings. Just an alert. Just some early warning system or a nudge or whatever. When the message was clearer, he would share it with her.

He sighed. "Besides, with your being so competitive, I really think it boils down to the *shiny* comment. I know you are not a believer, yet, after seeing a lot of this from my viewpoint, are you upset that you can begin to see the validity of this woo-woo stuff? No matter what, just forget about that part. *You* are a hell of a good investigator, and, if you don't want any help, then that's fine too," he pointed out. "I'll definitely try to avoid giving you my help." He chuckled, and she giggled too. "Although I must admit, it hadn't occurred to me that you needed me to keep any information I get to myself. Am I correct in thinking that?"

"Yeah, you're right. I really don't want you to hold back. That would be foolish because the overall goal is to solve these murders. It's not about my ego. It's not about recognition for the job I'm doing. Those are secondary, if that," she explained. "It's about the victims, and that's all it needs to be. As we've seen, solving these cases isn't just about justice for the victim but closure for the family and, all too often, can prevent future victims. Thus I need to embrace any information I can get, no matter how unfortunate the source."

When he broke up in delighted laughter at the terminology, she couldn't help but join in.

BRIGHT AND EARLY the next morning, Kate and Rodney stood outside the office door of Rebecca Harrison, the witness who had called in about the drowning she had seen. As they stepped through the doorway, both flashing their badges, a woman looked up, frowned, then hastily looked away. "If you're looking for Rebecca, she's not here."

"She wasn't at home either," Kate replied. "Do you have any idea where she would be?"

The other woman looked at her, suddenly forgetting the papers in her hand she had been seemingly so engrossed in. "She should be home. She called in sick again today."

"I'm pretty sure she is sick," Kate clarified. "It just might be more emotional than physical." When the other woman frowned, Kate went on. "It's not really for me to say, but she saw something fairly distressing yesterday, and she called it in to the police. So we need to ask her more questions about the incident."

Obviously confused but concerned, the other woman nodded. "If you've already been to her house, then I don't know what to say. Her mother's place, I guess. If Rebecca's upset, maybe she would go there."

"Do you have any contact information for her?" When the woman hesitated, Kate added, "Obviously this is something that we're concerned about, and we also want to ensure that Rebecca is okay."

"Yes, yes, of course," she replied apologetically. She wrote down an address on her yellow sticky note. "This is all I have. It's her emergency contact, and I hope you can figure it out from there."

"Good enough," Kate said, with a smile.

As they stepped back out again, Kate noted they weren't very far away from the address for Rebecca's mother's house. "It's about a ten-minute drive from here," she told Rodney.

Rodney nodded. "Good thing I'm driving. Even injured, I'm the best one for the job today."

"Why?" she asked, glaring at him.

"Because we'll get there in ten minutes, maybe even fifteen, but we'll arrive alive."

"I am not a bad driver," she declared, still glaring at him.

He held up both hands. "I absolutely did not say that. However, when it comes to traffic, you have a tendency to get a little road rage."

She snorted at that. "Most people on the road are idiots and should be banned from driving."

"I won't argue that either," he added, with a chuckle, "particularly when you could be one of them on the road."

She shook her head and then laughed. "Hey, I've gotten much better."

"Glad to hear it," he stated, but his expression screamed that he didn't believe it. "Still, I'll do the driving."

She snorted. "You're just making a big deal out of nothing."

He laughed. "It's absurdly easy to bug you. Had you grown up with even one sibling, you could handle a little teasing a whole lot easier."

"Thanks for that," she said, with a smile that didn't

reach her eyes.

He looked over at her and winced. "Oh, crap, Kate. I'm sorry. I keep forgetting about your brother."

"Which is why his cold case file sits on my desk, … so I don't forget," she explained. "Because it's just too damn easy for the days to roll from one to the next and to still have absolutely no idea what happened to him. It's just one of those things where I never get any answers. So, I keep it there, keep it fresh in my mind, and hope that maybe one day I will come up with something that makes sense."

"You will," Rodney replied. "I'm sure of it. However, in the meantime, just make sure that whenever that happens, you let us help. Whatever it is, we're there to support you and to assist you however we can."

She stared at him. "A few months back I never would have thought that would be on the agenda."

"A few months back," he noted, with a small smile, "it probably wouldn't have been." He glanced at her. "It's taken us a while, but we got there eventually."

She nodded. "We still have one more team member in theory allocated for us, don't we?"

"We do," he agreed. "At least if it's still in the budget, and I'm never quite sure about that. So, for now, we're all functioning without Andy, but it's a lot of extra work."

"Maybe another analyst might help."

"Maybe," Rodney replied. "I won't argue with that concept, but, if we had someone to pick up more of that research and gathering work, that would take a load off too."

"Which is what our analyst does."

"Yeah, but she's completely run off her feet too, so—"

"Oh, wow, what a novel idea," she muttered, as Rodney drove too slowly to their witness. "Just think. We could have people who aren't run off their feet, who maybe come in fresh with, you know, brain cells that function, instead of being completely exhausted because of the work they've done overnight."

He burst out laughing. "You're welcome to take that up with the higher-ups anytime you want."

"Always the charmer, and *my* talking to the bosses won't help," she noted, with an eyeroll.

"Glad you know that," he said, "but it would be a whole lot easier on all of us if *you* do it."

She shrugged. "I'm not sure I'm ready to have anybody else come on the team anyway."

"That could very well be why we haven't gotten Andy back. I'm not sure if he's even coming back. His leave just keeps getting extended. Does he not want to come back or is he looking to shift to something else right now?"

"Lilliana told me how Andy's divorce sent him into his hump-and-dump phase, but now he has a serious girlfriend, right? Or at least last I heard. Maybe he is looking for changes in his work life as well. I guess that's always an option for people, isn't it?"

"It can be," Rodney pointed out. "He can always ask for a transfer to another department. Not everybody wants to be in our division, although there is a certain amount of prestige in being a detective," he shared. "However, we also have a high burnout rate."

"Of course, what with our crazy long hours," she pointed out, "and mostly I would think that lack of support, … emotional support, when it comes to facing murder every day. That alone has got to be a factor."

"Ah, you've been talking to the shrink again, haven't you?" She glared at him, and he just laughed. "You'll have to talk to him again eventually."

"I talk to him about work."

"You're supposed to talk to him about your cases, your mental state, and how you're handling all these depressing situations around here."

"Yeah, well, *supposed to* and *doing it* is a whole different story." He frowned at her, and she frowned right back. "Don't even go there." She raised a finger to warn him. "I'm not too interested in having anybody get into my brain. Particularly after his predecessor ..."

"You're really going to hold that against him?"

"Nope, I'm not. I'm holding it against the entire damn profession."

He burst out laughing at that and said, "With an attitude like that, you may almost get away with it."

She grinned at him. When he gave her a side-eye glance, she knew what was coming, as he put it in words.

"I'm pretty sure the department has rules and regulations, so eventually ... it will come back and hit you in the throat."

"Jeez, did Colby put you up to this? Wait. Don't answer that."

Thankfully they arrived at their destination just then, shifting the conversation.

She walked up to the small front door and gave it a hard knock. When the door opened to reveal a late fifties or more like a sixty-year-old woman, Kate smiled, held up her badge, and introduced herself. "Hello, we're looking for your daughter and are hoping she's here. We need to ask her a few questions."

The older woman looked at her and then turned and called out, "Becky, the police are here to talk to you."

As soon as she called out, an exhausted and stressed-out woman, clutching at her robe, appeared at the door. "How did you find us?"

"We're the police. It's what we do," Kate replied.

Becky flushed and nodded. "I'm sorry. I didn't mean it quite that way. I'm just really surprised to see you here."

"You made a police report, and we must confirm that we have all the details, so we can get to the bottom of the issue. If it's a crime, … then to find all the evidence we can, so we can get a conviction."

"And yet I don't have any good way to describe him, except that he was a white male or potentially a mixed race or maybe just had a suntan," she shared, raising both hands. "He had come off the beach, right around the corner from Wreck Beach."

"Hang on. Are you saying he wasn't at the beach?" Kate asked, her voice sharp.

"No, he was just around the corner a little bit," she clarified, clutching her hands. "Whenever I go down there, I don't …" She tossed a half-worried glance at her mother. "I don't go there so much for the beach itself, but for the privacy," she replied reluctantly. "If you continue to walk around the point a little way, you can sit and really commune with nature at a couple places on the rocks."

Kate thought about that and nodded. "Okay, so you went around this corner, and what exactly did you see?"

She sniffled. "A woman, at least I thought it was a woman," she added, taking a moment. "She was on the rocks, fully dressed, and then this man came up beside her. I don't know if he pushed her or what happened. I wasn't looking, but the next thing I know she's in the water, and he looks like he's trying to help her. I wanted to believe he was trying to help her, and I'm standing up on my feet and cheering him on but not saying anything, wondering if I should call for help or what I'm supposed to do," she muttered, half-worried and half-clutching the lapels of her robe, tighter and tighter. She looked lost for a moment.

"Go on, please."

"So it looks like he's almost got her, but ... instead he seems to push her back in the water. I couldn't clearly see, as they weren't close to me. For all I know, she fell back in."

This wasn't what Kate expected to hear.

Becky flushed and shook her head. "I know that sounds terrible, but there was such a creepiness to it, especially when she went down the second time." Becky shuddered. "It looked to me as if he wasn't helping her at all."

"And what did you do?"

"That's partly why I've been bawling my eyes out because I feel terribly guilty." She cried out, "I don't even know what I was supposed to do, but, since I didn't do anything, I'm just as guilty as he is."

"Think about it. If you had gone down there, would you have made it in time?" Kate asked her.

"No, I don't think so. Or that's what I want to believe because that's the only way I can really absolve myself of the guilt," she admitted, "but I don't really know."

Kate understood that. It was hard to go through something like that and then wonder *what if.* She needed to confirm with Rebecca what a normal reaction that was.

She said as much to the young woman. "Just remember. You were not trained to rescue someone. It's natural to freeze, questioning what to do next. I think the what-ifs are the worst thing when something like this happens. *What if I could have gotten there in time? What if I could have saved her?*

What if I had done something different?"

Kate held a hand out to her. "I don't think in a circumstance like this that you could have reached the woman in time or that it would have made any difference. We don't know whether this man was helping her or hurting her. For that matter, we don't know if he could swim. He may have been dealing with his own trauma from some previous scenario or something."

"Oh, I never thought of that," Rebecca muttered, staring at Kate. "I guess that's possible too, isn't it?"

"It's absolutely possible," Kate agreed. "It's quite a common reflex for anybody who has come close to drowning or has watched somebody drown or has been in any kind of scenario like that to just go to pieces, and they freeze up. They can't help because it's not within them to pull themselves together once the shock and/or trauma takes over. As sad as it may sound, they aren't the right person to be helping."

"So, if I had been there, maybe I could have helped?"

"You phoned the police, and I'm here to determine just what it was that you saw. I don't know if you've heard, but her body was recovered yesterday morning," Kate shared. "An autopsy has been performed, but no other obvious factors, like a gunshot wound or anything like that, could be found on her body."

"Right." Rebecca wrung her hands. "My God, I just … don't ever want to see something like that again."

"Of course not," Kate murmured, "and, with any luck, you won't. Can you remember anything to help identify this man? Anything at all? Did he leave right away, or did he sit down on the rocks and cry or pray or anything?"

"He stood there and watched her as she went down. He

didn't try to phone the police or anything." And then she stopped and added, "I don't even know that for sure because I was in such shock myself. That should teach me a lesson. I was in shock and didn't know what to do. So, if he was there on the spot, I can't imagine how he must have felt."

"Exactly. I don't want this man doing something to himself out of guilt or despair either," Kate noted. "So, if we can contact him or find out who he is, that would be helpful."

"I don't know." Becky shook her head. "And that just makes me feel like an even bigger idiot."

"Hush now," her mother said from behind them. "You've already been through enough trauma. Don't make it worse."

"And yet, how much worse was it for that young woman?" Rebecca wailed.

Kate didn't have any argument for that because Rebecca was right. As Kate stood here, she noticed just how bright and comforting the front room was. That said much about Rebecca's mother's personality. She smiled at the other woman and added, "I presume she can stay here with you for another day or two."

"Oh, of course," the mother replied, as she pulled Rebecca a little closer to her. "She just needs a couple days to get over this."

Kate nodded. "I presume you left before he did."

She nodded. "I bolted," she confessed. "I don't even know what else I could have done anyway, but I just ... bolted." She shook her head. "I'm really struggling with who I am and what I did or didn't do," she admitted, with a sheen of fresh tears. "I did phone the police, but I don't know if that was enough." And her voice trailed away.

"There was nothing else you could do," Kate declared. "So let that go, and just remember. As this investigation goes on, I might need to contact you again. In the meantime, if you do think of anything else, please call and let me know." And she slipped over her card.

Rodney gave her one as well and added, "I work with Kate, so the two of us will be on this case until we sort it out."

"Thank you," Rebecca said gratefully, looking over at the two of them. "Thank you so much. I really hate to even imply that this guy might have done something wrong because who the hell am I to judge? Apparently I didn't do anything right either."

"You absolutely did something right," Kate reiterated. "You contacted the police, and I'm not sure anybody else could have done anything, short of being a doctor or somebody with life-saving skills." She gave Rebecca a reassuring smile and went on. "It's not really something that you had a choice over, as you just happened upon this event. Plus, the water is cold, and the current is strong. You could have easily drowned yourself."

Her mother frowned. "I don't remember hearing much about Wreck Beach. Where is it?"

"It's right on the banks of the university," Kate supplied, as she eyed the older woman and then the daughter, who looked resigned to an explosion about to come. Kate smiled and added, "One of many popular places down there."

Her mother turned to Rebecca. "Surely enough beautiful beaches are close by that you don't have to go into these isolated ones, honey. You know better."

Rebecca nodded. "I'll certainly reconsider it now, won't I?"

"So you should," her mother stated crossly. "I mean, look at what happened. Stay on the true and narrow, and you'll be in much better shape."

Kate, with a small smile on her face, nodded at Rebecca, who seemed relieved, as if the storm had been averted. "We'll see ourselves out." She turned to leave, and Rodney did the same. "Remember. If you think of anything, just let us know."

Grateful, Rebecca nodded. "Thank you, Detective."

Kate understood exactly what she meant, as she headed out to Rodney's car.

Once outside on the sidewalk, Rodney asked her, "What was that all about?"

"A young woman not wanting her mother to know that she had been frequenting a nude beach," Kate explained, with a knowing smile. "A very appreciative daughter, since we didn't tattle."

He chuckled. "It's always the quiet ones who surprise you."

Kate snorted. "Only because you already expect that behavior from the other ones."

He nodded. "The quiet ones have to do it on the sly, so nobody knows."

***

SIMON WAS HARD-PRESSED to put the thoughts of the lovely little vessel *Running Mate* out of his mind, though it wasn't so little at all. He absolutely did not need it, unless one considered the benefit of getting out on the water to relax. No doubt that stress was one of the biggest issues he needed to combat. And Kate too.

Even if he handled his stress on a day-to-day basis, it was

an insidious disease going on in the background that continuously worked to gain a foothold, with the intent of eroding his health. Not something he was prepared to lose at this stage of his life. Baxter himself looked to be quite happy and content, and it was an interesting choice to sell a yacht that he had enjoyed with his family for decades. However, with the march of time, Simon knew and understood all too well that families changed, that priorities changed.

Simon didn't even have a family, so this family-size yacht was clearly too big for him. Yet his affinity for the *Running Mate* never dimmed. He would buy that yacht, but, for now, he put the thought out of his mind, as he walked from project to project to inspect his building rehabs. He also stopped in at several suppliers today, where he had a couple arguments over some invoices that were paid, yet the suppliers weren't. Just a typical business day for anybody who did this kind of work. The biggest problem was often the damn phone calls that just never left him alone.

He stepped into a popular coffee shop and waited in line, and, when it was his turn, he quickly ordered a coffee to-go. As he waited in yet another line for it to be made, he heard a shout behind him.

He turned and there was Baxter, walking up to him. Simon laughed. "What the hell?" he asked, as they shared a handshake.

"I know, right? But that's what happens when we live in the same area. You put any more thought into that yacht of mine?"

"You mean that *barely a yacht* thing?" he teased.

Baxter rolled his eyes. "You know I always wanted bigger."

"Of course. You wanted a faster sports car. You wanted a

better motorcycle and everything else. I know all about it all too well." Simon laughed.

"Yeah, especially once I hit middle age, and the kids hit, like fourteen," Baxter shared, thinking back. "Just something about seeing a stretch of freedom ahead but not quite being there, something that I could taste but I couldn't eat yet because it was in the future. It was attainable, but I couldn't have it yet." He shrugged. "That was kind of painful. I needed time to assimilate through my kids' teenage years and then their college years. Now they all have families of their own"—he sighed—"and my wife wants to travel. I'm torn, but happy to do it her way for a while."

"Are you though?" Simon asked curiously. "The last thing I want to do is take away the freedom that the *Running Mate* gives you, then have you come back in five years and whine about how much you miss her. I'm not sure I would be ready to let her go in five years."

Baxter chuckled. "And with good reason," he agreed, "but that's the way I would want her to go, you know? To somebody who would get out there and enjoy life. You work too hard."

"Yeah, I've been told that a time or two," Simon conceded, with a smile. "Yet I also know that the years will pass by very, very quickly."

"I think, in a way, they pass by even more quickly when you have kids. Your days are so full that you don't quite ever get a sense of time *without* the kids. Then suddenly there's spring break and summer holidays and Christmas, and the years tumble by without your thinking about the culmination of all of them and those experiences. It's this never-ending rotation that never stops. ... And then it does."

Simon nodded. "As I don't have any kids, I haven't really had a whole lot of that cyclical thing going on, yet time does seem to go faster as I get older."

At that, Baxter laughed, and then he grew serious, with an expression on his face that Simon couldn't place. "What are your thoughts on the boat?"

"You mean, on the *Running Mate?*" he asked, with a pointed smile. "You sure you're ready to sell? I do hear a hint of upset over the whole thing."

Baxter gave a one-arm shrug. "It's been my baby," he admitted. "But, just like her babies have flown the coop, it might be time to have mine go as well." Then he looked at Simon and smiled. "We had a health scare this year, and that means we get to reevaluate some of the things that we still want to do, while we have the time. As much as I wouldn't mind keeping *Running Mate*, we need the money from the sale to realize some of these other travel plans."

"Ah." Simon nodded at that. "That makes a whole lot more sense."

"The trouble is, we have all these things that we want to do and could do, but then we have to decide if we'll actually do them." Baxter eyed Simon with a certain seriousness that surprised Simon. "If you don't make those decisions soon, and then something happens, it's too late."

"I gather the health scare must have been pretty bad."

"It was. She was in treatment for nine months," Baxter shared, his voice dropping with emotions. "But she's free and clear now, so we'll spend the next five years doing a lot of what she wanted to do. She spent her life raising the children, and I could get away occasionally. Sure, a lot of them were business trips, but it was still a break, and it was a change for me. It was something that I could do but that she couldn't. We've talked about a lot of things over the years that she was counting on me to continue to do or to keep us on a plan, even though I may have changed my mind a time or two," he admitted, with an eyeroll. "So it's time for us to do a few other things. I might buy another yacht down the road, when we get there. You never know. Maybe I'll come knocking on your door, seeing if you're still as happy with your purchase then as you might be now," he added, looking at Simon intently. "Maybe you'll be willing to sell it back to me—though I doubt that will be anytime soon."

Simon smiled. "In that case, let's talk price."

After that, it didn't take long to hammer out a price that made them both happy. When Baxter stood, he shook Simon's hand and stated, "There's another advantage of your getting her too."

"What's that?" Simon asked, as he sent a text to his lawyer to draw up the paperwork.

Baxter laughed. "I'll come and visit you and her over the years," he shared ruefully, as Simon chuckled at his tone. "This last year I've hardly taken her out."

And, with that, and a promise to come and crack a couple beers down the road, Baxter walked out, leaving Simon with a smile and a sense of completion and joy. He'd bought something that had been on his mind for a very long time, but he hadn't quite got around to doing something about it. Now finally it had been the right time to do this.

Something about being in a relationship with Kate made Simon feel more settled. It made no sense because she seemed to also have sparked his psychic abilities in a way that made him way less settled. Still, she'd helped him to find a sense of value from them. A purpose.

As he got up to toss his plate and napkins in the garbage, a strange prickling raced along the back of his neck. Curious, he turned and looked around. A line of people were at the coffee counter again on both sides, one to order and another to await their drinks being made. They were mostly young, laughing, some of them on their phones. But one man, probably in his mid-fifties, just stood there, his hands in his jacket pockets, glaring but not necessarily seeing what was around him. It was weird.

Suddenly he turned and stared directly at Simon.

Simon jolted with the power of his gaze, before it slipped past him, almost as if releasing him. Such a strange and unnerving experience. He took note of the gentleman—nondescript brown hair, nondescript brown suit, nondescript brown shoes. Everything about him was kind of *nothing*. *Average*. Simon was more than a little disturbed by the realization that he couldn't find something more distinctive about him, so he quickly walked out of the coffee shop.

CHAPTER 5

KATE, WITH RODNEY at her side, pulled up to the first of the witness addresses they'd been given regarding the multiple drowning files. She double-checked her notes to confirm the address and frowned. "It doesn't look like a great area," she noted cautiously.

"You mean because we're in the commercial district and this looks more like a homeless shelter?"

She nodded. "What are the chances that it *is* a shelter?"

"Let's go find out." He hopped out of the vehicle, and she quickly raced to catch up.

As they walked in, she nodded. "Either it's a halfway house or something similar." At the front desk, Kate introduced herself and asked if they could see Norman Rogers.

The woman frowned. "I'm not sure that he's around," she noted tentatively. "Were you expecting him to be here?"

Kate nodded. "This is the last address we have on file."

"Ah." The woman's expression cleared. "We only keep residents for one night. They're welcome to come back the next day," she explained, still shuffling papers around. "Sometimes they use our address for mail and things, but we certainly can't say that they live here all the time."

"Right. So is this a halfway house, or is this a ..."

She interrupted, "It's a homeless shelter, and we start

taking in people again at three. Everybody needs to be out by nine in the morning, and then they can start filtering back here, depending on how much space we have at three o'clock."

"When do you close your doors?"

"For the evening, at ten o'clock," she replied, "*or* when we fill up, usually by six every night."

"So, you have a huge demand for this service."

"Absolutely," she stated. "We serve two meals, breakfast and dinner. They can go to the nearby soup kitchen for lunch, if they want."

"Right, so I presume you have a lot of regulars."

"We have mostly regulars," she admitted. "That is not optimal and can cause trouble with other homeless people in town because they can never get in. There are other centers of course, but not here, in this area."

"So back to the person who we asked for," Kate nudged.

The front desk lady looked around carefully. "Right. He has been here most of the last few months. I don't think he's around just now, but you could come back later today, and odds are you'll probably find him."

"Okay, and I suppose if we left a message for him, the chances of it getting to him aren't great?"

The woman winced. "It's not that I wouldn't try," she said in an apologetic tone, "but we don't have a system set up for that. Even though you might leave a message, I couldn't guarantee that he would receive it, and, if it were private, personal, or in any way important, I absolutely could not guarantee that he would get it or that he would respond to your message, if that is something you need."

"Right." Kate nodded. "We'll come back later this afternoon. How many people do you have here on a regular basis?"

"We accommodate one hundred and fifty a night."

"Oh, wow," she murmured. "That's a lot to deal with, isn't it?"

"I've worked at smaller homeless shelters, where they hold only thirty or forty residents," she admitted, without any hesitation. "We did several expansions on this one because this area deals with more homeless people."

"Wow. One hundred and fifty ..." Kate repeated. "That's a lot of people to keep track of. Not to mention trying to keep track of their things and the rules and all the fights and everything else that must come up."

The other woman nodded. "Exactly. I prefer a smaller center, but the need here means that it's full constantly."

As she walked back outside into the fresh air, Kate took a deep, slow breath. "Hard to imagine how so many people are in need that they have to go to a place like this every night and stand in line to ensure that they get a bed to sleep in. They can't leave their stuff, so are always carrying around whatever they have with them. If they don't get a bed before the place is full, they're out on the street." Kate shook her head. "This was a men's shelter, right? Or maybe it wasn't just for men." She frowned at Rodney. "Maybe that's why it's so big. Maybe they take in both. If coed, that would cause all kinds of additional headaches," she muttered.

Rodney chuckled. "Yeah, let's hope they also have the morning-after pill."

"Oh God," Kate muttered.

As they headed back to the car, he asked, "What's the next address?"

"Over in Kerrisdale," she replied, checking her notes.

"Who is it?"

"Sheila. Sheila Walker."

"Why do I know that name?"

She frowned at him and shrugged. "No clue. Why do you think that you know that name?"

He pondered it the whole trip, as he pulled up to a very appealing house in Point Grey.

She asked him, "Do you know the area?"

He nodded. "I used to live here."

"Maybe you know Sheila Walker then."

"I don't know for sure," he admitted, as they got out and walked up to the front door.

The door opened before they ever had a chance to knock, and a woman stood there, fully dressed and clearly ready to go out. She frowned at them, as she snapped, "I don't know what you're selling, but I don't want any of it."

"That's good," Kate replied, with a smile, "because we're not selling."

The woman stamped her foot impatiently. "I mean it. I have to leave."

Kate pulled out her badge and held it up.

The woman froze and looked at her in shock. "What's the matter?" she asked, almost in panic. "Did something happen to my daughter?"

"No," Kate said. "Our visit has nothing to do with her."

Sheila sighed, righting herself for a moment. "In that case, I don't have time for this shit."

"Where are you going?"

"I'm off to work, providing I still have a job when I get there. I've already had more than enough time off, and he is being a dick about it."

"I suppose being delayed by the cops won't be excuse enough for him."

"No, he'll think I made it up."

"Who's your boss?" Rodney asked, frowning.

Sheila turned to him and then stopped. "Rodney?"

He looked at her and slowly nodded. "Sheila. Oh, my God. I just told Kate, my partner here, that your name sounded familiar."

She rolled her eyes. "We did spend a lot of time in school together, but, of course, you forgot me," she stated crossly. "Story of my life right now. Look. I don't know what this is about, but I really need to go."

"It's about a drowning that you saw a few months ago and related ones. I would like to show you some photos."

The woman froze, closed her eyes. "I really don't want to talk about that." She shook her head vehemently. "I'm already seeing a therapist so I can sleep at night, instead of reviewing the drowning memories constantly plaguing my evenings."

"Did you see what happened?"

"That was the part that bothered me most. I didn't know if what I saw was real or something my mind was making up. I don't know. There was a wharf, a guy at the end of the wharf, and what I thought was a man in the water. The man on the wharf appeared to be trying to help the man in the water, but the man kept slipping away or something." Sheila stared between them impatiently. "At the end, he stood there, with nobody to pull up," she stated bitterly, then took a deep breath. "I phoned 9-1-1 and took off as soon as I could." She shuddered at the unpleasant memory. "It was terrible."

"Of course it was," Rodney agreed. "Can you describe the man? Did you go down to the water?"

"No, I didn't, and, as I already told you, there was something … You may think I'm a terrible person for this, but something was off about it. I didn't want him to know who I was. I didn't want to know anything about it. So, I took the coward's way out, raced back to the parking lot, and waited for the cops."

Then she eyed them both suspiciously and stated, "That was seriously months and months ago. Why are you coming now? What's changed?"

"It's not so much that something's changed," Rodney replied, "but we do have a couple other suspicious drownings. We would like you to look at a few photos and see if you recognize anyone." He fanned out the handful of victims and showed them to Sheila.

She stared at them briefly, then back at him, waving her hand, as her gaze widened. "Oh my God, oh my God, you think he murdered them all, don't you?"

"We don't know anything yet. That's why we're here," Kate stated in exasperation. "We don't have very much information, except your eyewitness account."

"But I didn't see anything, and that's the problem," she said bluntly. "I saw, but I didn't see."

Kate nodded. "Right. So, you saw something, but you don't know exactly what you saw."

"Yes, that's exactly it. So I can't help you." Then she stepped forward, pushing them both back down the walkway. "And now I really do have to go to work." She quickly locked up the door and bolted to her car.

Kate faced Rodney. "So, is that the effect you have on all women?"

He rolled his eyes at that. "That's not even a good joke."

"No, but that wasn't a good interview either," she declared, looking back to where the woman had disappeared.

"It was in one way," he muttered, his voice sober.

"What's that?"

"I think she's terrified."

"What could possibly have terrified her?" Kate asked.

"Did you see her expression when I showed her the other victim photos?"

Kate nodded. "She's not telling us everything."

They had four more witnesses to go and drove to the next address on their list. One had produced no results. The second one had just brought more confusion, and the third one they were heading to now, close by the university.

Rodney shook his head. "I don't understand what was going on in Sheila's head back there. It makes no sense. Yet she seemed truly terrified."

Kate wanted to say something about it, but she didn't know the woman enough to understand what was going on, yet something was off for sure. "Do you think she wondered if he had had something to do with the death, but was too scared to say anything in case he found out she had said something?"

"Oh, it's possible. You never know what goes through people's heads," Rodney replied. "You can't really hold it against her either."

"No, I'm not saying that, particularly if she does have any fear of reprisal."

"But why would she have any fear of reprisal? That's the question," he pointed out.

She gave him a flat stare. "Because she recognized him."

"Even though she's telling us that she didn't see him clearly enough?"

"She either knew him, recognized him, or could identify him."

"In which case, the question is, did he even care? Because he seems to have left her alone so far."

"But we don't know that," Kate pointed out. "She took off before we had a chance to find out further details from her."

"So, what now?"

"We come back around again to Sheila," Kate declared, with an eyeroll. "Seems to be our day for it."

And it was. By the time they got through the third interview, it was more of the same. This was a male teenager who kept holding out his hands, as if to ward them off. "I don't know. I don't know what I saw. I called the police because somebody was drowning."

"Yet you noted at the time that it seemed suspicious."

He winced. "Yeah, it was months and months ago. I was kind of a pathetic kid back then," he shared, "and I might have just been looking for attention."

"*Might* have been?" she asked.

He glared at her. "I don't remember."

"Or are you too scared to tell us?" Rodney asked curiously.

The kid flushed with temper and turned his anger on Rodney. "What is that supposed to mean?" he growled.

Kate replied, "I guess we're wondering if you recognized the guy trying to save him or if you were afraid for your own life. Did he come back and threaten you or anything like that?"

The kid stared at her. "Hell no. Why would he? We were trying to save that guy."

"*We?*" Kate repeated.

"Yeah, *we,*" the teen confirmed, looking at Kate cautiously. "I was down there too. I went and called for help, and then I raced down to the dock. I don't swim all that well, but I was willing to go in. By the time I got there, he was still standing there, calling out for help, but no sign of the kid." As he spoke, fear was evident in his voice and clearly written on his face. "Crap, that's the reason I turned my world around, you know? To clean up everything, after seeing him drown like that. The kid was around my age."

Kate nodded slowly. "He was your age. Exactly."

He winced at that and nodded. "So, as much as I understand that his death was a tragedy, it also woke me up a little bit and made me realize that everything you just assumed would be there forever might not be."

"And that's a good lesson to learn," she agreed. "Would you recognize this guy again?"

He stared at her and shrugged. "I'm not sure I would. It was getting late in the afternoon, and it was all a big panic. I talked to the police, and it was all kind of a blur that I didn't want to remember."

"What do you remember?"

"My parents came down and dragged me away from there. They didn't want me involved either," he said, with an eyeroll. "That seems to be a standard response, doesn't it?"

"Unfortunately it's exactly that," Kate confirmed. "Avoid it, run away, hide, and don't get involved." She pulled out the other victim photos and showed them to the kid.

He took a quick glance at them, probably figuring out these were pictures of dead people. He shook his head.

"If you do remember anything later, call me." She handed over her card.

"Right. That's kind of what I figured. Maybe if I keep my head down, maybe fate will miss me on its next pass."

She grinned. "That's not a bad way of looking at it. I think a lot of people have a similar hope regarding fate."

"Like she's a bitch, but she's our bitch?" he asked, with a droll smile.

She burst out laughing at that, liking the kid even more. "Something like that. Have you seen the guy trying to save the kid since the drowning?"

"No. God, no," the teenager replied. "Never, though I'm not sure I would have even recognized him if I did."

"Any idea on height? Skin color?"

"Yeah, he was white. Maybe older, like mid-fifties, late fifties, something along that line. Wasn't terribly big, kind of thin and scrawny. If he'd gone in after the guy, I think he probably would have drowned himself."

"I'm presuming he couldn't swim very well since he didn't go in after him," Rodney pointed out.

The kid shrugged. "I don't swim, but I was prepared to go in. And I know it's the wrong thing to think or to say, but I'm glad I wasn't put in that position. By the time I got there, nobody was there to save, you know?"

"You did not go into the water then, is that correct?"

"No, I didn't," he said. "Believe me. That's a decision I have questioned many times."

"Of course you have," Kate replied gently. "That would be normal under the circumstances."

"If I had gone in, I may not have survived myself, but I don't really have any reason to believe that. I think it's probably just straight-up fear," he admitted, now shivering. "I can tell you one thing though. I haven't gone back in the ocean."

"Not at all?"

He shook his head. "No way. After something like that,

it changes you," he stated. "I haven't gone back, and I'm not sure I ever will," he murmured. "That's just the way my life is now. It's kind of a pisser because I used to meet my friends down on the beach all the time, but now? Now it's a bit more than I can handle." He looked away.

Kate wondered, *Was he hiding something? If so, what?* "Do your friends understand?" she asked.

He looked at her. "I don't know how they could. I never told them. It's just not something I wanted them to know about."

She stared at him.

He flushed and then finally shared, "Look. I didn't go in after the guy. I didn't try to save him because I'm not that good of a swimmer. But I'm sure my friends, at least the big jocks, would have, and they probably would have saved the guy."

Clearly he was ashamed, and that was understandable.

"So, that just makes me feel even shittier, and I didn't want to tell them."

"Got it." Kate nodded. "We did find the teen's body, which does bring some closure for his family, at least."

"Yeah, closure for his family," he muttered bitterly, "but what about closure for those who watched him die?"

Back at their vehicle now, heading to the last witness's address, Rodney added, "The kid has a point."

"He does," she agreed. "Not the easiest of things to deal with, whether a car accident or something much more graphic. Seeing death happen right in front of you like that is always shocking. You go home and hug your child or kiss your spouse because you don't know what'll happen from one day to the next. You just don't know."

"How about you?" Rodney asked. "Is that what losing

your brother was like?"

"It was partly like that," she replied. "Then came the aftermath. The guilt, the distress, the blame, the knowing that *You don't deserve to live because you're not good enough, because you didn't do enough to save him, because you weren't the person who you came here to be*, which was to look after him apparently," she shared, a strong bitterness to her tone. "I shouldn't let you drive if you'll just bring up this shit."

"I'm sorry. I didn't think."

"You're just always bringing up the wound, and not just you. Everybody does it," she said, with a headshake. "I just don't understand why you care."

"We know that it's still an open cold case, and it's understandable that it would wear on you. You've obviously got some feelings about it."

"Oh, I've got a lot of feelings about it," she snorted. "You know my mother's still alive, but she won't talk to me because she blames me for her precious baby being dead," she snapped, then groaned. "And that just makes me sound and feel even worse because I don't know that Timmy's dead. However, after all these years, I have to assume that he is." She sat back.

"But there's always still that glimmer of hope, isn't there?"

"There is. Sometimes having hope is good. Yet sometimes having hope is brutal because you always look at the door when it opens, and you always reach for the phone when it rings, and you always have that eternal hope that maybe somebody just wanted a child. Maybe somebody just wanted to adopt him. Maybe, maybe, maybe."

He nodded and went quiet for the rest of the trip.

As they pulled up to the next address, she stared up at

the ramshackle house and muttered, "This doesn't look like a good sign."

He turned and followed her gaze, and, sure enough, the front door sagged drunkenly off the hinges.

"I wonder what this is all about?" he asked, pulling off his seat belt.

She pulled up the respective witness report and stated, "The drowning happened in a nearby lake." Then she looked at the name and read further. "Oh, no. No, no, no. This was a long time ago, like fifteen years ago."

He looked at her, pulled the file over where he could see it too, then nodded. "Interesting," he murmured.

As they walked up to the front of the residence, a dog tore out of the front door, barking like crazy. Kate just kept on walking and ignored him.

Rodney, however, stopped and asked her, "You think it's safe?"

"I don't care if it's safe or not," she stated, with a dismissive wave at the dog, who calmed down at her side. "I do find that a lot of these barks are tests. Some dogs will be out there to kill you, sure," she added, as she pointed to the one now sitting down, "and others, like this guy, he's just looking for a friendly hand."

She reached down to pet him gently, and the dog rolled over in ecstasy, giving her a belly.

She laughed, gently stroked his belly a few times, and then straightened. "Now, where's your master?" With that, the dog took off running in the direction of the house.

Rodney shook his head. "I wouldn't have given you two chances for walking into that place without getting bit."

She shrugged. "I know perfectly well that the worst predators in the world are the ones on two feet, not four."

SIMON FINISHED THE day, yet still with an odd sense of disquiet from his earlier encounter with the nondescript man at the coffee shop. Simon kept looking behind him, trying to figure out what was bothering him, but he had no answer, no explanation. Ever since the coffee shop and that weird sensation, he just didn't get it. But most definitely something was off.

Maybe the guy was off, maybe the coffee shop; he didn't know. Something was just off, and often *off* was what he got before the visions, yet it wasn't enough of an *off* to be an explanation. Confusing as hell. Yet was this related to his weird nudging dream that had no details too? Maybe someone was trying to communicate with him but wasn't getting through? Simon shook his head. He needed an instruction manual on this stuff.

As he walked away from his last rehab jobsite, his foreman Joe called him back and asked, "Whatever happened about Bartlett's company?"

Simon shrugged. "It's largely in the hands of the lawyers now, but it looks like the company will survive."

His foreman grinned. "Now that's good to know. With family companies like that, you really don't want to see them go down the tube, without anybody trying to help out."

"Oh, I think people were ready to *help*," Simon quipped. "Unfortunately most of them had a hand in the till and were helping themselves."

At that, his foreman winced. "And that's the world around us, isn't it?"

"Unfortunately it appears to be, but it just doesn't have to be," Simon retorted. "You would think that enough decent people were in the world out there that we wouldn't have to deal with this kind of crap," he snapped. "Still, that appears to be the state of affairs with Bartlett's company." He asked his foreman, "Are you guys doing okay, you and your wife and the kids?"

The foreman nodded. "Yeah, we're doing fine, at least for the moment." Then he laughed, as if he was not sure what to say. "We're happy to be in the moment, instead of dealing with God-only-knows what nightmares the kids come up with. I got four, all boys." He took a moment to savor that fact and looked a bit proud of himself. "When they were little, I thought that my life would be easy because they were boys. I would understand them and thought for sure I could handle it, but Holy Hannah," he replied, with a grin. "I was never the hellion that most of them are." He shook his head. "My youngest is a sweetheart, but he's young yet," he added, with an eyeroll.

"I bet your wife is thrilled."

"No, she kept saying that we should have girls, as if it were some conscious choice." He laughed. "At least then she could have kept them quiet with a shopping trip to the mall. It's just that the boys, they all want things that could kill them. They want racecars, motorbikes, drugs, alcohol." He shook his head. "Definitely not the same as it was in my day."

Simon chuckled. "Joe, nothing is the same anymore."

And, with that, Simon headed back to town. He would drop off some cash at the women's shelter on his way, since he'd been informed they'd had several new arrivals and might need some extra assistance. He also hadn't checked in on the owner, Lisa Sands, in a while, and he probably should do that. It just brought up more of those bad memories. Yet she remained there, carrying on solo, even after the bad situation with her business partner. Lisa was still helping everybody, so the least Simon could do was stay and help as well.

She had suffered terribly, and now she was trying to make amends for her partner's doings, but Lisa had spent her life making amends. As he walked to the center, he went around to the back alley and quickly knocked. When Lisa opened the door and saw him, tears came to her eyes.

He nodded. "I know." He raised his hands. "It took me a little while to work my way back around here again."

She asked in a hushed whisper, "Do you want to come in?"

He shook his head. "Nope, I'm fine here," he said politely, knowing most of the women in these shelters had been abused, and a strange man could scare them. "I'm tired. I'm just heading home." But he held up the roll of bills and added, "It's not a whole lot, just what I happened to have on me."

She accepted it, with a quiet thanks. "There is just me now, so I don't need quite as much."

He knew what she was referring to because he suspected that the shelter was bound to be in hot water when one of their own went on a murder spree. "Yes, but there will be more clients who need it," he told her in a reassuring tone. "Can you keep this place going alone is another question, or should you seek another partner?"

"I know," she admitted, "and the jury's still out on that."

"Take it day by day. You know how to reach me," he replied, as he quickly backed up, then turned and headed through town.

He took a couple shortcuts, wondering just what route he should take and whether he wanted to stop and eat while he was out. He saw one of the homeless shelters up ahead, one he passed on a regular basis, but what caught his eye was the ray of sunshine that he cherished all too well. Right there in front of him was Kate.

He stopped to watch, and she appeared to be talking to somebody standing outside the shelter in a loosely formed line. Simon wanted to approach but didn't want to interfere, only he was riddled with curiosity now. What was she doing at the homeless shelter?

As he approached, the man Kate had stopped just looked at him and growled, "The center's full."

Simon smiled, then nodded. "Understood. I should be okay tonight though. Are you?"

The other man shook his head. "She won't let me go inside," he whined.

Simon turned, looked at Kate, one eyebrow raised.

She sighed. "I have a couple questions for him. That's all," she replied, treating Simon as if he were an interested bystander. "He's not being terribly cooperative," she added, with a hard glance in the young man's direction.

"I don't know anything," he whined. "I don't know what I saw."

"And yet," she pointed out, "your hands are shaking."

He shoved his closed fists into his pockets, then argued, "They are not."

She groaned. "But they are, and that tells me that you're scared, which means either you're scared of me or scared of what you saw."

"A guy drowned," he snarled. "I didn't like it. It left me really shaken up," he muttered, and, indeed, he looked like he was quite unsteady. "I saw something. I don't even know what I saw exactly, but this man was trying to pull a kid out of the water. I don't know how old the kid was, or maybe it was a small woman," he replied, raising both hands out of his pockets. "I don't even want to know because I already have bad-enough nightmares."

Simon understood that. "Maybe you could tell her if you would recognize this guy or something, and then she would leave you alone, and you could go in and get a meal."

He turned and looked at her.

She nodded, eyeing him intently. "Can you identify him?"

He shook his head. "No, I told you that."

"How old was he?"

He stared at her, his bottom lip trembling, but it appeared to be a gaze of concentration on his face. "Maybe in his fifties?" he muttered. "He was small in stature. The guy in the water was screaming for help, and people were running away, so the other guy was trying to use a stick to pull him forward." Then the witness stopped and admitted, "I was high on drugs. I've been clean ever since, honest," he claimed, his gaze going anxiously back from one to the other, as he turned toward the center to ensure nobody heard him. "If they think I'm on drugs, they won't let me in."

"I didn't hear you say you were," she noted, "and, if you've been clean since, it's got nothing to do with me."

He seemed to relax at that. "It seemed to me … God, it's been giving me nightmares."

"What?" she asked intently.

He lowered his voice, leaned forward, and whispered, "It seemed to me that he was using the stick to keep him down, to keep poking him under the water, instead of helping him out."

And, with that, he dashed into the shelter, leaving Kate and Simon behind, staring after him.

CHAPTER 6

"**S**HIT," KATE SNAPPED, as she tossed her jacket on the small hook that Simon had placed at the front of the hallway in his place and then threw her wallet on a small table with a beautiful, probably thousand-dollar collectible on it to hold keys. As she studied the bowl for a minute, she shook her head, realizing that people with money had no concept of what life was like for people who didn't.

"What's the matter?" Simon asked, with a note of amusement. "Even my bowl is pissing you off today?"

She turned and glared at him, but, when his eyebrows shot up, she groaned. "Maybe I should go home." She looked away from him. "I'm probably not the best company right now."

"That may be so. Still, it's probably even more important that you stay and visit, even though you're not in a great mood," he shared, studying her intently. "Something about this case obviously bothers you."

"Yeah. All the stories, although they vary with slight differences, have just enough similarity to really, really worry me."

"How many are we talking about?"

"Seven," she declared. "We talked to a total of seven witnesses to date, and it was pretty much the same thing. Everybody, every one of them, was traumatized by the incident, but not a one of them could identify the person who was desperately trying to help somebody who was drowning—or maybe not. And the last guy, as you heard, thought that maybe the supposed Good Samaritan was using the stick to keep the kid underwater. When they dragged him up again, he was dead," she added in exasperation. "It's the same kind of story in each case. In every case the same Good Samaritan was there, whoever he is, this white male in his fifties, small in stature, who apparently didn't swim well, if at all, involved in trying to rescue these people."

"And you don't think he was rescuing them?" Simon asked bluntly, putting it right out there in the open.

"No, and the question is whether he was murdering them or putting them in a position where they could save themselves," she suggested, with an eyeroll. "Or some other godforsaken nightmare of an excuse for whatever it was he was doing."

"But you're pretty certain that you've got the same guy showing up at each drowning event?"

"No, not at all, because not a one of them could identify him. ... No, that's not true. One was an old school friend of Rodney's, someone he hadn't spoken to since way back when. I definitely got the impression that she was hiding something."

"What would she be hiding?"

"Honestly? I think she got a good look at him, and I think that's why she's been kind of a mess ever since."

"It seems like the guy I saw you with also saw something that made quite an impact."

"Wouldn't you react that way too? If people see someone die, that's already traumatizing, like if you witness a car accident. However, when it's something like a drowning, where somebody is struggling to survive, and then they don't," she explained, "it can be so much worse."

"Seeing somebody on a bridge ready to jump was terrifying enough for me."

She nodded. "Exactly, now imagine if that person had jumped, and you were in the water, but you couldn't get to her in time. Then you watched her struggle and struggle and drown, before you could save her."

He walked over to the fridge with a headshake, then pulled out a bottle of wine and popped the cork on it. "I don't need to imagine," he replied, his voice flat. "I've got enough shit going on with the dead on the other side that I don't really want to deal with that too." Then he looked at her with misery clearly visible on his face. When she went oddly silent, he frowned at her. "What?"

"You said you've got enough going on *with the dead* on the other side."

He winced. "I don't know where this information comes from, where these visions come from, and there have been enough cases involving you that I wonder if these people talking to me, or trying to talk to me, are already dead," he shared, shaking his head. "I know you don't want to hear about that any more than I want to tell you. But, hey, I'm already up the shit creek of crazy anyway. The question is whether you're coming along with a paddle to rescue me."

She stared at him, her eyebrows slowly lifting. "I've never heard you talk like that," she noted, her earlier mood completely changing, as she studied him and realized something else was going on. "Did something happen to you today?" she asked curiously, as she watched his expression change.

"Not so much today." And then he acknowledged,

"Yeah, some weird thing was going on today, but I don't even know what to say about it." Then he looked away and groaned. "It was just a weird day, a weird couple of days."

"Why don't you tell me more about this?" she offered. He looked over at her and glared, but she shrugged. "It seems to be the evening for it."

"Why? Because you've been talking to all these people about drowning victims?"

She nodded. "That's my life. I talk to people about dead people. Remember?"

He looked at her, and then a smile broke across his face. "God, we're a pair, aren't we?" He held out a full glass of wine.

She walked over, took a sip, then set her wineglass on the counter. Smiling at him, she pointed him toward the couch. "It seems like we are," she replied, walking over to see the view. "I didn't really think we were going to be anything close to a pair, but it does appear to be that that's where we're heading."

"*Heading?*" he asked, with a wry note.

"Fine, that's where we are already," she snapped. "Happy now?"

"Not anywhere near close enough." He snorted, then took a sip of wine. "Yet, hey, that's progress, so I'll take it."

She sighed. "It shouldn't be this hard."

"Nothing should be this hard," he stated, looking at her.

"So, why do we keep making it that hard?" she asked, glaring at him. "Seriously, why does all this stuff keep coming around in circles, and why are people such shits?" She landed on the couch with a *thud*.

Simon nodded, as he joined her on the couch. "What you're trying to figure out is why would anybody want to do something like this, and how could they?"

"Yeah, I do want to know," she said. "I can't, for the life of me, understand in what way watching somebody drown is something someone can get off on."

"Maybe if somebody's been traumatized by a drowning early in life ..." And he let his voice trail off, staring at her, as if willing her to fill in the blank.

"Meaning that, if somebody already was traumatized, ... they're recreating it somehow?"

Simon nodded, encouraging her. "What if they're recreating it, hoping that they'll get a different outcome this time?"

She stared at him and then laughed. "That's just crazy enough to be possible."

He smiled. "Apparently *crazy* is what we do."

She winced. "The *what-ifs* with you are painful."

"The *what-ifs* are painful no matter who they're with. But think about it. What could possibly cause somebody to want to recreate these scenarios?"

"Because he lost somebody, and he wants to either save somebody in order to redeem himself or ..." She thought about it, shaking her head. "To recreate a situation just once is one thing, but to do it over and over again? Let's go with your theory. What if he *is* recreating it, so he can save the person he couldn't save before?"

"Meaning, he's caught in some sort of time loop?" Simon asked.

Kate nodded. "Yeah, but doesn't recognize that the person he didn't save isn't coming back regardless."

"Exactly," he agreed, with satisfaction and a smile. "Did you talk to anybody today who said something along that line?" Simon twisted in his seat on the couch to face her.

She took the glass of wine out of his hand, took a sip, and then handed it back to him, ignoring hers on the kitchen counter. "But, according to one man, he watched a little boy drown in a lake some fifteen years ago. All kinds of people were around, and everybody tried to save him. The boy was eventually pulled from the water, but it was too late. People screamed, shouted for a doctor, all kinds of stuff, but he couldn't be saved."

Simon shook his head. "You're right though. What the hell is going on that any one person could witness more than one drowning?"

"That was my problem too," she noted, with a smirk. "But the witness wouldn't talk after that, not with Rodney there."

"So, you're going back tomorrow."

"Absolutely," she declared, with a smile. "I'll start there in the morning. Rodney was like, *Yeah, you go on your own. I don't want to see that dog again.*" She laughed. "The dog *really* didn't like Rodney, so it's probably just as well to keep the two of them apart."

"Is the dog safe?" Simon asked hesitantly. She cocked an eyebrow at him, and he shrugged. "You can't blame a guy for asking."

"I might not blame a guy for asking, *unless* he's asking because he assumes I'm not capable of looking after myself with a little dog."

He groaned, his shoulders sagging, as he replied in a firm tone, "I would never make that mistake."

She chuckled, and then she stared at him. "We didn't pick up any food. You have any leftovers?"

He shook his head and laughed. "No, I don't think I do, but the sky is not falling, and there are options. We can go pick up something, or, hey, maybe we should go out to have a meal for a change."

She groaned at that. "Can't say I'm up for that."

"A few local places are around here, and, there's always Mama's, and she's been asking about you."

She hesitated. "Italian would be good, but ..." She looked down at her clothes. "I'm not dressed to go to a restaurant."

He eyed her up and down, shook his head, and pointed out, "Mama would have your head on a platter for saying that. She doesn't care if you come in your nightclothes. She just wants to encourage you to come."

Kate burst out laughing. "You could be right, but first you need to tell me what the hell happened to you today." He glared at her, and she nodded. "I'm not a cop for nothing," she stated, with a smile. "Lots of things happen that I might miss, but, when it's dodgy, suspicious, or something to do with one of my cases, believe me. My antenna's on full alert."

"It's got nothing to do with one of your cases."

"Yeah? How do you know?" she asked.

"Because I know it's not."

"Then maybe you should tell me the good news first."

He sat back and frowned at her. "How the hell did you know there's something good?"

"Because there's a bubbliness to you, but then something is underneath. It's almost as if you're dying to tell me and wanting to go out and celebrate something," she noted. "I don't know what it is, and I'm not sure what's going on, but it would be good if you just told me."

"Shit," he muttered. He picked up his glass of wine, tossed back the bulk of it, and admitted, "Fine, I bought the yacht today."

"*Running Mate*," she said in delight.

He asked, "You remembered the name?"

"Sure, it's kind of unique."

"It is a unique name," he agreed. "I kind of like it and might keep it. Baxter's happy that he'll get to visit her in the marina. I need to contact him about the berth as it is. Maybe I can lease that from him too," he shared, giving her a smile. "Finding a dock is a whole different story in this town."

"I'm sure you have lots of friends to help you find a place."

He smiled, then nodded. "I've got a couple to check out first. I want something within walking distance, so I can head down with a picnic basket and just go."

"That sounds absolutely lovely," she declared in delight.

"Good, then make it a date for Saturday."

She frowned. "What do you mean? This coming Saturday?"

"What? Do you really think we're not going out on it?" he asked in exasperation. "I figured a picnic on Saturday would be perfect."

"And yet," she began, with a note of warning.

"I know. You're on a case, so it all depends on work."

She nodded. "Okay, so that's the good news. I'm kind of looking forward to it."

"Good. Maybe one day we'll bring the rest of your team."

She rolled her eyes at that. "Let's not get too excited."

He chuckled.

"But I'm still waiting," she stated, firmly refusing to budge, until he fessed up.

He relaxed back on the couch and thought about what

he could even tell her. "It's nothing that I can even put a finger on, but just today I had this strange feeling. I was at the coffee shop and had just finished my boat-buying business with Baxter, and somewhere along the line I had this strange sensation of, I don't know. ... I don't even know what to say, but it was a weird feeling of something going on. Maybe it was a person. Maybe it was not the person but the place." He frowned, shaking his head. "But I got a weird feeling coming off one guy in the coffee shop, a smaller person, slight in stature, maybe in his fifties or so. It may have been the wariness that made him seem older. Anyway... he stared at me for a long moment too."

She froze and asked, "Are you sure it was him?"

"We were at a coffee shop with other customers," he explained, sipping his wine. "I tried hard to figure out who was emanating this weird—I don't even want to call it a *signature*—but this weird ..." He threw up his hands. "Energy, a feeling, coming from somebody in this coffee line, and, when he looked at me, it appeared to be coming from him."

She nodded, her gaze intent.

He frowned at her and admitted, "Okay, so normally I know what that look means, but today? ... You've got me flummoxed."

She sighed. "Normally you wouldn't be this dense." His jaw snapped shut, and he glared at her. She added, "So, what did I just tell you about all those witness descriptions?"

He asked, "What do you mean? The drownings?"

"Yeah, the drownings."

"Oh, he was in his fifties maybe, slight in stature, white." And then he sagged, his jaw dropping, and he was hit hard, "In his fifties. Oh, hell no." She just waited. "No, no, no, no, no, no, no, no, no. This is not connected to one of your cases." She didn't say anything, and finally he glared. "Do you really think it could be him?"

"I have no idea." She eyed him in astonishment. "Maybe that's a question you should be asking yourself. Do you really think it could be him?"

"No, hell no," he replied in frustration. "Why the hell would it be him?"

She shook her head. "I don't have any idea, and it doesn't make sense to me. But, for whatever reason, you picked up on the energy of somebody who matches the same description that seven people gave me of somebody who could be drowning people in order to try and save them or to watch them expire," she repeated calmly, "and the only thing I now have to ID this guy is on you."

Simon wasn't so sure.

"Will you sit with the sketch artist? He can bring out more than you think."

Simon frowned, yet shook his head. "I can if you need me to. I did see him at my local coffee shop. I'll keep an eye out for him there and will let you know."

CHAPTER 7

A N HOUR LATER Kate and Simon walked into Mama's restaurant. She took one look at Simon and came running, throwing her arms around Simon with all the same robust love that Kate remembered from before. When Mama saw Kate, her face lit up even wider, and she gave Kate a huge bone-crunching hug as well. Considering the woman couldn't have been more than five foot four and almost as round as she was tall, Kate was amazed at the amount of force she could generate in that hug.

When Mama finally stepped back, her face was flushed with pleasure and pride. She nudged Simon. "I'm glad to see you brought her back." Then Mama beamed at Kate. "Come, come, come. Let's get you food." She frowned, as she walked beside Kate. "You're still losing weight."

"I'm probably not losing weight," Kate corrected, "but I will give you that I'm probably not gaining weight either."

Mama sighed. "It's no good. You'll waste away to nothing."

Kate chuckled at that. "I am a long way from wasting away to nothing," she countered, with a smile. "A very long way from that."

But Mama wouldn't listen. "You're too skinny."

Such a note of surety filled her tone that Kate knew there would be no arguing with her. "I'm sure dinner will help," she replied gently.

Mama's face lit up, and she nodded. "It will, indeed," she declared, practically beaming. "It will, indeed." She gave her a look and added, "You go sit down. I'll bring you coffee." She stopped and looked at Simon. "Or do you want wine? I'll bring a bottle of wine," she declared, not giving him a chance to even answer, and she quickly raced into the back room.

Kate sat and looked over at Simon. "You know, considering the way that she moves, I don't understand how she could possibly have a weight issue."

"For one, she doesn't think she has a weight issue, and that's a huge distinction," he pointed out, with a smile. "And the other is, … she moves constantly, but she also loves her groceries. So, I think moving just stops her from getting any bigger."

"That's a good thing," Kate noted, "so her health is not an issue." Yet she was such a happy person and seemingly so comfortable in her body that Kate wanted to cheer her on, but she didn't want the woman to die early from a heart attack or any other complication either. Still, she would never say that to Mama. That was definitely not happening.

Simon patted her hand and nodded. "I know you're just concerned about her."

"I am," she agreed. "She's a lovely lady, and I don't want to see anything going wrong in her world. Not to mention the fact that you wouldn't have any food to eat for the rest of your life if something did happen to her," she teased, with an eyeroll.

He looked at her in mock outrage. "*Me?* We'll see who eats the most tonight."

She groaned. "Don't challenge me. I'm starving."

"Exactly."

Before they even had the words out of their mouths, Mama returned with a big board full of wonderful sourdough bread and butter in one hand and an ice bucket with a bottle of wine in her other hand. She quickly unloaded everything on the table and disappeared.

Kate looked down at the bread and smiled. "It's worth coming just for this."

Simon picked up the bread knife and started slicing the loaf, and nodded. "It is, isn't it? But then the rest of the food is also divine."

They settled into a wonderful evening of ravioli, homemade in the back, and a beautiful salad. Only as the evening was almost done did Simon ask, "Mama, where's your husband?"

"Ah," she muttered, her face frowning with sorrow. "He's struggling with the loss of a family member today," she shared, tears in her eyes. "I told him to take off the evening and to spend it with his family."

"What happened?" Kate asked, not sure if she should.

"His nephew drowned," Mama shared, her tears threatening to spill, "and all of us are horrified."

"Of course, of course," Kate agreed, patting her shoulder. "Locally? Was it here in town?"

"Yes, yes," she said, "down at the beach. I don't even know which beach," she shared animatedly. "But he was out playing on the rocks, and he went under, and everybody tried to pull him back up again, but …"

"Ah, so Stanley Park? But they weren't jumping, were they?"

"I don't know," she replied, tears in her eyes. "Maybe. He's young and stupid enough."

"Right." Kate winced. A mermaid statue and a couple other very popular places were down on the seawall that a lot of people, both locals and tourists, liked to jump from. Some of those places were quite dangerous, particularly if the water levels were low. Nobody ever seemed to consider the rocks that were underneath, so Vancouver had more than its fair share of accidents. "I am so sorry," she murmured gently to Mama.

Mama nodded. "The family is devastated of course, the poor soul," she muttered, wiping the tears away from her face. "So young."

"So, a group of boys were there?"

"A couple of them and young, yeah, but older than him, but all too young. By the time it was all over with, I think half the city was there," she stated, with a sigh. "A doctor was trying to save him. Several others were trying to save him. I don't want to ask too many questions because it all just makes my husband so sad." Mama sniffled, as she returned to the kitchen.

Kate winced and nodded but mentally noted that she should look it up in the morning. Drownings like that wouldn't likely have any effect on her case. Still, considering it was yet another drowning, as far as she was concerned, it was a little too much coincidence for the day. As she turned, she caught Simon's gaze and the acknowledgment in his. She winced and nodded. "You think it's connected?"

His gaze had a far-off look with something weird, something otherworldly about it. When he slowly tilted his head to the side and looked at her with a strange intensity, she realized that's exactly what he thought.

CHAPTER 8

BRIGHT AND EARLY the next morning, Kate walked into the office and sat down at her desk, grateful that the bullpen was empty at the moment, and she could get in a few minutes of research—before anybody came in and questioned why she was working on another drowning case. It probably had nothing to do with the ones she'd been asked to look into. Yet being asked to investigate something was a far cry from finding something curious about another incident.

She didn't want to be paranoid, and neither did she want to make assumptions. So a few quick clicks should dispel any sense of disquiet about this drowning case involving Mama's husband's nephew. Stanley Park and the seawall were both popular places for swimming at any point in time. However, it didn't seem to matter how many public announcements anybody made or how many warning signs were put up telling people not to jump off the wall, particularly in low-lying water areas. Still, every year a certain number of deaths happened from just that.

With just a couple clicks of her mouse, she found the report filed yesterday. She quickly printed off a copy to read. It was categorized as an accidental death, a drowning down at the seawall, right at the very spot she had expected. She wasn't surprised, considering one or two deaths a year always occurred there. It's seriously sad that, even after all the education and sincere efforts to try and warn people about these areas, still that group—almost always young males, with the occasional young female thrown in there—continued to ignore the warnings.

Per the report, according to three friends, they had all been there on a dare. It was far from beach season, although a warm fall for Vancouver. Yet this young man didn't want to jump off the rocks but had been swimming in the area. They had all been splashing and playing, but nobody saw whether he jumped off the rocks or not. He had been in the water with the rest of them, and another group had come to join them.

They'd all been talking and laughing, with a bunch of them jumping off the wall and into the water, having fun. A couple more went off the rocks themselves, when they realized one of their group was in trouble. An older man had come over to help, but he had been unable to do anything, until they got the swimmer to the shore, but it was too late. They had done CPR and everything else that could possibly be done. However, the head injury had potentially rendered resuscitation ineffective. That was declared the most likely cause of death.

Not a whole lot was in the initial report, including a few quick mentions of the observers. Nothing there suggested anything beyond a regular drowning. Relieved at that, Kate still decided to phone the detective and ensure she could write off this one.

When she introduced herself, he replied, "This one isn't yours. This was an accident, through and through."

"I'm glad to hear that," she replied. "I do have a series of cases I'm looking into that looked like drownings, but potentially were not."

He paused at that. "Crap, people are sick."

"They can be absolutely," she agreed. "I'm only calling to confirm this was an accident and not connected to a case I'm working on."

"The issue is that people are stupid, and no matter how many times we warn the public about not jumping into the water because you don't know what's underneath—even with warnings posted that hidden rocks are here—apparently he still chose to jump."

"He was seen jumping?"

He hesitated. "I didn't ask that directly, but the whole group of them were jumping, so that was the assumption. They were jumping, and he didn't surface very quickly. When he did, he was moaning a little bit, as if his head were hurting. Then he went under, rather than splashing around and looking for help. So they thought he was just kidding at first. However, after he didn't resurface soon, they managed to find him and to drag him to the surface, but it was already too late."

"Interesting," she murmured, relieved more than she could say that this probably had nothing to do with her case.

"Nothing was suspicious about it," he repeated. "It was just sad, damn sad. I know we live in an ocean town and all, but it would be nice if we didn't have quite so many of these accidental drownings."

"I agree with you there." Kate sighed.

"If you need anything else, you know where to reach me." And, with that, they rang off.

She stared at the report and wondered whether she should double-check things the officer admittedly hadn't specifically confirmed. On that note, she picked the first name on the list of witnesses, Alison Murre. When Kate dialed the number, it was picked up almost at the first ring.

"Hello," answered a woman on the other end.

"Hi, I'm Detective Kate Morgan. I'm with the Vancouver Police Department."

"Oh my, this is about Axel's drowning yesterday, isn't it?"

"It is, in the sense that I just need to confirm some of the details."

"What details?" she asked bitterly. "We thought everything was fine. Then we turn around, and it wasn't fine at all." She sighed heavily. "God. Nobody seemed to do anything to help him."

"What do you mean?"

"We were all jumping, laughing, and playing around in the water," she replied. "I got out because I was getting cold, and another group of people came over, and we were laughing and talking with them. They were on skateboards and whatnot. I wasn't even paying attention to what was happening behind me," she explained, a raw scratchiness in her tone. "When all the frantic yelling started, I turned around and realized that Axel was not with the group. When I called out, asking where he was, others were diving in, looking for him. When they came back up, another man was there, fully dressed, reaching out with shaky hands, trying to help."

"A man?"

"Yeah, he looked respectable too. I pulled him back because he didn't look very good, and I asked him if he was all right." He just gave me a weird look and told me how he was terrified of water, and I'm like, *Dude, get away from it then,* you know? Meanwhile, our friends and a bunch of other guys jumped in, and suddenly they brought Axel to the surface, but ... it was pretty clear he was already gone.

"Then the older guy jumped into action, stating he was a doctor, and started doing CPR, trying to save Axel. ... We wanted it to work. We really did. Axel was one of our best friends. But it was obvious, after ten minutes, no way to save Axel, but the older guy kept at it. He just wouldn't give up. They told him it was probably too late, that Axel had been under too long, but he wouldn't listen. He just kept shaking his head. And, when the ambulance arrived, they took over CPR, but they called it very quickly afterward because there were just no vitals," she added. "They grabbed Axel and took him away." Her voice broke at that point. "It was ... really bad."

"Of course it was," Kate said. "Would you recognize the man?"

"I'd recognize him, sure. Maybe. I'm pretty sure the police talked to him but maybe not. I don't know. He just disappeared, looking completely shattered that he couldn't save Axel, and I felt bad for him."

"Of course," Kate agreed. "A death like this, ... it affects everybody differently."

"It certainly affected me and my friends. We'd all been in there playing in that same water, enjoying the unexpected wave of warm weather, so to not even know exactly what happened or how, it was all just so distressing," she muttered. "I cried all day yesterday, and today my eyes are so worn out and tired. I just don't even know what to do." Then she started to weep again softly.

"This man, did he have a name?"

"I don't know," she replied, her voice flat, completely done with the conversation. "I'm sure it'll be in the police report."

"I'm sure it will be. Anyway, thanks very much for your help." She quickly disconnected and checked the report, but there was no name. She called the detective back, and, when he answered again, he stated, "Wow, this case has really got you hooked."

"I just talked to one of the witnesses, the young lady, Alison Murre."

"Yeah, she was pretty racked up about it," he admitted. "But then, you watch a friend of yours drown like that, it's hard. It's always hard. And young kids like that? They think life is grand, and they are immortal. Then, just like that, it's not quite so grand anymore. The reality is a bit of a bitch."

"Absolutely," she murmured. "She mentioned that a doctor was there, that he'd worked hard to try and save Axel. Did you guys catch his name or interview him? I'm not seeing it in the report."

He sighed. "Yeah, I looked around for him, but, not finding him, concluded he was already long gone. Understandably he was pretty upset at the fact that he couldn't do anything about it."

"It sounded like he was doing CPR, until he passed it off to the EMTs, when the ambulance crew arrived."

"Yeah, absolutely," he confirmed, "but I didn't catch the guy's name. I asked a few people, but they didn't know who he was either, and he had already left the scene. And, before you ask, absolutely no cameras are down there."

"Got it." She ended the call, pondering the scenario. Not able to leave it alone, she picked up the phone and called the second name on her list. It was a young man and another friend of Axel's.

"I don't know what I can tell you," he replied in a tone

that matched Alison's. "God, everything happened so fast. It was slow motion for the longest time in the sense that we couldn't find him, and then suddenly there he was. I know it sounds terrible, but a part of me wished we hadn't found him at that point because, after trying our best, we had to face the reality that he was dead. And none of us could deal with that either."

"So, someone tried to save him?"

"We all tried. This one guy tried so hard to bring him back, with CPR and everything, but nothing was working," he explained. "When the paramedics took Axel away, it was already over with," he shared, "but the doctor dude, he tried hard, so kudos to him for that."

"Nobody seems to have caught his name. Do you happen to have it?"

"Nope, I sure don't. It's not like we were doing introductions or anything," he snapped in a scathing voice. "We were all focused on trying to save Axel."

"Of course," she said. "I just wondered, since his name isn't on any of the reports yet."

"I'm not at all surprised. I know he was pretty upset when he couldn't save him. He was—*upset* doesn't do it justice. He was ... He was devastated."

"Right," she noted, "and understandably so."

"Yeah, absolutely," he agreed. "We were all really shaken up, and none of us wanted to see that happen."

"And you go down there a lot, do you?"

"We used to," he said. "I won't go back, and my mum is very much of the opinion that I shouldn't have been there in the first place," he muttered. "I've been reamed out many times over it, and I haven't worked up the courage to go see Axel's mom yet."

"Yes, it would be a nice thing if you would," she suggested. "I'm sure she's suffering."

"I'm sure she is, but I can't help her. Everything I could have done, we did, and there's just nothing else I could have done," he wailed, his voice starting to crack. "Look. I can't talk anymore." And, with that, he was gone.

She phoned a couple more of the bystanders and got the same response. Basically they came upon a group, obviously in a panic about somebody accidentally drowning, and efforts were underway to try and resuscitate him, but the efforts were unsuccessful, and wasn't it a terrible shock and shame for everybody? By the time she was done and got up to grab some coffee, the bullpen had filled up.

Rodney asked her, "What's going on?"

"Another drowning I heard about," she replied, trying for a casual tone. "I was just checking to make sure it wasn't connected."

"And?"

"I don't think it was connected, but I needed to check. If I could find the doctor who had been instrumental in trying to resuscitate the victim, I would feel a lot better."

"Why?" Lilliana asked curiously, off from the side. "If he was working to actively resuscitate him, doesn't that kind of go against everything that you think has been happening?"

"No, not in this instance." She thought back to the details. She raised both hands and grumbled, "I don't have anything, so I was hoping to find something."

"Right, got it." Lilliana nodded. "Those cases are the devil, aren't they?"

"They absolutely are."

Owen walked in just then. "Did you guys hear about that other drowning down in Vancouver? Down at Stanley

Park."

She looked up at him and groaned. "Yeah, I was just making some phone calls about it. Why? How did you hear about it?"

He shrugged. "It's on the news."

"Of course it is." She shook her head. "It would be nice if the media wasn't quite so quick to get on top of this stuff."

"Why?" he asked, perplexed. "Maybe it'll keep somebody else safe."

"And yet, with the water so low now, you would think they could see the rocks down below," Rodney pointed out, looking over at Kate curiously.

"Yep, you would think so," she agreed. "Apparently there's all kinds of ways and means of dying without thinking about them."

"We see it time and time again," Rodney noted, pointing at his computer. "How many times in a day do we have deaths that make absolutely no sense, yet people are gone in a flash? ... Too many are because of sheer stupidity."

She nodded. "I know. I get it, but this one's getting to me."

"Maybe you need a break from that. Work on something else for a while," Owen suggested.

"Wouldn't that be nice," she muttered. "But I've got an angle going on this one now, so I'll follow it through."

"Need any help? Unless vicious dogs are involved," Rodney added.

She snickered. "Not really, but how would I identify someone who helped at the scene of a drowning, but nobody got his name?"

He looked at her and frowned. "God only knows. I guess if you could find somebody who recognized him."

"Sure, but I would need a picture to show them," she pointed out, with a wry look.

"Exactly, so that makes life a little more difficult." And, with that, Rodney turned back to his computer.

She sat here, flipping her pen back and forth, trying to figure out an angle to even search for. "Yet again, no cameras, and nobody knows anything about it." Then she thought about it and muttered, "Video," under her breath. She quickly phoned the one girl back. "Yes, it's Detective Kate Morgan again."

Alison sighed. "I sure hope you're done soon."

"I know it sounds like a macabre request," Kate began, "but, in these cases, often people have their phones out, taking videos."

She gasped and cried out, "That's just disgusting."

"And yet cell phones capture so much these days."

"I certainly didn't take a photo of it," she declared in disgust. "A good friend of mine died. Why the hell would anybody do that?"

"We know why people do it because they're curious, and then there's that whole sense of *Hey, look what I got.* Then they show other people."

"That's just gross," she snapped.

"I don't disagree, and I'm not saying that you took photos. I'm asking if you noticed anybody with their phones out, maybe taking photos or video?"

The girl calmed down at that. "I didn't really notice, but you're right. Somebody could have caught it," she added bitterly, "even though it's wrong."

"But you also know how people feel about stuff like this and how much of it ends up on social media."

"God, I sure as hell hope not. That would be awful for

his family."

"That would be awful," Kate agreed. "Did you notice anybody who may have had their phone out and may have taken pictures of it?"

"I wasn't watching for anything like that, but the only ones in a position to do it," she shared, "would have been in the skateboarding group we'd been talking to. They left, but then they came back. I wouldn't be at all surprised if some of them had done something like that."

"But you didn't notice?"

"No, the only thing I was focused on was whether my friend was going to survive," she snapped, with a note of brutal honesty in her voice. "Would it help in any way to have a video of it?"

"Of course," Kate stated. "Any visual record gives us more than actual eyewitness accounts, right? It's far too easy, particularly when people are under stress, for important details to get forgotten or to be lost in translation from person to person."

"I suppose," she replied doubtfully. "I don't know if they would turn it over to you though."

"You let me worry about that."

"Right. I suppose it's a crime."

"If it was taken without anybody's permission, … what do you think? And, if it's posted on social media, then that's even worse."

"Crap," Alison whispered. "You should check with Benji then."

"And who's Benji?"

"He's probably the better person among that group. If somebody was doing that, he would know, and he's probably already reamed them out for doing it in the first place."

Kate quickly checked her list of witnesses. "Benji, here it is." Then she read off a last name and number.

"Yeah, that's him."

"I thought you didn't know anybody in that group."

"I don't really. I know Benji, but I don't know him that way."

"Meaning, you've never gone out with him."

"No, not at all, but he seems like a nice guy, and, if there is a halfway decent responsible person in that group, it would be him. The other bunch are just frat-boy wannabees."

"Okay, that's good to know. I'll call you back if I need to."

Alison didn't say anything to that.

Kate quickly disconnected and phoned Benji. When a sleepy, scratchy voice answered a few minutes later, she identified herself. "You were a witness at the drowning in Stanley Park yesterday, correct?"

"Yeah, I was there. That really sucked, man, holy shit."

"Got it. So, I'm looking for video of it."

Silence came on the other end, before he asked in a careful tone, "And you called me why?"

"Because you would know which of your friends took a video," she stated bluntly, "and, considering it's an ongoing investigation, I need it."

"Ah, crap," he muttered. "I don't need this shit."

"I'm sure you don't," she replied, "but, if that video has already been posted to social media, there'll be hell to pay."

"Crap," he muttered. "I told him to not do it, that it was gross, and that he should show a little respect for the family, but he didn't give a shit."

"Who is he?" Kate asked. When Benji hesitated, she added, "Or you can come down here and talk to me at the precinct.”

“No, no, no. It was Josh.”

“Josh Brinkley?”

“Yeah, Josh Brinkley,” he confirmed in a bummed tone. “The kid’s not bad. He’s just got a morbid sense of, … not even a sense of humor, but like a fascination with death or something.”

“*Sure*. A fascination with death, and then there’s a lack of personal ethics and privacy for families who are mourning,” she countered.

“I know. I know. I told him that he better not do anything with it, and he shouldn’t even be taking video at a time like that. He just laughed and said, *How else do I get something like this? It’s probably worth a lot of money.*”

“Oh, so now he’s interested in selling videos like that?” she asked, her voice lowering.

Instantly Benji added, “Look. I don’t know what he’s planning on doing with it, but I guess that’s bad, *huh*?”

“It is worse than bad. So just hold tight. I’ll go talk to your friend, Josh.”

And, with that, she ended the call, looked at Rodney, and asked, “What do we do when we have somebody who took a video of somebody dying, and now he’s looking to potentially sell it? This kid has decided it’s probably worth a lot of money.”

At that, Rodney turned and looked at her in fury. “Jeez Crap. Really?”

She nodded. “One of the kids who witnessed the drowning. Unfortunately he’s got the idea in his head and mentioned it to a friend.” She turned and looked at the rest of the team, and, now that she had their attention, decided what the hell, they ought to know. “Do you guys know

Mama?"

They all nodded.

"It's Axel, their nephew, who died. Mama's husband's nephew. And now we've got some kid who apparently took a video and has the great idea that it's worth a lot of money."

"*Nice*," Owen muttered. "Worst case is that it ends up on one of those big multi-user platforms for everybody to pore over when they want to see something awful, so you should talk to our internet group."

"Will do," Kate noted. "I need to talk to this kid and see if I can just get it. However, if he's already done something with it, what do I do about it?"

"First off, contact our in-house department," Lilliana reiterated, "and see what they say about it. That'll give you more confidence on a legal leg to threaten him with."

"I'll throw the book at him," Kate declared, staring down at her phone. "I mean, there's stupid, and then there's criminally stupid."

"He's a kid, so chances are, he'll think of it more as a lark," Rodney noted.

"Yeah, a lark. Except for the family who will be tormented by it," Lilliana added.

"Unless somebody were to buy it from him," Kate suggested, as she saw Rodney staring at her intently.

He nodded. "I know how Simon feels about that family."

"Yeah, and believe me," Kate replied. "Simon won't take kindly to some kid trying to sell something like that. And sure, Simon would probably buy it from him to keep it private and quiet, but he shouldn't have to. That kid shouldn't do something like that."

It didn't take long to talk to the Internet Crimes Division, and, with a better understanding of what she had in terms of legal options, it apparently depended on what he was planning on doing with it. Having something like this was a whole lot harder to do anything about than if it were child porn, revenge porn, or something like that. It still wasn't allowed, but the charges would be a whole lot different, if any at all, particularly given his age. Swearing at the possibility that this could get ugly, she was on the phone and contacting the person in question.

Just as he answered, she ended the call, looked at Rodney, and stated, "I suggest we go there in person right now, first and foremost."

He nodded. "You're right. It would be much better in terms of shock value, wouldn't it?"

"It sure would," she snapped.

Grabbing her jacket, she marched out to her vehicle and got into the driver's side. Rodney was quick to catch up, and it took them fifteen minutes to get to Josh's apartment building. When they walked up to the proper floor, she knocked on the door, and a young man answered, still wiping the sleep from his eyes and yawning. He looked at her, and, as she held up her badge, his face flushed.

She nodded. "Do you like taking pictures of people dying?" she asked in a conversational tone.

The color in his face flushed red, white, and then ended up red again. In the background an older woman called out, "Who is it, Josh?"

He looked even more panicked at that moment.

Kate called out in a loud voice, "Detective Kate Morgan, ma'am."

The woman came to the door. "What's going on?"

"Apparently your son took a video of a young man

drowning yesterday," Kate explained, "and had the *brilliant* idea that it might be worth a lot of money, so he should possibly sell it."

The mother looked at Kate in complete shock. Her jaw dropped, as she turned around and looked at Josh. "What?"

Josh looked from one to the other and shook his head. "I didn't say I was *for sure* going sell it," he argued. "I just thought that maybe it was worth a lot of money."

"You what?" his mother repeated.

His mom was obviously shattered to even hear that he had done what he'd already done. "First off, even taking a video or photo like that," Kate began, glaring at him, "is cruel and horrible to begin with. You should know that I already have Internet Crimes on the case to have a nice little talk with you about it, as we search the internet to see what you may have already done with it. There's also the family involved, but that's apparently not of concern to you, right?"

"Look …"

Kate didn't give him a chance to mouth off anymore. "All you care about is having some sordid little clip that you get to show all your friends and say, *Hey, look what I got. Let's go watch some kid drown.*"

The mother grabbed her son and turned him to face her, and demanded, "Tell me that you didn't do this." He opened his mouth, and she repeated hysterically, "Josh! Tell me that you didn't do it."

She was barely even giving the kid a chance to talk, and finally the kid looked from one to the other, and his shoulders sagged. "I didn't even think anything of it. We take photos, videos of everything," he explained. "You know that."

"So, some kid, somebody you know, *died,*" Kate broke

in, "but that just added to it, right? It's much more fun when you can get a video of a guy *dying*, right?"

At that, Rodney clamped a hand on her shoulder, and she shrugged it off, glaring at him. He gave her a look that clearly suggested she ease up, but she wasn't interested in listening. Nothing pissed her off more than seeing people take advantage of others, particularly when they were down and out. She glared at him, holding out her hand. "The video. Now."

"No, you can't. It's my phone." He had the phone in his hand. "I can't do without my phone."

His mother snatched the phone from his hand, then handed it over to Kate. "Please, take whatever you need, but we do need the phone back."

"Not a problem. When his phone has been searched, and we track down what Josh did with the video, you can have it back."

Rodney quickly wrote up a receipt and handed it to the mother.

And, with that, Kate turned to Josh. "Internet Crimes Department is on this," she added, a bit scathingly, "just in case you've already done something you shouldn't have." And, with that, she turned and stalked off.

In the background, she heard the mother lighting into the kid, and Kate smiled at that. If nothing else, maybe the kid would learn a hard lesson today. Yet he probably wouldn't even give it a second thought, after the moment had passed, especially once he got his precious phone back.

However, if Kate were lucky, he hadn't done anything with the video yet, and poor Mama wouldn't have to watch it over and over on the internet.

✵

SIMON LOOKED DOWN at the text from Kate, but it didn't make a whole lot of sense. He moved forward in the line at the coffee shop, where he'd been waiting for the last couple minutes to pick up a coffee and a bite to eat. He should have had breakfast, but then he should have done a lot of things today, and, so far, nothing had made the day any better.

When his phone rang, he answered it, and Kate asked, "Are you in a place you can talk?"

"I'm just in line trying to get a coffee," he replied. "What's going on?" When she hesitated, he asked, "Can you wait five minutes?" As he stepped up to the counter, he quickly placed his order.

"I can wait," she said. "It's fine. I can call you back later." And, with that, she ended the call.

He groaned as he stared down at his phone. Kate was as prickly as ever, but right now it seemed like something was bothering her even more than usual. He understood in many ways, but, in other ways, it was so Kate. He quickly finished getting his coffee and a muffin, and, as he headed outside, he called her back. "I'm outside. What's up?"

"I just wanted you to know that I looked into the drowning of Mama's nephew."

"Ah. It was accidental, wasn't it?"

"I'm still investigating because a person was there who I couldn't reach, couldn't find, so I confiscated a video from one of the young men who was there."

Simon groaned. "Of course somebody videotaped it. Crap."

"Quite possibly more than one. I don't know. I just got it off him, and he's busy dealing with his mother right now, and that may be the worst punishment I could throw at him. I just can't be sure that he didn't upload it already or that somebody else hasn't posted another one."

"Crap," he muttered, as he brushed his hair off his forehead. "Can you imagine?"

"I don't even want to imagine," she declared. "I went through this once already, and that's probably why I'm as prickly as I am over the media. Especially on something like this. While I do have the video, he may have already sent it to somebody. I don't know," she admitted, trying to get the words out. "We're going through his phone right now. Anyway I just wanted to warn you."

"So, the drowning was an accident then?"

"Unfortunately the video starts at a point in time when I can't see what may have originally happened. A man was there, who I'm trying to locate and determine who he is. However, so far, I don't have anything."

"He wasn't interviewed?"

"No, he left when the ambulance took over. He was doing CPR, and then, in the chaos, he walked away."

"Do you find that suspicious?"

"No, not at all," she replied in frustration. "It's definitely something that people do. Nobody wants to get involved with police. Nobody wants to give their name or address," she explained. "We deal with that all the time. I would just like to cross that off my list, crossing the *T*s and dotting the *I*s."

"Of course you would," he acknowledged. "Nothing bothers you more than to have something outstanding and niggling away at the back of your mind."

"I also feel particularly bad because of whose family it is," she admitted.

He smiled at that. "That's very sweet, and, if they knew, they would appreciate it very much."

"Don't tell them, for God's sake," she muttered. "It's bad enough what they're already going through, without having to go through more questions and discussions as to what could have happened."

"I certainly won't get involved," he noted. "If your tech guys have the video, you could always get them to catch a still of the man's face and use it to ask around."

She laughed. "*Gee*, that's a great idea. Maybe next time we just call you at the get-go and ask for advice."

He groaned. "I didn't mean that quite the way it came across."

"You were just being you. It came to your mind that maybe that's what we could do, so you went with it, without stopping to consider that we'd already thought of it."

He sighed. "Sorry."

"It's fine," she muttered. "They're in the process of doing it right now. I'll send it over when I get it." With that, she disconnected.

When it came in moments later, she sent it on to him as well, with a text. **Here's the man we're trying to find, if you happen to see him. Anyway, go sit down and eat your muffin. Drink your coffee and enjoy life for a few minutes because right now you have one.**

He walked over to a small table outside and sat down, even though he was short on time. He couldn't imagine how Mama's family would feel if the drowning had been recorded and the video put on social media.

Who knows how many videos might exist, though maybe from a different angle. As he sat here. sipping his coffee, he waited for the picture to load, so he checked his email. When he went back to it, he clicked on the picture, opened it, and froze.

He shook his head several times as he stared at it for a long time. Was it him or wasn't it?

He called her back a few minutes later, and she asked, "What? I suppose you've got another idea for me. Or maybe you've found out who it is already?"

"No, but I can tell you one thing."

"What's that?" she asked, laughter still in her voice.

"It's the same man who I saw at the coffee shop, ... when I had that really strange feeling."

Silence. "Are you serious?"

"Yeah, I'm serious," he snapped.

"Damn, I was just really hoping that this wasn't a woo-woo case."

"My plate is kind of full right now, so I don't need any woo-woo myself."

"And yet you got a weird feeling when this guy what, walked past you?" she asked, as if trying to remember the details.

"I was standing in the coffee shop, got a weird feeling from somebody in the line, so I looked up and saw this guy staring at me. When he walked past me to leave the coffee shop, I realized it was him."

"Where are you right now?"

"I'm just around the corner from Vancouver General Hospital, at one of the coffee shops on Broadway."

"Crap," she muttered, "and this guy was a doctor."

"So, in theory, yeah, it could have been him."

"It could have been," she muttered. "If you have any idea who he is, that would be wonderful."

"Why?"

"I really want to talk to him."

"Do you think he has anything to do with this?"

"I know for a fact that he's the one who tried to resuscitate Mama's nephew."

"And that's a bad thing?" he questioned.

"No, it's not a bad thing," she snapped in exasperation. "I just want to rule him out as not having done anything weird, suspicious, or whatever else," she stated in a clear, brittle tone. "This video doesn't give me enough to do that, so I very much want to talk to him."

"Do you think he's connected to the other cases?"

"We do have the nondescript man showing up at the other drownings. Do I know that it's this man, this doctor?" she asked. "Not right now. So it would be nice if I could find out who he is, and then we'll see." Her voice changed at that. "Colby's just arrived. Gotta go." And, with that, she was gone.

Simon sat here for a long time, just staring at the image, and then looked around at the coffee shop. If the man sending out weird vibrations came here on a regular basis, it's quite possible that somebody would know who he was. Should Simon ask around or would that just set off outrage on all kinds of levels because Kate might not want this doctor to have any advance warning?

Frowning, Simon closed the picture on his phone, picked up his empty wrapper from his muffin, plus his coffee, and headed to one of his rehab projects. As he walked up the hill to Twelfth Avenue, he looked around, sensing an odd disquiet, much like the one he'd felt earlier. Of course he was walking past the Cancer Center and multiple other large office buildings that housed all kinds of different medical specialties. Hospitals set off his connections to the dead and dying, and so did these outpatient centers.

Then he looked up to see a man walking toward him,

muttering something. Simon noted he wore an earpiece and was talking to somebody. He walked right past Simon without even seeing him, but it was definitely the man in the picture.

Simon made a quick decision, turned, and followed him.

CHAPTER 9

KATE SAT AT her desk, tapping her fingers on the surface, as she wondered about her next step.

"Problems?" Rodney asked, but he hadn't even turned around.

She glared at his back.

He chuckled. "No, I can't see you from the back of my eyes," he muttered, "but you only ever tap your fingers like that when you're pissed off." She stopped that nervous movement. He turned to look at her, nodded, and added, "It's a pretty reliable tell."

She stared at him and shook her head. "That's dangerous."

"Hey," Rodney pointed out, "you're not in a war zone here in the bullpen, and having a tell like that isn't necessarily a problem. You know that."

But she wasn't having any of it. "Having *any* tell is bad news," she muttered, as she stared down at her fingers. "This is probably one of the worst ones."

"Why? How do you figure that?" he asked curiously.

"Because, when we're interviewing people, anybody who is smart enough to figure out my emotions will pick up an awful lot more information than I want them to know."

He sat back and frowned. "Okay, so at some point in time you might be taking some of this a little too far."

She shook her head. "Or not far enough."

He groaned. "Jeez, what's got you in an uproar now?"

"Simon recognized the picture of the doctor."

"And?" Rodney asked, still working on his own computer. "That's good, isn't it? He can tell you who he is. So what's the issue?"

"No, he can't tell me who he is. All he can tell me is that he saw this guy a few days ago or maybe yesterday," she clarified, "and Simon got a weird feeling from him."

At that, she watched as Rodney lifted his head and slowly rotated to face her. "Seriously?"

She shrugged and then muttered, "Yeah, seriously."

"So, is this really another woo-woo case?" he asked, almost in delight. She glared at him, and he raised his hands in surrender. "Hey, look. It's always fascinating working with Simon."

"It's not that fascinating," she snapped. "Besides, this is a little more personal because ..." Then she stopped and winced.

"And yet it's causing you a lot of trouble," Rodney noted. "So you may want to step back a little bit from it."

"I know. I know," she grumbled, with a wave of her hand, hoping he'd go back to his own work.

He laughed. "And now you're basically telling me to piss off."

"No, I'm not doing that," she argued, "but I will see if I can find some way to track this person on social media."

"How are you going to do that if you don't have a name?"

"I was hoping somebody could run facial recognition."

"That's budget money," he pointed out.

She stopped in her tracks and groaned. "Fine, or ..."

"Or what?"

"Never mind," she muttered. "Besides, I have a bunch of other work I can do first."

"You're hoping that Simon will find out who he is."

"Knowing Simon, he's already on that track," she muttered, with a groan. "Not necessarily by choice, and I don't want him involved at all, but he isn't exactly somebody I can slow down easily."

"No, I don't imagine he is," Rodney agreed. "I would think he's kind of the opposite."

"Yeah, you're not kidding," she muttered and shook her head. "It's just frustrating, but I do have other things here that I want to go over."

"You really think it's the same guy?"

She hesitated and looked over at him. "I'm *afraid* it's the same guy. And given that this comes from Simon, it's now a whole different story."

"Oh, hell," Rodney muttered, as he sat back. "I thought you were on a wild goose chase, and I really didn't understand why Colby was even asking you to look into this because it's just so far-fetched."

"It is far-fetched, and it's ugly," she stated bitterly. "The trouble is, that's never stopped anything from being real before. Just because we don't think somebody out there is sick enough to do something like this doesn't mean there isn't."

"No, of course not." Rodney rubbed his temples. "This will definitely be a whole lot more challenging to prove."

"There's proving, and then there's stopping," she declared, with an eye roll. "And, in this case, as much as I won't like letting go of a convictable case," she admitted, "if this is what our nondescript man is doing, and, it's a big *if*, it still has to stop."

"Of course, but you're never going to prove that he's ... this guy, who's really doing something like recreating a drowning to save somebody."

"No, not unless I have an eyewitness account," she noted.

"But you don't, do you?" he asked.

"No, I don't. Not really. At least not now. Come on. You were there for some of the witness interviews. We have all kinds of eyewitness accounts, and several weren't sure what the guy was doing. Maybe he just had the bad luck to be in places where people happen to drown all the time."

Rodney gave her an odd look at that.

"I know, far-fetched at best," she said, "but then what's the difference between that and the guy hit by lightning seven times?"

"Oh, I remember that. Didn't he die eventually, and even his tombstone got hit or something?"

She nodded. "Exactly. So, some things out there we can't explain, and something completely reasonable, like this guy being around to save four or five people from drowning, is potentially also possible. But we do need to check our facts and go from there."

"Good God," Rodney mumbled. "Can you imagine?"

"I don't want to imagine," she admitted. "That's just too much pain for anybody to have to deal with."

"Exactly."

She kept the rest of what was on her mind to herself because it was hard to imagine that anybody was accidentally at all these drownings, ... unless they had done something to contribute to the events taking place.

SIMON WALKED QUICKLY behind the other man, who was moving at a fair pace. Simon studied the man in front of him. He had a slight build, short in stature, and yet he moved like a younger man, … a man with energy, with purpose. Maybe *determination* was a better word for it, as Simon wasn't quite sure how to describe it. But he was talking continuously the whole time, presumably to somebody on the phone, maybe even recording messages.

Simon had done that a time or two himself when he needed to take notes. He would often grab his phone and record his thoughts, even while he walked and talked. Yet so much purpose filled this man's steps that Simon wondered if it were possible to do something with that level of drive. … An awful lot to be said for this older man's ability to move at this fast clip, while continuously talking too.

It was fascinating in a way. As they came up to Broadway and the traffic light, the man stopped, but he also stopped talking, which also seemed to confirm that either he was talking to somebody or was dictating. Simon waited, close to the man's side now—even looking over at him once, catching his gaze, and immediately looking away. Just two completely disinterested business acquaintances out in the world.

As the traffic lights changed, Simon marched in step with him. When they got to the other side, Simon slowed ever-so-slightly and stepped out of the man's way, letting him step up ahead. The man turned and headed down to the very same coffee shop as before.

At that, Simon loitered outside at a table, until the man came back out again, with his coffee and what looked like a sandwich. Then the man turned and headed up the hill. Simon followed at a slight distance. When the man abruptly turned into a building, Simon raced in behind, but the lobby itself was empty. Frowning, he looked around for a directory, then winced when he saw quite a few doctors listed. But it did go a long way in confirming that the unidentified man was a doctor and that he did work here.

Pulling his phone from his pocket, he brought up the image, walked over to one of the security guards, and asked, "I'm looking for this man. Can you tell me which doctor he is?"

When the security guard looked at him doubtfully, Simon smiled. "You can phone Detective Kate Morgan for confirmation, if you like," he added easily.

The guard frowned even harder, so Simon tapped on his screen and helpfully provided Kate's number. As soon as he got somebody on the other end, the security guard asked about Simon. There were some further exchanges, then the guard confirmed, "Yes, he's holding a picture of Dr. Don Burnett in his hand."

"Oh, good. Thank you," Simon replied, and he checked the board of the listings of doctors again.

The security guard wasn't terribly happy, but Simon nodded, as he found Dr. Don Burnett's floor, the third floor, which was oncology. Interesting, a cancer doctor. With that, Simon took a photo of the directory information and sent it to Kate.

She called him a few minutes later. "Was that necessary?" she asked, her voice distracted.

"Nope, not necessary at all," he admitted, "but it certainly was helpful."

"Maybe. Did you chase him down?" she asked. "I really can't have any harassment complaints."

Simon snorted. "No. I was walking up the hill to one of

my rehabs, when I saw the guy coming toward me. So I turned around and followed him. He went right back to the same damn coffee shop. So I waited, then followed him into this building, but I had no clue which floor he went to, so I asked the security guard. And there you have it. The rest is history."

"I have to get down there and talk to him myself."

"I'm still in the area, if you want to do dinner down here."

She laughed. "In that area? I highly doubt anything is fit to eat. Sure, there are lots of lunch places, but I can't say that's my preferred dinner area."

"A couple places are around here," Simon noted, but he was a little hard-pressed to think of one at that moment.

"Besides, when I go there," she shared, "I'm usually heading to the morgue."

"Right. I forgot that you come down here a lot, don't you?"

"I do," she confirmed, laughter in her voice. "So, when I'm done at the office today, I may head to the morgue to see Smidge. If so, I might stop in and see this Dr. Burnett at the same time."

"Good idea," Simon agreed. "Let me know when you're done, and I'll see where I'm at." And, with that, they disconnected. With a smile on his face, he headed to his rehab project.

When he arrived, his foreman Joe looked at him and smiled. "You sure smile a lot more, since you hooked up with Kate."

He looked at him and then nodded. "I do, don't I?"

"You do, and it's good to see. That last chick of yours? ... She wasn't so good."

"No, she really wasn't," Simon agreed, with an eyeroll. "Apparently I have better taste now."

"You sure do."

"It's funny," Simon noted, as they walked up to the second floor to check on the current state of the plumbing issues there. "My doorman says the same thing."

"You should listen to your doorman. Those guys know people. They see them all the time and are generally a good judge of character as well."

"If I had listened to him, I wouldn't have hooked up with Caitlyn," Simon acknowledged. "He was against her from the start. Yet I sure as hell wasn't taking dating advice from him."

"Why? He's probably been married for thirty years."

Simon winced. "Yeah, more like thirty-two."

Joe laughed. "See? Even when we are presented with solid alternatives for our own bloody opinion, we refuse to take it."

Simon chuckled. "Don't worry. If I ever let him know that, he'll hound me about it forever."

"Then he probably should. At least with somebody like your doorman around, he knows the makings of a good relationship, and he'll at least try to keep you on the straight and narrow."

"Maybe," Simon conceded, "but I'm not planning on changing Kate out for a better model. I'm not sure there is a better model anyway."

"Oh, boy, that means you got it bad then."

"No, I think I'm just realizing the benefits of a very different kind of relationship."

"Yeah, there's a lot of those," Joe agreed, "a lot."

"How's your sister doing?" Simon studied him carefully.

Joe winced. "She'll be okay but the process? ... It's painful."

"It is painful, but it's all about a new start now."

"Yeah, and it's easy to say that, but she doesn't want a new start."

"Yeah, I'm sorry about that," Simon said, as they walked over to where they had four plumbers working.

Just as they got there, a shout came, and water shot upward. Simon groaned, as he watched the men try to cap the leak. He turned to look at Joe and asked in a harsh tone, "How long has this shit been going on?"

"Too damn long," he muttered. "Every time we fix one thing, something else happens. And this is the rehab that we were looking at coming out barely even on as it was. With the new supply increases," he muttered, "it's likely to be tough to do that. But every time we have a problem like this"—he motioned to the plumbers—"you realize that it's just not worth trying to chintz out because, every time you try that, some shit happens, and we're up in the soup again."

"We did increase the budget for this one," Simon noted, as he watched the men scurry around, trying to contain the flooding. "Do we need to increase it again?"

"I don't know that we need to increase the budget, but now that we have a few extra guys on it," Joe suggested, "I'm kind of hoping we'll bring the numbers in, and it'll look better."

"I'm glad to hear that," Simon muttered, his hands on his hips, as he looked over at the men still fighting the problem, and then he barked out, "Do I need to jump in there and stop this myself?"

One of the plumbers looked at him, sneered, and replied, "As if you could."

"Whoa, whoa, whoa," Joe called out, as he ripped into the belligerent guy.

Simon was already wading through the water, grabbing a sledgehammer, bending a pipe, and putting a stop to the flow. He turned and glared at the mouthy guy, who had the good graces to look ashamed, even while growing red in the face. "This is my job, my building, and I can assure you that I know what the fuck I'm doing. You don't like me and my suggestions? You can get the fuck out. I don't hire apprentices. Or, at least, if I do, I get rid of them."

Joe shook his head. "Sorry about that, boss."

"Who's the kid?" Simon barked, asking the three plumbers who weren't red in the face.

"Yeah," one admitted, with a sigh, "my nephew."

"I don't do family around here," he declared, with a warning note. "Especially not if they've got a mouth and if they can't get their head out of their ass to do the work."

"It won't happen again," the plumber replied.

"If it happens again, you get rid of him yourself. Deal?" Simon demanded.

"Deal," the plumber confirmed, then turned and glared at the kid. "You hear that?"

The kid shrugged. "I don't like plumbing anyway," he muttered, though his expression said otherwise. "Man, this job is the shits."

Simon snorted. "It can be. Depends which end of the toilet you're working from." He hopped back up to where Joe waited, and, in a quiet voice, he added, "Keep an eye on him."

Joe nodded. "We are short on plumbers."

"I don't give a shit if we are. You've got to have somebody who's capable," Simon barked, "and, if you have to let him go, just do it. Trouble like that will kill us."

"I know. I know," Joe agreed, hanging his head. "Let's see how it shakes out tomorrow."

"Says you," Simon murmured, as he took a step back and headed toward the next floor. "What the hell do we have for problems on the next floor?"

"You sure you want to continue this review today?" Joe asked, with a note of amusement in his voice. "You're definitely a little on the short-tempered side."

"Watching money blast out a plumbing pipe will make anybody short on patience. But watching this incompetence go around all the time, family hiring family, even when they're not good," Simon replied, trying to control his tone, "yeah, that'll never be my favorite part of the job either."

"Cut the kid some slack," Joe suggested. "He needs a chance."

"We all need chances," Simon stated, as he rubbed the back of his neck. "Fine, he gets to the end of the week to smarten up and to see if he'll pull through this, but, if not, he's out of here."

"I got it," Joe said, with a grin. "Up until now he's been fine, but you kind of lost your cool there for a minute."

"Really?" Simon asked, looking at him with a droll expression. "You know how I react with anybody who tells me that I can't do something. Particularly when the so-called experts were standing there, watching the kid."

"I do, indeed."

Then Simon turned to walk away, not even checking out the next floor, just leaving Joe handling the plumbers on his own. Simon felt that weird and strange sensation again. He turned around, looking to see if the doctor was anywhere close, but he wasn't. As a matter of fact, there was no sign of anyone but his plumbers and Joe.

A little spooked and uncertain as to what the hell was going on, Simon left the rehab project and stepped into the street and the bright sunlight, which was always a better place to be when the ghosties were starting to walk the scene. More to the point, why was a spirit or energy walking this place? It was an old building that had a long history, but he'd never felt that energy before in the building, and he sure as hell didn't want to feel it now.

With nobody around to hear, he sent out a whispered message, "I don't know who you are, or what you are, but take a hike. My building, my rehab. I'll do it justice, but I need you gone."

And, with that, he walked away.

CHAPTER 10

KATE, WITH RODNEY at her side, walked out of the car park, reoriented herself, and then headed toward the oncology building.

Rodney frowned at her. "You really think it's him?"

"We'll know soon enough," she stated, without turning around. "We do have a picture of him, so that will go a long way to helping make an ID."

"What if he denies any involvement?"

"Why would he?" she asked curiously. "He's a doctor and presumably working to save people is probably something he does on a regular basis. Maybe he left the scene just not wanting to get involved with the police, or maybe he was late for an appointment or just not wanting anything to do with the aftermath of a failure," she suggested. "Those are all possibilities as to why he left, but I don't understand why he would deny being there."

She took a moment and thought about it, realizing it was still possible, since he hadn't called in or anything and would surely realize the authorities would be trying to get a statement from a doctor on the scene. "And we have the video proof that he was there, so that should end any denials."

Rodney shrugged. "I just think it's a little dodgy that he left."

She laughed. "I wonder, if the situation were reversed, … what you would do?"

He looked at her. "I have no idea. I've never been in that situation."

"And that's one of the things we have to keep in mind," she murmured, as they walked into the large building.

As she approached the front desk, she smiled at the woman, held up her badge, and asked, "Where is Dr. Burnett's office?"

"The third floor."

Kate smiled, nodded her thanks, and headed to the elevator. Lots of other people were coming and going on a regular basis; some looked professional, and some looked to be patients. As the elevator doors opened onto the third floor, she walked up to study the wall of names in front of her, then headed to the right.

Rodney kept pace with her, looking around. "A place like this gives me the heebie-jeebies."

Kate just shrugged.

"Can Simon walk right into places like this?" Rodney asked.

She frowned at him. "I have no idea. Why wouldn't he?"

"When you think about it, it's full of pain and suffering." And then he lowered his voice and added ominously, "And death."

"I don't know how much death is really here though," she clarified, looking for Dr. Burnett's office. "I don't know that death is the trigger for Simon anyway. Those are things we really haven't talked about."

Rodney chuckled. "Not exactly pleasant dinner conversation?"

She shot him a look, as she walked into the office. Several people were in the waiting room, many of whom looked up, but several didn't even bother. They sat here in a slumped position, with that perpetual frozen gaze of trying to be polite, while they waited for a doctor who would always be late.

She walked over to the receptionist, who declared, "I'm sorry. You must make an appointment in order to see him."

Kate held up her badge. "We'll only need a few minutes of his time."

"He's really very busy," the woman said a little desperately, as she looked behind Kate at all the people waiting for their turn.

But Kate was adamant. "I understand that," she replied in a polite tone, "but again, we won't need very much of his time." When the receptionist hesitated, Kate stated sternly, "Or we could just walk into his office unannounced."

"No, no, no, let's not do that," the woman relented and picked up her phone and called the doctor.

It was a quick conversation in a lowered voice, and then Kate was motioned toward an inner door. She smiled and quickly stepped forward, ignoring all the glaring looks from the people who had likely been sitting here waiting for way too long already. As she approached the office door, she looked up to see a doctor sitting at a desk, dictating some notes in front of him. He glared at her.

She smiled amiably and held up the photo she had of him. "This, I presume, is you."

He looked at it and then winced. "Yes, of course it's me," he snapped, openly hostile, "otherwise you wouldn't be here."

"Exactly, and now you know why we're here," she stated in a firm tone. "Sorry to bother you when you obviously have a full waiting room out there."

He groaned, as he stared at the door behind her. "It's always a full waiting room, no matter what. This place is always overrun."

"And yet, I presume you provide a valuable service for those people."

"I provide a valuable service, yes, … but it doesn't necessarily have to be much of a service," he admitted, with a quiet groan. "The incidences of cancer are rising at a phenomenal rate, and only so many treatment solutions are available for anyone."

"Right, and, when it comes to drowning victims, apparently not always a whole lot anybody can do for them either."

He froze, and then his shoulders sagged. "It wasn't my fault," he muttered.

Surprised, she eyed him, seeing the look of defeat on his face—not so much anger but shame—that she had to put his mind at ease. "We know it's not your fault," she replied gently, "but, because you left, without us getting your statement, we don't have your take on what happened."

"Who cares?" he asked in a bitter tone. "The boy died, didn't he?" He looked up at her suddenly. "He did, … or he didn't?"

She nodded. "He passed away."

"Of course," he said sadly, "and such a loss. He was so young." He groaned, as he settled back in his chair. "So, what is so important that you had to come disturb me at work and set my entire schedule back God-only-knows how long, all over a drowning victim who didn't make it?"

"The fact that you didn't stick around for us to talk to you is a large part of that," Rodney stepped in. "Particularly, when you work on somebody like that, we do need a statement from you."

The doctor just stared at him, then his gaze switched back to Kate. "I was there and saw somebody drowning. I walked over to the water, trying to help, but I ... I don't swim, and I couldn't go in after him." He swallowed visibly at that point. "I waited until they brought me the body," he stated, deliberately using the word *body*. "I tried hard to revive him, until the ambulance arrived. As soon as they were on the scene, I handed off care. I stepped back, quite distraught over the loss of a young man's life, then realized I was extremely late for a meeting, and I booked it," he explained in an apologetic tone. "Sorry, I guess I should have left my name, but who would I have left my name with?" he asked, looking at them.

Kate replied, "A policeman was already on the scene. That was somebody you could have left a statement with. You could have left your card with one of the EMTs also."

"Maybe," Dr. Burnett acknowledged, "but I didn't look. So, there you go. That's my statement." His shoulders sagged some more. "If you want to print it up and send it to me, I'll sign it."

Kate studied him for a moment. "Have you had any experience with other drownings like this?"

He shrugged and replied in a low voice, "Unfortunately, yes, and every time it bothers me tremendously." He stared at the wall. "It's not an avenue of life I particularly like to work with."

"Death?" she asked curiously. "You're an oncology doctor, so therefore—"

"Therefore what?" he asked, challenging her with a hard glare. "Therefore what? I'm used to people dying? I don't see dying patients here. You know that, right? They come in. We do treatments. We sort out medications. I see them as follow-ups, or they don't make it, and I don't see them anymore as follow-ups, and they end up in the hospital. And, yes, I often go to the hospital to change medications and potentially to see people coming and going in their treatment plan." He was clearly upset at the line of questioning, "But being there physically witnessing the act of dying is not something I'm accustomed to."

"Ah," Rodney added, "okay, that makes a lot of sense. I can't say it's something I would want to stick around for either."

The doctor gave him a commiserating look. "You're the same, aren't you?"

"Yeah, I've seen a few people die," Rodney confirmed. "It's not something I particularly want to see again."

"Exactly. I do the best I can to keep people alive," the doc stated, "but I prefer *not* to be there when they die," He looked over at Kate and frowned. "Is that all? I really need to get back to my patients."

"Have you been around any recent drownings, outside of that one?"

He looked at her, narrowed his gaze, and stated, "I don't understand what you're getting at, Detective."

"It's an innocent question," she declared, keeping her gaze on him. "I just asked if you had been around any other drownings recently."

"Why would you ask that of me?" he asked, outrage in his voice.

"Because another drowning happened off Wreck Beach, one where somebody thought she recognized you."

He sat here, stunned for a moment, then opened his

mouth, but closed it again. Finally he answered, "Good Lord. I'm not famous. You know that, right? Absolutely no way anybody would recognize me outside of this office. How ludicrous is that?"

She stared at him steadily, watching him fidget in place, and then his shoulders slumped yet again.

"Fine, I was there at Wreck Beach as well." He pinched the bridge of his nose. "Who would have thought anybody would even see me?" he called out in wonder.

That was not a question she wanted to answer at this time, nor was his office the place for it. "And yet it bothers you that people saw you?" she asked curiously.

"Sure, of course it bothers me," he declared in mild outrage. "Would you like to be seen at the site of your failures all the time? It just goes to show you that you shouldn't try to help." He shook his head. "So, now what? Do you want a statement for that one too?"

"That would be very helpful," she stated smoothly.

"I was walking along Wreck Beach. I was out at the rocks, and I saw somebody who was looping from one rock to the other, and I called out and told her to be careful. She looked up at me and laughed, as if she were laughing at me. To say *arrogantly* would be a judgment on the poor woman, but ... she was, indeed, laughing at my admonition," he shared in a furious tone. "But then she reached out a hand, and there was no call for help, just splashing and all, and I thought maybe she was in trouble. So I raced a little farther down, but it was very rocky."

He stopped, closed his eyes. "You've got to understand," he added, and a sheen of tears gathered at his eyes. "I'm also terrified of water. So, getting too close isn't something I can do, and I felt even worse by the time she got swept away."

"So, you did try to help?"

"Yes, of course I did," he said in astonishment. "I had found a big stick, and I tried hard to get her to hang on, so I could drag her around the corner and up onto the rocks on the other side. I figured scraped skin wasn't anything to complain about if that were her only injury." He laughed in hysteria and then swallowed. "Unfortunately, as she went around the corner, the tide caught, and she got pulled under. At least I think that's what happened. I stood there and waited, calling out for her, hoping against hope that she would resurface, but ..." He swallowed several times, shook his head. "She didn't."

Kate studied his face and listened to the inflection in his tone, but nothing was off. It sounded normal. It sounded reasonable, and it sounded like something that could happen to anybody. She smiled and nodded. "That must have been very traumatizing."

"It was very traumatizing," he agreed, shaking his head, "and then to see the one at the seawall afterward." He shook his head. "I'll have to find forested places to go for walks instead of beaches, I guess."

"Wreck Beach is an interesting location for you," she said, with a note of humor.

He frowned at her and shrugged. "I see naked bodies all day long," he said. "They really don't matter one way or the other. What I do see there is the ocean and the rocks and the harbor, all in one stunning panorama. It's truly a lovely location," he murmured. "Besides, at this time of year, ... the beach is mostly empty, so it's more or less safe," he was using air quotes now, "to go down there."

She laughed. "I was thinking the same thing when I was there. It was lovely."

He nodded. "Now seriously, if there's nothing else, I need to get back to my patients."

She turned and walked to the door. "I need your email, and I'll write up both statements and send them over for you to sign."

"That's fine. Get the email from my receptionist and send them to me when you get them done. I'll review them and sign them. I guess, next time, I'm supposed to stick around for the reports."

"It would help us a lot, yes, rather than spending time tracking down all these mystery people."

"Is it something people do a lot?" he asked curiously.

"I don't know about *a lot*," she replied, "but we really do like to have our *T*s crossed and our *I*s dotted."

He shook his head. "Good to know." Then he muttered something so faint that she barely caught it.

Something about it never happening before. She spun and looked at him, unsure of what to make of it. "What did you just say?"

He frowned at her. "I didn't say anything."

"I thought you just mentioned something about it hadn't ever happened before."

He froze in shock. "No, I didn't say anything of the sort, I assure you."

She narrowed her gaze as she studied him, and he looked completely innocent, yet a furtive sense of guilt was in his gaze. "So, while we're on that subject, and before I walk out here. Have you ever been on the scene of any other drownings?"

He stared, then quickly shook his head. "Good Lord, isn't two enough for anybody?"

"Yeah, it sure is," she stated, "as long as it's only the

two."

When he just stared back at her, almost pinned in place with a hapless *deer in the headlights* look, she nodded. "You would tell me if there were any others, wouldn't you?"

"Yes, I would." His gaze went from one to the other. "Good Lord, you make me sound like I'm some sort of a criminal."

"Not at all," Rodney said a bit too quickly. "But, as Kate did point out, we do like to have our *Ts* crossed and *Is* dotted."

"Wow," he muttered. "But the answer you are looking for is no."

And, with that, Kate turned and walked out. She headed to the receptionist, picked up one of the cards with the email noted, smiled at her, as Kate turned and walked out. The receptionist got up and called somebody from the waiting room into the office.

Outside on the street again, Kate stood for a long moment, taking several deep breaths. Something about being in that building, something about even being around that level of illness was disturbing. With Rodney at her side, she just stood here for a long moment.

"Thoughts?" he asked.

"Besides the fact that he's lying?"

He nodded. "That was my take on it too, ... but I don't understand why."

"No, we don't understand why, do we?"

"And there's nothing criminal about it," he pointed out. "He tried to save two people on a beach. At one scene, he was surrounded by a ton of other people, and, at the other, he was completely alone. But he did look visibly alarmed at the idea of getting into the water."

"Yes, I think he was being honest about *that*," she clarified.

Rodney laughed. "I'm glad you think he was honest about something."

"You didn't?"

"I did and I didn't. I think our visit completely surprised him."

"Yes, and it's one of the reasons why I love to show up in person, without notice," she admitted, with a smile.

"Oh, I get it," Rodney said, with a smile on his gruff face. "Absolutely, and it was an interesting response on his part."

"Yeah," she murmured, as she looked at the street bustling around her. "Anything else we can do here?"

"I don't think so."

With one last look at the building, she said, "Let's head back to the office. I was going to drop by the morgue and see Dr. Smidge, but I'll call instead."

Rodney shrugged. "Yeah, I should go back to the office and grab my car. I've got to track down some other witnesses in a different case." He asked her, "You sure you're okay?"

"I'm fine. I'll go talk to Reese and see what we can come up with."

"Good enough," he said, with a nod.

And, with that, they quickly returned to the office. She left him in the parking lot, getting into his vehicle. She hadn't bothered to ask what he was working on because she wanted to continue working on her own case. If he needed help, he would have asked for it.

In the meantime, everybody plugged away on their own cases. Technically all cases were everybody's, but sometimes each one of them had an affinity and a drive to take on something that was a little bit more in their lane, and this one was in hers. She also knew that she would be running out of time if she didn't come up with something soon, as she was sure that Colby would eventually tell her to park this investigation and move on.

━━━ ∾∾ ━━━

AT LUNCHTIME SIMON sat outside one of his rehabs, enjoying the sunshine, not hungry but quite happy to take a break, just to let his mind drift and free itself from the calculations he'd been doing all morning. Two of his rehab buildings were running into cost overruns, mostly due to the supply issues and accumulating higher costs to get the same products he could have gotten last year—or at least two years ago, at a much better price.

He didn't want to sit here and deal in bribes to get what he needed by paying a premium price, but, if he had to, the suppliers had him over a barrel. It was frustrating and not how he liked to do business. He preferred to be a straight shooter, pay a good fair price, get a good product. It just worked better for him karmically. But, right now, things weren't exactly easy.

It's not that he was in a financial bind, but he wasn't exactly free and clear either. He was still dealing with Bartlett's company, and now that Simon had just purchased the yacht, he needed to sort out that money too, but it came from a completely different account. Even the thought of the yacht put a smile on his face. It wasn't his yet, and the paperwork still had to be completed, but they were close to finalizing that purchase, and that was exciting. With that satisfied smile taking over his face, he just sat here, kicked his legs out, and relaxed, looking around at the people as they walked by.

He was in a small corner lot that had been turned into—he wouldn't quite say a *garden* because there wasn't much of a garden about it—but a nice bench area. More could be done with it, if the city had the time, the energy, or the inclination, and he knew that they did not. In a way he understood that too. So he put in various little corner spots like this on all his properties, for the residents and for the people walking by, just to give it a much better look and feel. Not everybody appreciated it, and nobody understood the costs to maintain it, and that was one of the things he was considering now, what with these cost overruns.

How would he cut back? Where would he cut back? Were his garden spots something he needed to cut back or was this a temporary thing, and he could make up the money through different designs, different changes? Of course any kind of change issue on these rehabs and gardens also cost money and wasn't something he was prepared to do very often.

As he pondered it, something came over him. He'd heard the phrase, *a ghost walked over his grave*, but it wasn't something he'd ever really felt. Yet, at that moment, this wispy weirdness raised the hair on the back of his neck. He slowly sat up, then turned and looked around, not understanding where this was coming from, what it was, or why it was even around him. That was another question because it wasn't like he was a medium or something, and that certainly wasn't anything he wanted to become. Yet no doubt he was experiencing this sense of something reaching out to him.

It was an eerie feeling, not something he wanted to encourage. He got up and shook his head. *Hell no.* Then he turned and headed to his next rehab project. As he crossed the street, a bit distracted, there was a moment—where he wasn't even sure what had happened. Suddenly Simon was on his knees off to the side, as a vehicle honked its horn and came blaring around him, missing him by mere inches. He slowly shifted to his feet, walked across the street, and sat down on another bench, while he caught his breath.

He didn't know what that was, but it hadn't been—he searched frantically for the appropriate word. It hadn't been *malevolent*. At least he didn't think so, but what did he know? Definitely something had caught him and had tossed him to the ground, barely out of harm's way. So, whatever it was had been trying to help him, and, for that, he owed it. He nodded to the energy around him. "I'll say *thank you* this time, but it would really be nice if you weren't around."

And, with that, he got up, brushed off his pant legs, and, more than a little unnerved, determined to carry on for the rest of his day. However, knowing that he'd been distracted enough to get into that life-threatening situation was disturbing. The mysterious presence was something he didn't understand, but the fact that whatever it was had helped him out was even more disturbing.

Determined to put it behind him, he sent Kate a text, asking if they could do dinner tonight.

When she sent back a thumbs-up, he smiled, his day turning brighter, his balance returning. He took several deep breaths, looked around, smiled at the world, and whispered, "Okay, let's … let's start again."

And, with that, he set off with much more awareness of where he was going and how to stop whatever the hell had just happened from occurring again. When he arrived at the next jobsite, Joe waited for him. He took one look at him and asked in concern, "You okay, boss?"

He froze and asked, "Does it look like I'm not?"

Joe studied him for a moment. "You looked a little tousled, like you took the morning off or like you stumbled and fell."

"You called it with the *stumbled and fell* part," he admitted, "though I'm not exactly sure what happened."

"The potholes and ruts in the sidewalks around this place never get fixed."

"It's a good thing that I fell when I did because it sent me backward onto a sidewalk, as a vehicle was coming toward me, so maybe it was just instinctual."

"Whatever, … a damn good thing," Joe muttered, eyeing Simon.

"I know, and normally I'm very careful."

"Yeah, you are, but nobody's careful all the time, and you appear to be quite distracted these days."

"Do I?"

"I think that Bartlett thing really got to you."

"Yeah, it did, and it still does. I've been on the phone with them quite a bit this morning, in fact."

"And then there is Mrs. Bartlett too." He snorted and asked caustically, "Do you have to go to the sentencing?"

"No, I don't," he shared. "The last thing I need is to see her again."

"And yet it might make you feel better." When Simon turned and scowled at Joe, Joe winced.

"I've got enough things to feel better about without adding that." And, in fact, Simon felt exhausted. The fatigue from the adrenaline rush ending after whatever just happened had Simon all churned up and yet depleted.

Joe looked at him. "You have been under a lot of strain lately."

"Don't say it," Simon warned. "I'm not leaving, not going anywhere. I've got way too many projects happening."

"I know. I was just going to suggest that you might want to"—he hesitated—"I know it's a novel idea, but how about taking a day off?"

"A day off is possible, but not until the yacht is in my name."

At that, Joe frowned at him.

"I bought a small yacht off a friend of mine," he explained, as he shrugged and smiled. "The paperwork should be signed tomorrow."

"Now that is good news," Joe declared, with a bright smile. "Damn, a yacht, *huh?*"

"Not exactly. A schooner, maybe. Damn, I'm not sure what he even called her," he admitted, with a laugh. "I'll have to get my jargon right."

"You do that, but I like the sound of a yacht."

"That's what he called it. He named it *Running Mate.*"

"Ooh, and I like that too. I presume he's married."

"Happily married. Although they had quite a health scare, so now they'll be spending some quality time together but traveling in a different way. He was looking to sell the yacht to fund their next adventures and approached me about it."

"Why did he approach you though?"

At that, Simon stopped and looked at him. "No idea. I should ask him, I guess."

"Yeah, you should. Bet he says something about the fact that you work too much."

He snorted at that. "I don't think he would do that, but you never know."

"Maybe."

It was something Simon pondered throughout the rest of the day, and, when he had a chance, he sent Baxter a text asking him about that.

Baxter phoned him right back. "Really? I'm not allowed to ask an old friend if you're interested in my yacht?"

"No, it's just that somebody asked me out of the blue why you called me, and I didn't have an answer for him."

"I was thinking that maybe it was the time of life for you to look for ways to relax and to get out of the office," he shared, confirming Joe's idea. "It wasn't a deep-thinking roulette kind of thing, you know."

"Glad to hear it." Simon chuckled. "Anyway, I was just sorting my way through it as to why you phoned me directly."

"Honestly? We've seen each other on multiple occasions. You've been out on her with me more than once, and you've always seemed to enjoy it. I know that you don't own one, and you have the money. It was just one of those enlightened kind of answers."

"I don't suppose your real running mate had anything to do with it, did she?"

He chuckled. "She might very well have. I don't remember, but she's very intuitive herself, when it comes to things like that, which has been very helpful where my business decisions are concerned."

"Good," Simon replied. "That's all, just my curiosity."

"No, it's all good," Baxter replied. "You're not backing out of it, right?" He showed a bit of hesitation, but not much care.

"No, I'm not. Are you?"

"Oh, hell no," he declared, then chuckled. "I'm feeling quite a bit better about it now too. A couple of the kids need help financially, and we're doing some retirement planning and all that good stuff," he explained. "You don't really realize how the years go by, not until the kids are all gone, and then you're sitting here, wondering what happened."

"Yeah, I could see that," Simon agreed.

"You will soon enough, once you cross the forties line," he stated. "Of course I have crossed the sixties line, so you can imagine."

"And that in addition to the health scare."

"Yeah, you just add up all those milestones, and one morning you wake up, knowing it's time for a change," he shared. "However, if you do ever meet my running mate," he added, with a laugh, "don't, ah, … don't belabor the point, will you?"

"Why? Is she against you selling it?"

"No, she's very much in favor of me selling, but she's afraid that she pushed me into it and that I'll regret it later."

"Will you?" Simon asked bluntly.

First came silence on the other end, and then he replied, "I don't think so. It feels like it's time."

"Good enough," Simon said. "I've got an appointment with the lawyer tomorrow anyway, so we'll take care of the paperwork then."

"Sounds good." And, with that, Baxter rang off.

As Simon looked around, he still felt and heard the strange energy as it called to him. God help him because it was still calling him, and that was nothing if not unnerving.

CHAPTER 11

Back in the office, Colby called out to Kate, just as she walked to her desk. She turned mid-step and headed toward his office. "Any luck?" he asked. When she frowned at him, he raised an eyebrow. "You don't like me asking?"

"I don't have enough to tell you something yet," she replied irritably, "which makes me feel that I'm not getting anywhere."

He snorted at that. "That's not the way I want you to look at it. I just want to know if we're getting anywhere or if it's a wild goose chase."

"I'm not ready to say yes or no either way yet," she admitted, watching his expression.

"Yet that face you make means something's bothering you. Do you think something might be there?"

"Something's there, but I don't know what. I don't know whether it's guilt or something else. I don't know exactly what I'm seeing."

"Okay, then you need to tell me." He listened to her carefully, as she talked to him about the doctor lying to her. "You're thinking that he's involved in some way?"

"I'm not sure what he is yet," she said, "except suspicious and guilty of something."

"But it could just be feeling bad because he couldn't save people," Colby pointed out.

"Exactly—or if he's actively involved, or if he knows something, or, or, or," she added. "I'll do a full workup on him, now that I know he is who I think he is, and I'll go from there."

Colby asked, "And if any of your team needs help?"

"I've already told them to let me know," she stated, as she walked out of Colby's office. "Obviously this is a time frame that can't continue if something else comes in."

"Exactly," Colby agreed, with a small smile. "Yet I can also see that you are biting into this one."

"I absolutely am," she muttered. "And now it'll bug me until I figure it out."

He laughed. "Just be aware."

"I know. I know," she muttered, as she left. "We have other cases to solve, other things to do, and time frames are tight."

"Oh, you forgot to mention one more thing."

"Yeah, the budget's overwhelmed."

He burst out laughing and nodded. "Glad to see you understand the system."

She shook her head at that and headed back to her desk. She understood and knew she had no luxury for sitting here and delving into a case like this. If something was there, it was ugly, and it needed to stop.

She picked up a full cup of coffee along the way to the bullpen. Just as she sat down with it, Reese walked over. "Hey," Kate greeted her. "I was looking into those other cases you found."

"Did you come up with anything?"

"Some, not a whole lot. It seems none of the witnesses really want to say anything definitively as to what happened, or they can't say anything. I think we're probably looking at a *can't say.* Like nobody saw it clearly enough. I think accidents like this happen so fast that nobody really knows what happened."

Reese smiled at her. "That's a nice way to put it."

Kate shrugged. "Is there any other way?" she asked, with a wince in Reese's direction. "So much shit is going on here that it will be hard to prove either way, but I don't want to just let it go, not if culpability is involved."

"Understood."

As Reese went to walk out, Kate added, "So, I'm looking into this Dr. Don Burnett. Can you pull everything you can possibly find on him, please?"

"Sure. When do you want it?"

"Now would be good," she replied, with a laugh. "Otherwise I'll keep plugging away at it here."

Reese snorted. "Give me five." And, with a wave, she was gone.

Kate got an email a few minutes later from Reese. Her note read *This is the first run.* And, with that, Kate read through the attached case file. Dr. Burnett was in his fifties, with conflicting information on his parents regarding their vocations and/or social status. He had one sister who died while he was a teen. Kate needed more and picked up the phone. She contacted Reese. "Apparently his sister died. Can you roust up anything more on that?"

"Sure. I'll send you a first run on her in a sec."

Kate continued to read on the doctor. He'd had an average life. He'd been a decent student at school, but apparently, according to some of the notes here, plus an interview that he'd given years ago, he'd been pushed into medicine because his parents had poured everything into his life. As the only remaining sibling, they wanted him to be a success and at a level they hadn't been able to achieve themselves. Again Reese had flagged inconsistencies because some accounts described his mother as a highly regarded doctor, who came from a very wealthy family.

So Dr. Don Burnett had felt compelled to live up to the life his sister had lost, and that had put a lot of pressure on him to do better, to be better. That was the extent of his rare comments on the matter. She had read the interview, and it was very much verbatim from his older speech to a graduating class, where he came across very awkwardly. He hadn't been any less awkward in the meeting she'd had with him in person either. He was someone who didn't have much in the way of social skills, but that was often the case with brainy people. She wondered if Reese could find his IQ on file somewhere.

People like this doctor spent a lot of time studying and working to become whatever it was they were reaching for, often missing out on interaction with people, developing some social skills—or they were just introverts and suited this studious loner lifestyle, who still tended to have under-developed social skills.

She went through the rest of the interview but not a whole lot was there. Waiting for Reese to get back to her with more, Kate did a Google search to see what came up about Dr. Don Burnett. It revealed his position at the Oncology Center and at UBC's medical department, but it didn't share a whole lot else. Even as she looked for more hits and any Google links, there was just nothing.

It appeared that he was the kind of guy who showed up, worked his job, went home, and had little to no social presence. She couldn't find any records of marriage or divorce. Frowning at that, she called Reese back. "I'm struggling to find very much on him online," she admitted.

"Yeah, me too. I'm not seeing anything."

"How about social media? I can't find a marriage or anything like that. Have you found anything personal, like a social circle, marriage, girlfriends?"

"Nope. Nobody else comes up when I search his name, no children with his name. It seems his parents did pass away, and, other than that, there isn't much on the surface."

"Any idea when?"

"About thirty years ago from the looks of it."

"Interesting," Kate murmured. "Okay, send me anything you have on those deaths too."

"I can do that. What else?"

"Anything and everything. There's got to be more on this guy. There must be more, right? He's a doctor at the oncology center for the university, so who got him the job right out of the gate? Doesn't it take like sixteen years to get a specialized medical degree? Something landed him in that position at such a young age because he's been there since graduation—I would guess—since he's worked there like eighteen, nineteen years."

"Yeah, exactly," Reese confirmed, clicking away at her keyboard. "Finished his residency program at age thirty-five. He's fifty-three now, so eighteen years later."

Kate muttered, "Could be he was the best candidate at the time, and he's just stayed there and hasn't moved up, hasn't moved down."

"Not sure you do in a medical field like this one," Reese noted. "It's a specialty, and it seems he's very well-known for that."

"In a good way?"

"I'll take a look and see, but I figure most of his patients die from the cancer or the treatments or even old age," she replied. "Don't you worry. I'll dig deep." And, with that, she was gone.

As the day went on, it was just more of the same. Nice guy, everybody knew him or didn't know him at all, and those who knew him had nothing specific to say. *He's a nice guy, been working here since forever.* Couldn't tell her anything about what he was like outside of work, couldn't tell her anything of what he was like in his private life at all.

He was just kind of *there.*

Some had shared, *I'm sorry to say, but I don't really know him that well. He's always been there. He's always been a pleasant-enough guy. You ask him for something, and he's happy to help. He's got a good reputation in the department as a good, solid doctor.*

Essentially people were making excuses for not having any clue as to who this man really was. Obviously he was there. He showed up every day. He did his job. Yet, on a personal level, nobody had anything to offer, even people who had worked with him for almost two decades. *I don't know what it is you're asking. All I can tell you is that he's a good guy.*

Kate continued with her questioning. *Okay, do you know anything about his family life, a marriage, anything about his family or his parents or what he does outside of work?*

No, not at all came the comments, again and again with a sense of surprise to consider Dr. Burnett in that way. One thing that she kept hearing was, *Ask him. I'm sure he'll tell you.*

This latest call was basically the same as the others.

"I will ask him," Kate stated. "I was just trying to get a feel for him first."

"I don't know what to say. I've known him for a good ten or twelve years, and he's been there at various meetings. He's always quiet, doesn't really get himself into any trouble."

"Any problems with anyone?"

At that, the man she was talking with laughed. "No, he barely has an opinion. He doesn't get involved with arguments or office politics. He doesn't say anything negative about anyone. Even if you try to get him involved in something," he added, "he's just one of those nice guys." And, with that, he quickly rang off.

She was starting to realize that, no matter who she talked to, everybody repeated the same thing, and yet the conversation made them uncomfortable. As if they didn't know how to explain their lack of information on a coworker or didn't know what bothered them about these questions or really didn't have a clue what made Dr. Burnett tick. Seemingly Kate's questions made them feel worse because they had *known* the guy for a very long time and yet knew nothing of him.

All of this left Kate frustrated, angry, and way too suspicious. As she walked out of the office, she pulled out her phone and called Simon. Walking to her car, she asked him, "Do I need to come now, or can I go do a workout?"

"You mean, go have a couple rounds and get yourself beaten up?" He chuckled lightly, as he added, "Absolutely, go do that."

She hesitated, then asked, "Seriously? No reason not to?"

"No, not at all," he reassured her. "Dinner will be ready when you get here."

"Okay, give me an hour. I just need to go beat the crap out of something."

"Oh, by all means," Simon replied, with a note of amusement in his voice. "Get that out of your system before you come to visit me."

"Why?" she asked suspiciously. "You afraid I might beat you up?"

"Nope, not likely," he countered, with a hearty laugh. "A combative Kate is one thing, but an angry combative Kate is a whole different story. So I would rather not come between you and your workout."

She groaned. "Sorry, I really do need a workout." And she quickly disconnected the call.

She wasn't sure why she was so frustrated and upset. Yet she was, and it was all about that bloody Dr. Burnett. As far as doctors went, that's probably what you wanted in a doctor, except she would also want somebody to be an advocate for her, somebody who would fight for her cause, her treatment, somebody who understood and would go the extra mile. Was that what he was like? So far, she hadn't contacted any patients, and yet it was something that she felt she should do.

She just didn't want to start that whole privacy rigmarole if she didn't have to because she needed a reason to contact these patients, and right now all she had was a suspicion that the doc wasn't quite what he appeared to be. Yet she hadn't really seen any sign of aggression or even defiance. She groaned as she drove toward the dojo. All she really saw was ... *acceptance,* maybe a passiveness that bothered her. Somebody who didn't seem to care and was going through the motions of life because it was expected of him, not because he wanted to. He was a doctor because somebody else chose it for him. He did his job because he was supposed to. He showed up every day because that's what everybody did in life, right?

But there wasn't any spark, wasn't any liveliness. Yet who was she to judge him for that? Maybe the term wasn't *docile* or *passive.* Maybe it was *peaceful.* Maybe he was at peace with his lot in life, and he had no intention of changing it. Was that so wrong? She pondered that, wondering what about him set her off. Part of it was the fact that nobody was this perfect—in the sense of calmness, contentment, and zen—and she wasn't even sure that was it. It seemed more a case of … surrender? She didn't know, but she was happy to talk it over with Simon when she got there.

Her workout was intense, with no break, until she was physically drained.

Flushed, hot, and sweaty, she walked into Simon's penthouse apartment and called out, "I need five minutes for a shower."

"You got it." He stepped forward, gave her a quick kiss, and a searching gaze. "*Uh-oh.*"

"No, no *uh-oh.*" She frowned, feeling *something* hit her. "Just a, … just a …" She shook her head. "I don't even know what it is. I'll talk to you in a minute."

And, with that, she dashed into the bathroom, stripped down, and stepped under the hot spray. As soon as she was done, she turned off the water and found him standing outside, waiting to wrap her up in a towel. She stepped into the towel and sighed happily. "It's amazing how much just getting clean can do for you. The freedom of being able to wash off your own thoughts with the sweat, grime, and everything else. I've had days where things were ugly, like seriously ugly," she shared, as she nodded. "This isn't anything like that, but this case? It's just confusing. I don't understand."

"Come and tell me about it," he said, as he walked into the living room.

She still had just the towel wrapped around her. "Wait. I need clothes first."

"Or you could just come as you are." He waggled his eyebrows.

She laughed. "Chances are, I'll end up like this anyway, but, … in the meantime, I would like to throw something on." She found a light summery shift of a type she almost never wore. She pulled it out and looked at him, frowning. "So, this is supposed to be my side of the closet, where you allocated space for me," she said pointedly, "but I didn't buy this."

He looked at it and smiled. "No, but try it on anyway." When she hesitated and eyed him searchingly, he rolled his eyes and admitted, "Yes, I bought it for you."

"You don't know my size."

"I will try not to feel insulted by that."

He didn't say anything else, as she slipped it over her head, stepping out of the towel. She still didn't have anything on underneath. This fabric was smooth and silky. She brushed at the dress and asked, "What's this material?"

"Silk," he replied, with a casual indifference that left her gaping.

"Silk?" she repeated. "Why the hell am I wearing silk?"

"Because I happen to like silk," he explained, "and I saw that and thought of you." She didn't know quite what to say, but he tapped her gently on the lips and suggested, "All you need to do is say *thank you*, assuming you like it."

She nodded, knowing she would need to think about this a little later, and added, "Thank you."

He beamed at her. "See? That wasn't so hard."

And yet, it was hard. Quite hard, in fact. After brushing her hair and finishing getting dressed, she walked into the living room and smelled something aromatic and yet completely different. "I can't place that smell. What's for dinner?" she asked, with a questioning look in his direction.

"It's a Lebanese dish," he replied, "from one of those little shops around the corner."

"How come all these shops are around your corner," she asked, "but not around mine?"

"Maybe because of where you live," he deadpanned.

She winced at that. "Fine, fine, okay. I'll give you points on that one. I don't exactly live where the best culinary experiences are available."

"You're in a commercial district," he stated, "so it's really not a surprise."

"Maybe not," she muttered, "but this has quite an intriguing aroma."

"As it should." He chuckled. "It's ethnic food, with a difference."

"If you say so," she muttered, as she sat down in a dining room chair, her nose inhaling in delight. "Wow. … It smells wonderful, whatever it is." He quickly dished up the rice and meat dish, with some weird vegetables. She shook her head, frowning. "I can't identify most of this food."

"So, just taste it first," he suggested.

She quickly had several bites and then sat back with a happy sigh. "Don't even tell me what it is. Just tell me it's good for me."

"It's good for you," he repeated, with a knowing smile.

She rolled her eyes. "Okay, that was just a little too fast."

He chuckled. "Not at all," he argued. "Nothing in there could give you any cause to squeak or scream or squeal." He shrugged. "It's just good food."

"If you say so." She took a bite of a different dish and asked, "Is that raisins I taste in here?"

He nodded. "That is one of my favorite dishes. Enjoy."

With no interest in doing anything but, she tucked into her plate. After the first flush of hunger had been abated, Kate sat back a bit, then ate at a much slower pace, enjoying the wine, enjoying the change of flavors and foods. When she finally sat back, pushing away her empty plate, she muttered, "That was lovely."

"Good." He gave her a beaming smile. "I'll add it to our regular roster of restaurants we can order from."

She shook her head at him in amusement. "I suppose you keep a list, don't you?"

"Of course. Don't you?"

She contemplated the question and shrugged. "I guess maybe in a way I do, but not consciously."

"Of course not." He laughed. "That would make way too much sense."

"Now, now," she teased, "you don't have to be nasty."

"Hey, we all do it." He shrugged. "We keep a mental list of places that we're happy to go to, happy to order from. I just added this one to it."

She nodded. "And a good choice it is. I still don't know what all those flavors were, but, wow, even now I still want more, but I'm just too full."

He laughed. "I know, and that's a good thing."

"It is," she agreed, with a happy smile. She got up and helped him clear off the table.

When the dishes were done, she picked up her glass of wine and headed for the couch, the view from the window starting to sparkle with the evening lights below. Happily, she sat down, curled her legs underneath her, and whispered, "You do lead a charmed life." At the silence from beside her, she looked over at him and frowned. "Did I say something wrong?"

"It's not that you said anything wrong," he clarified. "However, it just seems you've had a frustrating day, in a way, something odd happened to me too."

"Sounds like we need to talk."

"You first," he said, trying to delay the inevitable. "Let's talk about your case, and then I promise I'll tell you some of the weirdness going on in my world."

She frowned at that and then slowly nodded. "Okay, and when you say *weirdness* ..."

"You first," he repeated firmly.

She groaned, then nodded. "Okay, fine. It's this case with the drownings."

"Right, you're still working on that."

"I am, ... mostly because I have the time to do it and because I'm concerned that there may be more to it than we have even considered," she began. "It's a disconcerting kind of a case because we don't really have any proof, and we don't even know, honest to God, that a crime was committed."

He just stared at her.

"First, let's talk about the boy from Mama's family." She explained about what happened and how she had gone to the doctor's office to confirm the reports.

"Thank you for checking in on Mama's case."

She nodded. "I just don't know that I have anything concrete here. Axel's drowning is too messy, and there's not much in terms of details."

"Come on. Spit it out. What is it that's bothering you?"

"When I was at the doctor's office, talking to Dr. Burnett, I did ask him whether he had seen any other drownings recently, and he did get a bit irate about it."

"Which I would expect in somebody who was innocent," he stated pointedly.

"Absolutely," she agreed, "but then he finally admitted that he had been the person seen at the Wreck Beach drowning as well."

At that, Simon sat back, stared at her, and whistled.

"Exactly," she stated. "So now I have the same doctor who tried to do CPR at the one drowning and apparently tried hard to save somebody at the other."

"And your impression of him?"

"Meek, accepting, or maybe not even accepting, more like somewhat detached from the world around him, as if … I can't put my finger on it, but something is there."

"Do you think he deliberately killed these people?" Simon asked, voicing what she was afraid to get out. "That is not what I want to hear in regard to Rosa and Henri's nephew."

"I know. I understand that, and I don't have enough data yet to say that," she conceded, "so definitely don't go down that pathway just yet."

Such a warning filled her tone that he held up a hand. "I'm not. I won't. It's a little bit much to think that somebody is involved in two drownings within the span of what? A couple weeks?"

She nodded. "One week even. So seriously bad luck doesn't cut it for me."

He winced at that. "There's bad luck, and then there's the fates-hate-you variety of bad luck."

She chuckled. "You know there's no such thing as coincidence, right?" Returning to their serious conversation, she added, "Right now I'm looking at all avenues and pulling up everything I can about this guy. Everybody at his work says that he's a nice guy who is always there, who helps out when he can, that sort of thing. He's been working for the department forever, almost two decades, yet not one of his colleagues really knows him. They didn't have anything to say or anything to offer in terms of information on the guy."

"So maybe it wasn't so much that they know who he really is, but they see the persona that he has established at work."

"That's part of it, no doubt," she replied. "Still, how do you work with somebody for all that time and not know a single thing about him? Nobody knew whether he was married, divorced, or had been in a relationship. One person said, *I'm sure he's married. I'm pretty sure I heard him talking about it at some time.* And yet, the more we talked, she backtracked. *Oh no, that was somebody else, wasn't it?* She asked me, as if I was the one who was supposed to know, and I don't. And that was basically echoed by everyone I spoke to."

"So, this guy is just ..." Simon winced. "I can't believe I'm saying this, but it's like he's a ghost of sorts. He shows up every day, does the job, and goes home every day, interacts with people as needed, but not contributing beyond what is required, and ultimately nobody really has a clue who he is."

"Yep, that's about it," she agreed, with a sigh.

"And that, of course, makes you suspicious," he shared, with an eyeroll.

She glared at him. "I'm not sure that I'm being suspicious about him as much as I would like to know a whole lot more, and it's always hard when you don't have anyone who can give you further information."

"What about family? Can you talk to them?"

"His parents are both deceased." She frowned and pulled out her phone. "Wait. I didn't get any information back on that yet."

"Any siblings?" he asked.

"A sister who died when he was a teenager."

He frowned at her. "So, nobody is in his world, which means this guy is probably lonely, seriously lonely, and probably never learned how to make friends and gave up trying."

"Maybe," she said, with a sigh. "I don't have a good grasp on who he is, and because I don't—"

"It pisses you off," he stated, with a nod, understanding in his tone. "That's why you had to go kick some ass at the dojo."

She groaned and then looked at him with half a smile. "And you're happy with that, aren't you? You've figured out what makes me tick, and, as far as you're concerned, it fits nicely into the profile you've got of me."

"I don't have a profile of you," he declared, with a laugh. "You're the one person in this world who I do not understand, don't know what makes you tick, and haven't a clue how on earth you've survived doing the work you do," he admitted, with a warmth that made her smile. "But what I do know is that, when you get a smell and a hint of something, you're like a dog with a bone, and you just won't leave it until you've figured it out."

"I was thinking that about him today. If you had cancer, what kind of doctor do you want?"

He nodded. "I would want an advocate. I would want

somebody who is there to find the best solution to my problem and to help me through it. Basically I would want somebody willing to fight for me," he stated, and then he looked at her. "You don't see that in him, do you?"

She shook her head. "No, I don't. I almost see like ... a passiveness."

"And yet you don't know that for sure because you haven't talked to any of his patients."

"Not yet, I haven't. Which is something that I am having a hard time getting to, you know? Like, how do you talk to patients of a doctor like this, without setting off alarm bells or making them even more stressed at a point in their life when they don't need to be stressed and maybe can't even handle any more stress?"

He nodded. "And, if this Dr. Burnett is your oncology doctor, isn't a lack of confidence in him the very last thing you want?"

She nodded. "I'm with you there. If I have any kind of serious disease, I want a doctor who will fight ... for me, for my cause, for my life. Not just hand me a prescription and say, *Here try this.*"

"What you're really saying is he doesn't seem to have the kind of personality of a doctor you would want to go to," Simon pointed out and then shook his head. "However, that's a hell of a long way from somebody who's actively putting people in danger and killing them."

"I can't really see him doing that either," she shared. "There's such a passiveness to him."

"So maybe it's nothing then," Simon suggested. "Maybe, once you've done all your digging into this, you'll walk away and realize there's nothing to it, and it just needed somebody like you to check it all out and to put it to rest."

"Maybe," she muttered, taking a sip of her wine.

"However," he added, with a note of warning, "something's still bugging you because clearly you can't let it rest."

She nodded and slowly looked at him. "You know what it's like when something is just eating away at you on the inside, and you can't quite figure out what the problem is?"

He knew exactly what that meant. "Yeah, I do unfortunately, and a lot of the time it has to do with that crazy ability of mine."

She looked at him, startled, and then nodded. "Yeah, so you do understand, and the problem here is, I can't let it go because I sense something. I don't know what it is, don't know if it's even something illegal. I just don't know." She sighed, throwing back her wine. "I just know something's there, and it'll drive me nuts until I figure it out."

"In that case," Simon replied, "you need to pursue it."

She smiled and scrunched up her nose. "I wasn't *not* going to, but thanks for the vote of approval."

He chuckled, as if approvals meant anything to her. He knew her better than that.

"And now"—she turned her gaze to him—"what on earth is going on with you?"

He faced her and winced. "Yeah, that's a whole different story."

"No, it's not," she disagreed, putting down her empty wineglass. "It's going to be all about you, so let's hear it. What's going on in your world?"

CHAPTER 12

IT HAD TAKEN Kate hours to fall asleep. Simon's ghost kept her brain circling way too long before she finally managed to part it and crash. She woke in the early hours of the morning to her phone insistently buzzing at her side. Groaning, she reached out, slammed her hand on top, picked it up, and growled into the phone, "Kate here."

Rodney sounded way too cheerful for whatever time of night it was. "I know you won't like this, so don't shoot the messenger," he began, his voice upbeat. "We have another drowning."

Her eyelids flew open, and she stared up at the darkened ceiling. "And I care about that why?" she asked cautiously.

After a moment's hesitation on the other end, Rodney replied, "Because we have a witness who says a small middle-aged man apparently tried to help the victim, only it didn't work, and the victim was washed away."

"Jeez Crap." She sat up in the darkness. "Surely not."

"That's the problem."

"At this hour?"

"The body washed in earlier tonight around Stanley Park," he explained, giving her time to get it. "The police were present, and this woman came over and shared how she had seen it happen the previous night."

"And of course she can't identify the man trying to help?

Right?"

"Bingo. Not only that, she was full of awe that somebody was working so hard to try and save him. Presuming he didn't call for the EMTs, she dialed 9-1-1, as he was busy trying hard to help, but he didn't go into the water."

"Of course not," Kate replied, "because he's afraid of the water."

There was silence for a moment, then Rodney came back cautiously, "You really think it's him?"

"I don't know," she admitted, her voice ever-so-soft. "If it wasn't Dr. Burnett, who the hell was it? Is it just one man or are there several we consider to be one man? We have so little information, not much else to go on."

"That's the problem," Rodney agreed. "Hence this lovely wake-up call to you."

"Why did you get called in?"

"I know one of the paramedics," he shared. "He called me after he happened to overhear this woman, telling everybody who would listen that this brave man had been trying to help but apparently couldn't save the drowning man."

"Great. So now we have somebody hero-worshipping this guy, and we don't know if he's doing something to deliberately put these people in a position where he could help, but then isn't able to help, so they drown."

"Which, when put that way," Rodney noted, "sounds pretty disgusting."

"Ya think?" she muttered, as she shifted in the bed and noted that Simon was still sound asleep beside her. "Give me a few minutes. I'm getting dressed."

"We're down here at the main parking lot," he shared, giving her the location, "and I've already spoken to the witness, but I'm pretty sure you'll want to speak to her yourself."

"Why is that?" she asked, stifling a groan.

"Because she's got this infatuation thing going on, and, therefore, she may very well have a few more details than we do."

"Okay, give me twenty."

She disconnected, hurried to the bathroom, used the facilities, and quickly got herself dressed and prepped for the day. She checked her watch and saw that it was ten to five. Ten to five, and yet the body had washed ashore hours earlier, and people were already there collecting it. Which was good in the sense that the public wouldn't be exposed to something like that, but bad in the sense of *What the hell? Didn't anybody sleep anymore?*

She left Simon a quick note, let herself out of his apartment, then headed to work. At the last minute, she remembered she had to go to the beach instead and caught the correct turnoff. She pulled into a public parking lot and walked to where the small crowd had gathered.

Even as she arrived, she saw the gurney being loaded into the ambulance. She walked over, held up her badge, and asked to see the victim. The sheet covering the victim was partially pulled back. She took a quick look at him, nodded, then turned and walked to where Rodney waited for her.

"This guy was older," she shared, "which kind of surprises me."

"Why?" he asked her.

"Just the time of day, I guess."

"It's quite possible that this doctor had nothing to do with it."

"Had nothing to do with what?" she asked absentmindedly. He gave her a look, and she shrugged. "Anything is possible at this point, and nothing makes any sense. I still haven't got what I would consider a solid motive for this."

"Not surprised," Rodney muttered, agreeing with her point because she was right. "How many motives can we have when it comes to this shit?"

"I don't know," she admitted. "When you think about it, the whole thing seems far-fetched."

"You're still pursuing that fake savior angle though?"

"I am because, every time I turn around, there's this fifty-something-year-old smaller-framed man. After tracking down Dr. Burnett, who could possibly be our guy, there's absolutely no motive. There's nothing so far that would suggest he's had anything to do with it."

"Which doesn't mean that he's not involved, just that you haven't *found* any reason."

"No, I haven't," she muttered, with a nod.

He pointed to a little old lady sitting bundled up on one of the benches. Kate walked over, sat down on the bench beside her, held up her badge, and introduced herself.

The other woman's face lit up. "Oh, so lovely that you're here, dear."

Kate stared at her, nonplussed. "I don't know about how lovely it is, but I appreciate any help you can give us in trying to find the man who was working to save this guy."

"Oh, he was trying. He was really trying. I kept calling out to him to see if he could change his grip or something. Yet every time he got the stick and the poor person drowning was to be dragged to shore, something would happen, and he would slip away again. It was just heartbreaking," she said, and her voice trembled. "I'm terrified of the water myself, so I didn't even go down over the seawall at the end of the pool.

It was just … awful," she added, "and he tried so hard."

"Did you talk to him at all?" Kate asked.

"No. No, I didn't. I would have liked to have taken him home and given him a strong cup of tea. He looked quite devastated by the end of it."

Kate nodded. "I suppose you didn't recognize him, did you?"

"No, dear. No, no, no. I wish I did though. He really worked hard to try and help, but to know that he got so close and yet failed …"

"Right," Kate replied. "The failing part is the hardest, isn't it?"

"Oh, it is, my dear, it is. You can be in the right place at the right time, and everybody talks about miracles, but they often forget about the fact that being in the right place at the right time doesn't necessarily give you the right assistance at the right time. My sister, … her vehicle went into the water when she was trying to get onto a ferry one day. She had her two kids in there with her, and she was almost paralyzed because she didn't know which child to help first. As it was, both were good swimmers, and they both got out on their own and had to help her out," she shared, with a headshake. "She was completely frozen, worrying about which child to help. She kept going from one to the other, but they were doing much better than she was, and, by the time everybody got back to the shore, she was the one who was really struggling."

"Goodness," Kate muttered. "I think that would be one of the hardest decisions ever. But there wasn't in this case, correct?" she asked, "There wasn't another drowning person, there was just the one?"

"Oh, no, no, no, there was just the one," she confirmed.

"I didn't mean to imply that a second victim was here," she said. "No, it's just that poor man was working so hard to try and save him. Then, when the guy went back under for the last time, I really felt for him," she shared, tears coming to her eyes. "There are few enough good people in this world as it is, and then to have something like that happen. You know it will affect him for the rest of his life."

"Of course," Kate agreed, staring at the other woman. "I don't suppose you have a description that we could go with, do you?"

"Oh, dear, no. He was just a slight-framed man," she replied, but still, that element of awe filled her voice. "And it was so sad, just so, so sad."

"Of course." Kate gave an inward sigh. "But sad doesn't get us anything that we need in this instance, does it?"

"No, no, it certainly doesn't. I felt so bad that I kept calling out to him."

"Did he respond at all?"

"He looked over at me once or twice, realized I was still there, and then he just seemed to … I would like to think that my being here made him try that much harder."

"So, he had a stick or something?"

"It looked like he had a cane," she clarified, "and was reaching out to get this person to grab the cane, so he could pull him in. I know there was at least one time when they connected, and he was trying to drag the man around to shore where he could help him. He bent down at one point in time, and I think he was literally giving him his hand, but something happened. I heard a shout, and the next thing I knew, he was standing up again with his hands in the air, looking terribly upset."

"He probably lost him at that point in time," Kate suggested, unless this guy was happy that he'd managed to force this guy under long enough to know he wouldn't pop up again.

Long after the lady had left, Kate sat here, staring out at the water. It was still glassy looking, after last night's storm. Surely the drowning wasn't during the storm, was it? Still, if the storm were coming in, that would add to the distress of the drowning person—and the supposed Good Samaritan.

She got up and carefully walked around the swimming pool wall. It was a unique swimming pool in that a massive brick wall ran right into the inlet, and the pool washed over the wall, so the water was ever recirculating with the seawater outside, but it kept them safe from boating and any marine life. She stopped at the location where the woman had pointed out, but there was nothing to see, and, during a storm, it would be even more problematic.

If the victim could have made it around the corner, it would have made it much easier to get him free of the force of the tides, plus any heavy winds and waves, all smashing him against the wall. She walked back around to find Rodney waiting for her.

He stared at her. "Did you really expect to see anything out there?" he asked, a dubious note in his tone.

"Nope, just doing my due diligence. I need to understand the scene, so I can understand the witness statements."

"Your due diligence is way more than a lot of people's due diligence," he muttered.

She shrugged. "Hey, I can't be responsible for what other people do," she stated, with half a laugh. She stopped, then looked back at him. "It's so far-fetched that you can't really believe it. Yet, because we keep hearing it over and over again, how can we not consider it?"

"Exactly," Rodney agreed, with a nod. "Hence the call from my paramedic friend. He's somebody I play hockey with over the winter, which kind of complicates matters sometimes."

"No, it doesn't," she countered, with a shrug. "If something is here, we need to track it down. If there isn't, we also need to know that there isn't anything nefarious."

"You got any suggestions for that?"

"I'm not so sure," she noted, staring around the park. "I didn't ask her if she had taken a photo." She pondered that, as she turned to look around, but there was no sign of the older lady. "I did feel like she was hiding something though."

At that, Rodney turned to her. "You rarely let anybody go if you think they're hiding something. Did you show her a picture of our suspect?"

"No, but I didn't have any real reason to keep her, and she was getting tired. It occurred to me that we might be better off to give her a chance to think about it a little more first, then contact her about whatever it is that may be bothering me," she suggested. "And that will give me a chance to sort it out in my head. I'll show her the doc's picture then."

She turned toward the paramedics, then asked Rodney, "Did you talk to your friend?"

"I did. He doesn't know anything outside of the fact that they got this call and that the woman was telling anybody who would listen about the brave man who tried to save him."

"But he didn't talk to the supposed Good Samaritan?"

"No, he disappeared very quickly afterward."

"Which is definitely par for the course, like every other one we've had," she noted.

"I know that, but again we don't have any proof. However, neither do we have any reason to doubt the stories."

"No, and the stories are getting a little odder every time," she admitted, "and, if it is the same guy, we have yet to ask the right questions. Why is he striking so quickly? What is this need that's driving him to do it in the first place? And, more important, why does he do this as regularly as he does?" With a sigh, she looked back at the beach. "At some point in time, somebody will get very suspicious."

"You mean, like you?" Rodney teased.

"Absolutely like me." Kate turned to face him. "And the thing is, even when I'm suspicious and even when it's the same guy, he still came out and did it again—after I'd already spoken to him."

"But did he do anything, or was he just taking advantage of the scenario?"

"So, by withholding help, is he still actively hurting someone?"

"If you do not render aid, that's a crime in itself. But if he called 9-1-1, he is rendering aid. We don't want anybody jumping in the water who can't swim because they'll create another emergency and potentially drown themselves."

She nodded. "I know that's the sensible way to look at this," she said, her tone doubtful. "I'm just not so sure. So, what the hell is it that's driving this guy?"

"Do you think he's trying to drown people or is drowning people?"

"I don't know," she admitted. "I don't understand this element of failure to all this."

"Yeah, I don't even know where you came up with that," he shared, frowning at her. "Nobody's talking about failure here."

"Except, in every case there's the failure to save some-body," she declared, turning to him. "If he's not helping them, that is failure, too many of them."

"Maybe. Yet, if you come across somebody who is drowning, and you don't swim, and they die in front of you, how is that your fault?"

"Technically it probably isn't," she replied.

"There's no *technically* about it," he replied, with a shake of his head.

"Except," she argued, as they headed back to their vehi-cles, "what if he did something so they couldn't get out?"

"You mean, kept them in to drown them? That sounds terrible. So, what then? He comes upon somebody who's drowning, but, instead of rescuing them, he makes sure they can't be rescued?"

"Something like that, yeah." She frowned, as she stared off in the distance, because that sounded lame, even to her.

"You know what that sounds like, right?"

"Sure, conspiracy theory through and through, if not outright craziness," she muttered. "However, if you look at our track record, *crazy* is apparently something I specialize in."

"Yeah, you seem to. Does Simon have any connection to this?"

"I hope not," she replied, restraining herself. "He just bought a small yacht. I think we're heading out there this weekend to catch some fresh air in the harbor."

"A yacht?" he repeated, looking at her. "Must be nice to have somebody in your life with money."

"Maybe," she muttered. "But it's his money, not mine."

"Oh, I heard you the first time you mentioned that, and I do appreciate the fact that means something to you, but it is nice to have money available for you to go out and to enjoy life a little."

She looked at him suspiciously, but he appeared to be earnest in his choice of words. Then she shrugged. "I'll have to see how I feel about the yacht when I'm out there. Who knows? Maybe it won't even be something I particularly enjoy. But what I do enjoy is his ability to afford to order takeout every night."

He laughed at that. "I'll see you back at the office."

"Will do."

He got into his vehicle and headed out of the parking lot.

Stopping to look around, she wondered what the hell was bothering her about this place. Well, it was the same location again. She headed down to the beach, wondering if she could pick up on whatever was bothering her. Getting there, with the wind picking up, her face staring at the water flowing swiftly all around her, while knowing that somebody had just passed away, she noted this weird airiness. But that was more of Simon's domain than hers.

Shaking it off, she turned and headed back to the office.

***

SIMON WOKE WITH a start, a weird sensation of water flowing around him, over him, and under him. He was floating, and yet he wasn't drowning. He was just in this weird, almost cocoon-like space, and, while that felt nice, he was shaking. He shifted from side to side, and everything appeared to be normal in his bedroom, yet he heard the water, constant water flowing, soothing, smashing up against a wall of some sort or something. He wasn't even sure what that something was.

He shook his head to get rid of the vision, now noting Kate was no longer here.

With a sigh, he touched her side of the bed. It was cold. He reached for his phone and realized it was almost nine in the morning. Swearing at that, he hopped out of bed and quickly raced through his morning ablutions, smiling at her note before he headed downtown. Yet always in the background was this sense of water, this splash of the ocean somewhere along the line. It made no sense to him.

By the time lunchtime rolled around, he had been buried in work and needed to stop and get some food because he had skipped breakfast. Still, he wasn't even sure he wanted to take the time for such a thing. When he popped into a coffee shop and grabbed a sandwich, an eerie feeling came at the back of his neck. He turned slowly and looked around, trying for a casual look, only to find the same doctor he had seen before, standing in line beside him. He spun back to look ahead, hoping the doc didn't notice.

As Simon glanced back a little later, he realized that the doctor appeared to be completely consumed with something else in his *inner* world, not even aware of what was going on around him.

Certainly not aware of the vibe he was putting out to Simon.

Yet the doc was awake and standing there, waiting his turn.

It made no sense to Simon that he felt this almost instant rejection of who or what the doctor was because nothing was fearful about him outwardly. He was just this drab little man in a drab suit—and it looked to be the same suit he'd seen him in the previous day. Simon watched as the doctor placed his order and then stepped off to the side, close to where Simon waited for his coffee to be made.

His gaze drifted to Simon and then almost darted away again, which was interesting.

Simon didn't tend to make people feel threatened, at least he didn't think so, yet this guy didn't want to draw any direct attention to himself. Simon smiled at him and said, "At least it's not too busy today."

Dr. Burnett looked at him, then around hurriedly, as if to double-check that Simon was talking to him, and then he nodded. "It's quiet today."

His voice was soft, almost faint. Yet Simon heard him loud and clear. "We have the weekend coming, so that'll help." The doctor looked at him with a frown, and Simon explained, "It's nice to think we have time off coming up."

"Time off?" he repeated in a questioning tone, as if that were something he didn't really understand.

At that, Simon eyed him and nodded. "Yeah, I'm heading out on the water this weekend. I just got a boat, and I'm going to do some sailing."

The doc just stared at him, confused again.

Simon wasn't sure whether the guy was confused that Simon was talking to him or confused that anybody would want to go out on the water.

"I don't like the water," the doc stated almost instantly, as if trying to shut down Simon.

"I love it," Simon shared affably. "I absolutely love being out in the deep."

The other man shuddered. "Not me," he muttered faintly. "I watched someone drown as a child. I don't … now I'm terrified and I don't go in the water at all."

"Oh, I'm sorry," Simon replied, not sorry at all. "That must have been fairly traumatic."

"It was," he agreed. "I don't do well with any water now."

"No, of course not. An experience like that is enough to keep you out of the water forever. Of course you can learn to swim in the meantime, and then it won't have that power over you."

"Power?" he repeated, looking at Simon nervously.

Simon narrowed his gaze. "Yes, power," he repeated, trying for a simple tone. "When you give in to a fear, … you're giving it power over you." Simon nodded. "Only by learning to control it can you regain that sense of control over it, … over that hidden aspect in your life."

Dr. Burnett stared at him in fascination.

Simon frowned and asked, "Does that not make sense?"

He only shrugged in response.

Just then, Simon's name was called, and he walked a couple steps to the side counter, picked up his sandwich, then smiled at the doctor. "It's true though. You should try it." And, with that, he turned and headed outside to the table out there.

As soon as he sat down, he turned to look back at the doctor, who even now watched Simon as he sat outside. The doc's gaze shifted away, so Simon wouldn't know he had been watching, but it was hard not to notice it.

Simon started on his sandwich, while he waited for the doctor to come back out. But he didn't exit, which meant he was sitting inside, either hoping that Simon would leave or just choosing to have his sandwich inside, but why? And yet there could be a lot of reasons, including the fact that Simon was outside.

Turning to the work at hand, using his phone and a notepad, Simon quickly went through the things that he had to do. He sent off some orders, fixed a couple invoices that needed corrections, wrote a bunch of emails, and by the time he was done with all that, his sandwich was gone and so was his coffee.

He stood up, put away the few items that he carried around all the time into his briefcase, pocketed his phone, then turned back to see that the doctor had taken up a chair right behind him, his gaze steadily on him. While he'd been busy working, Simon hadn't even noticed. He looked over at him and smiled. "Have a good day."

The doctor looked at him and then hastily down and mumbled something, but it was obviously a *go away and leave me alone* response. And yet Simon had not been the one to stare.

Simon took a moment to really sort out the guy's energy, wondering why it didn't affect him the same way it had before, and then he turned and walked away. He could almost sense the tension easing in the doctor, the farther away Simon got, which attracted his interest even more. Why was the real question here. What was it about Simon that caused the other guy trouble? Simon gave him no reason to be upset about anything, unless ... unless what?

Simon pondered that *unless* part, as he walked to his next jobsite. The weather was starting to get a little bit ugly up ahead, and he worried that the whole weekend would be shot and that he and Kate would have to stay docked. He didn't want to start out in rough weather, not when he was still relatively green at this. He had lots of sailing experience, but not for a while, and it would take him a bit to get to know the *Running Mate*. He really just wanted to take Kate out and spend some time with her, and, of course, the whole *Running Mate* name was stuck in his head as well. He'd already signed the paperwork digitally through his lawyer, so it was his now.

It was such an interesting name, especially considering that Baxter was still married to his running mate, even after all the trouble they'd been through. It revealed a lot about their marriage, and that was something that Simon wanted himself. He just wasn't sure how to get it, or if Kate was even it. He knew that she would be furious, or at least horrified, to know he was even contemplating such a thing at this point in time. He didn't want to do anything to upset the apple cart, and that meant taking Kate as she was, without pushing for anything more. At least not until she was ready, and that might be never.

He almost laughed at that, as he neared his next rehab. As he walked closer, he felt strange, sensing something akin to a beckoning, a silent calling, but he couldn't make any sense of it.

As soon as he got to the job, his foreman was arguing with someone. The argument ceased when Simon walked in, and the other man took off. Simon walked up to Joe and asked, "Problems?"

"*Nah*, just one of the suppliers trying to screw us out of some of our parts."

"Yet he didn't wait for me to arrive or hang around once I did," Simon noted in a mild tone.

"Yeah, he prefers to bark at me. Believe me. He doesn't like confrontations with bosses, I suspect. You seem to have the ability to completely neuter him in a way."

"Neuter him?" he repeated, with a tongue-in-cheek tone. "That's a hell of a way to describe it."

"These guys talk among themselves, you know? And it's true. You have this ability to squelch people in their tracks right off the bat," he shared, "so this guy just wasn't up for dealing with you."

"Too bad," Simon muttered. "Anyway, what have we got for problems today?"

"You always come here expecting a litany of problems, don't you?" Joe asked, with a grin. "How about none today?"

Simon frowned. "Seriously?"

Joe nodded. "Seriously. In fact, unless you have something for me, I'm heading back inside, and you can take off and do whatever you need to do. I do not anticipate needing anything from you regarding this job today."

And, with that, Simon smiled, turned and headed back toward the marina to head home. The closer he got to the aquabus, the more the sensation of water built up in his head. Just that weird floating sensation, not drowning, which was a good thing, but just a float on the bay. Yet it felt as if he were fully in the water and not just sitting on a sailboat. He hopped on the little aquabus, until it got to the stop closest to his home, then hopped off and headed up to his apartment.

At the entrance, his doorman, Harry, walked over and gave him a typical afternoon greeting, with a bright cheerful smile. "So, you're alone, are you?" he asked.

Simon knew perfectly well how much both of his doormen liked Kate. "Yes, but I'm trying to convince her to come here tonight, so we can go out on the yachtearly tomorrow."

"Right, I heard about the boat," Harry replied. "Sounds like it could be fun."

"I hope so. I'm not going too far or pushing it on the first couple times out," Simon shared. "At least not until I have a chance to see how she feels out there. Plus it would be nice to get Kate out for a day or two."

"She works too hard," Harry stated, with a nod of his head.

"She does, indeed, and I'm hoping to change that." Simon laughed. "Wish me luck." Still smiling, he headed up to his apartment. He'd made it to his living room, right before he felt a weird sensation of water rising. Only this time, it made him choke. He cleared his throat several times from the uncomfortable feeling, but it continued, until he was on his knees, gasping, trying desperately to breathe in air. When no more air came, he pitched forward to the floor, out cold.

CHAPTER 13

K ATE'S DAY HAD been busy, checking in on the family of the most recently drowned victim and making another visit to the little old lady to see if she could potentially identify the man from a group of photos. She clearly identified Dr. Burnett and was thrilled to find out he was a doctor.

Kate smiled. "He does work hard at saving people. He's an oncology specialist."

The lady's mouth went into a rosebud O shape, and her eyes lit up with a quiet pride, almost as if she'd had a hand in him choosing that career. Kate never really understood taking pride in other people's lives. You could be proud of them for the sake of them having done something they wanted to do, but it really had nothing to do with you. Yet she saw it often, particularly in relationships. In this case, there wasn't a relationship, and this woman would do well to remember that.

As Kate got back into her vehicle and headed home after her very long day, she already felt the effects of her short night. She debated whether she should go to her place or to Simon's. When her phone rang, as she pulled out of the parking lot, Simon's doorman, Harry, was on the other end.

"Kate," he said, his voice trembling. "Can you come to Simon's?"

"Sure, I can," she stated, switching lanes and heading in Simon's direction. "What's the problem?"

"He hit a panic button," he began, "and, when I went up, I found him not very coherent. He's on the couch, not making sense, and yet he was very clear that I'm not allowed to call the doctor."

"Right," she muttered, her tone turning grim. "Is he hurt?"

"Not that I can see, but he keeps putting his hands around his throat, as if he's choking."

"*Great*," she muttered, guessing what was going on. "Okay, I'm about"—she checked the clock on the dashboard—"ten minutes out."

"Okay, good. I can't stay here long."

"Are you all alone downstairs?"

"Yes, I am."

"I would appreciate it if you could ensure he's okay, but I understand if you need to go down to your job," she stated. "I'm on my way and will get there as quickly as I can."

"I'll just go down and make sure everything's okay, then pop back up again."

"Yes, please do that," she replied, before disconnecting. She swore and then punched the gas pedal to the floor. "Dear God, Simon, now what?" To have him half unconscious and incoherent could be any number of things, from an allergic reaction to some food he'd picked up, especially since he loved any weird and wonderful new and different thing he could find.

However, it could just as easily be a vision that he'd got caught up in, also not something she particularly wanted to consider. Still, on any given day, just no way to knock that off the list of possibilities. By the time she pulled into the parking lot and headed up the steps, Harry rushed to open the front door for her. "Hey, Harry. When did you last see him?"

"About four minutes ago," he said, worried to a fault. "He still wasn't very coherent and was still mumbling something about no doctor."

Kate nodded. "I'm on it."

She raced to the elevator. As soon as she entered his penthouse apartment, he seemed to be waving over the back of the couch. She wasn't sure if he was trying to wave at her or was fighting off something. She dashed forward to see him flat on the couch, one hand at his throat, as he gasped and coughed, as if he couldn't get any air. She checked his gaze, but nothing was clear or coherent there. Wincing to herself, she hauled back and smacked him hard across the face.

Instantly the flailing stopped.

Then, in a normal voice, he whispered, "I wish to God you would find another way to wake me up."

With a note of humor in her voice, she replied, "And I wish to God I wouldn't find you in the middle of a seizure, wondering if I should be calling an ambulance."

He opened his eyes wide, and that magnetic gray gaze landed on her face. A glimmer of a smile was on his face, as he added, "You could at least kiss the *owie* all better."

She rolled her eyes, but leaned over and kissed him gently on the cheek. "Do you want to tell me what the hell just happened?"

"Not particularly," he muttered, as he gently stroked his throat. "I'm not drowning, right?"

At that, she winced and sat back. "Oh, God," she murmured. "Please tell me that you're not connecting to this case."

But his gaze was steady, as he stared at her. "I don't know what I'm connecting to, but it ain't fun."

"No, it doesn't sound like it," she agreed. "Is that where you were?"

He pondered that, his gaze slowly moving around the living room, before zipping back to her face. "If I'm home, and I'm acting strange, and I'm feeling like I'm choking, then yes."

"Harry found you. Apparently you hit some sort of emergency button."

He winced at that. "*Great.* I must have really been choking."

"He came up to find you on the floor and incoherent. He helped you onto the couch and wanted to call 9-1-1, but you apparently kept saying something about no doctors."

"Of course," he muttered, and then he frowned. "That would imply that I was cognizant and capable of thought, even while I was caught up in a vision."

"That's why I'm asking if you were caught up in a vision." She couldn't smell any alcohol on his breath and no drink glasses were around or any funny powdered substances. She sat down beside him. "I presume you're not taking any weird drugs or anything."

"Crap, can you imagine? With these bloody visions I already have, adding something like LSD to them, and I would be tripping out all the time."

"Sometimes I think you *are* tripping out all the time," she pointed out gently. Then she got up, walked into the kitchen, poured him a glass of water, came back, and handed it to him.

He looked at it skeptically. "I really don't know that I want to try getting water down my throat, not after I've spent all this time feeling like I've been drowning."

"Maybe, but your throat has got to be sore," she suggested, "so why don't you try."

He shifted into a half-sitting position, accepted the glass from her, and took a sip. It took him a minute or two to swallow, but, as soon as he did, he took another sip and then finished drinking all the water. He sat up fully, curling up in the corner, as he assessed the condition of his physical body.

She sat beside him, waited until he was done, and asked, "Well?"

He looked over at her with a droll expression. "You do know that most people would ask, *What the hell are you doing, or why do you look so weird, or what are you thinking?* In your case, you're just like, *Yeah, so are you done yet?*"

She snorted. "I was more concerned that you were doing an assessment and finding something wrong."

"I never find anything wrong," he admitted in exasperation. "Never. It's just these weird things overtake me at various times, and all too frequently they're somehow connected to you." He glared at her.

She nodded. "And I've told you before that maybe, ... if we didn't have a relationship, they wouldn't affect you as much."

He grabbed her hand and rested it on his thigh and declared, "That is no reason to break up with me."

"I'm not breaking up with you," she replied gently, "but these events, Simon, they are very traumatic. I hate to see you in this kind of a state."

"And I wouldn't be in this state ... or I don't know why I'm in this state anyway, since normally they just pass." He shook his head. "I kind of went from one to the other to the other." When she stiffened, he looked at her knowingly. "In other words, you've had too many drownings, haven't you?" he asked her.

"There are always too many drownings," she noted. "I don't know why one versus another would affect you."

He sighed. "I really want past these visions. Drowning is some scary shit." Then he snatched the phone from her hand and called down to Harry in the front lobby and asked him to put in a large order from Mama's.

She stared at him, wondering.

When he put down her phone, he eyed her, understanding her confusion all too well. "I'm feeling remarkably better and hungry all of a sudden."

"I wonder if you'll feel even better after you eat *past it.*"

He looked at her. "Why?"

She didn't say anything, but she wondered if this was connected somehow to Mama's nephew? She stood up again and now paced.

"You don't have a problem with Italian, do you?" he asked suddenly.

"No, I sure don't." She smiled. "You know me. I'm happy to eat anything, anytime."

"As long as it's not too weird and wonderful," Simon clarified.

She rolled her eyes at that. "Yeah, you're the one who does the weird and wonderful."

"I like to try different cultures," he shared absentmindedly, as he walked over to the window and stared down at the view.

She walked over, looped her arm through his elbow, and looked up at him. "Are you sure that you're okay?"

He squeezed her arm tight against his body and nodded. "I'm fine." He turned to stare at the city bustling down below. "It would be lovely, one of these days, if I wasn't the person you had to rescue. It does make me feel fairly odd."

She frowned at him. "That has never occurred to me."

"What? Having to rescue me?" he asked, with a laugh. "How many times have you found me in a situation like that?"

She shook her head and shrugged. "I don't know." She stared at him. "I don't keep count. Do you?"

He turned her so that she faced him, his hands on either side of her cheeks. "Doesn't it bother you?"

She shook her head, her cheek coming up against his hand, as he wouldn't let go. "No, it doesn't bother me, and it shouldn't bother you. Do you want me to keep track of the number of times you reach out and help me? Is that what you want to do? We can have a tally on either side of the page and keep track of who finds the other in the worst scenarios. That sounds like a rough way to have a relationship."

"I didn't mean it that way," he said too quickly.

"I know you didn't," she replied gently, "but no. ... I'm not keeping track of how many times I'm here to rescue you. And, if you don't keep track of how many times you have to rescue me, I'll take it as a favor."

He stared at her, and then he started to grin. "And, for you, it really is that simple, isn't it?"

"Of course it's that simple," she declared. "That's what life is all about. It's not about keeping track of who owes whom, and I don't ever want to owe you. Can you help me with cases sometimes? Sure, occasionally I would gladly take a hand, even though I have trouble asking. I don't have trouble accepting the information, but I do have trouble figuring out how it can be useful," she admitted, looking at him intently. "Often it's cryptic and definitely not clear. It's not like we can say, *Hey, Dr. Don Burnett drowned Axel Peterson, and he did it in a way that makes perfect sense.* Wouldn't it be nice if you could give me something that useful?"

"What about when you come in and find me completely spaced out in some sort of weird trance or waking up in the middle of the night, where I'm sitting there pounding nails into people's hands?"

She knew what he was talking about, as she had told him about that, recalling a recent case where Simon had helped her catch the pair of killers.

She shook her head. "I think you traumatize yourself way more than you could ever traumatize me. I mean, yes, in the beginning, I wondered what the hell I got myself into. I'm sure there were times when I looked at you and said, *That's not possible.* Are there times when you say things and, I'm like, no fucking way? Absolutely, but that's about the psychic part, not the other part. I deal with death every day at work. But the woo-woo part? I'm working on it. I am learning, and I think the bottom line is acceptance. I take every little bit one day at a time. I came in, found you in a weird state on the couch. Big deal," she snapped. "I am not planning on seeing you as a victim. Hell, I can't ever imagine such a thing." She wasn't able to comprehend for herself, much less put into words what all this meant for her and how to relay it to Simon, not without offending him. "So, if you want sympathy or pity or anything else along those lines, you're out of luck."

"God, no," he said, glaring at her.

She chuckled. "Good thing, because that's in really short supply." She leaned over and kissed him quickly on the cheek. "I don't know how long until dinner is here, but it's been a very long time since I had any sleep. So, if there's time, I wouldn't mind maybe having a ten-minute power nap."

And she walked over, threw herself onto the couch, mumbling, "Wake me up when dinner comes."

And, with that, she literally closed her eyes and crashed.

SIMON PICKED UP a blanket and gently covered up Kate, while she took a quick nap before dinner, wondering at her ability to essentially just power off, as if she had a switch that clicked off and on. He loved it, absolutely loved it. If ever somebody needed a chance to recharge, it was Kate. No doubt that she gave it her all each day, and they hadn't even talked about what kind of day she'd had.

He was still dealing with that weird sensation in the back of his throat. The feeling of drowning was one of the most horrific he'd ever dealt with. When stabbed, and God help him for saying that, the pain was sharp, was sudden, and was almost always fatal. But this drowning thing? It was a slow death, constantly gasping for air, then coming up and thinking that maybe he would be okay, only to find himself going under and fighting to the surface again and again and again.

He didn't know what this particular vision meant. He didn't know if it pertained to multiple victims. He didn't know if it was just somebody trying to keep him under. He felt a stick, some object reaching out for him, him trying to grasp it but not able to. It was such a weird thing. When his phone buzzed not very long afterward, Harry called from downstairs, telling him dinner was here. Simon asked the delivery guy to bring it on up, meeting him at the elevator with the money, if he had the bill with him. As soon as the delivery guy came upstairs, Simon recognized him as Mama's husband. "Henri, are you okay?"

The older man nodded and smiled. "When I knew it was you, I wanted to bring over the food and to thank your girlfriend for looking into the case for us."

Simon frowned at Henri. "Did she?"

"She's been out there actively questioning everybody. We didn't ask her to do anything special because we wouldn't ask for favors, because we're already struggling with our loss," he explained, as he handed over the large bag. He chuckled as Simon raised his eyebrows at the amount of food. "Mama's pretty sure you're starving and not looking after yourself, and she knows Kate never does."

"As it is, Kate is sound asleep on the couch," Simon whispered, "but I do appreciate this." He quickly checked the bill and handed over the money.

"You should just set up an account," Henri suggested. "Then you could pay once a month."

Simon laughed. "That would probably shock me to see how much pasta I eat on a monthly basis."

Henri rubbed his tummy, then laughed. "Not as much as I do." And, with that, he was gone.

Simon carried the bags into the kitchen, and, as he put them down, he heard Kate in the living room.

"Was that Henri?" Kate asked, poking her tired face over the back of the couch. "He didn't deliver dinner, did he?"

"He did," Simon confirmed, "and it's ready. So get up, sleepyhead. Come and eat."

She slowly rose from the couch, stretched her long, lean length, and then stumbled toward Simon.

He looked at her in concern. "You really are tired, aren't you?"

"I'll be fine after I get some food," she stated. "I don't remember whether I ate today or not." He stopped in the act of pulling out containers, then turned and frowned at her. She shrugged. "I think I found a granola bar in my desk, but I don't really remember. The days run together. Then, once I get into the research," she explained, "I forget everything else."

"Jeez," Simon muttered, as he walked over to the cupboard and pulled out a couple plates and then grabbed some cutlery and brought it over to dish out the food.

"We don't have to use a plate, you know?" Kate noted.

"I prefer a plate," he said in a dry tone, "rather than eating from a takeout container."

She just shrugged and accepted the plate. When she opened the container, she said, "I'm not even sure what this is."

"It's manicotti, I think." Huge shells stuffed with something, and it smelled divine. Also a big container of salad.

So, with several of these big stuffed shells and a massive salad on her plate, she dug into her meal.

He let her get several bites in ahead of his question and then murmured, "So, what took you out of bed so early this morning?"

She looked up at him briefly, cut a bite, and swallowed it. "Another drowning." He froze, as he picked up his own bite. She nodded. "Unfortunately with way-too-similar circumstances too."

"How did they know to call you over something like that?"

"In this case, the paramedic knew Rodney and plays

hockey with him. I don't know whether the EMT had been at another of these recent drownings or if he had talked some about this issue with Rodney. Somehow, having heard the witness's explanation of the older Good Samaritan, … his EMT buddy called Rodney and gave him a heads-up on this one." She stared thoughtfully off in the distance. "I need to ask Rodney about that, but the EMT called Rodney, and Rodney went down to the scene and called me."

"And was it worthwhile?"

"Our witness identified Dr. Burnett," she stated. Simon put down his fork and stared at her, as she nodded. "Right? What the hell do I do with that?"

"Yet, the witness confirmed that the doc was trying to save this person?" Simon asked.

"Yes," she replied, "I can hardly arrest somebody for failing to rescue a drowning victim. Crap, I would have to arrest all kinds of people for something like that, particularly when Dr. Burnett does not swim," she murmured.

"Crap." Simon shook his head. "That's absolutely bizarre."

"I know. What I don't know was if anybody else was there."

"Meaning? Another drowning person or a partner working with Dr. Burnett or a second witness?"

"Any or all. I don't know. I just do not know," she replied, with a headshake. "None of it makes any sense."

"And yet you seem to have these cases that don't make sense," he shared, a pointed reference to her other cases solved this year. "Then eventually all the pieces fall into place, and it makes perfect sense."

"Eventually, yes," she acknowledged, with a quick nod. "The problem is, … that's an eventuality, not something that

I get to work with right now. So this doctor was there at the scene of way-too-many recent drownings. He doesn't manage to save any of them, but that doesn't mean he's actively trying to kill them either—like the lightning person." She waved her fork in the air, as she tried to remember the name of that person.

"You mean, the person who got hit by lightning seven times?"

"Yeah." She nodded. "Rodney mentioned the same thing, how some people attract the same thing over and over. Someone may escape a horrific forest fire one year, but then they're in some torrential flooding two years later, and, after the passage of more time, they're caught up in some horrid hurricane. There are individuals who go from disaster to disaster to disaster. So it's not out of the realm of possibility that this doctor is going from drowning to drowning to drowning, particularly if he's always out looking for those events, especially when walking the beaches."

"What was he doing out there at that hour anyway?"

"*That*," she noted, "is a question I haven't been able to ask him. He didn't show up at work today. He called in sick, and, when I went to his house, he didn't answer the door," she shared. "He's not answering his phone either."

"I saw him at the coffee shop again. He admitted almost drowning as a kid. Not sure that's relevant. So what do you think he's doing right now?"

"I don't know. If he were a religious person, he might be in church," she suggested. "I would certainly not be answering my phone, particularly if I knew that the detective was leaving messages."

He looked at her, then slowly nodded his head. "At the very least he doesn't want to get involved."

"He keeps leaving the scene, so we know he doesn't want to get involved. Now, whether it's okay that he keeps leaving is a whole different story, since leaving the scene of a crime …"

Simon half laughed. "But *was* it the scene of a crime?"

"That's the problem. Drownings are generally accidental, and that's just a fact of life. Water is water."

"Speaking of water," Simon asked, "any chance you're off for the weekend?"

"I am," she said, looking over at him. "At least tomorrow, providing we don't get any more craziness."

"I thought maybe we could take the *Running Mate* out tomorrow."

She looked at him with delight. "You do know how to run her, right?"

"Yes, I do," he stated, "and, if I run into trouble or we need a hand, Baxter will be around, at least for the next little while, until they start traveling."

"That sounds good. As long as nothing else blows up, this would be a great idea," she replied, smiling broadly. "We should pack a picnic and take it out on the water."

He nodded. "Or we could get the deli to pack up a picnic."

"I don't care who packs it up," she said impatiently, yet excited. "What time do you want to go?"

"I thought we could maybe get some decent sleep tonight, then head out in the morning around eight*ish* or so?"

"Eight is fine. Maybe phone the deli tonight and have it ready to pick up."

He nodded, grabbed his phone, and dialed the deli that they both loved to use. When the owner answered the phone, Simon quickly identified himself and asked for a picnic basket for tomorrow to take out on the boat.

With the arrangement made to pick it up just after eight tomorrow morning, which was when they opened, Simon disconnected. "That was a really good idea. I'm really looking forward to this."

"I kind of am too," she admitted, giving him a bright smile. "If nothing else, I'm really looking forward to having a day off."

"But will you enjoy a day off?" he asked, with a knowing smile.

"If I asked to travel around some of the beaches, you wouldn't mind, would you?"

He laughed. "I thought we would stay around the harbor anyway and see what we might see."

She looked at him and narrowed her gaze. "You were half expecting me to ask that, weren't you?"

"Let's just say, I know my Kate very well," he shared, with a big smile.

She rolled her eyes. "Do you?"

"If you hadn't asked to go to the beaches where these drownings were happening, I would have been surprised— even though you know perfectly well the chances of the good doctor being out there are slim, especially with you wanting to speak to him so badly."

She nodded. "Beyond slim. It's stupidly slim."

"Right. Does he have any favorite haunts? Does he have any places he likes to go?"

"I don't know. Wouldn't it be nice if I could talk to him and find out?"

He nodded. "You could always try him again."

She reached for her phone, even as Simon put another big stuffed shell on her plate. When her call went to voice mail, she left yet another message. She sighed, as she put down her phone. "He really doesn't want to talk to me."

"Is he forced to?"

"No. His actions are considered those of a Good Samaritan." She shrugged. "And, in that sense, he doesn't have to talk to me. It would be nice if he did, but it's not mandatory. So unfortunately he has the liberty to decline any such request."

CHAPTER 14

AT EIGHT O'CLOCK Saturday morning, Kate and Simon headed to the deli, picked up the picnic basket, and grabbed several bottles of water, some juices, and a little bit of fruit to go with it all, then popped into the café next door, got a big thermos of coffee, and an assortment of several muffins and croissants. With everything loaded in the car, they headed to the harbor.

Once they parked and carted everything they needed to the boat, she suggested, "We need to get organized and get some large carry bags for our stuff."

Nodding, he turned his attention to orient himself to the workings of the boat.

Once out of the marina, she stepped up beside him, as he sat in front at the wheel. She sighed happily, as she crashed beside him with a cup of coffee in her hand. He turned and grinned at her happily. "It's been on my mind for a while," he murmured. "I was thinking of a catamaran, and I really loved that idea, and that still might be something that I get to at some point. However, right now, this gets me where I want to be, and I can just relax and float as need be." He asked her, "Did you happen to put away the perishable food downstairs?"

She nodded. "Yeah, I couldn't believe a fridge is down there and everything," she murmured.

"It's a high-end little unit," he murmured. "I've been out several times with Baxter, and the *Running Mate* always struck me as the perfect size."

She smiled, as she looked around and asked, "She sleeps what, eight?"

He laughed. "Okay, so it's a little bigger than I may require."

"Yeah, ya think? But, even with it sleeping eight, it's got a beautiful bedroom. We could do weekends out here," she murmured, as she stared around. "That's a pretty incredible thought."

"It is," he agreed, "and I agree. Today was intended to be a day trip," he began, looking at her questioningly, "but we could certainly stay out overnight if we wanted to."

"We didn't bring clothes or anything though," she murmured. "So, we're probably better off to just stick with the day trip idea and then plan for an overnighter next time, since more groceries will be needed."

"Of course. More groceries will definitely be needed." He chuckled. "But you're right in that we don't have everything we need. Besides, we could find ourselves completely worn out from all this fresh air by the time we've been out a few hours."

She laughed. "I suppose you bought fishing stuff too."

"I didn't," he said, with a shrug. "Do you like to fish?"

"I've never fished before," she admitted, looking over at the dark water all around them. "I haven't the first idea how."

Right now, the marina was getting smaller and smaller in the distance. They were heading out in the direction of the big tankers that always dotted the inner harbor. "You don't realize how big those things are, until you come up close to them," she murmured, as she stared at them up ahead.

"They are incredibly huge," he agreed, as they came up alongside one.

They moved past, out to the wide-open water. "I don't even know how far we can go in this thing," she noted, wondering out loud.

"A long way," he replied. "She's seaworthy. If you want, we can go over to the island sometime. Really, as soon as we have time off, or we both arrange to take time off, we can do whatever you want."

She nodded.

He glanced over at her and added, "But today, you probably want to stay close and go up and down the harbor, right?"

"It's stupid," she acknowledged, "because he won't be out there, particularly because I'm looking for him. It's not as if I'll see him in the act."

"You can't let it go from your mind, can you?"

She frowned. "It's my day off," she reminded herself firmly. "He's not responding to any of my phone messages," she confirmed, "so there's a darn good chance that he's holed up in bed and feeling sorry for himself."

"Good," Simon replied, "then let's leave it be for now and just enjoy the day."

And that's what they did. They stopped, they sunbathed, they laughed, they motored on a little bit farther, and they just generally enjoyed the day. Then he finally looked over at her and asked, "Ready to turn back?"

She nodded, looking at the cloud cover coming in. "It's a typical Vancouver day, so we're about to get a ton of rain very soon."

He nodded. "Let's head back to the harbor then."

When he headed in the direction of a different moorage, Kate asked, "What's up with this?"

"It's closer to my place." He pointed out his apartment building. "I had arranged to take over Baxter's moorage, but then switched with somebody else, so I could get closer to home."

She frowned. "So, by rights, can we stay here overnight?"

He nodded. "We're not allowed to just move in and live on these boats," he explained, "but we could absolutely stay overnight on occasion." He looked at her, then waggled his eyebrows. "We can go back out too."

"Not with the storm coming in," she said nervously. "I guess I just need to get a little more comfortable first, before we willfully brace bad weather."

He smiled. "Don't worry about it," he told her, with a nod, "although I do like the idea of staying here overnight." He finally pulled up to his new moorage spot, hopped out, and tied up the boat, then hopped back in again. "See? We're all safely moored in."

She looked around at the docks and the other boats and smiled. "I imagine it's really pretty down here at night."

"I see a lot of houseboats. Therefore, lots of people stay on their boats while they're here temporarily, traveling up and down the coast," Simon shared. "So it's certainly an option."

She was tempted to stay overnight; she really was. Then he took the decision away from her.

"I think we should just stay here. We should order in dinner, plan for a night on the boat, and then we can head on home tomorrow morning if you want, or we can go back out again."

"I'm still off tomorrow," she shared, "at least if nobody

calls me."

"Right." He headed downstairs, and, when he came back up with two fresh cups of coffee, she smiled.

"Now that's a good idea."

Then they sat under cover, as the rain poured around them. They enjoyed the hot coffee and the rolling of the yacht out on the waves. It was a unique and very special event. When a shout came from the shore, Simon looked at Kate, grinned, and said, "That's dinner. I'll be right back."

He dashed out amid the drizzle, then raced down the wharf and met somebody standing at the other end. He accepted several bags, paid the delivery guy, and rushed back. Kate watched with interest as he returned. As soon as he was here, they slipped downstairs to the big kitchen area, where he quickly dished up Greek souvlaki, Greek potatoes, and a Greek cucumber salad.

She looked at their dinner spread and smiled. "I guess it really doesn't matter where you are. You can order in dinner delivered regardless."

"You absolutely can," he agreed, with a chuckle.

They'd just barely finished eating when another shout came from outside. "Ahoy, permission to come aboard?"

Kate looked over at Simon, and he grinned, then called out, "Come on in, Baxter."

Baxter, a short man in his sixties, popped down, took one look at the two of them, and grinned. "Now this is pretty cozy, don't you think? You don't know how many times my wife and I have done this exact same thing. She's never really liked being out in bad weather, so we sat in the harbor a lot," he added, with an eyeroll.

"We live in Vancouver, so I don't consider this rain bad weather." Kate chuckled. "I'm Kate," she added, "and I can't say I've spent very much time on the water, so Simon's basically humoring me."

"We were out all day," Simon shared, "and then the weather started to get a little ugly. We didn't plan to stay overnight, but, the longer we sat here, the more we started thinking that this might be a nice day to stay put."

"It is, indeed," Baxter agreed. "I like the new berth, by the way. Closer to home, isn't it?"

"It absolutely is," Simon stated, with a smile. "I wasn't sure if you could find me."

"Oh, I would recognize this yacht anywhere." He chuckled, then held out a package to the two of them. "I brought you a little something, like a housewarming gift. The yacht is like a new home in a way."

Kate opened the bag and pulled out a lovely bottle of red wine. "Oh, now this is great. Thank you."

Simon nodded, appreciative. "Will you have a glass with us?"

"Oh no, no thanks," Baxter declined, raising his hand. "I just wanted to pop in and to say hello and to see how your virgin cruise went."

"It was wonderful," Kate replied.

And, with that, Baxter gave a cheerful wave and was gone.

She looked over at Simon. "He's the first nice friend of yours I've ever met."

He winced. "Wow," he muttered in mock hurt.

"Think about it," she stated, with an eyeroll. "Some pretty strange characters have been in your life."

He reached a hand across the table to hold one of hers. "Yes, they were, but they were all past friends. I think most of the people I have around me currently right now are pretty decent people."

"Good," she declared. "I'll take the credit for that." He looked at her, and she flashed a grin in his direction. "After all, I'm in your life now."

He grinned and nodded. "Exactly. Now what do you think about giving that berth downstairs some good old testing?"

She batted her eyelashes at him. "That's all you've been thinking about, isn't it? The whole time, all you could think about was giving that bed a try."

"Hey, we took the yacht out for a romp. Now I think we should take the bed for a romp too."

She burst out laughing and added, "Good idea." Only her next words were muffled, as he half stood and half leaned across the table, sealing her lips. Minutes later they were beside the bed, shedding clothes as fast as they could get them off, yet hampered by the need to touch each other as more skin was exposed.

He nudged her backward, until her knees hit the bed and she collapsed on it, her arms reaching up for him. He sank down on her, his lips immediately latching on to a pouting nipple, suckling deep. She cried out, her hips rising up against him, but he wouldn't be deterred. His hands reached for hers to hold them high above her head, as he poured his attention on both breasts, ignoring her mewling cries for relief.

Then she laughed, arching up beneath him and flipping him onto his back, scrambling to sit astride him, before he could protest. All protests died as she sank deep onto his erection, making them both shudder in an agony of joy.

"Now move, damn it," he groaned.

And she did. Taking them both to soaring heights, she

matched her rhythm to that of the waves rocking the yacht—carrying them both higher and higher, before crashing them over the cliffs to the waves below.

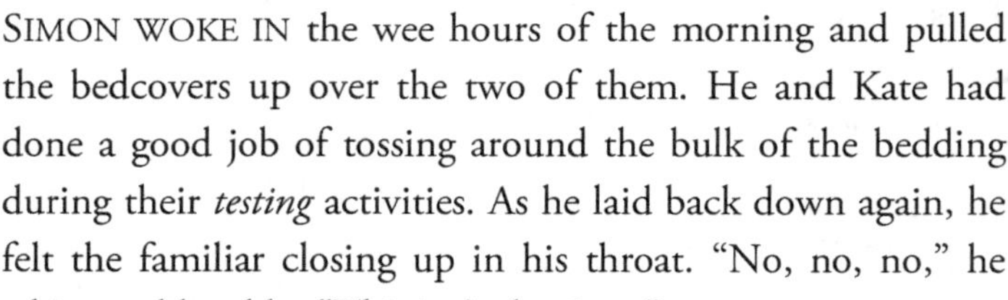

SIMON WOKE IN the wee hours of the morning and pulled the bedcovers up over the two of them. He and Kate had done a good job of tossing around the bulk of the bedding during their *testing* activities. As he laid back down again, he felt the familiar closing up in his throat. "No, no, no," he whispered harshly. "This isn't the time."

Hell, there was never a good time. He gently massaged his throat, trying to get that horrible closed-in feeling to disappear. Almost as soon as he touched his throat, he felt the water gurgling up on the inside. He sat up and started coughing and coughing, trying to clear his throat, feeling the same damn panic rising.

Then Kate's hand, firm, calm, and patient, landed on his shoulder. She whispered, "See through it, Simon. Just relax and don't get sucked into it."

He shifted and was no longer sitting on a bed. He was floating in the water, and nothing was around him. It was completely jet-black, and nothing was out here. He shook his head and whispered, "I'm in the middle of the ocean. Nothing is here, no one's around, nothing I can see."

"But there is," she stated. "Someone is there. Someone who either put you there, someone who dropped you there, or somebody who left you there."

"He's gone. Whoever it was is gone."

"Take a closer look," she murmured soothingly. "Don't let your fear stop you."

He wanted to argue that it wasn't fear and that nothing

was stopping him, but she was right. When he turned and looked again, he saw a dock, and sitting on the dock was a little boy, staring down at him.

"A little boy is on a dock," he murmured, as if afraid of speaking too loudly would make the vision disappear in front of him. "He's just sitting there."

"Talk to him. See what his name is and why he is there."

"He's staring at me in horror."

"Of course he is. Maybe, just maybe, you're in trouble, or maybe you've suggested he go in the water. Who knows," she said. "Talk to him. See what his story is."

Simon swam a little closer. The little boy pulled his legs up from below the dock, so his hands were around his knees, as he stared down at him. Simon smiled up at him, but the look of horror on the little boy's face made Simon realize that, whatever the little boy was seeing, it wasn't nice and calm. Simon whispered, "Hello."

The little boy shrieked and bolted to his feet, still frozen in place, as he stared down at him.

Simon gave the boy a smile, then asked in a whisper, "What do you see?"

"A ghost," the boy cried out, his lips trembling. "It's a ghost. Mommy, Mommy, Mommy, it's a ghost." Then he took off, racing to the end of the dock.

Simon snapped out of the vision and looked around, feeling his heart constricting in his chest. "Crap," he whispered, as he rubbed his temples.

Kate squeezed his shoulder and asked, "What was that?"

"A little boy on a dock saw me, and I clearly freaked him out. He said I was a ghost and took off screaming, calling to his mommy."

"Oh," she suggested, "maybe that little boy saw a body

come to the shore."

"And yet he talked to me?"

"No," she clarified. "Seems you talked to him."

"Right. I guess that's the difference."

"How did you feel in the vision?"

"I was just floating, like I had no control over where I went."

"Which could mean either you were a drowning victim or … somebody lost in the water, before he drowned."

"It was pretty awful," he murmured.

"Did you recognize the little boy?"

Simon shook his head. "No, but the vision was gloomy, dark. I don't know why I would see a vision of the little boy."

"I don't know either," she admitted, "unless maybe you were connecting more with a victim in the water and not with the little boy."

Simon nodded, then laid back down, taking several deep breaths to try and calm his system. When he lifted a shaky hand, he whispered, "I can't believe how cold I am."

"Cold, as in the body that you were connected to was cold?" Kate asked.

He frowned at her. "That's right. I was connected to the body. Maybe that was the weird *floatiness* I felt. The body, … it wasn't alive."

She winced and added, "So, chances are, the little boy may have seen a dead man floating."

He stared at her, nodded slowly. "I think so. I think that's exactly what happened. He saw a dead body."

"And then, when you spoke, either that little boy recognized the body or heard your voice."

"Maybe," Simon agreed. "I don't know. You would have

to talk to the little boy, not me."

She smiled. "Except that *you* were talking to the little boy. Did you get any thoughts, any impressions from the body?"

"Yeah, *cold*," he repeated, then shuddered. "Cold, motionless. I was just floating in the water, and I had no control."

"And that's because you weren't alive any longer, correct?" she asked.

He nodded slowly. "One would think so, yet why was I then able to connect to the little boy through a dead body?"

"Oh, right," she said, staring at him, and then shook her head. "Who knows, Simon. The vagaries of your gift elude me at times."

He snorted at that. "The vagaries of my gift elude me all the time," he complained, with a groan. "But I suspect the answer in this lies in the fact that the body was probably recently deceased, and potentially the spirit was still attached."

"Maybe," she replied, looking at him doubtfully. "You're sure you weren't connecting to the little boy or maybe to this man's connection to the little boy?"

"I don't know." Simon shook his head, feeling a chill from the water that no longer surrounded him. He felt the yacht rock gently under them. "Seems that the storm's gone."

"I don't know," she murmured, as she cuddled up close, pulling the blankets up over both their chests. "It's a very peaceful way to sleep regardless."

"It is, isn't it?" he murmured, as he held her close.

She whispered, "Your skin feels clammy."

"That's how the body felt too." When she shivered ever-so-slightly, he gently rubbed her back. "I'm not dead. Remember that."

"It's a weird thing to think that you may have connected with a dead man, or maybe he was just unconscious?"

Simon frowned. "I guess that's possible too, but then he wouldn't have been alive for long."

Kate took a deep breath, then asked, "What are the chances that this little boy was Dr. Burnett from years ago?"

Simon sat up slowly and stared at her, … clearly in shock. "I have no idea why you would even say that."

Clearly he was disturbed at the very idea.

"Maybe the floating body was unconscious and is still alive?" she asked, her voice rising with the question.

"Crap. I don't know. Nothing ever makes any sense in my visions. Not at the time anyway."

"No, but what does make sense is, you saw a little boy on a dock today, and you were stuck inside a floating body."

"*Great*," he muttered, as he looked at her. "You expect me to sleep better after that?"

"Hell, I don't know," she said in mock horror, "but, if we're going to get some sleep, we should try because it's already four in the morning, and that tends to be the witching hour in my world. I often get phone calls between now and six."

He settled back down on the bed again, pulling her into his arms. "Sleep then. Either sleep or we can find something better to do with our time than talk about visions that make no sense."

She chuckled, then kissed him gently. "We already spent many hours making love," she murmured. "Let's get some sleep. It would be best for both of us."

She curled up tightly against him, closed her eyes, and drifted off. He soon followed.

CHAPTER 15

KATE WOKE SEVERAL hours later and stretched, then smiled as she realized where she was and that she'd woke on her own, without any frantic phone calls from her team members. Simon was still sound asleep, yet Kate got up, dressed quickly, and walked out on the deck. Looking around to see what the day would bring, she noted it was sunny, warm, and yet a typical mid-November day, so definitely not bathing suit weather, at least not at this hour.

She made coffee and took her first cup and sat on the top deck, thoroughly enjoying both her coffee and the change of venue. She was pleasantly surprised at how quickly she'd adapted to the yacht. Wanting to walk a little bit, she refilled her cup, then headed down the wharf and walked along several of the marina docks, looking at all the boats tied up for the night. Obviously a few people had stayed on board, but, for the most part, the boats were empty; some were even covered up. As she walked toward one of the beaches, the marina and its boardwalk kept going around the corner. As she got to the other end, she heard shrieking.

Instinctively she ran toward it and found a little girl, clutching her mother. The mom was telling her, "It's all right. It's all right."

Kate asked her, "What's the problem?"

"She thought she saw somebody go into the water over

there. I can't go over there and look, not with her."

Kate dashed to the other end, where the rocks were, and somebody bobbed in the water at the other end. Kate called out, "Are you okay?"

The man nodded and replied, "I just came for an early morning swim."

"Okay, good," Kate noted. "Just no drowning, okay?"

He laughed. "No, no drowning," he hollered back.

As she turned and headed back, the mother waved and took off with her child. Kate wandered along the wharf area and noted somebody at the other end of one of the docks, where the boats were. Her cop's instincts got a hit, and, as she got closer, she realized he was calling out to somebody.

"Are you okay? Are you okay?" He had a walking cane in his hand. He reached out, as if encouraging the person to grab the cane. Yet, as soon as he grabbed it, he fell back off again.

She ran to them and watched that happen a few times before she got there, along with a lot of shouting that she couldn't make out. She neared the two men, just as they both lost their grip on the cane, after another failed attempt. Moments later a large wave came in and pushed the young man toward the dock and high enough that he could scramble up onto it. He was still here, coughing and shiver-ing, when she got there.

The man who had been trying to help was gone. Kate heard his footsteps running away, but she had to deal with the victim.

She checked on the young man, still sputtering and trembling as he sat up on the dock. She squatted beside him. "Hey, are you okay?"

He nodded. "I think so." He was shivering hard now.

"It's so stupid. I just fell in. I was walking along here, enjoying my morning, then I tripped on my own two feet and fell into the water."

"And the man who was here?"

"He was sitting on one the benches, and, when I went down, he came over to try and help."

She looked down at him and nodded. "Glad to hear that. Do you need a hand?"

"No, I'm fine." He got up, took off his shirt, and wrung it out. "My car is just up there." Kate walked with him, picking up the discarded cane, as the victim slowly made his way back toward the parking lot. "I'm okay."

"Good to hear. I'm a cop, so let me just confirm that you get back to your car okay."

She waited until he got into his vehicle, then looked around but saw no sign of the other man. She wasn't sure that it was Burnett, yet she couldn't stop thinking that it was him. With that, she slowly walked back toward Simon and the *Running Mate*.

As she got closer, Simon stood out on deck, looking around for her. His face lit up when he saw her. However, when he saw the cane in her hand, the smile fell from his face. He looked at her, horrified. "Don't tell me. Not another one?"

She shrugged. "Maybe not. I'm not exactly sure what the hell that was."

"Explain, please."

When she did so, his eyebrows shot up. "So this young man, Danny you said his name was, ... he's okay then?"

She nodded. "Yes, he drove off just now. He's young and looked incredibly healthy and fit. So no reason to think he would need help from someone, when he supposedly fell in the water. Still, I don't know why the other man left."

"You can be intimidating," Simon noted, with a gentle smile. "So, there could be all kinds of reasons."

She rolled her eyes at that. "He's missing a cane," she noted, as she held it out to him.

When Simon grabbed it from the lower end, he frowned and took a step back.

"What?" she asked, frowning.

"The end has been oiled. Anybody who grabbed that to pull themself up couldn't hang on." He took the cane from her and pointed it her way. "Try it. Pull."

And she pulled it, her hand sliding off. "Ah, shit."

"Yeah," Simon replied. "I don't know what kind of a Good Samaritan that was, but, if he expected this cane to be of any help, he was mistaken." Simon shook his head. "If nothing else, it could be a self-defense weapon of sorts, but not something useful for a rescue."

***

KATE HAD HOPED she could walk away from the encounter and enjoy her Sunday, but, after all that, no way. She fussed around, trying to get herself comfortable with the idea of not following up, until finally she turned to Simon, and her shoulders slumped.

He smiled, then nodded. "I know." He looked at her, with a knowing twinkle in his gaze. "I've just been waiting for you to say you need to go."

"The thing is, I don't have to go," she replied. "I don't have any reason to follow up on this. I don't really even have anything I can even go on—except my instincts."

"What would make you happy?" Simon asked.

She frowned at that and then replied, "I want to talk to

the young man who was in the water. That would be first."

"I like that plan," Simon noted. "Any idea where he lives?"

She nodded. "I got his contact information. It's a habit at this point," she muttered. She pulled it up and then smiled. "Hey, he doesn't live very far from here."

"Let's go for a walk," Simon suggested.

She frowned at him and added, "You don't have to come. It's your day off too."

He just rolled his eyes. "Let's go."

She laughed and added, "We can always come back here afterward."

"And that would be lovely, if we could make that happen."

"But you don't want to count on it. Got it?" she stated, with a groan. "I'm a bit of a trial, aren't I?"

He wrapped an arm around her shoulders, pulled her in for a quick hug before releasing her, and pointed out, "I'm pretty sure we're equal in that regard."

She looked at him and then smiled. "Yeah, sometimes we pretty well are." She didn't pull her punches; she had things to adapt to with him as well.

He quickly locked up the boat, cast a glance at it, and smiled. "I don't know about you, but I really enjoyed being out here."

"I did too," she said, excited to have the experience. "It kind of surprised me. It was unique, and I'm sure we're not allowed to stay overnight all the time or maybe you probably need a different license, just so we can."

He chuckled. "Could you stop being a cop for just a minute?" he teased, with a smirk. "We will figure that out as we go along."

"Sounds good to me."

Hand in hand, they walked down the wharf up onto the land. She walked around, eyeing everything. "It's such a different world for me here."

"It's not all that different for me," he noted casually. "I've been living and working around this area for the last ten years, but now, being a yacht owner myself, that part is different."

"And something you take great pride in," she noted, with a chuckle.

He pulled her to him and kissed her cheek. "I don't want to say *prideful,* but it's definitely something I'm happy about."

"Maybe *prideful* isn't the right word," she murmured. "You're allowed to be excited about reaching a milestone, and it appears that this is something you've wanted for a long time. The *Running Mate* is beautiful."

"She really is, isn't she?" he agreed, with a big smile.

"Baxter seems to be pretty happy that you've got it."

"I think he is. He's at a different stage of his life, and I think there's a certain nostalgia about walking away from this era, but to know that I'm happy with his yacht and that it'll still be around so he can see her on a regular basis should bring him some peace and solace."

"You guys talk like the yacht is some sort of pet or even a relationship."

"I think for many people it is. Just think about some guy who's had the same vehicle since he turned sixteen, worked on it all his life. Now here he is at sixty-five, looking at a vehicle he almost never takes out anymore, but it's still his pride and joy, and it has a space in his garage, unlike anything else."

They walked along in the early afternoon sun, enjoying just the freedom of being out and walking in this area.

She squeezed his hand at one point and shared, "I didn't even realize how much of a difference it would make to be on the water or to sail in this area. I must be deeply in my daily grind. I may walk the beach for work, but I never come to swim. It never appealed or even crossed my mind."

"That's a whole different story that it never appealed," he pointed out. "But, if you've never been sailing, you can't properly make that determination about sailing until you're out there. Plus, you never thought this was a possibility to begin with."

She laughed at his wording. "I guess. If you don't have any experience with boats, then it's not like a marina here in your posh False Creek area will be something I have any exposure to," she murmured. "I live in my apartment because it's close to work, and that's important to me." She shook her head.

"Yet you're not even at home all that much," he pointed out.

She glanced at him sideways. "Is that a problem?"

He looked at her and shook his head, getting where that was coming from. "Not for me, no. Is it a problem for you?"

"What? No. That I'm not there? No," she repeated. "I still pay the rent. I still pay the bills. So, whether I'm there or not shouldn't make much difference." She frowned, as she pondered that. "Yet I guess in a way it does."

"No," he countered firmly. "It doesn't. And I don't want you to start worrying about something like that."

"Something like that?" she asked, with a note of amusement. "I'm not even sure I know what *something like that* means."

He chuckled. "I don't want you making things way the hell more complicated than they need to be."

"Yet in some cases—most cases probably—I think they need to be complicated." She stared up ahead. "It's the only way we figure out shit."

He looked at her. "But sometimes you don't have time to figure out shit."

Surprised, she could only nod, as she contemplated his words. "Meaning that, people plod along on a day-to-day basis, and we just ignore everything else?"

"I think that many of us bump along quite comfortably, and on a day-to-day basis as you put it, not realizing how much of a rut we're in or how much of a problem that rut can become, simply because we don't have any reason to be bumped out of our comfort zone. Then, when we are bumped out of our comfort zone, it's this rude awakening as to how much is out there in our world that we didn't know about or partake in. You had no idea that there was so much to love about boats, marinas, and spending a night on the water, even if we are just in the harbor," he stated, with a smile.

"I suppose it's that much nicer when you're really out of the harbor, isn't it?"

"It can be," he said, giving her a smirk. "I absolutely love it out there. I've spent quite a few weeks out there at a time." He gazed out to the ocean. "I have rented different vessels over the last ten years, just to get away, to get some time and a bit of space, to figure out what I'm doing with my life and where I'm going," he shared, with a pensive note in his tone. "It's not something everybody does, and it certainly isn't something that I do all the time. However, when I could make it happen, it's always brought me an element of peace that I hadn't found any other way."

"*Peace*," she murmured. "I get it, and, given all that plagues you on a regular basis, I would imagine that peace is one of the biggest goals in life for you."

"Peace and happiness," he stated. "They should go together."

"I wonder. I think people can still be very happy and not be at peace because they thrive on that kind of chaos. It's not my style, but I've seen lots of people who just love constant shakeups, interactions, and almost a craziness that would completely turn me off."

"And me too," Simon agreed.

She laughed. "That's because we're both the same in many ways."

They meandered their way up to the address, which Simon seemed to navigate without even looking it up. "Do you have a building around here?"

"I'm always looking at older buildings to rehab." He added a chuckle.

"I've never met anybody with such an affinity for older buildings," she noted in mock horror. "Almost every other developer I know just wants to drop them."

"Yep, they do, but that's not my style," Simon stated. "I like to see what can be saved, what can be salvaged. I see value in the original design. Sometimes nothing can be done because the buildings have been lost to time and neglect," he shared, sorrow creeping into his tone, "but, when something can be done, I like to consider whether it's feasible."

"Even if it's not financially sensible?"

"Now that's a whole different ball game," he admitted, with another smile in her direction. "As you know, I have to do what makes overall financial sense, but I often make decisions that aren't necessarily what my accountant would agree with," he shared, with a sideways glance.

She nodded, as they headed up to the apartment building. "I get that, but it is still a unique concept to think that somebody cares about the origin, the history of a building, and all the time and effort that went into making her in the first place."

"It's those roots that so many people forget all about," Simon stated. "I'm not even sure that *forgetting* is the right word. Rehabbing just never even comes into consideration, as if anything old is to be discarded, so anything new is to be embraced." He shrugged. "I'm not of that mind-set and think that everything has a lot to offer, and—not always, but sometimes—what was there just needs a little bit of attention," he suggested.

"I get it," she said, "kind of, anyway."

"Sure, you do, but that comes with a big price tag, so it's not always doable, but I don't necessarily always buy the buildings that I can't work on either," Simon noted. "I'll admit that there is a certain amount of emotionalism for me when I buy a building, and I can indulge that emotional feeling a little more than some people because I have the money for it. Most builders take emotion completely out of the decision and look at it from a purely credit/debit point of view, as to whether that building will make them money."

He stood still to look at the place before him. "I don't like to look at it from that point of view, so I come at it from a different angle. Realtors don't always understand. I've bought buildings that they couldn't sell for the life of them because they just needed to be dropped, and the market wasn't ready to handle the cost of putting in a new one in addition to the purchase price. I'm content to wait. In a lot of cases, old buildings will go for a very cheap price, and, because I know that often I can fix them up and that they've got another twenty, thirty, forty years, if not hundreds of years to go," he noted, "I can make it work, where others cannot."

He pointed to the four-story apartment building before them. "That's the address you're looking for."

CHAPTER 16

K ATE FOLLOWED SIMON to the main entrance. A buzzer system was there, so Simon looked at the number on her notes and rang it. When a young man answered, Kate stepped up and explained who she was and that she had a few more questions for him.

A note of complete exasperation filled his tone, when he said, "I told you that I'm fine."

"That's nice," she replied, keeping her tone mild. "That doesn't change the fact that I need to ask you a couple more questions."

The frustration in his voice boiled over when he asked, "And what if I don't want to answer any questions?"

She looked over at Simon and grimaced. "Then I guess I would have to ask why," she replied, her voice calm but determined. "That would make me suspicious."

"For crying out loud," he snapped. "I just want to forget the fact that I was such an idiot this morning, okay? I don't like drawing attention to myself to begin with, and this morning was a particularly bad scenario."

"I do want to talk to you about it," she repeated, her tone inflexible. "So let us in or you come down to the station tomorrow."

The buzzer rang in front of them, allowing them in. Simon didn't say anything and just hung off to the side. She quickly walked in, and Simon followed. Together they walked up to the second floor, where the apartment was.

He was waiting at the doorway, his arms crossed, glaring at her.

"Do you want to do this outside or inside?" she asked.

He frowned at that and stepped back, but he didn't let them in.

"So be it. I'll ask my questions out here in the hallway." She nodded. "I'm not trying to make a scene, okay? And I'm definitely not trying to make you feel even worse. I don't know why you would feel like what happened was such a problem," she explained. "You don't need to feel stupid because accidents do happen."

"I'm young, strong, and healthy," he declared. "I sure as hell didn't need any attention being drawn to the fact that I was supposedly struggling to get out."

"When you say *supposedly*, what does that mean?"

"That's the way the old man kept acting, you know? Like I was drowning or something," he snapped in a clipped retort. "Obviously I wasn't, but he was in this weird state, like he just didn't understand what was going on and was trying to help." He paused and took a deep breath, as if to control his outburst, and then added something that really caught her attention. "Yet the help he was giving me ... was definitely not at all helpful."

"Meaning?"

He groaned. "Just, you know, it's embarrassing."

The words flew out of his mouth, and she finally realized what his problem was. "So, you're upset because you got caught up in a situation, likely to attract undue attention, and was then misconstrued from the start, since you were never in any kind of distress or danger."

"Exactly, and I was right. I mean, ... look at you. I have a cop at my door."

She gave him half a smile. "And the only reason I'm here is because I was there with you earlier and saw the aftermath."

"And I told you," he stated flatly, "I'm fine."

"But you're not fine," she argued, eyeing him carefully. "You're obviously upset and stressed out about the entire thing."

He glared at her. "How would you feel?"

"If I'd been in an ugly situation where I might have drowned?" She snorted at his attitude. "I would be grateful. If I was feeling stupid for having done something that might have got me into trouble? ... I might try to brush the whole thing off," she suggested, with a nod. "If I was just going for a swim, and I had this old guy try hard to save me, when I didn't need saving, then I probably would be quite pissed."

He stared at her and nodded. "The last two are definitely true. I can swim. I was fine. He was making a big deal out of nothing, and, with all his fumbling around, he wouldn't let me out of the water."

"Ah," she noted, "and that is the crux of the matter."

He flung back the door and finally stepped aside to let them inside the apartment. She walked in to see a blanket on the couch, a gray sectional sitting in front of a big TV. She motioned at the blanket. "Are you still cold?"

He shrugged self-consciously. "More upset at this point," he admitted.

She nodded. "There is something called dry drowning," she shared, "and I want to ensure you don't run into any problem like that."

He frowned at her. "I was in the water, and that sounds

to me like it would be considered a water drowning, not a dry drowning."

She gave him a hard look, and Simon interrupted their pissing contest. "It happens after the fact, when you get a little bit of water in your lungs, and you don't realize it. You feel just fine. Then suddenly you don't feel fine," Simon explained. "So, if you have any trouble breathing, any issues at all, … please don't let your ego stop you from getting checked out."

Danny looked at Simon, then sat down hard on the couch. "Jeez, I feel like such an idiot."

"I'm not so worried about your feelings of being an idiot," she shared, "as much as what you thought about your Good Samaritan." She sat down gingerly on the couch beside him, assessing his color. He did seem to be okay and was quite pissed off, and that energy would help him get through this next little bit.

"What about it?" he asked in a brooding manner, as he pulled the blanket up over his shoulders.

"Was he trying to help you?"

"Sure, of course he was," he stated, giving her a hard stare. "What else? It's just that he was old and obviously couldn't really help me out of the water. He wasn't strong enough to lift me up or to really give me a hand. If I had grabbed his hand, I would have accidently pulled him in, and we would have had an even worse scenario. I was hanging on to the side of the dock, so I didn't need anybody to pull me up."

"And yet he tried?" she asked carefully.

"Several times. He kept trying to give me his cane, hoping that would help, and I guess at one point in time I did grab it, but it slipped right out of my hand."

"Did he try again and again?"

Danny nodded. "Yes. He kept telling me to grab the cane, and he kept poking me with it, I presume because he thought I was too worried or too panicked and couldn't see it," he said, hanging his head, "but I don't know for sure. It was kind of ... It didn't do any good, and, if I had pulled on it, he would have ended up in the water too."

"Yes, of course," she agreed. "So your hand slipped off the cane?"

He shrugged. "Yeah, I couldn't seem to grasp it."

"And that was probably a good thing."

"I don't know. It was just a weird scenario that I really don't want to spend any time thinking about. It all happened so fast."

"Instead I'm here hounding you."

"Exactly," he agreed pointedly. "So, you can leave any time, you know?"

She laughed, then nodded. "And I will." She got up and asked him one last time, "Did you at any point in time feel threatened by this guy?"

He looked at her and then exploded, "Jeez, what the hell? This guy was old." She just stared at him and continued to wait for his answer. "Why would you even ask something like that?" He frowned at her.

"Because I'm curious, and I want to know," she declared. "I know that you're sitting here, trying not to think about it, but it's important."

"Why? It's not like he was trying to drown me or anything."

"That's a good point, and I'm glad that you just brought it up. Was he trying to drown you?" she asked pointedly.

"No, he was just trying to give me the damn cane to help

me out."

"Though you yourself told me that the cane was slippery, and you couldn't get out."

"Yeah, well, that was probably more my fault because I didn't want to put any weight on it. He was an older guy."

"Older like … ?"

"Had to be at least fifty, maybe," he replied, with a note of disgust. "Could have been younger, I guess, but the guy was too damn small and skinny and didn't seem like he would have much strength. He would have been far better off to just call for help."

"Did he call for help?" she asked.

He looked at her. "I don't know. I didn't hear him call for help, but, by then, I was more concerned about getting myself out of the water."

"Did he at any point in time push you back into the water?"

"No, of course not." Then he stopped and frowned. "At one point I did wonder. It must have been an accident with the cane because somehow I ended up back in the water again, after I had spent a lot of my energy getting out. I was in there too long. That damn harbor is colder than you think," he shared, as he pulled the blanket closer, shivering some more. "I hadn't intended on going into the water in the first place, and, once I was in, … fully dressed, it was a lot harder than I expected to get back out."

Simon nodded and added, "That's one of the problems with drowning. It's already mid-November, and the weather may not be as cold as it usually is, but it's cold in the water. Nobody expects the ocean to sap your energy and strength as fast as it does. So, even at a dock, being fully clothed like that and potentially"—Simon eyed him cautiously—"also drinking a little last night …?" Simon left that hanging there.

The young man glared at him. Then his shoulders sagged, and he nodded. "I'd only had a few beers. Yeah, I was probably a little hungover, and I accept that's probably how I ended up in the water in the first place," he acknowledged, "and I suppose that's why I felt the cold so much faster."

She nodded. "That's definitely true, and I know you're probably not ready to hear this, but you really did have a lucky escape."

He sagged deeper into the couch cushions, pulled the blanket up tighter, and nodded. "Yeah, I'm starting to figure that out," he muttered.

"I am still quite concerned about your lungs," she murmured. "So, I will be calling you several times today to check in and to confirm you're doing okay."

He looked at her. "I've never known a cop who gave a shit."

She shrugged. "Did the older man say anything to you?"

He looked at her. "I don't quite understand what the problem was with this guy, but I wasn't necessarily picking up everything he might have been saying. He muttered something like, *I've got you. I've got you. This time it'll work.*"

She smiled and nodded. "Thank you for your cooperation. I'll leave you now, but seriously, I want you to stay warm and to get some hot fluids into you." She walked into the kitchen and asked, "Do you drink coffee?"

"Yeah, I do," he said. "I haven't put any on yet."

She quickly made a pot based on his instructions and soon brought him a cup back out. When she handed it to him, he looked at her and shook his head. "I really don't see you as a cop. You've got to be shitting me."

"Doesn't matter whether you do or not," she stated. "I'm just a human being helping another human being in distress, whether that person wants to admit it or not." When she was ready to leave, she pulled up the picture of Dr. Burnett.

He looked at it and nodded. "Yeah, that's him. Who is this guy anyway?"

"He's a doctor. An oncologist."

"Ah," he said, as comprehension crossed face. "I think he mentioned something about that, like, *I can help. I'm a doctor.*"

She nodded. "He is."

"Why are you so concerned about him?" he asked.

"He's turned up at the scene of several recent drownings," she shared, "situations where unfortunately the people in question didn't survive. He was seen trying to help them too."

"So, what's wrong with that?" he asked her curiously.

"At what point in time is it abnormal for one person to repeatedly be at the site of different drownings?" she asked, "Once, twice, three times?"

"I guess if you've got really bad luck, yeah."

"But what about four or five, even six times?" she asked, tilting her head to the side.

He swallowed hard. "Yeah, that's kind of weird."

"Weird is right," she added, nodding in agreement. "So far you're the only one who survived to talk about what he may or may not have done."

"He didn't do anything," he stated in confusion. "It seemed like he was trying to help. Maybe he was, or maybe he wasn't, but I certainly wouldn't go on record and say either way."

"Ah ..." She smiled. "That's all right. Look after yourself. And the next time you're out drinking," she stated pointedly, "stay away from the water."

"Yeah, don't worry," he muttered. "I've learned my lesson on that."

EVEN THOUGH THIS was technically her day off, Kate walked into the office later this Monday morning, pondering what she was supposed to do about Dr. Don Burnett. Per everything she'd found to date, she still only had this odd hint of suspicion that something was off. He had made rescue attempts, using that lovely but oily cane. And yet it was made of wood, so maybe somebody had recently oiled it as part of its proper care. She didn't know.

She had the cane with her. Yet she wondered about returning it to him, but then considered it might be better to hold it as evidence, and yet evidence of what? She didn't have a case; that was the sticking point. As she walked in and poured coffee, Colby called out to her. She winced, headed to his office, and sat down with a harder *plop* than necessary.

He looked at her and asked, "So?"

"So, what?" she replied crossly.

"You're here on your day off, so what is bothering you?"

She then took a deep breath and told him about her Sunday morning.

"Again, the same doctor?" he asked.

"Yeah, the same doctor ... again."

"So, is this guy just going around looking for opportunities to try and save people?"

"That's possible," she admitted, "and I gather from everything I've heard, read, and gotten directly from him is that he's alone and doesn't have any family. So, maybe he just has this thing about water, a compulsion or whatever, and he's stuck trying to help people."

Colby nodded slowly. "Which isn't a crime."

"No," she agreed, glaring at him. "It isn't a crime."

He half smiled. "But you're not happy with that conclusion either, are you?"

"It feels like I'm spinning my wheels. Yet every time I try to walk away, I keep coming back."

"So, to you, something is still very suspicious about this situation."

"If he were only at the scene of one or two deaths, I probably would think, *Shitty luck on his part.* Nobody wants to see anyone drown, much less to see multiple people drown, but at what point is that shitty luck something more?"

He stared at her in fascination, and then he voiced the words that she dreaded hearing. "Did you ask Simon about this?"

"I don't like asking Simon about things," she snapped, glaring at her boss. "It's good old police work that gets cases solved, not the things we cannot prove." His lips twitched, and she realized how defensive she sounded. "We've talked about it," she conceded, shaking her head, "and he was with me when we went and checked on this young man."

"Is he okay?"

She nodded. "I talked to him twice this morning, and I will probably call him a time or two more later today. I think I can probably leave it alone after that. … However, Danny was hungover or maybe still drunk when it happened. Plus, he didn't want to admit it, but maybe he struggled to get out of the water more than he let on at first. He was fully dressed."

"So, he didn't want to lose face and admit that he'd been stupid enough to fall into the water as a drunk. Then, because of his altered state, getting out was more of a challenge than it would have been otherwise."

"Exactly," she agreed, "and this old guy wasn't much help. I think Danny started to panic when he realized that the old guy was the only help he had out there and that he wasn't enough help. It was a hard incoming wave that got Danny up and out of the water, before he succumbed to the cold."

"Jeez." Colby shook his head, as he stared down at the notepad in his hands. "And yet, how do you charge somebody with trying to help?"

"Exactly," she said. "As far as I know, the doc's in the free and clear, and we're just messing up his life."

He gave a shout of laughter at that. "I think a lot of criminals would say that same thing." He took a moment to think and then nodded at her. "Why don't you return the cane to Dr. Burnett and see what his reaction is."

"I can certainly do that because I don't really have any legitimate reason not to, although I was wondering about getting forensics to take a look at it first."

He frowned at her and asked, "Why?"

She told him what Simon had pointed out and about the strange feel of it.

Colby asked, "Did you bring it with you?"

She nodded and, going back out to her desk, retrieved it and brought it back to his office. He ran his hand over it and, as she expected, it came away slippery, but not with any noticeable substance on his hand.

"It has definitely been oiled," Colby noted. "Yet it could

be on a completely innocent level, since it's a wooden cane with no factory-style finish, almost like somebody made it. Therefore, it does need regular care."

She smiled and nodded in agreement. "See? And that's my problem. Every time I turn around, there's an innocent explanation."

"And yet you still can't leave it."

"No, I can't. With his family issues, I'm questioning his motives."

"You know what that means," Colby said, with a smirk.

"I don't need to see the in-house shrink about this case. I'm at a dead end, so I should just work on my other cases, until something further comes up."

"Return the cane to the good doctor, see what he has to say, and then you might just need to park it."

"You're the one who brought me in on this."

"I did," he confirmed, "and you're the one who grabbed on and can't walk away. Tell me no crime has been committed, and I'll believe you, and you can move on. If a crime was committed, we need to figure out in what way it's been committed, who's responsible, how to stop it, and how to charge them. Short of any of that, leave it."

"Yeah, sure," she grumbled, staring at him. "Did you want to give me an easy job perchance?"

"No," he declared. "I want to give you the job you've got because I know you can handle it."

She shook her head at that, as she walked out. "Complete bullshit," she muttered.

"I heard that," Colby called out.

"Exactly as I intended," she replied and then laughed because their relationship had really eased in the department to the extent that she could do something like that. It was obviously not offering him the full measure of respect his position required, but occasionally such levity lightened the load and eased some of the stress.

As she sat down at her desk and set out to get to work, her attention kept going back to the cane. Shaking her head with a grumble, she decided she had to deal with that right off.

As it was, she needed to go to the morgue and check on another case, so she would get Dr. Smidge to check the cane first, before stopping off at Dr. Burnett's office to return his cane. He worked four on and four off at the morgue. Hopefully he was on today. She left a note for Rodney, grabbed the cane, and headed out. She caught Dr. Smidge and got him to examine the cane on the spot. He frowned but did it, then shooed her away. "You'll get my results in an email later. Now stop bothering me."

Next stop, the Oncology Center. She asked to see Dr. Burnett.

His receptionist looked at her with a worried expression. "He's really, really busy today."

"It won't take long," Kate replied, as she held up his cane.

The woman's face lit up when she saw it. "Oh my," she said, with a nervous laugh, "he'll be really happy to get that back."

"Will he?" she asked, with a questioning tone. "Anyway, I need a few minutes with him."

Kate was buzzed through, and the doctor looked up in annoyance, when she walked in. However, when he saw his cane, his face lit up like a Christmas tree. She stared down at the cane, wondering if she had missed something, but it appeared to be a simple cane, carved from a single piece of wood. As she held it out to him, she announced, "I believe this is yours."

He got up and came out from around his desk in a hurry, with the most enthusiasm she'd seen out of him yet. "Yes, absolutely." He smiled when he picked it up.

Kate noted, "And yet you don't need a cane."

"I use it when I go for my walks," he explained. "Sometimes it's just nice to have extra support, in case I get tired."

"Do you get tired?" she asked.

He shrugged. "Sometimes. Sometimes I go for long walks and find that I've taken it a little bit too far, and it's just nice to have this to depend on." She didn't say anything. "Where did you find it?"

"You left it at the marina in False Creek."

He frowned at her and asked, "How could you possibly know it was mine?"

"I saw most of the drowning event. The person survived that dunk into the harbor," she shared, taking her time to look at him as she spoke, searching for anything, "and identified your picture."

He just looked at her in shock, as she held up her phone, showing him the photo. "Good Lord, you never really know who is watching or following you out there, do you?"

"Oh, I don't have time for either, especially if you don't have anything to do with my cases," she shared, "but considering that you've been on the site of so many recent drownings and near drownings, you definitely have become a person of interest."

He looked at her with an almost unwavering intensity. "Why on earth would I be of interest?" he asked, staring at her.

She wasn't exactly sure what was wrong with the way he

asked it, but definitely something was wrong. She smiled as she replied, "Because, when I get somebody who shows up a little too often, they become a person of interest."

"Good Lord." He shook his head. "Is your world so empty that's all you have in it?"

She frowned at him and added, "Or yours? Regardless, my professional world is full of cases, which leads me to see bad guys everywhere."

"Ah." He smiled and nodded. "You probably should see a therapist about that."

Just hearing the word *therapist* along with the suggestion she should go to one reminded her of the one on staff that she had been avoiding for far too long again. Colby would not be happy about it either. Shaking her head, she took control of the conversation. "What was the reason you were down at the harbor earlier this Sunday morning?"

"Good Heavens." He remained standing, eyeing her in frustration. "Do I need an excuse to go to one of the most beautiful locations in the area? I mean, … why were you there?"

"Because I slept on one of the boats overnight," she shared in a dry tone. "I presume you did not."

He stared at her and slowly shook his head. "Though that would be an interesting experience," he murmured, "I haven't had the pleasure yet."

"No, and I wouldn't have either, except a friend of mine recently purchased a small yacht and is keeping it at the marina."

He nodded. "It must be nice."

"I don't know about that. It's not my boat, not my expense. I just happened to get an invitation, and I accepted," she stated. "And your reason to be there?"

He shrugged. "It's a lovely area to walk, although I have this love-hate relationship with water. I love the sound of it. I love to watch it. I love the reflection on it," he said in a dreamy voice. "But, because I can't swim and because I've seen way too many people go in the water and get into trouble, that's the hate part." He gave her a sad smile. "I can assure you that nothing is untoward about my being at the waterfront," he stated. "I just love being close to the water, and, maybe because I'm there more often than anybody else, it stands to reason that I would see more drownings, or near drownings, than other people, and that is not suspicious at all."

Just enough common sense filled his explanation to make her doubt herself.

Yet she wasn't convinced.

"The oil on your cane," she asked, "what is that about? And why doesn't it have a rubber tip on the bottom? It hardly seems safe."

"It used to have a rubber bottom," he replied, looking at his cane affectionately. "As for the oil, it needs regular coats to keep the wood from swelling. It also stops it from absorbing water, when I walk in the rain or when I get it wet, which, as you well know, I've had to do several times recently."

As it had, indeed, gotten wet several times recently, she didn't have any response, other than a nod. Truly he had been getting it wet a lot. Was it on purpose? Was there something nefarious about it? Why did everything seem so innocent, as he made it all sound? She didn't know, and she had very little way of determining just what the hell was going on. She had enough to make her suspicious, yet nothing to give her any foundation to base those suspicions on, making her feel even more of an idiot. Finally she stated, "Maybe you could avoid the water for a while, and we could avoid having drowning victims."

He looked at her in horror. "Surely you're not implying that I'm causing these events to happen, are you?"

She looked at him, saw the absolute shock on his face, and tilted her head. "I'm not implying anything." And, with that, she turned and walked out. The problem was, she wanted to imply that he very well may have had something to do with these deaths, and yet she couldn't find any solid motive, issue, or reasoning that would suggest he had pushed those people in or was doing anything other than trying to help them.

That part still drove her nuts when she got back to the office.

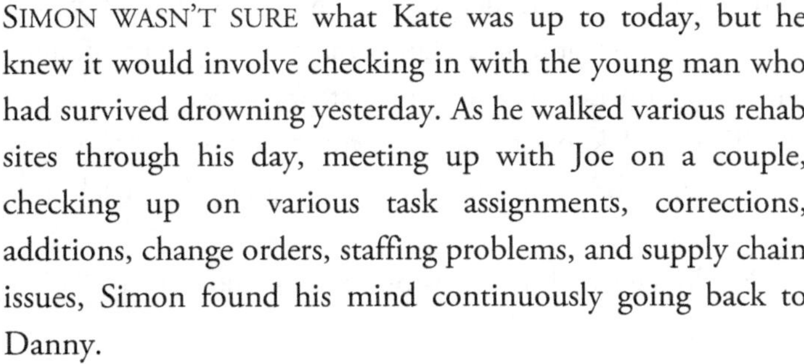

SIMON WASN'T SURE what Kate was up to today, but he knew it would involve checking in with the young man who had survived drowning yesterday. As he walked various rehab sites through his day, meeting up with Joe on a couple, checking up on various task assignments, corrections, additions, change orders, staffing problems, and supply chain issues, Simon found his mind continuously going back to Danny.

Finally he sent Kate a text, asking for his number. She phoned him right away and asked, "Why?"

"Because I've got this weird feeling that I need to speak with him right now, before I go check up on him."

She gave him the number. "I sure as hell hope that feeling is wrong."

"I'm not that far away from where he is, so I just

thought that maybe I should."

"Go for it." Then she was gone.

He chuckled at that. It's not as if he needed her permission, but he thought it might make it easier on the young man if he called first. When he phoned, the call was answered in a raw voice.

"Hello, my name is Simon, and I was there this morning with Detective Kate Morgan. I was just checking up to confirm you're doing okay."

"Yeah, I'm fine," he replied warily.

Simon continued. "I'm just around the corner. Is it all right if I stop in?"

"Hell." He replied in a resigned tone, "Fine, come on by."

A few minutes later, he walked up, rang the buzzer, was let into the building, and as he walked up to the second floor to see Danny, Simon found him leaning against the door, with a belligerent attitude, yet something was incredibly fake about it. Simon motioned Danny inside the apartment, and, caught by surprise, the young man stepped back.

"Danny, I know that there's more to this story, so I'm giving you a chance to tell me before I bring Kate back into it."

He looked at him in astonishment and asked, "What more could there possibly be?"

Simon shrugged. "I don't know, but I can feel it."

"Good God." He dropped his head into his hands. "You really operate on feelings?" he asked, with a snort.

"Yeah, I absolutely do," Simon stated, looking at him, "and, if you did more of it yourself, you wouldn't be quite so messed up."

Danny got ugly and snapped, "What do you mean,

messed up?"

"I guess the question I have to ask is whether that trip into the water, into the harbor, was accidental or deliberate."

Danny froze, as he stared at him. "Why would you even say that?" he asked in a ghost of a voice, completely confirming Simon's concern.

Speaking casually, not wanting to alarm him in any way, Simon went on. "So, it was an attempt at suicide, wasn't it?"

"Jeez," Danny yelled, getting in Simon's face. "Are you mad?" Seconds later, his shoulders sagged, and he stepped back. Walking over to the couch, he collapsed down on one end.

Simon sat at the other end and just waited.

"Why the hell would you even say something like that?" Danny muttered.

"You could say that I have this affinity for spying trouble," Simon said, with a wry look, when Danny turned to stare at him in shock. "I get feelings. I get information from people sometimes."

"You mean, like you're a psychic?" he cried out, horrified.

"Oh, I don't know that I would call myself psychic," Simon clarified. "Let's just say that often shit is going on that I can sense, but I don't really have answers for."

"Holy crap." Danny stared at him. "That is the last thing I expected. You look like you're completely normal on the outside."

Simon gave him a nod. "I do, don't I?" he stated in a cheerful voice. "It surprises everybody constantly."

"You mean, you tell people?"

"No, not very often. I'm telling you now because I sense that something is completely wrong in your world and that you potentially need help."

"Oh, and what, you're here to help me?" he asked, with bitterness in his tone.

"Is that so hard to believe?" Simon asked, looking at him curiously. "I know that men tend to miss out on that whole *needing help* cycle, but the reality is men do need help at times."

At that, Danny looked at him and clarified, "I've got my own apartment. I'm independent. I have everything I could possibly want. Why the hell would I have done something like that?"

But his very defensiveness was also what gave Simon a little more insight into what was going on in his world. "Maybe that's the very question you've been sitting here asking yourself. If you have all this, why did you think what you needed was a swim in the harbor?"

"I fell because I was drunk," he replied in a quick effort to cover up.

"Sure, sure, I hear that. I also hear something in your voice that tells me that I'm on the right track. So, tell me about yourself. What is going on in your world that's making you doubt where you are."

"Crap. You do understand how absolutely ridiculous you sound asking these questions."

Simon nodded. "Yet I am not afraid to ask the questions," he stated smoothly. "I am not afraid to have you tell me to take a hike or to have you burst into tears and tell me the truth. I've heard it all, and, if I haven't heard it all, believe me. Kate has."

"*Kate,*" Danny muttered in disgust. He slumped back onto the couch, shook his head, and added, "I can't believe I'm in this situation."

"You mean, the fact that somebody tuned in to what you were looking at doing, and, because of the old man, you ended up not doing it."

He pivoted to stare at him. "I could have brought that old man in with me. I could have drowned him in two seconds," he declared flatly. "Believe me. At the time I considered it." Simon didn't say anything, just waited. "And that doesn't surprise you at all, does it?"

"No, not really," Simon replied, with a casual tone. "Again, we've heard and seen a lot, but you probably didn't have any reason to hurt him, outside of the fact that he was starting to piss you off."

"Yeah, you're not kidding there. He sure was," Danny retorted. "He wouldn't leave me alone, and yet, if he was trying to help me, every effort seemed to be making it worse. I was starting to panic, and he kept poking me with the stick, trying to get my attention to grab it. Then, every time I grabbed it, my hand would slip, and I couldn't get up anyway. The only reason that I survived was that a huge wave came up, hit me broadside, and halfway lifted me up." He shook his head at the missed chances. "At the time, I was just grateful and grabbed on, dragged myself up onto the dock and just collapsed there. If not for that, I don't know what would have happened. Then I jumped up and tried to act like everything was normal, but I was shivering pretty badly."

Simon just nodded and listened.

"You don't look or sound in any way surprised."

"It's not that I'm *not* surprised," he explained, "because that would completely invalidate everything you're saying. What I am surprised about is the fact that you wanted to pretend it didn't happen."

"Believe me. As soon as I got into trouble, I wanted to live pretty-damn fast," he stated, his voice deepening in pain. "And that's when you realize that you may not have that choice any longer."

"That makes it even harder, doesn't it?"

"It sure does," he muttered.

"Does the booze bring it on?"

He looked at him and asked, "Does booze do that?"

"Absolutely. Sometimes we drink to feel better, but it has the opposite effect. It brings up all those repressed negative emotions that we haven't learned to handle, and then we end up bawling and realizing that everything we had hoped and wanted to go our way didn't. In some cases there's just no better answer, no good answer. Suddenly life seems like a really shitty deal, and you just want to check out," Simon shared.

It didn't take long for the young man to break down and to give him the full details about all the things that had gone wrong. He'd lost his job, and his girlfriend had left him, and his parents had passed on earlier in the year, and he was just lost. Simon sat here and listened, knowing perfectly well that it had probably been a very long time since anybody had given this young man any time to really hear who he was and what he was going through. His losses were not nothing.

After he finally ran out of words, Danny looked over at Simon and asked, "Why the hell do you even care?"

Simon smiled. "You would be surprised. There are a lot of reasons why people need to do things in this life, and often that has absolutely nothing to do with making money or pretending to be somebody other than you are."

"Everybody pretends," Danny stated instantly. "Everybody always pretends."

"Sounds like you've met some interesting people in your life."

"No, I'm not sure I have," he muttered, his voice getting faint. "Or maybe I've been getting it all wrong." He got up and started to pace. "When I was in the water, as soon as I realized I wanted to live, it seemed to be snatched from my hands. I just … I couldn't grasp the enormity of what I'd done, and the reality that there was no going back," he admitted, as he kept pacing, "It was … I had chosen this one-way ticket, and I couldn't figure out how to get out again, and I was panicking. Then the old man came along. I don't know what he was trying to do, like whether he was trying to help me or trying to hurt me. But I guess, in the end, he tried to help me," Danny said. "Whatever he did doesn't matter at all. I still owe him for trying."

"You don't owe him anything," Simon declared. "However, if you managed to have an awakening through this process, that can only be a good thing. Now the question is, what will you do from here?"

Danny looked over at Simon and sat back down again. "I still don't understand why you care."

Simon smiled. "You don't have to understand why I care. Just know that I do."

Danny shook his head. "Jeez, I can't believe any of this."

"What? The fact that you're this strapping—what are you, twenty-four, twenty-five?"

Danny nodded. "Twenty-five," he replied ruefully.

"Okay, so you're a healthy, physically active, strong in-dividual, and now here you are, contemplating suicide or trying to somehow reconcile the fact that you made an attempt at suicide, and it just makes no sense. You can't judge yourself based on simply your physical strength,"

Simon noted, "because mental and emotional trauma is a whole different story, and you have to let yourself off the hook for not being as strong as you seem to think you should have been."

Danny just stared at him for a long hard moment. "I guess. … Believe me. I'm feeling very different about the whole thing right now."

"You are, but what happens the next time you get drunk?"

"Meaning, I need to stop drinking?" Danny asked.

"Oh, I would," Simon said. "If there were ever a wake-up call for stopping, this would be it."

"And yet would it be? So what if I drink myself into the water? What does anybody care?"

"The real question is, what will it take for *you* to care?" Simon asked. "What would it really take for you to care enough to make it through today, to make it through tomorrow, and the next day?"

"I'm here aren't I?" he asked, a solemn note in his tone.

"You are. But, when I walk out this door, will you be gone again?"

"No. I'm not going anywhere. As I told you, nearly drowning was quite the eye-opener."

"I'm glad to hear that." Simon smiled. "What kind of work do you do?"

"I was a laborer, until I got fired."

"Why?" Simon asked.

He looked at him and asked, "Why the hell do you care?"

"I care, okay? Why did you get fired?"

He groaned. "I got into a fight with the foreman. I hated his guts. He was an asshole, and apparently I don't handle authority well."

"*Hmm*, what a surprise," Simon quipped.

Danny shook his head, not sure what to say to him. "I still don't understand what you're even doing here."

"I know, and I get that," Simon replied. "But the thing is, I am still here, and we can figure this out."

"Why? Because that warm fuzzy side of you is looking for a way to get me another job?"

"I don't have to look," Simon stated. "I have multiple jobs going at any given time. I own a construction company. If you want to go back to work as a laborer, that's easy." He smiled, as the shocked expression crossed Danny's face. "I can get you a job, but you'll have to keep it on your own. If you walk away a second time, that's on you."

Danny frowned at him and asked, "What company?" Simon told him, and Danny shrugged. "I don't know anything about it."

"My focus is the rehab of old buildings," Simon shared, with a chuckle, "much to the disgust of a lot of people who think I should drop them and build new."

"Oh, maybe I do know your company then." Then he mentioned a building down on Granville.

Simon nodded. "Yeah, that's one of mine."

"Well, damn, I really love that building. I thought for sure it would get dropped, but you did a hell of a job on it."

"Yep, that's what I do," he said. "I care about old build-ings."

Danny just eyed him in shock. "You know that doesn't make any sense, not when everybody else is leveling these old buildings to make money."

"What they fail to understand is that you can make money without destroying something that's elegant and beautiful and has a history worth saving," Simon explained, studying Danny intently, "Sometimes you won't make as much money, and, to be completely transparent, every once in a while I screw up, or we find out there are bigger issues, and I end up wishing I hadn't gone in that direction." Again Simon laughed. "Generally it works out okay in the end. So, if you want a second chance, you've got one. All you have to do is reach out and take it."

CHAPTER 17

KATE STARED DOWN at the text on her phone, then got up from her desk in the bullpen and stepped out into the hallway, going onto the neighboring deck outside, for the smokers to use. Thankfully nobody was here, and she could breathe and speak freely. She phoned Simon and asked, "Did you just say you gave Danny a job?"

"Yeah, I did," he confirmed. "That accidental trip into the harbor? Let's just say, it wasn't an accident."

"Aw, shit. That never even occurred to me."

"I kept getting mental reminders to check on him. I knew something was off about him. I just wasn't sure what."

"Oh, that famous Simon intuition again, *huh*?" Humor filled her tone, but she was still castigating herself for not having picked up on it. "Damn, but seriously I was just so focused on Dr. Burnett and his presence there that it never even occurred to me that the kid was in trouble."

"Hopefully he's a little bit less in trouble now, and he can manage to show up for work tomorrow morning."

"Do you think he'll be okay?" she asked. "Now I'll really worry about him."

"Not half as much as I am," Simon admitted, with a sigh, "and for good reason too. I'm just leaving his apartment building now."

"How did he take your visit?"

"I think, in one sense, he was relieved that he could talk to somebody about it. Yet it's also not something he wanted anybody to know, and, because he did survive, he figured he had safely managed to keep it a deep, dark secret of his own, … until I barged in and brought it into the light." He shook his head. "As you know, bringing things into the light doesn't necessarily make anybody happy, until they are well and truly on the other side of it."

"Yeah, but we can't heal if we don't bring it up and admit how we got there in the first place," she murmured.

"Let's hope that Danny's a little bit closer to looking at that now."

"And, of course, you offered him a job," she added, with a knowing tone.

"Well, yeah, I did," he said happily. "It was a no-brainer, since he's a laborer, and God knows I need them."

"Keep an eye on him and maybe warn your foreman too."

"I'll give him a warning to some extent," Simon replied, "but I did promise Danny to keep that confidential."

"Except for me," she noted.

"Yeah, he knew I would tell you, and I don't really think he wants to see you and go over that whole scenario. So, if you don't have to, please don't broach the subject."

"No, I don't need to talk to him about that. Attempted suicide triggers all kinds of responses, medical and legal. Burnett says that he wanders these areas all the time, and, because he's out there more than anybody else, it only makes sense that he would come across these scenarios more than anybody else."

"He has a point. If you go for a walk once along the water versus ten or twenty times a day, you're bound to see that much more."

"But what is a normal amount?" she asked.

"I don't know. That's for you to figure out," Simon declared. "I need to go. I'm running behind now."

And he quickly ended the call, leaving her staring down at the phone in her hand, wondering exactly what she was supposed to do with that information. As she wandered back inside to her desk, Rodney looked at her.

"You don't usually walk out and leave us hanging."

"It was Simon," she replied, "wanting to talk to me in private."

"What's the problem?"

She hesitated and then explained, "The kid who was rescued earlier this morning—and keep this confidential, please—he didn't fall in accidentally."

Rodney's gaze widened. "He was trying to commit suicide?"

She nodded. "Simon has already talked to him at some length and pulled him up out of whatever funk he was in at the time. Now the kid is left to deal with the fact that, as soon as he did go in the water, he knew he'd made a huge mistake. He's grateful that he made it out, but he's still feeling fragile. He had some major setbacks in his life, plus was laid off recently, leading up to all this, so Simon gave him a job."

"He needed a job, ... so Simon gave him a job?" Rodney repeated, frowning.

"He's a laborer, and Simon would probably agree that he wanted to keep an eye on the kid. Not to mention the fact that Simon always seems to need more workers."

Rodney smiled. "Simon really is a good guy, isn't he?"

She winced. "*Thanks*, I don't need to hear any more accolades in that department. Especially not the *Hey, you should hang on to him* messages. It gets old, you know?"

"You know you should," he teased. "So, your case is pretty well not a case. Is that what I'm hearing?"

She frowned, then sighed loudly. "Let's just say that there isn't anything I can seriously move forward with at this time. I don't have anything to charge Dr. Burnett with. I don't have … Jeez, even with this latest guy, who survived, it seemed like the doc was trying to help, and yet his very act of helping was probably not helping."

"And yet the kid wouldn't come out and say that the doc was trying to drown him?"

"Nope, he absolutely would not come out and say that."

"Will he say that in another day or two, once he's a little more balanced, or will he push all this behind him and try to forget it all?"

"I don't have a clue."

"Either way, if there's no murder …"

She nodded. "If there's no murder, then effectively I'm just fishing, and I don't have a case."

"What about the rest of the stuff on your desk?"

"I got all the reports off, and I'm pretty well back on track with everything. So, if you want help with yours, I'm all over it."

"Good," Rodney said, "because, yeah, I'm kind of swamped."

"Good enough. What have you got?" she asked.

He looked up at her in exasperation. "Why don't you come with me? I need to talk to a bunch of people. They saw a hit-and-run, but they're not doing so well at identifying anything about it."

"Right. Five people, so five different descriptions of the

car? That sort of thing?"

"Exactly. You know, trucks, black or blue, nobody can tell you what kind. One says Ford. One says Chevy, and it's almost as if that's the only brand name they know, so that's the kind that this must be."

"Oh, *great*," she muttered. "Witness accounts are sometimes the worst."

"They absolutely are, and this seems worse than normal."

As she hopped into the car beside him, she quickly brought up her phone and started tapping away.

After a quick turn or two and a bump, she barked at him, "Jeez, can you lay off the potholes? I'm trying to get an email done here."

"Sorry." Rodney chuckled. "What's so important that you try to email on the road? You know the roads are crap out here."

"Just a couple questions for Dr. Smidge," she said. "He's looking into things for me."

They reached the house in question, a crowd already outside. Rodney started talking to the people there, a group arguing over what kind of vehicle it was. Kate stood on the outside of the crowd, watching as Rodney tried to get as many individual statements as he could about the vehicle, but she had a weird suspicious thought, as she observed the group's behavior.

Finally Rodney turned to her and raised an eyebrow. "Do you have anything to add?"

She smiled, as she eyed the group, still lingering around. "Yeah, I do." She paused, looking from one to another, then at Rodney. "I think you're all lying." A cacophony of overlapping outbursts ensured, until she barked out, "Shut up. You all concocted this deliberately to confuse the police, and I'm fed up with it." She looked around, making eye contact wherever she could. "So, you have to the count of five, before I start hauling every one of your sorry asses down to the station for questioning, and you will all need lawyers. So, the count starts now." Then she held up her watch and started, "One, two, three …"

The crowd erupted again, and one guy was like, "What the hell are you talking about? How dare you come in here and threaten civilians?"

But a young girl spoke up in a high-pitched tone that cut through the chaos. "She's right." She was beyond hysterical. "I didn't want to do it in the first place, but she's right." At that, everybody stopped and stared at her in horror. She shrugged. "We've got absolutely nothing to hide, and all we're doing is messing things up with the police, and there's no reason for it."

"What the hell?" the older woman yelled at her. "Since when are the police on our side?"

Rodney looked from one to the other and replied, "Seriously, this is your idea of helping? Some young woman gets hit by a vehicle, and all you people are doing is deliberately obstructing justice?" He was furious. He looked over at Kate and just shook his head.

Kate took over from here. "So, now that we have your signed statements, proof that you deliberately falsified statements to the police, who among you are willing to change your statements to the actual truth and avoid perjury and obstruction of justice charges?"

At that, the same young woman spoke up. "Me. … I have no clue what kind of vehicle it was." She spoke quickly, as if trying to get it out before the cops changed their minds.

"I can tell you that it was a deep-blue pickup, and I can tell you what kind of grille it had, but I don't know anything else."

"Why were you told to make up a false statement and confuse us?" Kate asked.

"Because they figured that we would get charged, since we're black."

Kate looked at her. "That's not happening," she murmured. "However, we are looking for the person who is responsible, and, as far as I'm concerned, if you're covering up for the driver or willfully trying to create confusion, whatever the reason, that makes you an accessory," she explained. "Now, that's a whole different ball game. So every one of you is about to get charged with obstructing justice *and* accessory to this hit-and-run."

At that, the place erupted in chaos again. When Rodney finally had everybody calmed down, not one of them was willing to stay with their original statement—except that older woman.

He grabbed the original statements, handing them off to Kate, and muttered, "You hang on to these, and we'll compare statements when we get back to the office."

Then he went through the process again, and this time it was a completely different story. When he got to a young man at the other end, with a sullen look on his face, Rodney asked him, "And what's your story?"

First came silence. The teen looked around at everybody, shrugged, and finally admitted, "I was driving."

"No, no, no, no," the older woman exclaimed, bustling over. "You can't say that."

"If he did it, then, yes, he should say it," Rodney snapped, glaring at her. "It will be much better and easier on him if he admits whatever the hell happened."

Now completely fed up with the entire lot of them, Kate once again stepped in. "I'm taking him down to the station," she told Rodney. "I suggest you pack up every one of these people. They can come down and give their formal statements at the station, especially now that we know for sure they were withholding evidence. They knew perfectly well he was the driver the whole time."

"I didn't," shrieked the young woman who had started the whole honest approach. "I did not know he was involved at all." She turned to him and asked, "How the hell could you even do that?"

"It was an accident," he roared. "I didn't know she was there."

"But then you took off. I mean, … what if that had been me who you hit? What if that had been Sandy?" And she pointed to the other young woman in the front yard.

He shrugged. "I just panicked. I didn't know what to do, and … I just took off."

"So, everyone here then lied to hide your involvement?" Kate asked, staring at them.

Several of them looked ashamed, but not the older woman.

"I presume you're his mother."

She nodded and glared at Kate. "My statement stands."

"That's fine. You can get a jail cell right alongside your son then," she snapped.

When the backup cops and several transport wagons arrived, the group cried out again.

Kate yelled, "Shut the hell up. Do you think this is just a joke? An innocent young woman is on life support, and you guys think you can just sit here and have a little fun with your false statements and waste our time. You think you can just mock the police, mock your own involvement in all this? No," she declared. "That's not how it works. Every one of you is going downtown, and your statements will be formally reviewed, and then we'll look at the charges individually."

"Even me?" asked the young woman, who had been the first to recant her statement. She stared at Kate.

Kate shook her head. "No, not likely. But don't forget that you did make that original statement and that wasn't the truth. Once you go on record as a liar, it's not that easy for anyone to start believing you."

She nodded. "You're right, and, if I would have had any idea that my cousin was the one who ran her down," she explained, "I would have told you right off the bat." She turned and glared at him. "I suppose you were drunk again too. Were you?"

He shook his head. "I'd only had one beer. One, for God's sake. I wasn't drinking."

Kate already knew it was too late to use a breathalyzer. Regardless she packed up everybody in various vehicles. As Rodney stood here and stared from the sidewalk, watching all the vehicles pull away, he shook his head. "What the hell just happened?"

"The entire family conspired to lie in an attempt to confuse the police and to shield the driver," Kate replied. "And in among them are a couple more innocent victims because they didn't even realize who had done it. You can bet the driver's mother is behind everybody being told to lie. So, the mother needs to have the book thrown at her.

"Plus, the driver's definitely getting charged with hit-and-run. We may not get drunk driving, since we can't prove it now, but what a mess. The lawyers will have to sort all that out. It will be up in the air, while the victim is still on life support. It sure would have gone a lot better for him if they would have given him some tough love and had him turn himself in, instead of creating this fiasco. I don't know how it'll all come out now. Jeez, what a mess."

Kate shook her head and added, "The prosecutor will see what we can make stick on that, but his mother needs to be charged with obstruction of the case for sure." She looked over at Rodey, punched him on the shoulder, and said, "You're welcome, by the way."

He glared at her. "That was a mess. You about caused a riot, you know."

"Yeah, but it wasn't my mess," she defended herself. "You could tell they were lying. Every single one of them was lying."

He shook his head. "I had my suspicions, but I didn't know which ones."

"All of them," Kate stated, "every frickin' one of them."

"Since you have such an ear for the truth, you're coming down to the station to help me interview every one of them."

She rolled her eyes at that. "*Great*, thanks for that."

As they drove back down to the station and pulled into the parking lot, her phone rang. She answered it. "Dr. Smidge, what can I do for you?"

"You need to come down to my morgue," he snapped.

She looked over at Rodney, who rolled his eyes, and she replied, "I'll be right there." She hopped out, then walked over to her car.

"What the hell?" Rodney complained. "You spark this shit storm, then what did you do? Text Smidge so he'd call just in time to get you out of going in there?" Rodney glared at her, disgruntled.

She laughed. "Oh, come on. Lots of people in there can help take statements," she murmured.

"You're the only one who ever gets to talk to Smidge anyway."

"Not by choice," she pointed out, "but, hey, I'm not turning down the gift. Our coroner's got good timing. What can I say?"

"Yeah, lucky you," Rodney muttered, hanging his head. "Jeez, I don't want to go in there and deal with that pack of liars on my own."

"Come on, Rodney. You can do this. Just split them up and start with that young one, the girl who broke it open in the first place," Kate suggested. "She's not having it, so odds are, you'll get more truth out of her, more so than the rest of them. Then you can use that to call out the others. I would leave that momma bear to stew for a while," she advised.

He glared at her, rolling his eyes. "You do realize that I've been doing this for a while now. A lot more years than you, as a matter of fact."

"I know," she agreed, with a beaming smile. "Isn't it nice to know the young learn so quickly these days?" And with that, she headed to her car, leaving him laughing and shaking his head in her wake.

It wasn't long before she walked into the morgue and joined a pissed-off Dr. Smidge. "Okay, so what's wrong?" she asked, as this demeanor was relatively normal for him. Kate had her own frustration and temper issues, so she had no problem with his.

"One of the drowning victims you asked me to look into? I found the same oil on their fingers, as the sample from the cane. It's a normal wood treatment to stop wood from drying out and to protect it from soaking up water, when wet."

Kate swallowed. Then she asked, "And the other three?"

He nodded. "Autopsies weren't performed on all the ones you've mentioned but on these three? Yes."

Damn. She hated it when she was right.

But what the hell was she right about?

She considered that, as she instinctively drove to Simon's apartment, where they ordered in dinner, discussed their day, enjoyed a glass of wine on the couch as dusk descended, then fell into bed together.

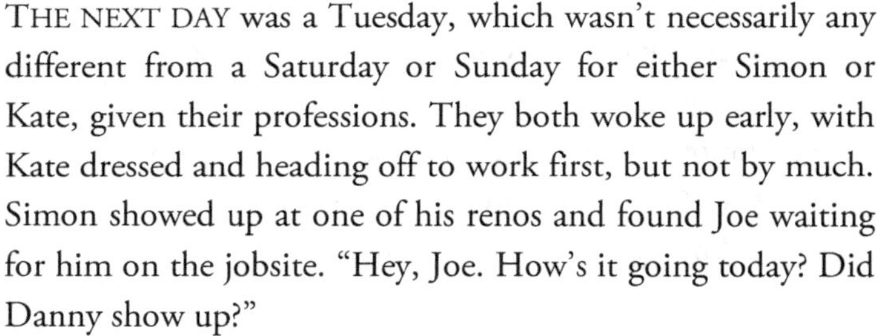

THE NEXT DAY was a Tuesday, which wasn't necessarily any different from a Saturday or Sunday for either Simon or Kate, given their professions. They both woke up early, with Kate dressed and heading off to work first, but not by much. Simon showed up at one of his renos and found Joe waiting for him on the jobsite. "Hey, Joe. How's it going today? Did Danny show up?"

Joe nodded. "He did. I've got him working on the additional panels, and that task is happening out in the back."

"Good. Don't give him anything too dangerous or potentially psychologically damaging. He told me that he has trouble with authority at times, so let's not set him up to fail here, not while he's getting his feet on the ground."

"I get it." Joe nodded. "He's reporting to me for now. He looks a little lost."

"Yeah, that's a good word for it."

"As long as he's not a danger to others," Joe stated, eyeing Simon intently.

"I don't see that at all. I think he's just somebody who needs a friend."

"I don't know about that," Joe quipped. "We need workers way more than friends, and good ones at that."

"Let's give him some room and a fair chance to show off what he can do. If it works out, it works out. If it doesn't, he'll go down the road like everybody else."

Joe laughed. "Come on. You rarely fire anybody, unless they really screw up."

"Maybe, but sometimes I wonder if we should do more of it."

Joe shook his head. "As long as they're all working, we're golden. You have a knack for matching up a guy who's having trouble with a situation he can succeed in, and I think it's rubbing off on me. It's when they stop working that we have to reevaluate."

"That should never happen on a job like this."

"Most of the time it doesn't, but you know, with that bloody pandemic dropping people in their tracks," Joe noted, "it changed the workforce pretty drastically. They are expecting a lot more benefits these days and a lot more extras in general."

Simon nodded. "I get the whole *extras in life* thing, providing there is some way to provide it without stripping ourselves of the ability to be solvent. We still have to pay our suppliers and the insurance and taxes on these properties," he murmured.

"And that's your problem, not mine." Joe chuckled. "Anyway, I've got quite a list of things to go over with you. So let's get started, if you're ready."

When Joe reached the end of the review of all the things to deal with on his list, Simon's head was reeling. What should have been an easy day didn't sound like *easy* would be a part of it. He stopped at the coffee shop to pick up a to-go cup and, sure enough, saw Dr. Burnett standing there. He didn't want to say anything to him, since this man most likely didn't remember him at all.

But he did seem to recognize Simon because he walked right over straightaway. "You're the one who travels around with Kate all the time."

Simon nodded. "If you mean Detective Kate Morgan, then I would say that's true. She's my partner."

Dr. Burnett nodded. "She came to my office and returned my cane."

"I'm glad you got it back," Simon replied, with a polite smile. "I was down at the harbor with her when she came back with it."

The doctor didn't say anything at first, just staring at him intently.

"Can I help you with something else?" Simon asked, trying to get back to his work.

"Is she trustworthy?" the doc asked.

Simon nodded. "Absolutely. She is one of the most trustworthy people I've ever met. Why?"

The doctor seemed to ponder that. Then he gave him a nervous smile. "I was just thinking of something." And, with that, he quickly turned and walked away.

Simon called after him, "If you need to talk …"

The doc just lifted a hand and kept on going, but his pace picked up, as if he wanted to get as far away from Simon as quickly as he could. It was such an odd encounter that Simon didn't really know what to do or say. He wanted to send Kate a text but also knew he shouldn't interrupt her day for such a strange encounter, with no facts to share. So Simon continued with his morning work, had his lunch, and, when he stood up again, his thoughts once again went back to the doctor.

Something was very unsettling about the man, something about that weird look in his eye and the odd words he kept spouting. Yet Simon didn't have anything against him. That was the thing. No reason to have anything against this man, so the question Simon really needed to answer was why the hell did this doctor bug him? And again, there was no rhyme or reason for his wariness where the older man was concerned. It was just that something about him seemed off.

As Simon headed to his afternoon, he sent Kate a text, asking how her day was going.

She phoned him. "Hey." There was a bit of excitement in her voice and a note of something going on.

"Sounds as if you're getting somewhere."

"I am. I absolutely am. At least on some cases."

"Good. Has it got to do with Dr. Burnett?"

"Why do you ask that?"

"Because he approached me today, asking if I was the same man he assumed I was, who routinely accompanied you."

"Good God, that's a surprise."

"You're right. I wasn't expecting anybody to recognize me, especially him. He's always off in his own little world. When he's not silently involved in whatever, he's always dictating into his Bluetooth."

"*Hmm,* interesting. I guess it's kind of a problem with both of our careers."

"Maybe. By the way, Danny did show up for work today."

"Really?" she asked in delight.

"Yes, and, so far, so good. He's working out well."

"That's wonderful news," she said warmly. "Thank you

for that."

Just as she went to ring off, he added quickly, "Hang on a minute."

"What?" she asked, with a groan. "I need to get going. What's up?"

"The doctor asked if you were trustworthy."

"What? … Why the hell would he ask you that?"

"Believe me. I have no idea. I just thought that maybe you should know."

"Well, okay. Thanks for telling me, but it means nothing to me, and I don't have a clue why my ethics would matter to him."

"I don't know, but definitely something is off about this man."

"I know," she retorted. "I'll probably find out something eventually. Anyway, I do have to get going." And, with that, she disconnected, leaving him wondering what was going on in her world and potentially in his as well.

He headed to his next job, and, with every step he took, he felt this weird compulsion to turn and look behind him. Finally he detoured into an alleyway and just waited, wondering what he was feeling. When nobody came and no vision arrived, he stepped back out again, looked around, expecting to see the doctor, given the adverse reaction Simon usually had to him. Yet Dr. Burnett was not around. Simon shook his head. He was pretty sharp, but right now he felt downright foolish. But that sense of *someone* being around continued for most of the afternoon. If not a person following him, maybe it was someone trying to connect with him. In his mind.

Once he reached the jobsite, he got busy enough that this prior episode was just a minor irritant.

Until his feet directed him back into the alleyway again. Swearing and wondering just what the hell was going on, he looked around, but nothing was here to see, and nothing in any way, shape, or form alerted him to a problem.

Except for the single problem at hand; his feet, they just wouldn't move.

He closed his eyes, straightened up, and pretended to stand here, looking normal, or at least less odd than a lot of people might seem, given this scenario. Eyes closed, he reached out with his mind. *What the hell is this?*

Answers. There are answers.

When he opened his eyes again, he looked around, and his feet were moving, taking him to a lone bench. He sat down and wondered just what the hell somebody was trying to tell him. *Okay, so I'm here. What on earth do you have to say?*

The same voice reached back to him. *You just need to listen.*

Simon closed his eyes and tried hard to blank out everything else from around him. *I'm listening.*

Immediately came screams and cries of terror. Shivers raced up and down Simon's back, and his gaze flew open. Instinctively he looked around to see who and what was going on because, based on the sounds, it seemed like somebody was dying, screaming out of fear and panic. However, no matter how real that vision felt, the area around him was empty, completely empty, except for Simon sitting on a bench.

He waited a few more minutes, hoping that something more was coming. He closed his eyes several more times, trying to hear the mental voice again, but there was absolutely ly nothing. He pulled out a notepad and quickly jotted down the little bit he'd heard, the little bit he'd picked up on, and then, as he went to stand, his butt slammed right back down onto the bench. His breath came out with a hard *whoosh*.

"Fine," he muttered because he knew all too well he had no choice in this matter. *I'm right here, if you have something else you need to say.*

Simon felt that same sense of having somebody there, but nobody was talking. There was almost an impatience to this presence, as if Simon were the one being dense. It was enough to piss off a person, to be honest. Simon glared around, then heard sobs and tears in his mind, but thankfully no longer screaming. *Okay, so somebody died. That much I can gather from all the screams. I am so sorry, but what do you expect me to do?* He got no answer from this person, this energy, whatever it was.

As he started to walk away, the voice whispered, *Answers, I need answers.*

Yeah. Somebody died. But where and how long ago? Who are you, and are you related to the person who died?

I want answers! The voice, now a scream, was too loud and rang through his ears with force. *Answers, then peace!* The voice got louder and louder, but there was no stopping it.

Simon sat back down again, closed his eyes, and willed it to stop.

As soon as it did, that same voice suggested, *You need to help me.*

And if I can't?

Get answers. You get answers. I get peace.

CHAPTER 18

KATE STARED DOWN at her phone. "So, was this a victim?" she asked. "I thought you didn't really connect to dead people. At least not normally."

There was silence on the other end, and then she heard Simon's voice, harsher than normal. "I never really know and still don't know exactly what I do," he snapped.

"Look. I'm not trying to categorize you," she said. "Any information is good information. You know that."

He snorted. "What you really mean to say is that you only want me to give you information that's helpful, and the rest of this shit I can keep to myself."

She winced at that, then stared around in the parking lot, where luckily she stood alone. "That's not fair. I didn't say that nor would I ever. Obviously some of this I'm uncomfortable with, but I've come a long way in trying to understand it … and you."

After a few more moments of silence, Simon groaned. "You have," he admitted, taking his irritability down a notch. "I'm just being a shit."

"You are," she agreed. "So, take that attitude to somebody else and don't cloud up my day with it," she muttered.

"Look. I'm sorry," he said in a much calmer voice. "I didn't know what to even think of this, and instinctively I called you first to help me figure it out."

She rushed to say, "It's a good thing you did. I don't want you sorting through this stuff on your own without any help. I just don't know what I can do besides listen."

"Listening without judging would be a good start," he suggested, a note of humor creeping into his voice again.

Her shoulders relaxed at that. "You're right. I need a series of pat answers that I can give you that make sense because God knows none of this makes sense to me."

"It doesn't make sense to me either," Simon countered, his voice getting heavy again.

"And that's the problem. We're both awash in a sea of confusion, as we try to sort out whether this is helpful or you've just got crazy on a string."

"*Crazy on a string?*" he repeated in a neutral tone.

She winced. "Okay, so that may not be the best description," she conceded.

"No, it may not be the best, but you do have a way to turn a phrase," he noted. "The trouble is, not everybody will understand."

She groaned. "Believe me. I know. I wasn't trying to piss you off either," she muttered.

"Look," he replied, with a heavy tone. "Let's just shelve this until dinnertime."

"We can do that," she noted in relief.

"You don't have to sound quite so happy about it," he muttered.

She burst out laughing. "It will give me a chance to adjust somewhat and to find some questions that may help push us a little further toward getting answers."

"Yeah, that would be good," he replied, "because I don't have any answers, and I sure as hell don't know what questions to ask to get them."

"I guess that's another thing, isn't it? You don't really have anybody you can converse with on all things psychic. You don't have anybody who can answer when you ask, *Hey, I got a problem with a ghost. Is there like a 9-1-1 for the ghost helpline?*"

His tone became almost comical, as he responded in a questioning voice. "A 9-1-1 helpline for a ghost?" he repeated, "Honey, do you hear yourself?"

She snapped back, "Do you hear yourself?"

He groaned. "Okay, this is how we started this conversation. Let's go back to shelving it until tonight. You go off and do your thing, and so will I. Have a great day." And, with that, he was gone.

She stared down at the phone and turned to look around the parking lot. Rodney was a few feet away, respectfully giving her some space.

He looked over at her and asked, "Trouble in paradise?"

She shook her head. "Trouble in ghost world. I may have overstepped by suggesting it would be helpful if he had access to an emergency line, you know, like a 9-1-1 for ghost problems."

He stared at her in shock, then burst out laughing. "Good God, if there was a helpline for that, it would be somebody like Simon on the other end, answering the questions."

"That was exactly my point," she stated, looking at Rodney with a bright smile. "When somebody like Simon has a problem, who does he go to, who does he call to say, *Hey, I can't understand these messages. Is there somebody out there who can help him?*"

"Definitely other people out there do this psychic work," Rodney noted, "and certainly lots who work with cops."

"Right. But, if he doesn't belong to that group, who does he call? There should be some sort of association or something."

"Maybe they're unionized," Rodney joked.

"I don't know what is out there. I made the mistake of asking if he could talk to someone about this, and unfortunately he apparently thought that was who he'd called."

It took Rodney a moment to get it, and then he winced. "Oh, ouch."

"Yeah, Relationship 101, and I just failed again," she muttered, as she motioned at the office. "Are we going in or out?"

"I'm leaving," he said. "You, on the other hand, still have a bunch of messages piled up on your desk."

She frowned at that. "Why?"

"Because you had your desk all cleared off, when you came with me earlier, and you've been out of the office ever since. And you know how nature abhors a vacuum," he added cheerfully.

She groaned. "In that case I'm apparently heading inside to see if there is anything interesting."

He escaped into his car, and she headed up and walked in. She sat down at her desk, wincing at the stack of messages in front of her. Pushing those aside, not giving herself a chance to question it, she brought up a search engine and typed in *psychics union*. Of course that wasn't clear enough, and she got a million hits, everything from psychics finding various messages at Union Square to psychics marrying in a blessed union.

Groaning, she typed in *Do psychics have a work union* and got a new batch of weird things again. Then looking up from her latest search, she found Colby, her sergeant, standing in front of her.

"You have a good day?" he asked.

"Oh, yeah, *sure*." She glared at him.

"Why not?" he asked, staring at her.

She hesitated, then added, "You got a minute?"

"Yeah, I sure do."

They headed to his office, and she threw herself down into the visitor's seat.

"Leave out the part about Rodney's case," Colby began. "I already heard all about how you helped with that, and I realized it was probably my fault because I told you to park yours."

She snorted. "Any word on the hit-and-run victim? That freaking mother was the whole cause of that mess of people lying in their initial statements. I wish these women would realize that going to these extremes makes it worse for their kids instead of better. But forget that. I wanted to mention more about the drownings." Then she went into some of the details she hadn't mentioned before, including Dr. Smidge's findings.

He stared at her. "You do realize that your criticism and suspicion of the good doctor could also be applied to you."

"Hardly," she cried out. "I saw *one* in progress. That's all."

"But what happens when you see another one," he pointed out smoothly. "That makes it a coincidence, doesn't it?"

She closed her eyes, counted to ten, and when she opened them, he was grinning at her. She narrowed her gaze.

Colby laughed. "You do have to keep an open mind with the doc."

"Sure, but it's not all that easy." She wondered whether

she should tell him about Simon's new revelation, then decided against it.

As soon as she got back to her desk, she started in on the stack of messages. There was one from Danny, the kid now working for Simon. She quickly returned the call.

He did answer the phone, but he couldn't talk. "I'm at work. I don't want to lose my job."

"Good, I understand you're working for Simon."

"Yeah, he seems like he's an all-right guy."

"He is an all-right guy, and he helps a lot of people," she noted. "Yet you had a reason for calling me, and I'm guessing it wasn't about Simon."

"I do, and I'm not … Can I talk to you after work?"

"Yes." She made an appointment to meet him at a coffee shop near one of the jobs he was working on. "Do you want me alone, or is it okay if Simon comes?"

"It's okay if he comes. He seems as much a part of this as you."

"I don't know about that," she said, with a chuckle. "I'm definitely the legal side of it."

"I get that," Danny said. "But, if he's around, it's … not an issue for me." And, with that, he rang off.

She made a note, then sent Simon a quick text, explaining about the appointment.

He called her to add, "He's off work at three, unless they put him on overtime to finish something."

"If I have to wait a little longer, that's fine," she murmured. "Though he did seem a little upset."

"Damn," Simon muttered, with a sigh. "I hope it's not affecting his work."

She sighed. "I doubt it, but you can always let Joe know that some shit is going on with him."

"Joe does know, and he's keeping an eye on Danny for me."

"Let's not have a meeting with me that costs him his job," she stated. "I wouldn't want to be the cause of that."

"Of course not. I'll meet you there." And Simon disconnected.

———

SIMON HEADED TO the next project. He could be a good couple hours at this one, but Danny was working here, and Simon would have a chance to check in with Joe about him.

As he approached, Joe looked up and smiled. "Hey, guess what? We're more or less having a decent day." Then he knocked on a stack of two-by-fours, sitting to the side.

The two of them sat down and caught up on business, as always. Simon quickly went through the work in progress, and then, in an undertone, looking around to see where his new hire might be, Simon asked, "How's Danny working out?"

"Just fine so far." Joe nodded. "He's here on time. He's doing his job, and, so far, he seems on the up-and-up, and I can't fault him for a thing."

"Good," Simon replied. "He has a meeting with Kate today at three. So, if he's not quite done, let him off anyway, if you can."

Joe nodded. "Sure. Problems?"

"Not that I know of. It's related to that scenario over the weekend, so we'll have to see."

"Ah." Joe shrugged. "Yeah, that's something bound to haunt the kid for a while."

"It'll haunt a lot of us," Simon stated, with a flat look in the direction of the workers. "I can only help somebody who wants help."

"But you can't take on the responsibility for those who don't," Joe pointed out.

"No, and I have more than enough on my plate without that," he noted, with a smile in his direction.

"Yeah, you sure do. Any new buildings happening?" Joe asked cautiously. "We're about 60 percent through with this one."

"I haven't bought any others, though I do have my eye on a couple. I was thinking I might take a look this afternoon," he shared. "I wanted to confirm we were well on target with all our supply issues, before I put up the money on something else."

"Not a bad idea, after all the pandemic-related troubles," Joe agreed, with a nod. "This one needed a close eye for sure. The other one over on Davie Street is breaking ground and holding. I was there this morning, and I'll head back over there in a little bit."

"Are you still okay to take on both of them?" Simon eyed his foreman, who'd worked for him for such a very long time. "Otherwise I can put someone else on that job."

"No, I think we'll be okay," he replied, with a hard laugh. "But you pay me well, and my four boys have plans for that money that I don't really want to give up on, not yet anyway."

"No, maybe not," Simon noted, with a laugh, "but we must keep both jobs on track. Plus, I don't want to burn you out."

"I know, and I appreciate that. These two rehabs aren't that far apart, which will save me some time going back and forth," he shared. "Don't worry. If we run into trouble, I'll be the first to let you know."

Simon nodded and headed up to look at the work that had been done over the last couple days. He saw Danny up ahead, who frowned at him, then put his head down and kept working. Simon walked past Danny and said in a causal tone, "You're doing fine. Just relax."

Danny's shoulders dropped in relief, and Simon realized just how hard it was for the kid to pick up and to carry on. Even though that was exactly what he wanted to do and was the best thing for him, it wasn't all that easy to make it happen. Having somebody like Simon around, who knew what had happened, wouldn't make it any easier on Danny, but somebody needed to keep an eye out on the young man.

"I also heard about the meeting this afternoon, so I'll see you there."

Danny just nodded and kept on working.

Simon checked up on a couple guys nearby as well. Most of the time he had a decent relationship with his staff, until all kinds of issues with the hired help had turned out on one project, all that Simon hadn't known about. So now he wasn't prepared to get too far removed from the finer details of his operations, just to make sure he didn't end up with staffing trouble like that again.

He had a quick talk with some more of the guys for a couple minutes to see if there were any problems or concerns, checking in with some subcontractors and tradesmen too, and, with everything on track for the moment, and everybody appearing to be happy, Simon moved on.

So far, every situation had required a certain amount of communication and some adjustments, but, by investing the time to hear the details from people on the ground, Simon gained the understanding that he needed to resolve the issues. He made some calls and worked out a few supply and delivery details, making sure that a scheduling problem was cleared up.

Then, with a much better grasp on the details Joe had asked him to help resolve, Simon turned in the direction of the café. He had to admit that heading there was partly because of the doctor and partly because Simon was getting damn hungry again.

He noted an appetite increase every time he had one of these weird connections with these spirits, and he didn't know what the hell that was about and who the spirits were, especially this most recent one. He could almost hear his grandmother's voice in the background, telling him that he must pay attention. Of course he had been just a child back then. Simon's attention span had been incredibly limited at the age of six, making it almost impossible to remember anything he might have picked up psychically. However, this was also his current problem, as he tried to navigate through this situation.

As he walked in, he smiled at the owner, quickly ordered some coffee and a muffin, and took up residence at a small table outside the restaurant, where he could sit and watch. Sure enough, it wasn't very long before the doctor came bumbling through, in worse condition than he had been in before, to such an extent that Simon was quite surprised. The doctor looked more unkempt, more stressed out, plus muttering to himself—not the Bluetooth this time. Dr. Burnett made his way through the line, placed his order, and then stepped off to the side. Something was seriously off about him today, more so than any of the other days.

Either something had severely upset his life or was in the process of doing so. Simon didn't know what was going on, but the man looked like he had completely lost whatever anchor he had previously had.

Dr. Burnett, as if sensing Simon's gaze, looked up and stared directly at him, then frowned and walked over. "Do I know you? It's Simon, right?"

Simon shrugged. "Yes, that's correct. We've spoken a couple times, but briefly."

The doctor nodded absentmindedly.

"Are you all right?" Simon asked. "Do you need something? You look like you've just lost your best friend."

"A brother," he muttered. "And not so much lost but on the verge of losing." He shook his head. "A mainstay I always thought would be there and now, all of a sudden, maybe not."

Simon just nodded, not sure what he was supposed to say, then added his condolences to the conversation. The doctor's order was called just then. He walked over, grabbed his items, then stepped out of the café and headed back toward his office, still looking shell-shocked, but maybe a tiny bit more alert. Simon picked up his phone and called Kate.

She sounded distracted when she answered, "What's up?"

"I just saw your doctor. He looks like his world's fallen apart. I did ask him if he was okay and if he needed anything. He mentioned something about being on the verge of losing his brother. I didn't realize he even had a brother, but anyway he seemed pretty rattled. Then he grabbed his order and walked out."

"A brother," she repeated. "What the hell? I don't have any information on a brother."

"Which is kind of what I was wondering," Simon noted. "It's not exactly something you can hide, is it?"

"No," she replied, "which is another reason for the work we do. There was no mention or record on my reports of a brother, but the whole family history thing has been giving Reese fits because nothing adds up." She took a moment and added, "Thanks. I'll get back to you on that." She ended the call with a *click*.

Simon got up, still quite perturbed at the doctor's appearance, and, acting on an impulse, half ran to catch up with the good doctor. He watched as the older man unsteadily headed back to his office. Simon frowned as he watched him head up the elevator. Simon followed slowly behind. He didn't go in at first and couldn't hear any of the conversation with the front desk, but Simon thought he'd picked up on the shocked tone in the receptionist's voice. By this time, Simon entered the building and headed to the elevator. He got out on the third floor and then stepped inside Dr. Burnett's empty waiting room, figuring that the doctor should have had enough time to get to his private office.

The receptionist looked up at him and frowned.

He nodded. "I was just speaking with Dr. Burnett, as we were both at the coffee shop, but he looked like he was having a tough time. I just wanted to confirm that he made it back okay."

Her face softened, and she nodded. "He does look upset. I left him some messages that may or may not help. I don't know." She sighed. "All we can do is hope that the news isn't bad and that he will come through it just fine."

"What does Dr. Burnett's schedule look like today?" Simon asked, waving around at the empty waiting room.

"He asked me to clear most of it for the day, so if you're hoping to get in to see him—"

Simon smiled and shook his head. "No, that's okay. I just see him at the coffee shop all the time and was worried." And, with that, he gave her a small wave, and, coffee in his hand, he stepped back out into the main hallway and walked toward the stairwell, stopping to look out a third-floor window.

There was nothing really that Simon could do, but it did feel as if he should do *something*, and he hated that. He absolutely hated that feeling of knowing he was supposed to do something, but not knowing what it was. It always panicked him. Even as he stood here, the doctor came out into the hallway, not completely distraught but obviously still upset.

Simon wondered if he should say anything, but the doctor quickly took the elevator and headed downstairs. That was enough for Simon. He dashed down the stairs, and, when the elevator didn't open on the main floor, he swore and ran down another flight of stairs to the parking level. There, he watched the doctor get into a vehicle, and, with very little care or concern about looking out for other traffic, he exited the parking lot and took off.

Simon phoned Kate back. "Look. I know it really has nothing to do with you, but the doctor just took off in his car, as if he had horrifically bad news, and he's quite distraught."

"What would you like me to do?" she asked, her voice gentle. "We have no reason to even follow him, much less question him."

"Yeah, that's a good point." Then he groaned. "I feel like it probably has to do with the doctor's brother."

"And I can't even find a brother so far. I would like to see Danny a hell of a lot earlier than three o'clock, hoping he has more info on the good doctor."

"I can go and check with him," Simon offered, "but Danny was a little bit hesitant to even talk to me in front of the other guys."

"Of course," she said. "He wouldn't want anyone to know that he even knows you personally. I can understand that. In the meantime, this doctor's world is coming apart, and we don't really know why."

"If you can find out if he really has a brother, that would help because this definitely had a personal feel to it."

"We're on it," she said, and, for the second time in one hour, she ended the call.

CHAPTER 19

KATE GOT UP, walked over to Reese's office, a space allocated to the analysts on the job. She smiled at her and began, "So, this Dr. Burnett …"

Reese nodded. "What about him?"

"We didn't come up with any other siblings, correct?"

"Just the sister who died when they were teenagers."

"I have it from a good authority," she shared, almost wincing, "that something may have happened involving a personal family member, and the doctor mentioned a brother in this conversation."

The analyst started clicking the keys on her keyboard. "As far as I'm aware, there wasn't any brother."

"What about …" Kate added. "What if we have somebody in a care home or somebody who potentially had a different name or something going on?"

"And yet, why would that be?" Reese muttered, as she clicked away.

"I can't answer the why part," she replied. "All I can do is question whether there is that possibility."

"Sure there's a possibility, but I'm not sure why it would be a name change for a brother. Sure, with women, some change their names when married and such."

"Right." Kate sighed. "Anyway, maybe take a closer look and see if you can come up with a brother, a birth certificate, a death certificate, something."

The analyst nodded. "Okay."

Kate walked back to her desk, and almost immediately her phone rang. It was Reese.

"I found a birth certificate, and you're not going to believe it."

"What?"

"There's definitely a brother, and he drowned."

"Drowned? So, you have a death certificate?"

"No, that's where the interesting part comes in, given the case that you're looking at. He was resuscitated, only he was never quite right afterward, so he's under full care."

"Ah, so there was brain damage?"

"Yes. I am pulling his medical records right now."

"Give me a location," Kate said, as she picked up her keys and grabbed her wallet. "Also, why did that not show up in the initial search?"

"There was a name change. I'm still working on that," Reese noted, confusion in her tone. "Oh, here it is. He's at the Haven Center, a full-time skilled nursing care facility. Looks high-end." She shared the address. "Do you want me to phone over there?"

"Nope, I'm heading over there myself," Kate replied. "I want to see this brother and find out what I can."

"Okay," Reese said, "but you know that you may not get in there without a warrant. Looks like it might be a private facility. Plus, if he's badly disabled, you may need his guardian's permission to see him. Then you have all the HIPAA laws to navigate too."

"That's fine," Kate noted. "Just gather as much information as you can."

"I'm on it."

Kate walked out to her car, hopped in, and, with a quick text off to Rodney and Simon, headed over to the nursing home. Pulling into the parking lot, something about the place surprised her, but she couldn't put her finger on it. Except … it seemed awfully quiet.

As she walked into the home, she immediately saw that *home* was a misnomer and that *facility* was far more accurate. She turned to the receptionist, who had a plastic smile on her face. "I'm here to see Roger Burnett," she murmured.

Quickly checking a file, she looked back at Kate with a shrug. "I'm so sorry. We don't have anyone here by that name."

Kate nodded. "I believe he may be here under the name of Roger Burnside."

"Oh, Roger," she said, with a knowing smile. "Unfortunately my directive here says family visitors only for him, so unless you are fam—"

Already weary of the fake airhead receptionist routine, Kate pulled out her badge.

The woman's face went blank. "Excuse me. I'll have to get the director." And, with that, she dashed off.

Kate wasn't exactly sure why a director was needed, but he soon came bustling out, in his most officious form. This was something that Kate recognized as a frustrating and time-consuming yet unavoidable step when dealing with organizations. She sighed, as she nodded at him and held up her badge for his inspection.

"What's this all about, Officer?"

"It's Detective Morgan, and that would be none of your business," she replied equally politely. "I would like to see Roger Burnside, please."

He frowned. "We do have very strict policies, and only

the family is allowed to see that patient at this time."

"I understand policies," she noted, "and that's fine. I can definitely get a search warrant and bring a team down to go through *all* things and to ensure you're following *all* your policies as carefully as you're following the one on visitation. I am certain that the public and the families of your patients will be happy with the transparency that will bring."

He frowned and retorted, "That sounds like a threat."

"I came to find out about *one* person, who you have been looking after," she explained, "and I'm going to do that, one way or another. It's your choice if we do it the easy way or the hard way." When he hesitated, she added, "I'm sure you could check with his brother easily enough."

"Oh, do you know Dr. Burnett?"

"Absolutely I know Dr. Burnett." She smiled. "I've spoken to him on several occasions. I understand he was on his way over here, so he's likely already on the premises."

"Yes, his brother has, *uh*, … taken a turn, and that's another reason why I don't really … why I haven't got clearance to let you in to see him. He's not in very good condition just now, so it's really just not a good time."

"What happened?"

He shrugged and then hesitated.

In that moment, she saw his countenance change, as if he were playing a role.

"It's a case of time. He's not … Roger was severely injured after a near-drowning incident some years ago, and, as it is, we never really expected him to live this long. It's really quite amazing."

"Is he nonverbal?" Kate asked.

The doctor frowned at the phrase and stated, "We don't like to classify our patients in that way." He took a moment, then continued. "However, to answer your question, most people would consider him nonverbal. He does have the ability to make sounds, and he does at times communicate with some people very well to a degree. Most people can't understand him, and, in his current condition, any additional disturbance would be ill-advised. Routine is most important with our patients."

"Of course." She nodded. "So, how old was he when it happened?"

"I would have to pull his file."

"Then do so, please," she stated, giving him a flat look.

"Let's go into my office." And, with that, he led her out of the main reception area. She looked around as she walked to his office, trying to see just how busy the place really was. It seemed oddly quiet and somewhat eerie.

Once in the director's office, she sat down before his desk and stated, "I get the impression that this is a very discreet location, perhaps for people who may prefer that information on their family members were not available to the public."

He stared at her. "Discretion is always among our best practices," he replied, with a nod. "And stringent patient privacy laws, of course. The motivation of our family members is never something we pass judgment on, and every situation is unique. But legal or medical mandates or family preferences aside, I can assure you that excellence in patient care is paramount, 100 percent of the time."

"And are most of the people here, the patients, are they all in a similar … situation?" she asked, with a wave of her hand, stumbling over the proper terminology.

"We are a full-care facility," he replied cautiously. "We have people who are comatose and have been for many,

many years, who are not likely to ever come out of that state. We have people who are, as you say, nonverbal and in many ways are not asleep but are in more of a vegetative state," he described, "for lack of a better word. Then we have people who, like Roger, have episodes of improvement yet mostly stay in a vegetative state only to come out once in a while to give us all hope, only to once again decline."

"Right," Kate said, grasping Roger's situation. "Got it. So, your entire facility is geared toward this type of patient?"

He nodded. "Yes, we take on those special long-term cases, including those who are on life support."

"So, cases where people are prepared to pay for accommodations like this."

"We do fulfill a need that goes beyond what general medical facilities provide. As such, our entire staff has exemplary medical credentials, and we maintain the most rigorous protocols to ensure we provide the very best of care to our patients and their family members. While we are a private facility," he acknowledged, "we choose to operate in conjunction with a medical board."

"Meaning, you get some government-related grants or funding along the way, requiring oversight of such a board. No need to sugarcoat it for me, Doctor. This is clearly a very specialized facility. The files on Roger, please."

She could only imagine the issues involved and would have to give some thought to what she would do if by some miracle she ever found her brother for example, and he were in a similar place. Would she want to do everything to keep him alive, even on artificial life support, or would she choose to let him go? It was a ... It was a difficult decision to make, she was sure. She sat and waited for the doctor to pull the related files.

When he finally had them in hand, he shook his head. "I really don't like sharing this information."

"Of course not," she said, with a smile. "However, much of it should be public information anyway. In an accident that serious, there should have been a police report."

He looked at her and added, "That's a good idea. You can pull the police report."

She gave him a flat smile. "That is why I'm here. We could find no such report."

The look on his face was not only one of shock but it was clear that the revelation made him extremely nervous. He moistened his lips several times and then added, "You do know that has nothing to do with us."

"I understand that," she said, "but I do need to get to the bottom of it."

"He's been a patient here," the director explained, "for a good share of four decades, since the Haven opened."

"Are you sure about his dates? He must have been what? … In his late teens at the time of the drowning?" she asked, trying to mentally calculate how far back this would have been.

"I believe eighteen at the time of the accident," he confirmed. "He was among the first patients at this facility, when it opened some two years later, I do believe." He hesitated.

"Don't stop now."

"Due to this young man's need for such a service, this center was brought into existence."

She stared at him. "Now, that is interesting, isn't it?"

"Sometimes unforeseen circumstances," he shared, "make for unusual responses, but since then clearly we have found many other families also determined to keep their family members alive and well."

"*Well?*" she questioned.

He flushed. "I will not be entering into a discussion of that nature with you today, Detective. Of that I can assure you."

"I'm not saying that this is a bad idea by any means," she clarified, "but I do want to know more details about Roger's accident."

"I have nothing here, except he was in a drowning accident but survived."

"I'll need a full copy of that file."

He hesitated, then swallowed. "Not without a court order. I really can't, and I shouldn't even be telling you what I've already shared."

She nodded and pulled out her phone.

"Wait. You're not going to get a search warrant, are you?'

She looked at him in astonishment. "Doctor, have I not made myself clear? I assure you that I didn't come here to waste my time."

"But what could this young man possibly have to do with anything current? He has been here since the facility opened and has largely been in a coma state."

"Tell me about his brother."

"Oh, Dr. Burnett is devoted to him. He comes constantly, looks after him, even makes personal recordings for him to listen to at night. Dr. Burnett provides free medical care for others as well. The family has always been very supportive and concerned, very caring of everything dealing with Roger. His mother was his first doctor. So I am quite certain that the mayor's office would be disappointed that we were spending our valuable time on such an inquiry. In a word,

Detective, I can assure you, nothing untoward is going on here."

"Maybe not," she replied in a very gentle voice, "but I do have questions." He frowned at her, and she nodded. "And, no, I won't go away. Nor do I respond to threats well. It will be much better for you to just deal with me, and then I can leave."

"I would love to *just deal with you*, but we also have patient confidentiality to consider. That will bite me when the proverbial other shoe drops."

"Hence the need for the search warrants," she declared. "That covers both of our proverbial asses. Or you can just go and ask Dr. Burnett yourself and see how much information he would allow me to have, without taking further time and trouble to get warrants."

He looked at her and brightened. "He is here. Are you on good terms with him then?"

"Why would you assume otherwise? If we can agree that he is, indeed, here and has the authority to release the information I seek, it would seem prudent for you to go speak to him now," she suggested, with half a smile. He frowned at her. "I'll stay right here."

He hesitated, obviously very undecided as to what route he should take. Then after quickly replacing the files, he dashed from the room.

She had no idea what Dr. Burnett would say about his brother's case, but it did give her an opportunity to see just how he would handle it. Was she prepared to request a search warrant? Maybe. It was certainly on the docket, depending on what more she found out here today. Why there was no police report was the main thing she needed to sort out. She needed the truth regarding the circumstances of the events that left Dr. Burnett's brother in this situation.

Kate quickly texted Reese and shared what she had learned, hoping that might lead Reese to a police file. With Reese's assurance that she was looking into that exact issue, Kate wondered if maybe back then there was no requirement to even file something like that. Since it was an accident and there was no death, maybe that was the end of it. She pondered that. When the director came back, he had Dr. Burnett in tow.

Dr. Burnett looked at her and frowned.

"Hello, Dr. Burnett," she greeted him politely. "I understand your brother is having a bad day. I'm very sorry to hear that."

His bottom lip trembled, and he nodded. "It's really not a good time, Detective," he muttered. "I have family in need."

"Of course it's not. There is no good time when it comes to ailing family members," she noted. "However, I am looking into the circumstances around your brother's incident." She took a moment, then continued. "So, either you can allow the director to release more information or you can sit down and give me the information that I need yourself. Then I'll be on my way. Either way is fine with me."

He stared at her in horror. "You want me to relive all that?" he exclaimed in extreme distress.

She replied, "Or you could let the director here tell me all about it."

The director shook his head. "That is not within my mandate."

"I don't know what your mandate is, sir," she stated bluntly, her gaze going from one man to the other, "and the longer this remains some sort of mystery, the more interested I get."

"Are you telling me that you really don't have any other cases to work on? Cases of murderers, serial killers, drunk drivers, hit-and-runs?" the director asked, regaining some of his voice, as he could see how devastated Dr. Burnett looked at the mention of the subject.

"That is quite true," she stated, and Rodney's case came to mind, as she wondered again about the hit-and-run victim on life support. "Yet it is quite amazing just how far back the impetus behind some crimes begins." Dr. Burnett squeaked at that. She looked at him and asked, "So, gentlemen, what will it be?"

Dr. Burnett looked from her to the director and finally stated, "He can tell you. Please, just let me go and be with my brother." And, with that, he dashed out.

She looked over at the director. "Looks like you're it. Shall we begin?"

He sighed, sat down at his desk. "I guess I'm not surprised that he would choose that route. It's obviously a very difficult subject for him and always has been."

"I'm sure it is," she agreed, "and the more you make this out to be a big mystery, the harder it is for me to untangle and to sort out the need for secrecy."

"Quite understandably, it's because Dr. Burnett was with Roger and the sister at the time," the director shared bluntly.

"The sister was there? I thought the sister was dead."

"The sister was drowning, and Roger jumped in to try and save her, but Roger ended up killing his sister in the process."

"Meaning?" Kate asked.

"When somebody is drowning, they instinctively grab on to anything or anyone they can. They aren't rational at the time of course and not easy to subdue. Sadly, in the attempt to save her, … she drowned and nearly drowned Roger too."

"And Dr. Burnett was there as well?"

"Yes, he is younger than Roger and had never learned to swim and was in no way capable of saving either of them."

Kate grimaced. "So, Dr. Burnett watched his sister die, and his older brother—drowning, deprived of oxygen—sustained severe brain damage. The family opted to keep him here essentially in a vegetative state for nearly four decades."

The director winced at that summation. "That's an unpleasant way to describe it, Detective, but technically speaking, yes."

She nodded. "How often does the doctor come here?"

"Very often. Weekly, daily at times, and sometimes more often than that."

"What does he do?"

"He spends hours talking to his brother. I think he is still holding out hope that his brother is in there and will one day come back to a normal world. The land of the living, so to speak."

"And yet that's not likely to happen?"

He gave her an ever-so-gentle headshake. "I won't say that miracles don't happen, but I will say that I haven't ever seen anything occur that would rise to the level that Dr. Burnett is hoping for. … I know that sounds terrible, but we haven't seen the level of positive change in Roger's condition that would indicate the potential for such an acute reversal. That's not to say he hasn't had good episodes arise but nothing long-term."

She pondered that for a long moment, then nodded. "Why all the secrecy? Presumably his surname is not Burnside."

"The family wanted it that way," the director replied, "and because his family imagined such a wonderful facility to meet the needs of their beloved son and others like him, then miraculously arranged to bring it into existence in a remarkably short time frame, a modicum of privacy for the setup of the center and its patients seemed an easy thing to promise."

Again she was left with multiple questions about why anyone felt the need for something like that, but it probably wasn't fair to ask him about someone else's motivations.

Checking the file, he added, "I'm sorry. I don't have any more information on that."

"What did his father do?"

"He was a policeman. As I mentioned earlier, their mother was a doctor and treated Roger and essentially set up the Haven Center and got it running."

"Tell me about them. Did you know them?"

"Sadly, neither of his parents lived long enough to see their son come back the way they had dreamed of. They died not long after the Haven was set up and Roger was placed here."

"Didn't you just say that his recovery was unlikely, if not nearly impossible?" she murmured.

"I don't recall saying it quite that way. However, it's not uncommon for family members to refuse to hear our professional opinions."

"Understood," she said, with a wave of her hand. "So who treated Roger after his mother's death and before Dr. Burnett became a practicing doctor?"

The director swallowed before answering. "I did."

Kate's gaze lingered on the director's face for a bit longer than necessary. She asked the director if she could see Roger, just through the viewing window into his room.

He frowned at her. "I would need his brother's permission for that."

She gave him a flat stare. "I want to confirm that he really is here."

He looked at her in complete surprise. "Of course he is. Where else would he be?" he asked in confusion.

"That's not what I asked," she clarified. "I want to confirm he is who you have here. So, tell me. Is that Roger Burnett in there?"

He hesitated, clearly insulted. "Let me talk to Dr. Burnett, and you can come back another time, when he's not so upset." He could barely disguise his repressed fury. "The poor man's beloved brother has taken a turn for the worse, and I would like to ensure that Roger pulls through this. Otherwise all of your interest, whatever this is about," he pointed out, opening his hands wide, "is all for naught anyway."

She pondered that and nodded. "Fine, get back to me this afternoon, please. I would like to at least confirm who is in that bed." He stopped and stared at her. "Chalk it up to the suspicious mind of a cop."

And she wouldn't elaborate any further than that. She didn't have anything to elaborate on. Period. Just something was cooking in the back of her mind, something that really didn't make a whole lot of sense, even to her. Even if it did make sense, it didn't apply to the current drownings, the subject of her actual case. She'd stumbled down some rabbit hole and couldn't seem to get herself out of it. At least not right now. Still pondering that, she headed to her vehicle and slowly drove back to the station.

When she got in, she walked over to Reese's office and brought her up-to-date. "According to the director of the center, the parents are deceased, and the mother was a doctor, and the father was a cop. There was a sister who drowned, and her older brother tried to rescue her but nearly drowned himself, becoming incapacitated."

At that, Reese's eyebrow shot up. "That's all very interesting, but it still conflicts with much of what I've been coming up with."

"So, which account has been doctored?" Kate asked.

Reese frowned. "It could be either, or it could be both."

"Then the question is why? Why go to all this trouble? I understand HIPAA laws and privacy issues, but why all this added secrecy? The parents created the Haven Center specifically for Roger. Yes, it was a horrific accident, but apparently no police file was ever created because nothing was sinister about it. It was an accidental death. Maybe back then it was easier to sweep things under the rug. But why go to all that trouble?" Kate asked Reese, staring at her.

"That's your department," Reese said, with a headshake. "God knows it's not mine."

"But it *is* yours," Kate pointed out.

At that, Reese laughed and admitted, "I know. But I do much better on pulling the data, not so much on analyzing it. Making sense of it *is* up to you."

"I think you're selling yourself short in that department," Kate murmured. "You're pretty gifted when it comes to this stuff. My initial thought is that they had access to a lot of money, which would buy a certain amount of privacy. Back then it was easier for files to get tampered with, for dates to be changed, surely for names to get changed. If they were a little paranoid, it might make sense to blur the lines a bit. I'm sure you'll figure it out."

Leaving a very surprised Reese behind her, Kate returned to her desk, where Rodney was just scooping up his wallet and heading back out.

He stopped when he saw her and asked, "Where were you?" She explained about the visit to the center. He frowned at her in confusion. "Why would they do all that?"

"That's the same question I just asked Reese. We have way more questions than before. Like, who's lying, who lied originally, why lie in the first place, and what purpose does it serve after all these years to continue lying?"

Owen came up behind her and added, "Because once that lie is out there, it's almost impossible to reverse it. So then you have to perpetrate it in order to maintain that you weren't some psycho at the beginning of the whole mess," he declared, with a half laugh.

Kate nodded. "I understand *perpetrating* the lie. I don't necessarily understand using the lie in the first place." She pondered that, as she put on a new pot of coffee and sat down, only to realize that she'd run herself tight on time. "Dammit." She stood, then stared wistfully at the coffee. "I've got a meeting at three."

"Take some with you," Owen suggested nonchalantly.

That was Owen for you. "I don't have time to wait," she muttered. "Besides, I would probably just spill it in my car. So, dammit, there you go. Have a fresh pot of hot coffee on me."

Owen laughed. "Sure, thanks. I'll be here for a bit yet. Has this meeting got to do with this drowning case?" he asked. "Because yours sounds a lot more interesting than mine."

She shook her head at that. "I've been given a short leash. I'm down to a couple days at best. For the life of me, I just keep coming up with more weird stuff," she muttered.

"But you do weird stuff so well," he replied. "In fact, I'm jealous in a way."

She stopped, gave him a hard look, and said, "I doubt that."

"You would be surprised," he countered. "That weird stuff of yours is pretty compelling, and this regular criminal stuff is pretty boring."

"It's also not earth-shattering, but it's definitely on the weird side, which means that nobody ever believes you. It's not all it's cracked up to be," she pointed out.

He chuckled. "But people are starting to understand that when you say, *This is weird shit, and it won't make any sense,* they're almost lining up with joy because it's different, it's unusual, it's something that not everybody is dealing with," he explained. "So don't hold back when it comes to sharing information."

"Nothing to tell yet," she admitted. "I was at this special care center today, and I'm waiting to hear back from them. I wanted to see the brother for myself."

At that, Owen asked her, "Why?"

She gave him a half a smile. "This is really going to sound bizarre."

"Yeah, everything out of your mouth these days is bizarre, but go ahead and tell me, please. I can't wait."

She shrugged. "I just want to make sure it's him. That's all."

"But that makes no sense. Who else would be in a bed completely out of it from a drowning accident, if not the brother?"

"That's the million-dollar question, isn't it?" she asked, with half a laugh. "For all I know, it is his brother, but because nobody will let me in to see and confirm that, it makes me suspicious as hell."

And, with that, she walked out.

SIMON WAS AT the coffee shop with Danny, when Kate walked in. She glanced around and found the two of them, then smiled and walked over. "I gather it was tough to make this meeting," Simon asked gently.

She shrugged. "Some days it's tough to make any meeting." She looked at Danny and asked, "How're you doing?"

Simon smiled. Kate had greeted Danny in such an off-hand way that Danny seemed to relax, as if she weren't going to be a mother hen about his near drowning and make him feel bad about any of it. But then Kate was good at that. She was also a little more rushed right now, as she turned, walked over to the counter, determined to get a coffee. When she spied the muffins, he laughed as she snagged up three and brought them over. She plunked down with a happy sigh, then snatched one of the muffins, pulling the paper off the bottom of it.

She motioned at the other two muffins and offered, "There's one for each of you, if you want."

Danny picked one up and smiled at her. "Thanks."

"You're welcome. Since you're the one who called this meeting, what's up?"

He hesitated and then focused intently on his muffin.

Simon snagged the remaining one and just gave Danny some time, following Kate's lead. There were a lot of things about Kate to admire, but her ability to deal with people when she wanted to, choosing not to crowd them into telling her exactly what she wanted from them, was pretty amazing. He was incredibly proud of her for the way she was handling Danny right now.

After he took several bites of his muffin and a sip of coffee, Danny muttered, "I didn't tell you everything."

She looked over at him and nodded. "Okay. So, what didn't you tell me?"

Danny raised both eyebrows. "What? No condemnation? No, *How could you do this to me? Do you know you're obstructing an investigation?*" he added in an exaggerated voice.

She flashed him a grin. "I figured I would save all that for afterward."

He winced and nodded. "Yeah, I probably deserve it."

"Part of the equation will be why you withheld it, and just what it is, and why are you telling me now?"

He took a deep breath and explained, "I didn't understand what I was hearing, and, because I didn't understand, I think I didn't want to tell you, for fear you would think I was crazy."

"Yeah, I do *crazy* pretty well," she said, with half a laugh. "In my job you get to recognize crazy pretty easily."

"I didn't have any exposure to crazy up until now," Danny shared, "and I'm still not sure if the doc was all there or not."

"I think I can tell you right now that he's going through some difficult personal stuff. So it may not have looked like he was all there. However, if you don't tell me what the problem is," she added, "I can't explain any of it away."

"It was just the way he said it. He kept saying he was sorry, he was sorry, he was sorry," he muttered. "And I was like, *Stop saying that, just help me*, but he kept up with the *I'm sorry. I'm sorry. I'm sorry.*"

"Okay," Kate replied, "and we already know you were worried that maybe he was using his cane as a weapon of sorts."

"I was thinking about that too. It's not so much that it was a weapon, but that it just wasn't a help. That could have been because of his age and his stage of life, impacting his ability to physically help me. I'm a big guy and wasn't all that together in terms of what I was doing, so I can't really hold that against him."

She laughed. "And you don't want me doing it either. I get it," she stated. "So, what is it that was so important that it's been haunting you?" When he gave her a surprised look, she shrugged. "Hey, I don't have to be a psychic to see that."

He winced. "No, you probably don't. It just makes it all seem even more bizarre."

"Come on. Spit it out."

"He mentioned something about a brother. That he was doing this to help his brother."

She sat back and looked at him intently. "Did he say what *this* was?"

"No, and that's the part I keep coming back to that I can't explain. But he went on and on about it. He was doing it for his brother."

"I see," she murmured.

Simon wasn't exactly sure what she meant by that and knew it would be a while before she shared any of it with him. Simon looked over at Danny. "Something about him saying that really bothered you?"

"Wouldn't it bother you? I was already not too sure that he was trying to help me, versus trying to hurt me. But I survived, and I wasn't in a good mental state myself at the time, and I feel like I really do owe him my thanks instead of, you know, whatever this is," he noted, with a wave of his hand around the café. "So having this conversation makes me feel guilty too."

"Why? Because you think you're getting him in trouble?" Kate asked.

"I am, right?" Danny asked point-blank.

She smiled. "That depends on *him*, if he's done anything wrong."

"What could he possibly have done wrong? That's the thing I don't get," Simon admitted. "I understand that we're all beating around the bush here, and nobody wants to come right out and say anything, but do you really think he was trying to kill Danny?" he asked Kate.

Danny looked from one to the other and nodded. "My darkest fear is that maybe I created the scenario, through my desperation to end my own life, and I was somehow hoping that's what he was doing."

"Did you talk to him?" Kate asked.

"I did, and that's the other part I didn't make clear before. When I first fell in, and he rushed over, I told him not to save me," Danny revealed in a very low tone. He looked around the room as if in shame, then added, "And that's something I'll have to live with."

"Sure, but it's not something you have to sit here and trash yourself over."

He looked at her and then laughed. "You really don't mince words, do you, Detective?"

"No, I really don't mince words," she agreed, looking at him. "Life is far too short for that shit. There are times to be nice, and then there's just wasting time."

That also startled another surprised laugh out of Danny, and he smiled. "Thanks, I kind of needed that."

"Yeah, it sounded like you did," she agreed, with a head-shake. "The fact that you did is also something that interests me because what in all this is the part that brought you to call this meeting? What part of this information did you think that I needed to hear? Or was it just that you needed to bare your soul to avoid any judgment going forward? Was it done so you're free and clear to move on?"

He stared at her for a moment. "Wow. So, I really hadn't expected that conversation."

"I'm not going into all that. I don't do salvation conversations," she muttered.

Simon was interested, but she kept her gaze locked on Danny, without looking at Simon, which was probably a good thing because he didn't want to get into that conversation with Danny either.

Danny looked at her, and then his shoulders sagged. "I feel guilty as hell because, if this guy was doing anything that made you suspicious of him, I'm afraid it was my fault because of what I told him. He was just trying to help me."

"Okay, hang on a minute. So, you're afraid that he was trying to actively help you commit suicide, and, even when you changed your mind and started to panic and didn't want to go through with it, he didn't get the message and was still trying to assist in this endeavor? Trying to kill you?" Kate asked Danny.

"Something like that, yeah. It wasn't very clear in my head, and I'm not sure it was in his either."

"No, I don't think his was, and, if he was saying sorry, sorry, sorry, and that he was doing this for his brother, what the hell does that mean?" Kate asked.

"I don't know," Danny admitted. "Now I've told you everything I know. It really bothered me that I withheld that, and Simon has been so good at helping me to get back on my feet that I just felt that I owed you everything."

"You don't owe me anything," she stated, with a smile.

Simon added, "And, for the record, you don't owe me anything either." He gave him a pat on the shoulder. "The best thing for you to do is just pick up your feet and go forward. Keep doing that, and, before long, life will feel worth living again. As for Kate and me, it's not a debt thing, so just knock that off your list of worries."

Danny nodded and smiled. "I hear you say that, but still, in my head, I owe you."

"Don't confuse gratitude for a kindness, with payment due for a debt that is owed. We're fine," Simon repeated.

"And should you ever see somebody else in a situation where you can help," Kate suggested, "pay it forward."

Danny sat back and looked at her with relief. "You know what? … That is something I can do."

"I know you can. I have faith in you, Danny. You're a good person."

He gave her a beaming smile and added, "I feel like I could cry right now." When she looked at him in alarm, he burst out laughing. "Obviously bawling young men is not your thing."

"I don't think it's anybody's thing," she declared. "There's something incredibly difficult about seeing someone in so much pain. I've seen a lot of pain, but dealing with crying, with tears?" She shook her head. "I don't deal with that at all."

Danny chuckled. "I'm going to leave the two of you. Thank you for the talk." And, with that, Danny got up and walked out.

She watched him go and then turned back to Simon, who watched her reaction with interest. "What do you think of that?" she asked him intently.

"What part of it?" he asked, curious as to what in all of that interested her.

"The *Don't try to save me* part."

"I think it would have been very early on, which would mean that the doctor must have been there fairly quickly."

"That would make sense. I think Danny's change of heart didn't take very long to happen. If you think about it, the cold would have set in within a matter of a few minutes, maybe ten or fifteen. Enough for him to realize that this venture of his would have the ending he thought he wanted, but it wasn't going the way he imagined. He was probably very quick to decide that wasn't what he wanted after all. And I guess that clears up the idea, the incongruency I had about why he didn't get out right away. It didn't make any sense to me that somebody as physically fit as he is, even fully dressed, couldn't have gotten out without any trouble."

"He told me that initially," Simon interjected, "how he swam out away from the dock far enough to ensure the desired result, even if someone saw him and put out a call for help. But he expended a good bit of energy getting back, just in time to have his attempt to save himself helped or thwarted by the doctor."

"And that's the question. Was it helped or thwarted?" she muttered.

He looked at her and asked, "You still don't know yourself, do you?"

"No, I don't. As odd as that may sound, it's still not entirely clear."

"No, it isn't," he agreed, with a smile. "What did you do today?" he asked, hoping for a complete change of topic.

But she picked up her coffee, looked at him over the rim, and replied, "I went to visit his nonexistent vegetable-ish brother, Roger." She laughed. "His brother apparently was involved in the same accident that killed Dr. Burnett's sister." Simon couldn't believe it.

"The account I was provided by the director of the facility, with Dr. Burnett's approval, goes like this. The older brother, who was maybe eighteen at the time, went into the water to save his drowning sister, but he somehow was drowning too, yet, although saved, still incurred brain damage. All while the teenage version of our good doctor looked on. He was fourteen then but didn't know how to swim."

"Crap," Simon muttered. "No wonder Dr. Burnett always has that lost puppy look about him."

"Is that what it is?" she asked curiously. "That's not quite the description I would have used."

Simon nodded, with an understanding smile. "But you look at it from a very different point of view. I look at it more from a victim's point of view. You, on the other hand, tend to see everything but a victim."

"Right," she muttered. "Maybe because I'm always looking for the opposite of a victim. I'm looking for the victimizer."

"So, did you find it?" he asked curiously.

She shook her head. "No. Not only did I not find it, I'm not exactly sure what I'm even looking for now."

"It's really not even been a case, has it?"

"It's not been a case, and yet it clearly seems to be," she shared, with an odd smile. "It's not been anything serious, and yet it's very serious. None of it makes a whole lot of sense, and yet I had this insistent drive to see the brother today, and they wouldn't let me see him. Roger was having some sort of major setback in his condition, which to my understanding is a vegetative state anyway. That is why you saw the good doctor in that kind of frozen, shell-shocked capacity today. He was up there at the center, and I did speak with him briefly at the care home. Anyway, since the brother apparently took a turn for the worse, they didn't let me see him."

"But did they let you see him eventually?"

"No, the director was looking for permission from Dr. Burnett, who was locked in with his brother. I'd already spoken to him once and decided I would leave him be and try again tomorrow."

Simon sat back and frowned. "I really do admire that brain of yours, but sometimes your logic is very convoluted."

She snorted. "Only sometimes?"

He grinned. "Yeah, only sometimes. In this case, I don't understand why you would even consider wanting to see this brother."

"I don't know, but that cop instinct in me says I need to."

"Well then, I presume you're following up."

"Oh, I'm following up all right. If nothing's there, and I've crossed all the *T*s and dotted all the *I*s"—she shrugged—"then I can leave it alone and chalk it up to experience or something, just determining who and what happened here."

"And yet again, you're back to the reality that you don't even know if a crime was committed."

She placed a finger up against her lips and whispered, "Hush. Colby won't let me have this luxury much longer of investigating a case that is not even a case. So don't jinx it. I'm on borrowed time as it is. This is, what, day seven? That's unheard of in my department. Won't happen again, I bet. And somehow the other cases are being handled without much help from me, even with Andy still off on extended leave. That lull in crimes won't last long either. This is my window, and I'm taking it."

Simon smiled. "I am sure you are."

She laughed. "Oh, don't get me wrong. I've been helping on other cases as it is, but even Colby had me follow this up and check on it because it's, as he puts it," she added, rolling her eyes, "a woo-woo case." He stared at her, then nodded. "Anything that's weird and wonderful now apparently comes to me."

He chuckled. "Does that make everybody else jealous?"

"Maybe," she muttered. "I'm not exactly sure, but Owen did say something about my getting most of the select and lovely cases, but I'm not sure if he was serious or being sarcastic."

"And yet you're all on the same team?"

"Yeah, we are, and I'm not sure that he meant it in any other way. They've all got other cases, so they haven't been particularly involved in this one. Still, they're curious. They want to know what's happening, and several of them have asked about you."

"Of course they have," he muttered. "It's not as if I've helped you at all though."

"Nope, you sure haven't," she stated, giving him a sideways look. "I don't think you've had any hits on this one, have you?"

"Hits?" he asked in a strangely neutral tone.

She glared at him. "I'm not sure what we would call

something like this, so don't take me to task over it."

His grin flashed. "Nope, I would never do that, but it is interesting and fun, I have to admit, to watch you wrap your mind around this and find the words to express yourself."

"Glad you're enjoying it," she muttered, scrunching her nose. "And what about you? Any more requests for answers?"

He shook his head. "Nope. None so far."

She sighed, then nodded. "I wish it would tell me something. The great psychic Simon has to strike out sometime."

He rolled his eyes. "I'm going to forget you said that."

"You can try," she teased him, as she looked at him sideways. "Are you off work?"

He nodded. "What about you?"

She laughed. "I'm here, aren't I?"

"Are you going back to the office?" he asked cautiously.

She shook her head. "Nope, I'm sure not."

"In that case"—he checked his watch and found it was well past four—"let's go."

"Where are we going?" she asked, as she got up.

"I suggest we pick up a picnic and head out to the harbor. Maybe we could go up the inlet, head around to the university, where we can put some of this behind us."

"I'm all for that." She looked around the café and asked, "Do they have anything here? We could just pick something up and carry it out."

"We don't even have to do that. I've already got a place down at the marina that's pretty good. I'll call in an order, and we'll pick it up on the way."

"I have my vehicle though," she noted, with a chuckle.

"We'll take both back to my place, or we can both go straight to the marina," he suggested, pausing to think about it.

They worked out the logistics and headed to the marina. Within minutes, they were aboard the *Running Mate*. She laughed as she threw herself down into the pilot's seat. "There is definitely a sense of freedom in having this."

"I know, and it's something that I think we'll enjoy more and more, as we figure out what we can do, how far we can go, and how quickly we can get out onto the water with it." He shook his head. "Those are all things we still have to work our way through."

She shrugged. "I don't think it'll take a whole lot of *working through*. Honest to God, this is too much like an instant getaway, and God knows we could both use more of that." He turned and looked at her. She nodded. "I know. I work too much, too long, too hard, and it never seems to get any easier," she muttered. "But I'm also very aware that, if we can do something like this, it will help both of us mentally and spiritually. We'll probably live longer and happier lives because of it."

And, on that note, he started the engine and maneuvered the *Running Mate* out of the marina to the open sea. An hour into their cruise, her phone rang. She glanced down to see the call was from Colby.

Frowning, she answered, "Sergeant? Kate here. What's up?"

"Another drowning," he said.

"Oh, crap," she muttered. "I'm out on Simon's yacht right now."

"Well, good. You can motor your way right around the corner, if you want. It's out off of Locarno Beach. I don't have much for details," he shared, "but you can fill me in when you get caught up."

"Why were we even called?" she asked, suspicious because everything went through him, but this was especially quick.

"Because you know a person who was down there."

"Oh, no, not Dr. Burnett again."

"Yeah, so over to you."

"*Great,*" she muttered. "I'm on it." She disconnected, looked over at Simon, and said, "I'm so sorry."

He nodded his head. "Colby's right. We aren't very far from Locarno Beach. It might be an unorthodox way to travel, since you're a detective, but it can definitely get us there pretty fast."

Sure enough, it took only twenty minutes, and they pulled right up, as close as possible. She hopped out, getting her pants and shoes wet but not really giving a crap. As she walked over to the uniform at the scene, she flashed her badge. He looked at her, then at the yacht behind her. She shrugged. "We were out on the water already."

"Lucky you," he muttered.

She nodded. "Yeah, except the part about getting called back in to work."

"Right, sorry," he muttered. "That does make a difference, doesn't it?"

"It sure cuts the enjoyment factor."

She walked over, took a quick look at the victim, a middle-aged woman. She frowned and noticed that the woman was fully dressed, wearing a long skirt. "Anybody ID the woman yet?"

"We didn't find any ID on her, so nothing so far," replied one of the paramedics.

Kate frowned, then took a picture of the woman's face. "I might have an idea." She waited until the body was removed, then she walked over to see Dr. Burnett just sitting there, his head in his hands.

He looked up at her, gave her a small smile, and said, "Yes, it's me again."

She nodded. "Do you want to talk this time, instead of walking away?"

"Do I have a choice?" he asked, looking at her. "This is starting to be a habit."

"Yeah, and, as habits go, it's not the best. Can you tell me what this is all about?"

"No," he replied, his voice sounding surprisingly strong and capable. He looked behind her to see the yacht along the shore. "That's a nice boat. I saw you get off."

"Yeah, I was supposed to be off duty, but deaths do take priority."

He sighed. "She tried so hard to live there at the end."

"But she didn't want to at the beginning, did she?"

He looked at her. "Oh, you figured that out, *huh*?"

"Yeah, I figured it out. I just don't really know all the details."

"I'm sure not giving them to you," he stated. "Not after you demanded to see my brother and put a timeline on it."

"What's wrong with my asking to see your brother?" she asked.

"I don't really want you in there. I don't want you disturbing him."

"How is my looking through the window on his door going to disturb him?"

He sighed, then shrugged. "If you don't go in his room, that's fine, but I don't want him disturbed."

"How is he doing after taking a turn for the worse earlier?"

"I hope that he will pull through, but I don't know that

he will," the doc stated. "Another reason I don't want his last days, or hours even, disturbed."

"And yet could disturbing him potentially get you some sort of response?"

He frowned at her in shock and murmured, "No, no, no. … That's not the way you do it. I don't want it done that way."

"If you say so." She looked back at the harbor and then at him. "I do need to get your statement."

"It's getting late in the day. How about I come down to the station tomorrow," he suggested wearily.

"Give me the abridged version now, please."

"I saw her walk out fully dressed," he began, "and she just kept on going. I called out to her a couple times. Nobody was here, and she got pulled around the corner. See that set of rocks over there? I climbed out onto the rocks, trying to help her out. At the end she was really trying to help for herself." He shook his head, looking like the epitome of sorrow. "Then she just … went under." He sighed. "As a doctor, I know death, and I hear about it all the time. However, right now, I feel as if I've seen way too much of it."

She nodded slowly. "I can accept that, but have you had anything to do with causing these deaths? That's what I really want to know."

He looked at her in horror and shook his head. "No! Absolutely not. I wouldn't. I would never." Yet his fervent protestations didn't ring true. Suddenly he got up. "I'll come down to the police station tomorrow." And, with that, he booked it to the parking lot.

━━━∼∾∼━━━

LATER ON THAT evening, back at his place, Simon stared at Kate in puzzlement. "What difference does it make what Dr. Burnett's brother looks like?" he asked. "Particularly when you know very well that after God-only-knows how many years in this vegetative state, he won't look young. He probably looks as if life has been ravaging him. Can you explain your impulse here?"

She gave him a wry look. "Can you explain what you do?"

He stopped and stared, then cautiously asked, "Are you saying what I think you're saying?"

"No, I'm not," she snapped. "All I'm saying is that it felt ..." And even she winced at that. "I feel like I need to see this person. I don't know why. I don't have the slightest idea what I could possibly gain from seeing him. You're right. He won't look anything like I would expect, whatever that is. But ..." She frowned. "It's instincts, Simon. It's pure instincts pushing me to keep doing whatever it is I'm doing."

"Then you have to follow it," he stated.

"Exactly. But you're right that it makes no sense. I can't begin to figure out what difference seeing this person would make to the case. It doesn't make any sense, and that makes me angry because it leaves me trying to justify something that I can't begin to justify." She raised both hands in frustration, got up, and poured herself another glass of wine, then sat back down on the couch. "In a way, it's also giving me a little bit of an insight into what you go through."

"You mean the fact that this shit happens and that I don't have any way to explain it, or to understand what it is, or to take that judgmental look off everybody's face when they hear me and I sound ridiculous?" He nodded.

"And yet"—she twisted on the couch to look at him fully—"that's also what you're doing to me."

He froze and then slowly nodded. "Yeah, it's kind of like we just put ourselves in each other's shoes. So, when I ask questions, it doesn't mean I'm judging you, even though it probably feels that way."

"Maybe it's good. Maybe it's not good," she muttered.

"I can't see that it's bad. Not if it helps us to understand where we're both coming from," he added. "It's an interesting opportunity for us to sort it out, though."

She winced at that. "It doesn't feel like an interesting opportunity," she stated, with a wry look in his direction. "It feels wrong because I can't explain what I'm doing and why I'm doing it, and that makes me angry. I don't understand half of what I am hearing in this case."

"Have you ever heard the phrase, *We're never angry for the reason we think we are?*"

She frowned at him. "What is that? Some psychic mumbo jumbo?"

He laughed. "I don't know whether it is or not, but I've certainly heard it a time or two. It has to do with the anger being a front, and we show the anger because it's easier to deal with, when what we're really angry about is something within ourselves. In your case, I would say it's probably self-doubt." She glared at him, and he nodded. "And that hits home because the last thing you want is for anybody to see you as being anything less than strong and confident."

"Jeez," she muttered, staring at him and then turning to stare out the window.

"I can see from the line of your jaw that you're most unimpressed with my comment," he shared. "You're right. I had no reason to bring it up. It's not part of this discussion right now."

"You're saying it should be though." She turned to look at him. "You're saying that's what you think."

"No, I'm not. I'm saying that it's a strong possibility of what *you* are thinking and that if you would look at it a little more, you would realize that the anger you're feeling may not even have anything to do with this case."

"It absolutely has something to do with this case. What makes me angry is that I feel completely incompetent and that I'm wasting everybody's time. I want very much to solve this case, and, if I can't solve it, then I want to know that no crime is here, so I can walk away," she explained. "I'm also taking time to help my coworkers, and miraculously we have a somewhat light caseload right now, where we can even spend time looking at this issue. Otherwise it wouldn't even have been considered because we usually don't have time to think about shit like this."

"And yet there have been enough cases that you're not so sure."

"No, I'm not so sure," she muttered, then groaned. "It just doesn't make any sense."

"No. So where is it that you'll make some sense of it?"

"I don't know," she admitted, showing her palms. "Is it wrong to feel that people are lying to me?"

Surprised, he looked at her and shook his head. "No, of course it's not wrong to think that, and, chances are, they *are* lying to you. Isn't that a common thing in your line of work?"

"Yes, it is a common thing," she confirmed, "but it really pisses me off. These witnesses could clear up things so easily if they would just tell the damn truth, but they don't. Why don't they?"

"Because they believe they have to hide it, for whatever

reason," he replied. "Frequently because it will make them look bad because they did something wrong, and they're trying to save their sorry asses. You know as well as I do that there are a million reasons why people don't stand up and tell the truth."

She groaned and nodded. "Fine, but I need something to break in this case, and I suspect that it needs to break in a way that has absolutely nothing to do with anything else."

"In what way?"

"I keep going back to Danny," she muttered.

Simon winced at that. "And that's the one direction I really hope you won't keep going back to because he's on the mend."

"I know he's on the mend, but how is it that Dr. Burnett knew he was suicidal?"

"Maybe he didn't know. Did you consider that?" he asked, with a wry look in her direction. He got up, brought the bottle of wine over and gently topped up her glass before refilling his own. The wine was almost gone, and that was okay because this seemed to be one of those nights where the conversations fascinated and at the same time repelled, just because of the content. How did one make peace with something like this?

"Do you really suspect that Danny was suicidal?" she asked him.

He looked at her. "Oh, wow, you don't even believe that?"

She stopped, then shrugged. "It's not that I don't believe it because anybody can become suicidal. It doesn't matter that they're strong, healthy, and seemingly have everything going for them. You and I have both seen horrific cases of things like that. I just don't ... I'm calling him."

He grabbed her hand. "Do you have to? Maybe think this through a minute?" he suggested cautiously.

She stared at him. "Think what through?"

"Whatever is going through your head right now because the kid is slowly starting to get himself together."

"He is, … but I'm a little concerned that he's not sharing everything."

Simon frowned. "But he contacted you just today. And it's getting late in the evening as it is."

"I know, and that makes no sense either. Still, when I got there to meet with Danny, whether you were already there, or maybe because I was late, or whatever else, but Danny saw me and changed his mind. It very much feels like … I want him to say more."

"Even if he doesn't have anything more to share?" he questioned.

"Apparently a part of me believes he *does* have more to share, but he's either too scared, too upset, too worried, too *something*."

He shook his head, not comprehending. "I'm just not sure that Danny's got that level of duplicity in him."

She looked at him. "Of course he does. Everybody does."

"Fine." He took a deep breath. "I'll give you that point. But, even if he's hiding something, it could just be because he wants to move on. Or it could be because he isn't sure of what happened. Or doesn't know it's important. It could be all kinds of things."

"I know," she agreed, "but, more often than not, people's worries are minuscule, yet get built up to be massive in their minds and—"

"It doesn't stop you from wanting to call him."

"No," she stated, as she pulled out her phone and stared down at it. "I really feel like he is hiding something else from us."

He sat back, while she quickly phoned Danny.

When Danny answered the phone, he was in a jovial mood. "Hey, Detective. I told you that I'm fine."

She put it on Speakerphone. "That's good to hear. I'm glad you're fine," she began. "Don't mind me if I continue to worry for a while."

He laughed. "If I had had people worrying about me originally, I might not have gotten into this situation."

"Maybe," she agreed. "However, the cop in me feels like you're still holding something back."

He sucked in his breath, and even Simon heard it. His eyebrows slowly raised, as he stared down at the phone, wondering what the hell had just shifted.

"Why would you say that?" Danny asked, his voice nervous.

So nervous that she looked over at Simon with a shrug, and he agreed with a nod. This did not sound good.

"Because I'm a cop," she repeated, with a groan. "As much as I would like to leave it alone, I can't. I'm pretty sure that whatever is bugging you in your mind, you have made it into a major issue, and it's traumatizing you. Therefore, left to fester, it'll either get you fired, get your ass kicked, or something worse," she stated, with a hard tone. "I'm here to tell you that there's a really good chance it won't impact you if you just talk about it. If it does impact you? … This is the time to get it out and to heal it," she muttered. "So, I really do need to know what it is that you're still hiding."

"Why?" he cried out. "It's just me. It's my stupidity. It doesn't mean anything."

"Which is also why it's important for you to lance that boil and to let it out, so it doesn't become more than it is."

Silence came on the other end. "Why? Are you a shrink now too?" he asked almost belligerently, but it was definitely an attempt to redirect her attention and to get her to back off.

Simon recognized the distraction tactics in the young man, but she had called Danny and hadn't told him that Simon was listening in. Thus he didn't really feel that he could jump in and say something now. Even if he could, what would he say? What could he say that would help the scenario and not piss off Kate too?

Kate sighed. "Look. I know it has to do with that scenario, and only two people were there, you and him. You've already told me that you basically went out, ready and happy to commit suicide, then panicked, came back to the shore. The Good Samaritan was seemingly trying to help you get back on the dock again. So, one question I didn't ask you before, and I'm asking you right now for a clear-cut answer. Did you know Dr. Burnett before the attempted suicide?"

Dead silence.

She looked over at Simon, and he stared right back and slowly nodded. That was the question she needed to ask.

"What difference does it make?" Danny asked cautiously.

"Maybe nothing. Did you or did you not?"

"Yes," he replied reluctantly. "I did."

"Okay, and how did you know him?"

He hesitated again, then said, "I attended a suicide watch group."

She sagged back and stared at Simon. "So, the doc was there?"

"He was the one running it," Danny shared. "Didn't you … Don't you people find out that stuff?"

"Sometimes. But other times it's fairly well disguised under your privacy rights," she noted.

Danny said, "I only went the one time, but it was enough. When I saw him down there by the water, he knew that I was looking to commit suicide at some point in my life. So, I think he also recognized exactly what I was doing, when I went in the water."

"So, when you went in the water, what did he really say to you?"

He hesitated once more. "I told you the truth about that. He kept apologizing, over and over. The things that he said made no sense to me."

"Okay, so what in all of this are you still hiding from me?"

"Nothing. I don't understand."

"Neither do I," she stated, "but something is still not clear."

"I don't know what else I can do to help you clear it up. I really don't want to go down to the station. I really don't want anybody to know what I did—talk about impacting my ability to get over this."

"I get it," Kate said. "That's *not* what I'm trying to do. I am trying to see if something untoward was in the doc's behavior. Did he … Did he want to help you commit suicide?"

First came dead silence on the other end, then a *click* as the phone went dead. She looked over at Simon and asked, "What do you think?"

"Dammit," he muttered, "that sounded very much like a yes to me."

She nodded. "Yeah, me too."

CHAPTER 20

FIRST THING THE next morning, as Kate walked into the front door of the Haven Center facility, the receptionist looked up, and a visible wince crossed her face, but she immediately dropped her gaze to the computer in front of her. As Kate approached, the receptionist pasted on a smile.

"I'm sorry, but the director isn't in right now."

"Where is he?"

The receptionist's expression turned cool and her tone even colder. "He called in sick this morning."

"Then presumably he's at home," Kate noted. "What about Dr. Burnett?"

She shook her head. "He's not here either."

"Good enough." Kate turned and walked through the double doors into the patient hallways.

"Wait," the receptionist called out, running behind her.

Kate turned to face her. "If the director isn't here, then you'd better get him on the phone for me, hadn't you?" With that, Kate turned and continued to walk down the hallway. The receptionist raced back to the front desk, but Kate didn't care. With her badge out and ready, she walked up to a couple nurses and asked to be directed to the room where Dr. Burnett's brother, Roger, was kept.

One of the nurses took note of Kate's badge and nodded. "Come this way." Kate was led down to a small wing at the far end of the building. At the second-to-last door, the nurse pointed out, "He took a bad turn yesterday."

Kate wondered how someone in a coma could have good versus bad days. Did they thrash about on bad days and not on good ones? Was it just a determination by a reading from some machine of his brain functions, his lungs, his heart, his BP? She had no idea, but she wouldn't ask the nurse that question. "And how is he now?" Kate asked her. As she spoke, she peered through the observation window, but it was hard to see very much. The patient faced the big glass windows and the garden outside.

"He's much better today, but you do understand he's nonverbal."

"Yes, I understand. Is he even conscious?"

"No, he's not and hasn't been for many, many years." The nurse looked at her and asked, "Why are you here?"

"Just something we're checking out," she muttered. She knew that was an unsatisfactory response, but she didn't have a better one. When the nurse hesitated, Kate looked at her. "How long have you worked here?"

"Since about two years after it opened," she replied, with a small smile.

"Have you seen any change in this man's condition?"

"Not really. At odd times there appeared to be improvements, but it always ended up being a false positive," she explained, as she turned her own gaze back to the window, revealing the shell of a man inside the room. "He's been in this condition the entire time. We do have several others much like him here."

"Of course," Kate noted. "That's essentially what this facility is known for, is it not?"

"Yes. It was built specifically for the patients who don't

have anywhere else to go. It takes a lot of money to provide this level of care. These patients are physically alive, so there is always a possibility of their coming back."

"Is that a big possibility?"

"I don't think so," she shared, her voice soft. "For a while there we wondered, as it seemed Roger might be coming out of it, and I know that Dr. Burnett was excited. But his brother didn't seem to make the progress that everybody thought he would."

"Was this lack of progress immediate, or did it take some time before it was obvious that it wouldn't happen?"

The nurse shrugged. "I don't really know what to say about that, as it was up to Roger's doctors. However, I believe the diagnosis was made a while ago." She hesitated, before asking, "Has something criminal happened?"

"I'm not sure yet," Kate replied in a noncommittal tone, as she stared at the man inside. "How old is he?"

"Oh my, he's got to be fifty-plus, maybe even sixty," she suggested. "He was the first patient in this facility."

"I understand that. I guess I'm curious as to why here."

"Are you asking why people choose to keep them alive? Why they continue with life support for a decade or more? Each case is different, of course, but they technically are alive, and to remove their support is for many like committing murder. All easier said than done, Detective."

"Right."

"There are definitely patients who come back from these types of comas, but that's not been the outcome in Roger's case."

"Has the medication been changed at all in the last many years?"

"Oh, definitely," she stated, nodding in vigor. "He is Dr.

Burnett's patient, and he exclusively looks after him. It's wonderful to see that much care and attention," she said warmly. "We don't always see that. Sometimes doctors become almost numb to these patients." She hesitated and then added, "It's almost as if they … They turn off in a way and become almost neutral to the whole thing."

"Understood," Kate replied. "And what about Dr. Burnett?"

"Oh, he's very attentive, all the time," she declared, with a bright smile. "He's a really good man."

"I'm glad to hear that." Then Kate faced the nurse. "Now, if you don't mind me asking, have you ever had any suspicions working here? Any problems?"

"No, not at all. Of course not." She seemed shocked at the question.

"You haven't seen anything strange or different in Roger's medications or anything else he's given?"

"Nope, nothing." She frowned. "I don't understand what's going on here. Do I need to call someone down for you?"

"It's nothing at this point, and everything's all right," Kate stated, shoving her fists into her pockets. "I'm just investigating a case, and I need to address a few concerns that have come up."

"I can't imagine it would have anything to do with this place or Dr. Burnett," she replied vehemently. "The man devotes his entire life to his brother."

Kate nodded. "So, you're totally on board with the decisions and delivery regarding his care, correct?"

"Oh, absolutely," she stated. "It's a little different from the other patients here but not that much different."

"How so?"

"Dr. Burnett may prescribe a few more things to try and bring him back out of the coma, that's all. The other patients, the doctors tend to just leave them be. But Dr. Burnett, he's a doctor, and he's the brother, so he has full control over Roger's treatment, so it makes sense that he would continue to try."

"But nothing has worked yet?"

"No, nothing. In fact"—her voice dropped—"I wondered a time or two if maybe it wasn't making him worse." The nurse shook her head, as if it were a ridiculous thought.

"That would be difficult too, I presume," Kate murmured, once again eyeing the man in the bed.

"We don't know what these treatments will do individually, but occasionally you have to wonder if it's worth it."

"That's my question too, of course," Kate agreed, "but I'm not in the position of having a family member like this."

"There are definitely cases all over the world, where the patients are alive but asleep. And that has its own problems. There's a huge financial cost, but the doctor handles all that himself, for Roger."

"I heard that he was also instrumental, or his family was instrumental, in setting up this center. Is that your understanding?"

"Yes, it was all developed after Roger's accident," she confirmed, with a nod. "Of course that's what I've been told."

"Is there anybody here from back then?" Kate asked, looking at her.

"Yes, Alice." Then she stopped and thought for a moment. "She's worked here since the beginning, or at least very early on, I think. Her grandson is also a patient here."

"At least she knows that he's getting the best care possible, and he's close by so she can look after him," Kate noted. "I don't suppose that she's around or that I could talk to her?"

"I think she may be. I saw her not very long ago. Let me go see."

And she walked off, her pace steady and calm, nothing hurried or upset in any way, which was what Kate wanted to see. At the same time, she couldn't understand why she felt this need to push, why the need to have this drag out, but something niggled at her.

Something seemed to be so well hidden that nothing would break it loose. As she stood here and studied the man, all she could really see were wisps of light-colored hair and a prone body, nothing suspicious, nothing unusual, which didn't help her one bit.

Then she stepped inside the room, nearing the patient. She didn't really see the familial connection, as Roger had aged in an unhealthy way, under his circumstances. However, she noted the earplugs in his ears, leading to an old-fashioned cassette player. She removed them to listen for herself for just a moment or two.

And heard the doctor's cruel words recorded for his brother, blaming him for their sister's death. The same accusations were repeated over and over, including how he had raped their sister for many years.

Kate pocketed the device and stepped back outside into the hallway.

WALKING BETWEEN JOBSITES, Simon suddenly coughed, then got that feeling of drowning again. He quickly slipped into an alley and sank against a wall, trying to breathe and to keep calm. It was such a horrible feeling, and it was hard not to panic. Worse though was he felt drawn into the scene, aware of the cold water, the heaviness of his clothes, as he fought to stay afloat. More than that was the certainly that something was terribly wrong. Trying to cling to reality by focusing on the memory of Kate coaching him through a similar episode, he pictured Kate's face, the feeling of her hand on his shoulder, and her voice in the background.

Then her voice was gone, replaced by a call for help, over and over.

CHAPTER 21

K ATE SCHOOLED HER expression, as she noted the nurse returning to her.

When the nurse reached Kate, she smiled. "Alice is here, if you want to talk to her."

Kate nodded. "Yes. Let me follow up, so I can cross whatever *T*s need to be crossed, and I can put this to rest."

"It really is a good place," the nurse offered. "I know you have a job to do, but so do we. Obviously we want people not to be distressed to the extent possible. Anybody who is here visiting is here because a family member is in a heartbreaking medical condition, which is inherently upsetting in itself, no matter how long it's been."

"I understand," Kate replied, "and I can't begin to imagine how hard this must be on the family."

"Neither can I," the nurse shared, "and I'm immersed in it every day. It's bad enough when you have any event that affects your family, but when it's on a ... I don't want to say *permanent basis,* but, when it's something like this, it's just got to be devastating."

When Kate walked into another patient room, the woman seated inside beside the hospital bed looked up and smiled at her. The nurse introduced them. "Alice, this is Detective Morgan."

Alice nodded and motioned to the chair beside her.

Settling into the chair as invited, Kate began, "Hi, please call me Kate, and thank you for agreeing to see me."

"So, you wanted to know more about the history here?"

"Yes, that would be very helpful."

Alice nodded. "I did start work here way back when, at the time this facility started," she stated, with a soft chuckle. "It's hard to imagine it was all so long ago."

"Which is one of the reasons it's been hard to get some clarity about it."

"It was such a different time. Back then, certainly there were rules and regulations, but nothing like now, nothing like the headaches they have now, dealing with authorities and various agencies and HIPAA requirements and other legislation," she shared, with an eyeroll.

Kate looked over at the young man in the bed. "The nurse told me this is your grandson."

"Yes," Alice whispered. "He was in a bad accident and never really came out of his coma. So, I knew where he needed to be, and I arranged to get him here. I still work here part-time and do the best I can, but I'm definitely at retirement age. Frankly the expense involved in the care required for my grandson is overwhelming and another whole ball of wax," she muttered, worry in her tone.

"Is that going to change? Do you not have lifetime access for his care?"

She shook her head. "No, I don't. … I wish I did, and I've certainly been fighting for it, but somebody still has to pay the bills." At that point, the tears started to creep into Alice's eyes.

Kate winced.

"Yes, it's a worry," Alice noted in a casual and apologetic tone.

"What would happen if he can't stay here?"

"I presume he would be moved to a government facility," she shared. "And those aren't anywhere near as nice as this one."

"But are they bad?" Kate asked. "I'm sorry to ask, but I don't really have a point of reference."

"They're not bad necessarily, but, like anything, there's a range, and it depends on the management and the staff to a large degree. When you're in a place like this, the care is much more personal, so the family members have peace of mind, knowing their loved one is well cared for. The management and staff in a nicer facility like this tend to stay, so family can develop confidence and trust on a more personal level. But, if my grandson can't stay here, that will be a different story. The next facility will be farther away, so I won't visit nearly as often, and I won't know anyone there, much less what's going on."

"Of course. What about the rest of his family?"

Alice winced. "They were killed in the same accident."

"Oh my," Kate replied. "I am so sorry."

She looked over at her and nodded. "Me too."

"And yet I guess it's not something you can just let go of, is it?"

"No, it sure isn't," she muttered, as she stared down at him.

Yet something was off in Alice's tone. Kate faced her and asked, "So, what is it that you aren't telling me?"

She looked at her in horror. "What do you mean?"

"Something is going on here, and I don't understand it."

"Nothing," she said. "Nothing's going on, Detective."

But Kate wasn't so sure. She heard a noise and looked back at the door. There stood the director, frowning at her.

She smiled and nodded at him. "Just visiting with Alice here," she noted.

Alice turned, visibly jumping when she saw the director.

Kate stood and spoke to Alice. "Thank you for the company. Now I'll leave you all to get on with your day." She noted that the director stayed behind, presumably to grill Alice.

As Kate returned to the front desk, she asked the receptionist, "I need the full names for Alice and Alice's grandson, please."

The woman looked at her hesitantly.

Kate shrugged and added, "We can go the more difficult route, if you want. The names are public records," she noted, "so there really shouldn't be any problem with giving me that information."

The woman quickly looked around, then wrote down both names on a scrap of paper and slid it over to her.

Kate asked, "Any particular reason why you're so scared?"

"No, not at all," she hissed, adding, "I need my job."

"Got it," Kate said. "I haven't done anything to make you lose it, if that makes you feel any better."

"No, but me helping you could." And with that, the woman got up and walked Kate to the main entrance.

As soon as she was outside, Kate could have sworn that the woman locked the door behind her. But that wouldn't be possible, would it? Surely the Haven Center was open to the public. But then again, it was privately run, so maybe not.

Pondering that, she got back to her office, snagged Reese, and said, "Hey, I need some information." Then she quickly handed over both names. "First, see if you find a rape report by the twin sister before her death—or maybe some counselor or psychologist or psychiatrist or whatever that the family may have seen."

"Oh no," Reese muttered.

"*Yeah*," Kate replied. "Then there is another family to investigate. I met the grandmother, who also works at the clinic, and her grandson lives there. Apparently he was in a bad accident and I didn't get the date, as the director interrupted us. Anyway, the grandson never woke up from a coma. The rest of his family was killed in the same accident, supposedly."

"Oh, my God. What exactly do you need?"

"I want details about his accident, a copy of the police report, anything you can find, and a full history on the grandmother. She may well have been at this center since it opened."

"That's a long time."

"It is, and I know that I don't really have any answers, but mark my words. … Something is off about that place."

Reese looked at her and nodded. "If there is, we'll find it. I'll start digging now, but give me some time."

Ignoring the request for time, Kate followed the analyst to her computer. "How do they make their money? How does that place operate?"

"I would think some of the families pay a pro-rata portion of the bills for their family members, while the rich families pay it all. To help pay the bills with that presumed shortfall, often there are government grants, and, from what I've seen in the very few minutes you've given me, … private funding."

"But if all the patients are in a coma, with a need for constant care, what on earth does the Haven do to keep the money rolling in?" she muttered.

Reese nodded, turning to Kate. "The fees for places like that are astronomical. We're not talking a few thousand a month. We're easily talking tens of thousands each month and more, depending on the level of care needed."

Kate stared at her. "Good God."

"I know, right? It really is a place for the rich."

"Then I can't understand how someone like Alice can afford it. She doesn't strike me as wealthy."

"If she has been working there for decades, they may have made a deal with her because she was obviously a loyal employee, like her retirement benefits include paying for her grandson's care or something. That's not unheard of."

"Sure, but if they are at full capacity, having her grandson in that room could impact their potential bottom line."

"Maybe that's part of the problem," Reese suggested. "Let me look into that angle, and Kate? No offense, but I'll be a lot more effective if you give me some room."

Knowing she was right, Kate went back to her desk. As it was, Rodney was looking for some help. Kate sat down and spent the next hour working on his cases, helping him sort through another gang-related drive-by shooting. By the time she had gone through the traffic cams with him, they had found a vehicle, ran it through the DMV, and, sure enough, came up with a name and a face that matched the witnesses' description.

Rodney hopped up and said, "I'll go double-check to confirm we got the right visual here." He stopped, looked back at her, and asked, "You coming?"

"No, I'm waiting for Reese, unless you need me," she replied. "With any luck, I can get mine sorted out today too."

He raised an eyebrow and asked, "You need a hand?"

"No, go deal with your drive-by. I've got this."

He laughed. "If you say so."

"I do."

She watched as he headed out. Just as she was about to check her emails, she looked up to see Reese walking toward her, with files in her hands. "Well? What did you find?"

"I have good news and bad. Nothing on the supposed rape in the Burnett family, but that doesn't really surprise me with those attacks not always being reported to the authorities. Something interesting came up for the other family in question. Apparently her grandson was the driver of the vehicle, the only one who survived."

"Jeez, so he was what, sixteen, eighteen at the time?"

"Twenty-one, and the witnesses said he was frequently fighting with other members of the family, and there was a lot of distress among the entire clan."

"Okay, and that's important why?"

The analyst looked up and tilted her head. "There were suspicions that he deliberately ran the vehicle off the road, killing everybody but himself."

"In an attempt to kill them all, himself included?" Kate asked.

She nodded. "That's what it looks like, but he didn't succeed in taking his own life. But he did manage to wipe out the rest of the family."

"So, does Alice have anybody else left in the family?"

"No, she only had the one child, who was killed in the accident. She lost her sister a couple decades ago, and her parents and her husband have been gone for many years."

"So, she's alone in the world."

"She is, except for this grandson."

Kate stared at her for a long moment. "What lengths do

people go to in order to keep family close?"

She stared at her and shrugged. "The reality is, if the grandson wasn't in the situation that he's in, he would be in prison. If he was awake and cognizant, I mean."

"Right," Kate muttered, with a slow nod. "So, here's a really ugly thought."

"What's that?" Colby walked in at that moment.

She quickly brought him up-to-date on the case.

"So, what's the ugly thought?" he asked.

She grimaced. "What if these people are kept there in that facility on purpose? What if they've done something in this world that they should have gone to jail for or could otherwise be held responsible for, and they're being held in this comatose condition against their will?"

Silence. Both Reese and Colby stared at her in shock.

Kate shrugged. "I know. I know. Conspiracy theories all over the place."

"Why would you even think of something like that?" Colby asked in a harsh tone.

"That other family, with Alice, the grandmother, who has worked there at the Haven Center all this time. She seemed afraid, like really afraid. The receptionist was downright jumpy too. Dr. Burnett is the sole caregiver for his brother, and he is a mess. The director is a strange duck. It just seems that everybody involved with the center seems to be nervous as hell." Then she pulled the tape recorder from her pocket. "Plus, there is this." She handed it to Colby, who was already pressing Play so they could all listen.

When it was done, Kate turned to Reese. "Can we get a full rundown on every patient in that place, and let's see what we can track back as to how they ended up there?"

"I'm on it."

Colby motioned for her to come into his office. "I'm okay with thinking we might have Dr. Burnett out there potentially trying to kill people in his suicide group," he acknowledged, "but now you're suggesting that he's been keeping his brother comatose for decades against his will? And other families are doing this as well?"

"I don't know that it's possible for his brother to ever recover from his initial injury," she admitted, point-blank. "I don't know if there was ever a time when Roger would have been able to recover, and there's no time for speculation on this one either. I guess I'm questioning who these patients are at the Haven Center, why they are there, how they came to get there, and whether they are being held there or otherwise put in this position. Potentially, at this stage of their life, they are comatose, not capable of having a full life any longer because of what's been done to them. Some of these people have been there for decades. But what if they weren't comatose before they got to the Haven? What if *becoming* comatose is *the* medical regimen at the Haven? What if these predominantly rich families are protecting their name and their other family members by having the black sheep of the family drugged into a coma somewhere out of sight?"

"Okay, in theory, I can see that happening ... somewhere. Can you prove this at Haven Center? But let's get back to the primary family of interest. What possible motive would Dr. Burnett have for doing that to his brother?" Colby asked incredulously, looking at her. "I expect this shit in a movie or something, but this is not a movie."

She stared at him, but a growing conviction filled her. "I hear you. I suggest you listen to the tape further. I just don't like anything about what I'm seeing or hearing."

"Yeah, but what you're not seeing are facts," he reminded her, rapping his hands on the table. "We have no proof, nothing here but crazy supposition that something's going on."

"I know. Let's see what Reese comes up with," she replied, "and then, if it's nothing, I'll drop it."

He frowned, as he considered that.

Kate added, "Look. I know we have other cases. I just spent an hour helping Rodney screen some video footage. He's gone out to double-check with eyewitnesses that we have the right guy. So that's a huge break in his case. Lilliana parked hers yesterday, and tonight we'll probably end up with a dozen more murders," she noted, "but we're close here. I know it. Let me see this through to the conclusion."

"I'm afraid there isn't a conclusion for you on this one," Colby declared. "I probably shouldn't have asked you to take a look into this as it was."

"And yet you did, and I have, and what I'm turning up feels problematic."

"That's more like a housing thing," he suggested, "something for human services or maybe the medical board. It's got nothing to do with murder or drownings."

"Doesn't it?" she asked, with half a smile. "I suspect we'll soon find out that it's all related."

He shrugged. "You can suspect it all you want, but I need proof. If you find it, I'll buy into this craziness with you. However, in the meantime, it looks like you're casting your net wider and wider, broadening your theories, trying to make something stick."

She nodded and stood. "Wrap it up or shut it down. Got it." And, with that, she quickly escaped, before he ordered her off the case.

She walked in on the analyst, who looked at her and muttered, "I figured you would be right back here."

"Yeah, well, the sergeant wanted an update. He doesn't want me doing this, doesn't think I've got anything to go on, that I'm just creating issues where there aren't any, desperately hoping to paste something together."

"That is kind of you though, isn't it?" Reese noted. "With your woo-woo cases, it seems to be a baked-in approach."

Kate groaned. "Keep me posted. I'm on borrowed time."

"Got it," she said, with a smile.

With a wave and a nod, Kate returned to the bullpen, just as her phone rang. She looked down at her screen. It was Simon.

"You got a minute?" His voice sounded dark.

"Yeah, what's up?"

"It's Danny."

"What about him?"

"He tried to commit suicide again."

She swore. "Is he … Did he … die?"

"No, he's in the hospital. I'm with him, and he's currently bawling his eyes out about not having told you the truth. I need you to come down here."

"I'm on my way." As she ended the call, Reese approached her. Kate explained, "I'm headed to the hospital. Text me anything you find, even if it doesn't make sense."

"What happened?" Reese asked.

"It's Danny. He's alive for now. I'll get the details as soon as I get down there."

"Jeez," Reese muttered. "Too much going on here for a case that isn't even a case."

"Exactly, but I highly suspect it's all related."

SIMON SAT ON the edge of the bed and stared down at Danny.

He opened his eyes. Tears filled the strapping young man's gaze, and he whispered, "I fucked up."

Simon grabbed his hand and nodded. "And now you need to tell us how, … so that we can help you to fix it."

"Crap," Danny muttered. "I don't even know if it's possible now."

"So, talk to me."

"It's the doctor."

"What about him?"

"I've been going to these individual sessions with him, apart from his group meetings, … where he tries to work out why we're feeling suicidal, what it is that we hate about our lives and all that."

"And?"

"I think it's more than just me. I think a person or two in these groups, who have made the decision that suicide is the best answer, they're looking for permission, more or less, or maybe even the doc's help to make it happen," he shared. Then Danny blinked away the tears and stared off in the distance. "I suppose I should be telling the detective this."

"Oh, you will be," Simon stated. "Kate's on her way."

Danny closed his eyes and whispered, "I should have told her all this in the first place."

"Yeah, you should have, and I still don't quite understand why you didn't."

He looked at him, and such shame and pain filled his gaze that Simon sighed, squeezed his shoulder, and added, "Look. I don't know why you feel that there is nothing of value in your life or that this is the only answer you have.

But it's not, Danny. It isn't. You are a good person, and you were doing really well at work."

"Yeah, *right*," he snapped in a harsh tone.

Just then Kate strode in, her frown front and center, as she glared at the pair of them. "What the hell, Danny?"

Danny visibly winced when she snapped at him. He started to bawl again, and Simon whispered to Kate, "Hey, hey, easy." She turned and glared at him. Simon shook his head. "He was trying to talk about the doctor."

Her eyebrows shot up. Then she turned to Danny. "Talk to me," she barked.

After a few more big sobs, he took a deep breath, then calmed down enough that he could look at her. "You're going to hate me. I know it."

"I could never hate you," she declared, as she walked closer to his bedside, "but I sure as hell can't help you if you keep holding back information."

"I told you about the suicide group."

"Yes, you did. … And?"

He moistened his lips several times. "I've seen him since, in private sessions."

"Got it," she said, with a nod. "Why, though? What is it that you think he can help you with?"

Danny shook his head. "You don't know anything about me."

"No, I don't. I don't know a lot about your history. Do I need to?"

He shrugged. "I … I killed my brother," he muttered, "and my world's never been the same since."

"That would have been helpful to know ahead of time," she murmured, as she stared at him. "How did it happen?"

"I was driving the car. I had to pick him up late from

work, and I'd already … I had worked the night shift at the hardware store, stocking shelves. I was tired, exhausted really, because I'd been going to school during the day and working at night. He was working at the hamburger joint down the road. I had to go pick him up, but, on the way back, I made a poor decision while driving. I was just so tired," he cried out in sorrow. "Anyway, we got into an accident, and my brother died."

"So, that's why suicide looks like an answer for you?" she asked him.

"Yes. … I haven't told very many people about my brother."

"But you told Dr. Burnett?"

"Yes, and he told me …" Danny stopped, as if he was unsure how to put what he wanted to say.

Kate prodded him. "He told you what? Come on, Danny. Look at me." He was obviously trying to look anywhere but at her. "What did he tell you?"

Danny looked over at Simon miserably.

"Go on, Danny," Simon urged him softly. "Just get it out."

His chin trembling, he took a big breath. "He mentioned that maybe … I might … I would be happier dead," he whispered. "He told me that maybe then I would be at peace."

She frowned at him. "Is that what this is all about? So, that's why you tried to drown yourself earlier? Was Dr. Burnett there ahead of time?"

"I told him that I was going to do it, and he told me, by telling him, that meant I wasn't serious, that I wasn't … that I was looking for an easy out, that I wasn't ready for the change that I said I wanted."

"Which is quite true," she noted, "like a call for help, but it would have been much nicer if the doc had done something to try and get you the help you needed instead."

"Yeah, but I don't need help," Danny wailed. "There is no help to be had. My parents basically disowned me, and I don't have anything to do with them. My brother and I were close, really close, but after he, after the … I just can't come to terms with it."

"Was the accident ruled to be your fault?"

"The official cause was deemed poor road conditions. I got off, mostly because I didn't have any accidents or anything on my record. The roads were terrible, and there was a bit of a washout. I hit it and went into a skid. Anyway, I ended up wrapping around a pole, and my brother died," he admitted, openly crying.

She picked up his hand and nodded. "Then the guilt sent you into this spiral."

He nodded. "It's just such a horrible feeling."

Simon understood what he was saying and knew it was quite a normal reaction. He added, "But now that you've finally told somebody, you should start to heal."

He shook his head. "I told Dr. Burnett, but I didn't feel like I was healing at all." He shook his head. "Honest to God, it's almost as if he was intentionally trying to make me feel bad about it, like pushing me in that direction. As if he wanted me to do it."

"Any idea why?"

"No, but he seems fascinated with drowning though. He mentions it a lot in the groups."

"His sister drowned when he was a child," she shared.

Danny looked at her. "Seriously?"

She nodded. "Yeah, she did. So, he's quite fixated with

drowning."

"He told me that it was easy, that it was calm and quiet, that it was an easy way to die."

"As you know for yourself, that was a lie. It's not easy at all," she pointed out. "You get out there, and your natural instinct for survival takes over, and you fight for your life. Your lungs are burning for oxygen. You go under the water. You panic. You try hard to get up to the surface. Your mouth fills with water. You go back under again." She asked, "What's easy about that?"

Danny just stared at her, his jaw open.

Simon winced at her no-nonsense approach to everything. After experiencing the sensation of drowning through his visions, he was shocked at her insensitive description. He admired Kate in many ways, but then, at times like this, he wished she would stop and think first. In this instance, he felt the need to interject. "I don't think killing yourself is easy at any time, and it would be much nicer if you could find a reason to live and to do something to honor your brother's life, instead of it destroying your own. I don't think that's what he would want for you, is it?"

"No, God no," Danny wailed. "He was always so full of life and so damn responsible. But, when something like this happens, … all you want to do is turn back the clock, so you don't have to deal with it."

"Oh, I get that," Kate agreed, with a nod, "but turning back the clock isn't something we can do."

"I know," he cried out. "Believe me. I know."

"So, what happened that you ended up trying this again?"

"I was talking to Dr. Burnett and told him that I really didn't feel suicidal anymore, how I was feeling so much better—had a job and a chance to pick myself up and do something. But, as we talked, all that guilt came flooding back somehow, and I just—" He groaned. "All the sudden I needed it to just be over. I needed to end my misery and to find a way to … finally be forgiven and find salvation."

"And this came about in the conversation with Dr. Burnett?"

He nodded. "Yes."

"Did he drive you down there?"

"No, I went on my own."

"But you told him that you were going?"

"Yes."

"And Dr. Burnett didn't do anything to stop you?"

"No, but then he also knew that was what I wanted."

"Is it really what you wanted, though?" she asked. "Or would you rather embrace a scenario where you could look back on your younger years, see the pain and trauma you experienced, recognize that you survived and went on to honor the memory of your brother—through living a full and enriching life that included a good measure of service to others?"

He just stared at her and nodded. "Yeah, I would love that." He nodded, but his gaze was filled with misery too. "But getting there? That doesn't happen easily."

"No, but that's why we also have people around us to help," she shared. "Obviously you haven't had the right support around you to help process your grief, and Dr. Burnett took advantage of that and has been intentionally pushing you toward suicide."

"And yet I didn't feel like he was pushing me."

"That is his talent," she muttered.

"But why would he do that?" Simon asked, looking over

at her.

"It's got to be all messed up with his brother, who's still alive but seemingly comatose in a long-term care facility," she explained. "I don't really understand, but he's got a fascination with death. He's got a fascination with suicide, with drowning, and that state in-between."

"Which is pretty foolish," Simon admitted.

"Do you know anybody else in that group?" Kate asked Danny.

"I don't really know them. A few people are there though, some older, some younger."

On impulse, she pulled out her phone and brought up a few images. "What about this person?"

He looked at the photo and nodded. "Yeah, she was there."

With a sinking feeling, Simon watched as Kate pulled up several more, and Danny nodded each time.

"Yeah, they were there. Definitely. All of them."

She turned to look at Simon, her face hard. "Will you stay here and look after him?"

"I'll get him set up with a full-time nurse. ... I have work to do, as he knows," Simon added. "But I don't want him going back out on his own, not until he's got some help." With that said, Simon gave Danny a pointed look.

"I think the doctor can hold him, until adequate professional help is assigned and in place," Kate shared, turning to look down the hallway behind her. "But that is something you'll need to check into. I don't have any personal experience with this."

Simon nodded. "You go on ahead. I'll take care of it." She hesitated, and he waved her out. "Go. It's fine."

"Is it though?" She turned and looked at Danny. "I

don't want you to have any contact with Dr. Burnett from here on out. Do you hear me? Not *any*."

Danny nodded sheepishly.

Kate frowned. "How did you get pulled out? Like how did you end up okay this time? Obviously you're not dead. So, what happened?"

He hesitated, then turned and looked at Simon. She frowned at Simon, who just stared back at her, shaking his head. She closed her eyes and winced, as if silently cussing herself. "I'm sorry. That was insensitive. We can discuss it another time." She told Danny point-blank, "Simon can't be around to rescue you every time. You understand that, don't you? One of these times, you will succeed and will end up dead."

Danny started to sob. "I don't want to die."

"And that's why I don't want you to have any contact with Dr. Burnett. Not until I figure out what the hell is going on with him." And, with that, she turned and stormed out.

She got into her vehicle and phoned the care center, looking for Dr. Burnett.

"He's not here," the receptionist replied in a prim voice.

"If I come back out there and find that he's there and that you're hiding him, I will be very pissed," she snapped. "I need to be informed the minute you see him. Do you understand me? I hope you do because it'll be you being raked over the coals as to why you're protecting him."

"Look. I'm under strict orders," the woman cried out. "I've got a job to do, and I answer to a boss. We're just hired employees. I can't afford to lose my job."

"Why is your facility protecting him?"

After a moment of silence, a different voice came on the

line. "This is the director. Is this Detective Morgan?"

"Yes, it is," Kate replied in a calm voice.

"Why are you hounding us?"

"For a lot of reasons, but this is just a warm-up, so be sure to keep it in mind. Where is Dr. Burnett?"

"I have no idea," he snapped. "Probably at his job? He has one of those. Remember?"

"Yes, he does, at least for the moment," she stated venomously. With that, she disconnected, then quickly placed a call to his office. Sure enough, the doctor had been there this morning but had left soon afterward.

"He's still not feeling well."

"I'm sorry to hear that," Kate replied. "So, is he likely to be at home?"

"Yes, I would think so."

Kate phoned his home, but she got no answer at his house. Making a quick decision, she started the engine and headed to his address. She pulled into his driveway, then walked up to the front door and knocked. No answer. She called through the windows and doors, all locked, but nobody replied.

One of the neighbors popped out and said, "The doctor just left a little bit before you arrived."

"Of course he did," she muttered, under her breath. "By any chance, did you see where he was going, or did he say anything to you?"

"He told me that he was just going down to the harbor, that he had some deep thinking to do."

She stared at the woman in shock, then nodded quickly. "Thank you." Then she bolted to her vehicle.

SIMON EXITED THE hospital. He stood outside in the parking lot, taking several deep breaths. Danny would be okay now, but he needed serious counseling, and that would be a long road to recovery that wouldn't be easy for him. Simon felt both traumatized for the young man and pissed at himself because he hadn't seen that there was more to be done.

As he took more deep breaths, that same voice broke through his mind again. It had been happening more and more frequently.

Answers, I need answers.

"Sure, you need answers. Don't we all?"

She needs real answers, and she's determined to find them.

He hesitated and repeated, "She?" He had no idea who this *she* was that the voice in his head was referring to.

Yeah, she. *I can sense her, feel her. She's causing stress, causing my brother distress.*

"I'm sorry."

I'm not. Any distress is … Anything that hurts him is good.

"What?" Simon stopped, confused, trying to figure out who was talking to him, who was in his head.

Then the voice in his head laughed. *God, you're slow.*

"I'm not slow."

Yes, you are. The voice was getting stronger as time went on, and then he laughed again. *Of course I've got nothing better to do than talk to you, especially now that I know I can talk to somebody out there. Do you know what it's like to be isolated, as I have been all these years?"*

Simon hesitated, then took a deep breath and went for it. "Are you Roger Burnett? Dr. Burnett's brother?"

Yes, I am, he replied in delight. *Thank God, somebody finally connected the dots.*

"It depends on how many dots need connecting," he replied cautiously, as he looked around.

Oh, more dots than you could make or could really and truly understand. He laughed. *Nobody ever really knows what goes on inside people, do they?*

"No, they don't. What happened to you?"

Oh, it's not what happened to me that's important, but what happened to me since then, he stated, with a sneer in his tone.

"I don't understand."

I know you don't. You could come visit me though, he added, with a cheerfulness. *But be careful. If anyone thought we were communicating, you can bet my life would change, and not in a good way.*

"I don't even know that we are communicating," he muttered, sure that he was caught up in some sort of weird vision, yet the parking lot around him looked to be normal and real.

The voice in his head laughed. *Maybe, but you'll be shocked when you hear the truth.*

"How about giving me a little nugget of the truth, so I can get there faster."

Oh, that's okay. I think it's finally happening now. This cop's been stirring up trouble around here, he stated, with a hard laugh. *So maybe finally my brother will get what's coming to him.*

"Did you get what was coming to you?"

If you only knew.

"Tell me then. Maybe I can help."

A harsh gasp came from the other end, and then the voice disappeared from his mind, not just the voice but the feeling of his presence.

"Holy shit, what the hell is happening?" Simon leaned over his car, his head in his hands, considering this completely bizarre conversation in his head. Was he making it up? He didn't believe that, though anybody would think that was exactly what he was doing. When he got a phone call from Kate moments later, he answered it, but he was still confused and disoriented.

"Are you okay?" she asked.

"I will be, yes. Just rattled. What's going on? What's the urgency that you're up to?"

"I'm heading down to the marina. I don't know that I'm in the right place, and God help me, I hope I am, but that's where Burnett is headed."

"Okay, and that's a problem, why?"

"Because I think he's off to commit suicide."

"Jeez, do you think so?" He turned and looked around. "I'm still outside the hospital right now."

"Will Danny be okay?"

"He will be. He's agreed to go forward with some serious long-term counseling. I told him that I would have his job waiting for him, once he gets out and is ready."

"I would be a little worried about him, working for you."

"That's my problem," he said smoothly. "Once he's got his head on straight, it'll be okay."

"I hope so," she muttered. "Believe me. Right now I have a whole lot on my mind."

"Do you have any idea what's going on yet?"

"Lots, but nothing that makes sense."

"Here's more to add to your *doesn't make sense* BS," he said, as he told her about the strange conversation he just had, supposedly with Roger.

"In your head? Right now?" she cried out in shock.

"Yes, but I don't know if it was a memory or if it was from another time or what. I don't know. It's been happening for a while, a voice asking for help, for answers. This is the first time it was an actual two-way conversation, where he confirmed he was Roger Burnett."

"Jeez, you spoke to Roger?"

"I know. I know. I'm pretty damn sure … I was just talking to Dr. Burnett's brother. It had to be Roger, and he did admit that much. He said you were figuring it out. Then he was gone."

"Yeah," she muttered. "Really gone. Somebody may have pulled his plug. I'll send a uniform over there, but I have to get to the doc, before he does something stupid—something *else* that's stupid." There was shock in her voice, and he heard her driving into traffic, as she headed toward the marina.

Simon needed to go in that direction as well. For whatever reason, he was supposed to be there at the end of this. Whatever this was. "I'm on my way."

"Why?"

Such an odd note filled her tone that he wondered just what she was up to. "Are you okay?"

"Yeah, I'm just not at all sure what to think though."

"Of course not, and I know it doesn't make you feel any better, but neither do I."

"If you are now talking to comatose patients, I would probably think that you had, you know, finally crossed that line."

"I probably *have* finally crossed that line," he noted, with some amusement, "but not so anybody would notice."

"God, if anybody even overheard these conversations of

ours ..."

"I know, but it's me, the reluctant psychic. Remember?"

"I know. I know," she muttered.

He heard the engine change gears, as she shifted and moved through traffic. "I'm heading your way. I should be there in five." He got in his vehicle and headed toward the marina. Why was Dr. Burnett so consumed with suicides? He was a doctor after all. The part where he was trying to help people was one thing, but, if there was any sign of his assisting these people to commit suicide, that was a different story. Maybe Dr. Burnett was contemplating his own suicide and couldn't find the gumption to do it. Simon surely hoped not.

There was something almost pathetic about the doctor, and Simon didn't want him to be the bad guy. Yet it was probably already too late for that. And what little that Roger had said to Simon supported that theory. Jeez, was he taking advice from voices now? Maybe he was the pathetic one.

As Kate would say, it was no time to get soft now. It was just that sometimes Kate didn't see the whole picture, and neither did he for that matter, though not through any intent on their own. Often he was given insights that had absolutely nothing to do with what anybody else could see, and he was very worried that was exactly what he was looking at right now.

<h1 style="text-align:center">CHAPTER 22</h1>

K ATE PULLED INTO the parking lot, looking for an empty space, her gaze already searching the water more than the parking lot.

When her phone rang and Reese's name flashed on her screen, she asked, "What's up?"

"Several of the patients there were in horrific accidents," she began, "but, from just the four cases that I've managed to find so far, there is definitely an unsettling assumption here."

"Yeah, tell me about it," Kate muttered, knowing what was to come. "Tell me that every one of those four victims you're looking at now were involved in accidents where they hurt or inflicted pain on somebody else, potentially with criminal charges involved."

There was silence on the other end. "How do you know that? Is it because of Simon?"

"What?" she asked.

"Those insights," Reese said, "because, damn, you're right on. In one case we've got a woman who took a handgun and shot her entire family and then turned the gun on herself but didn't manage to finish the job."

"Right. So, another one of *those* cases," Kate muttered. "Can you go back over the last few drownings—*before* the ones that we recently saw—and check in every case to see if any of these victims were in a suicide group with Dr.

Burnett."

"But they weren't sui—Oh God."

"Yeah, can you just do that for me?"

"Yeah, will do, will do. I'm on it."

With that, she ended the call, parked, and walked quickly toward the water. She searched everywhere for any sign of Dr. Burnett. So far she couldn't see him. She was counting on his being here, but there were so many places where he could go around the city, and she had no way to pinpoint his location. She was just going by instincts, something cops had relied on since the beginning of time, and she wouldn't allow people to assume she was operating on anything but.

She walked quickly, heading to where the boats were tied up, even went as far as where the *Running Mate* was berthed. She smiled as she walked past and then turned to see if there was any sign of the doc. There were places in between all the boats, places where he could walk, places where she wouldn't see him. There were all kinds of options, if someone wanted to hide down here. She was beginning to realize just how hard it would be to find Dr. Burnett if he didn't want to be found.

Then she caught sight of Simon racing to her. She raised her hands in frustration and said, "I have no idea where he is. He may not even be here."

"He's here," Simon declared, with a quiet conviction. She frowned at him, and he shrugged. "I can feel it. I can feel him."

"Great," she muttered. "Just don't say that out loud."

He gave her a wry look. "That's the least of our worries right now."

"I know," she muttered.

With him at her side, they both searched the area for the

doctor. Ten minutes later, Reese called back. Kate answered, her voice frazzled and frustrated.

"No sign of him?" Reese asked.

"No, no sign of him so far."

"I think you need to find him a whole lot faster."

"That's nice," Kate snapped. "Send out an alert for me, will you? We're looking for him near all waterways, beaches, parks, ponds, anything. What did you find?"

"He's been operating that suicide watch group at that center for many years, and I mean a lot of years now. Apparently, for some people, it's been very good and, for others, not so much. Some people seem to degrade, if that's a term in this case, and several others have ended up committing suicide."

"It's never an easy thing to work with suicide patients," Kate noted. "And, in this case, we don't have any clue if he's had anything to do with these people committing suicide because only one survived, who is in the hospital, Danny."

"That may not be true," Reese noted. "I have two women I'm trying to track down. They were part of the group, and then they stopped attending."

"Maybe they got better? Or are they dead?" Kate asked, taken aback.

"I'll let you know as soon as I find out."

Kate quickly ended the call and looked over at Simon, who nodded.

He explained, "That does kind of match up to what Danny told me. The thing is, if you're determined to commit suicide, you can make it sound like you're doing it, then turn right around and not be doing it, and it's not the doctor's fault."

"I understand that," she said, "but Danny said something about maybe turning around the words, especially for those who are on the edge of seriously following through with their suicide plan. And, if that's what Dr. Burnett's doing, that's a whole different story."

"And yet why though? And what does this have to do with the clinic?"

"It's all related," she said. "I just don't know how."

Then something caught her attention, and she stared off in the distance and pointed. "There." Then she took off at a run.

CHAPTER 23

K ATE SPOTTED DR. Burnett, sitting on a bench off on his own.

She walked up behind him, then sat down on the bench at the far end. Looking over at him, she said, "Hey, Dr. Burnett."

He just nodded, as if he'd already seen her coming, which of course he had.

"Bad day, *huh*?"

His shoulders sagged.

"Does *bad lifetime* describe it better today?" she asked.

"Bad lifetime for sure," he confirmed. "I loved my brother. I absolutely loved my brother. But that is nothing compared to how I felt about my sister. … She was my twin, and, when he killed her, … I just couldn't handle it."

She let him talk, while she tried to work her way through what he was saying. "Did he really kill her? I thought it was an accident."

"She was drowning, and he went in, but, instead of saving her, he held her under," he whispered, his voice breaking. "She drowned right in front of me. He kept telling me that it's what she wanted, but I got so angry that I couldn't … I *didn't* believe him," he said, almost in a trance state. "When he tried to get out, I kept pushing him back in, kept knocking him back in, telling him that he was lying, that he had deliberately killed her. Then he would laugh at me."

She let him talk and noticed the fury building in his voice.

"He was sick of the twins being special, tired of being a single child, when everybody else was a twin, tired of listening to our parents go on about how much better twins were. Tired of the way everybody was googly-eyed over us and ignored him. And he was right. It was true," the doctor added, his voice going soft. "Everybody loved us. We were a unique pair, and we were so very close," he shared in a wistful voice. "I was so lost without her."

"And your brother?"

"I had a big stick, and I was poking him in the chest, knocking him down into the water. He would try to grab it, and I would pull it away. When my father raced toward us, he saw that my sister was gone but dove in to save my brother. My father knew I was petrified of the water, and I couldn't jump in. I couldn't save Roger. I told my father that Roger killed my sister. My father told me not to be stupid, that Roger would never do that, but I could see in his expression that he was worried it might be true. Afterward, when I explained to both my parents what had happened, my father just hushed me up and told me that we weren't ever to speak of it again. But, if I couldn't speak of it again, I couldn't speak of her either," he whispered, tears in his eyes. He looked over at Kate, as if hoping so badly that she, if nobody else, could possibly understand.

She just nodded and waited.

"I loved her so much. We were so special together. Losing her was like having my heart ripped out."

"And your brother?"

"He was never quite the same. My parents hired a specialist, a doctor who kept saying that Roger would … that he should come back, that he would be much better. At one point in time, I declared, *That's good. Then he can go to prison.* My parents looked at me in horror, and the doctor asked me what I was talking about. My parents tried to hush me up, but I told the doctor what I saw, what I heard from my sister. The doctor asked my parents, wondering if it was an actual possibility. He asked if there was another witness to Roger's actions and told them that, if there were, it would be a real problem. He looked at my parents and said, *I know it's a tough decision.*"

Dr. Burnett let out a sigh and then continued. "But my mother was not willing to entertain the possibility of taking Roger off life support. On the contrary, she proclaimed that everything possible be done for him. I knew they would side with him. The specialist understood though. He looked over at me, and there was this … this connection between us.

"After this consultation with the specialist, my mother was beside herself, screaming and crying, demanding why I had said that, proclaiming that she would do everything she could to bring my brother back. And I was just numb. I was fourteen, and Roger was eighteen when this happened, but he ended up going into this special hospital. We would go like three times a week to visit him, as a family, but Roger never seemed to get any better and was generally worse, rarely communicating anymore, even with our mother now being his main doctor."

Dr. Burnett took a deep breath, but Kate dared not interrupt. "My parents struggled with that. They spent every penny they had, trying to help Roger. The specialist told them how he could do so much more for Roger outside of the confines of that hospital and all the rules, so they built the Haven Center to ensure Roger got the best of care, hoping there would always be something there that they could do for him. Thinking, with their own specialist in charge, they would have more say, so he became the director, where he remains.

"At one point in time he took me aside and asked how I was doing. I remember telling him that I was slowly recovering, but that the loss of my sister was so hard. He asked if I knew what would happen to my brother if he did recover. I remember looking at the vegetable in the bed, thinking that was unlikely, but the doctor reminded me of a marked improvement he'd shown only a few days before. He shared that there were all these promising new techniques they were trying, and, every now and then, it seemed like Roger was doing better.

"I looked at him and suddenly knew that he'd stopped Roger's progress somehow, and I asked him why. He hesitated, then nodded. The director asked me if I wanted him dead or in a coma. *Yes, I want him dead or in a coma.* The director suggested that it wouldn't be good if Roger were alive and fully functioning, that I wouldn't be safe. But maybe I just made that up in my head. Maybe I just wanted to believe that's what the specialist was thinking. Maybe I just wanted to believe that somebody was out there championing me instead of Roger." He turned to look directly at Kate. "Roger got his wish to be the favorite again. You know that, right?"

She stared at him. "What do you mean?"

"He enjoyed being the center of attention as the only child. Then, when we came along, everything changed for him, at least that's how he always told it. He felt my sister and I overshadowed him. But, after this, he was definitely the center of everything, and I faded into complete insignificance," Dr. Burnett stated, with a broken laugh.

"That suited me to a tee, and I just ended up as a nobody. Mother had always been so focused on my medical career, even when I was a small child. She had decided that I was gifted and would change the world by becoming a brilliant doctor. Always pushing, pushing. When she turned her attention to Roger, it was a break for me from the perfection she always demanded.

"Still, I plodded along, signed up for a college I did not choose, for a major I did not choose. Meanwhile my brother, my injured brother, was awake at times, not fully awake or fully okay, but better. Sometimes it seemed possible that he might make a full recovery. Then he would regress for a time."

Dr. Burnett went silent for a moment, then continued. "My mother went from one extreme to the other, on an emotional roller coaster. When Roger took another very bad turn after things had looked promising, ... she couldn't handle it. In her family trust document, she left me the house and money enough for my education, but the bulk of the family fortune went to my brother's care, to keep the Haven Center open, to ensure that Roger got the best of everything," Dr. Burnett explained.

"Then she went home one day and blew my father's brains apart. Then she drowned herself in the bathtub, something she had seemed obsessed with and had threatened or tried so very many times," he shared. "But finally she did it and took my father with her, and my life has never been the same again."

"Sounds like it hadn't been the same since your sister died."

His body sagged at that. "Everything inside me died that day, my love for my brother, my love for my parents. And then my love for my sister, even though still there, what good did it do me? My love for her caused me the greatest pain," he whispered. "It's been so hard." He looked over at her. "I've done so much to try and help people. Seriously I have. I've tried to save people who wanted to kill themselves."

"And yet there's that suicide group, where you haven't done very much to save them."

"That's because they don't want be saved," he stated earnestly. "Some people come to the sessions, and they really want to be saved and to go on to have a good life. Those … Those people I can help." He shook his head. "But then there's that other group, who tell me in private that it doesn't matter how much I help them. They will still go home and do this, and they just want me to facilitate it for them."

"Do they ask you to help them commit suicide?"

He nodded. "Yes, they do, just like Danny did."

"And yet Danny says that he was just really confused through it all."

"Of course he would say that now, wouldn't he?" he stated, with a headshake. "That's the nature of it all. They're so confused. They're so torn up on the inside from all the things they did, the terrible things they did."

"You mean, regarding the center? The place that your family's money goes to protect?"

"The center was a large part of it. My mother was a big advocate of taking a life, if that's what everybody wanted."

"Wait," Kate interrupted. "Are you talking about turning off life support and letting someone go, if their body could no longer sustain them?"

"That certainly happens, but usually in the more traditional hospital setting. Most of those patients don't come to the center. I'm talking about euthanasia. That's what she called it, not suicide. But when it came to my brother and letting go of him, she couldn't do it. It was obvious that my brother would be in that center for as long as his organic body could last, with all the assistance the center could provide. I was okay with that," he said. "I reveled in it. I wanted him to suffer for what he did. I wanted him to pay for it."

"Yet your mother wished to prolong Roger's life, even while she committed suicide?"

"Yes. She couldn't handle the ups and downs and the constant negative comments about Roger. At the end of the day, ... she just couldn't handle any of it," he said. "She never recovered from my sister's death, or maybe it was more about Roger being so *horribly ruined* in that same incident. He was her firstborn, after all. Suicide, euthanasia, and death in general was a theme in her life, even before losing my sister—as was water." Dr. Burnett looked over at Kate, gave her a small smile. "And still, you haven't asked that one question."

She stared at him for a long moment, processing everything, well aware that Simon was behind her, listening in. "You mean, the question about why your sister was drowning in the water in the first place?"

He smiled sadly and nodded. "Exactly. That question. Because she was trying to commit suicide too. My whole world is caught up with drownings and suicide, and it's just so frustrating," he murmured. "All I ever wanted was a peaceful, happy life."

"And yet you don't want your brother to have that. Even

now, you don't want him to have any peace?"

"No," he declared, his voice hardening. "He doesn't deserve it."

"So why did your sister want to commit suicide?"

He nodded. "That's the other question you need to ask, and, for that, the blame can be laid at my brother's feet yet again."

"So, he's the reason she committed suicide?"

"Yes. And when he realized she'd told our parents and what the repercussions would be for him, he made sure that she didn't survive," Dr. Burnett stated. "It was so hard watching her go under and stay under and me frozen, not able to go in after her. Roger called me all kinds of names, but I couldn't save her, and I sure as hell wouldn't save him," he added, staring off in the distance. "Not that I could anyway. I'm so terrified of water."

"And years later your mother blew your dad's brains out?"

"Yes, with his own service revolver," he replied. "She'd already tried to drown herself in the bathtub a couple times before. Our home life was never, ever a good place to be," he murmured.

"I'm sorry. … I'm still a little confused on all the details."

He laughed. "You and me both. It's been a lifetime, but it's over now."

"In what way?"

"My brother is gone," he shared, with a chuckle. "I put him out of his misery earlier today, mostly because I knew you were determined to find the truth, and there wouldn't be any way to stop a full investigation into the entire center," he acknowledged. "You really should look at everybody there."

"I intend to. I believe people there are being kept against their will."

"Oh, absolutely, but it's probably way too late to bring them back now," the doc noted, with a smile that unnerved her. "It's how the center kept the money coming in. Very few places will do something like that, you know—keep a family member in a manageable state, out of the public eye, out of the hands of the law, or whatever it might be." He shrugged.

"That was also my mother's brainstorm, though she never told my father about it. That was the big fight they had at the end of their lives, when he found out and just couldn't believe what she had put in motion. The cop in him was horrified. He was going to destroy it all. She couldn't let him do that, no way, not when she had put her entire life into it. But my sister's death, my brother's ongoing condition, Roger raping our sister, all had damaged Mother and had made her *off*, for want of a better word."

Kate winced at that, thinking back to Rodney's hit-and-run case and the actions of the mother there. "A mother's love."

"Yes. She wouldn't believe anything bad that anybody said about Roger. Despite his belief that he wasn't seen as special, he really was the apple of her eye. But no matter what anyone said about him being full of hatred and doing terrible things because we twins supposedly got all the attention, Mother wouldn't believe it. We might have gotten her attention, particularly in front of an audience, and the twin thing was a novelty, but Roger, her firstborn, really could do no wrong in her eyes."

He sighed. "I think when my sister told our mother that

Roger was raping her, that's when our mother's mind completely broke. She didn't want any more children to begin with and had never wanted twins. She thought it was terrible and had completely ruined her life in terms of all the things that she had planned on doing. She didn't even want to get pregnant again. My father wanted a second child, and, when it was twins, he was thrilled apparently, but, for her, not so much." He gave Kate a droll look. "Can you understand that?"

She shrugged. "This isn't about me. This is about you."

"Not for long," he replied, with a peaceful sigh. "I came out here for a few quality moments, before the chaos."

"What chaos is that?" she asked him.

"*You*. I knew you would figure it out sooner or later, even if you don't know all the details."

"It would really help if I did know the details," she added, with a small smile.

"Most of them are lost in time," he murmured, as he lifted his head to the sun, now dancing between the clouds. "I'm just tired, tired of trying to ensure my brother paid every minute of his godforsaken life for what he did to my sister. And trying to help as many people as I could, whether that was to help them *not* commit suicide or to help them do it."

"How many have you helped to commit suicide?" she asked.

"Oh, not that many. Maybe a dozen."

"All of them by drowning?"

"No, goodness no," he said, looking at her as if she were stupid or something. "Pills are easier. You just swallow a bunch of pills and go to bed at night. Most of the time they just want to talk to me beforehand."

"So, instead of convincing them not to do it, you gave them your approval or encouragement to go forward?"

"Is that so wrong?" he asked, staring off into the distance. "Just like me, people are tired. Tired of the fight, tired of trying to do everything right all the time, and getting very little for it," he muttered. "I spend hours trying to help my patients, yet it all comes down to the fact that we have so little available for them in terms of treatments. There is so little I can do that it just, ... it wears on me," he admitted, turning to look at her. "Don't you feel sometimes as if your job is not even worthwhile and how the world around you should just crash and burn? You take criminals off the street constantly. Yet here you are, worrying about somebody like me."

"You don't consider yourself a criminal?" she asked.

"Oh, gosh no," he replied, looking out at the water all around them. "Sometimes I wonder if I even know what I'm doing and why I'm doing it anymore. At some point, it just all became ... this blur."

"Except for your brother."

He glared at her. "Except for my brother." His voice hardened. "I've always known exactly what I was doing there," he muttered. "That one deserved everything he got."

"But it's over now, correct?"

"It is. He passed on earlier today, just in time."

"What do you mean by that?"

"Any investigation would mean a series of blood tests, a series of secondary doctor reviews, *blah-blah-blah*. I've managed to fake it all this time. I have been giving him medications that would keep him partially awake and in as much pain as I could but unable to tell anyone. Not all the time, of course, mixing it up, making it look normal, natural.

Sometimes I would even forget about him for a while. Life just happens. Then I would remember and get angry all over again, and I would doctor up his medicine," he admitted, with a smile. "I enjoyed knowing that he would suffer as long as I was. Like my recordings I made specifically for him. I presume you have those now."

She stared at him in shock.

He shrugged. "Hey, not all doctors care about their patients," he muttered.

"I would like to think that you care about some patients," she murmured.

"Of course you would. Everybody wants to think that," he noted, "and to a certain extent I do, but I'm just tired. I'm worn out physically. I'm mentally exhausted. I'm finished." He waved his hand about. "Now, if you don't mind, I really would like to be alone for a bit."

"You know that's not happening."

"Of course not. You want to take me in, to force me to answer a million questions, and to admit all the things I've done wrong," he stated, with a smile. "Instead, here you go." He held out a USB key.

"What's this?" she asked, as she slid closer to accept it.

"It's basically everything I've done over the years. Who I've helped, who I stopped from committing suicide," he said, "since I really should get kudos for those. Still, I have also given you the people you will fault me for in assisting in their suicide plans. Then, of course, my brother, but I have absolutely no regrets over him, not after what he did to my sister." With that, Dr. Burnett stood.

She rose too, and he looked at her and nodded. "I get it. I really do. I realize that you're just trying to do your job, but this is one time when you really need to back off."

"Why is that?" she asked.

He looked behind her, saw Simon, then nodded. "Have a good day, sir." And, with that, he turned and walked toward the end of the pier.

She watched him, then called out, "Doctor, I need you to come back and talk to me."

"Look at the key first," he called over his shoulder. "I'll be around for your questions afterward."

She quickly realized that wasn't true at all and raced after him.

He took one look, startled to see her coming behind him, and, like a jackrabbit, he bolted down the dock. Just as she got to the edge, he threw himself into the water.

Simon dove into the water, fully dressed, even as she jumped in herself, but ten fruitless minutes later, both of them breathing hard and bobbing at the surface, she looked over at Simon, and he shook his head.

"No sign of him. Did you notice that his coat pockets looked funny?"

"Yeah, but I don't know why," she murmured, as she pulled herself out of the water and sat on the edge of the dock, staring down at the darkness below. The dark waves still rippled from their every movement, but there was no sign of the doctor.

"I'm betting he had weights in his pockets."

She frowned at him.

"I'm pretty sure that he planned this as a way to go, now that his brother is gone," Simon noted.

"So he killed his brother, not anyone else at the Haven?"

Simon nodded. "Yes, I would say that's a safe bet."

"Jeez," she muttered. "I feel like this has been a complete shit show right from the start."

"It doesn't matter if it has been or not," Simon noted. "It's not as if you had a normal case, but you managed to sort it out, and you'll have an awful lot more to sort out when you see what he put on that key."

He pointed to where she had tossed her phone, wallet, car keys, the USB key, and her jacket onto the dock. She nodded, as she hopped to her feet, then looked down at her completely soaked body. "Dammit, not exactly how I wanted to go through my day."

"You don't have to," Simon suggested. "The *Running Mate* isn't very far from here."

"But it's not as if I left any clothes there," she pointed out, with a laugh, but she did look over at the yacht wistfully. "Maybe when this is over ..." She looked at him hopefully.

"Absolutely. A few days out on the water, for sure. But even sooner, a few hours with a picnic dinner, just to relax out there and to remember all the reasons why we do what we do."

"Yeah," she agreed. "I'll need that for sure. This will get particularly nasty." She groaned, as she picked up her phone and made the required calls. She turned and looked at him. "You may want to disappear."

He shook his head. "I'll stay."

"So, that telepathic conversation you had with Roger? You were probably a witness to his death, at least in your head," she noted, as they stood, waiting.

"Yep." He stared at her. "After hearing Dr. Burnett's confession, there's not a doubt in my mind now."

"Crap," she muttered. "I don't even want to think about somebody locked in their own body like that, completely incapable of moving, yet knowing full well what was happening to him."

"Exactly," Simon agreed, with a nod. "Whether Roger had anything to do with the sister's death or not, whether Roger had been raping his sister or not, Roger paid a huge price for crossing the doctor," he murmured.

"I don't even want to think about Roger potentially being innocent. I would at least like to think that there was some justice involved in this mess."

"Maybe," Simon replied. "But that doesn't mean that there is or that we'll ever find out the whole truth. And we can't put too much hope into that USB key you're hanging on to either," he added. "Still, it should reveal the mental state of Dr. Burnett at the end of the day." Simon looked around and said, "If you're okay, maybe I'll do my statement later."

"Sure. What will you do now?"

"Go home and change," he replied, looking down at his soaked clothing. "And then I'll head to the hospital."

"To talk to Danny?"

"Yeah, I think he should hear what's been going on and why. Better that it comes from me."

"Good enough." Kate nodded. "Let me know how that goes." Just then they heard sirens in the distance. "Go ahead and go. I'll handle this, the way I always do," she teased, with a wry smile.

"You should at least be happy to know that the doc can't do any more of what he was planning on doing. You put an end to that."

"And yet I still don't have all the answers. These drownings, the ones that he helped *facilitate*, as he called it."

"Yeah," Simon agreed. "*Helping*. But who was he helping? And in what way was that help being administered?" he asked. "Because they're dead, we don't have any way to know, and, because he's dead, you won't have anybody to convict."

"Crap," she muttered, with a nod. "What a mess. Get going. I'll sort this out someday."

She watched from the beach, as he took off, probably for a quick stop at the *Running Mate*, knowing that he at least would get a hot shower and could change into something dry, before going to his apartment.

Rodney was the first to reach her. "What the hell happened?"

She shook her head. "You won't believe it, and, until I have a chance to look at this USB key, I'm not sure I can give you all the answers, but I can share what Dr. Burnett told me. Basically our good doctor killed his comatose brother in the Haven Center earlier this morning, before Dr. Burnett jumped in the ocean here, intent on drowning himself. Both Simon and I went in after him, hoping to save him, but we couldn't find him."

Hours later the divers brought up his body. It had caught at the bottom, and she was told that there were, indeed, weights in his pockets.

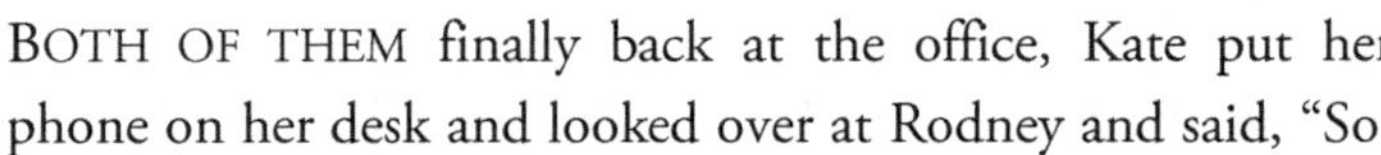

BOTH OF THEM finally back at the office, Kate put her phone on her desk and looked over at Rodney and said, "So, he really did plan it all. Hard to imagine."

"Of course he did. After everything you were uncovering, imagine what it would have been like for him in the public eye, once everyone found out what he'd been doing to his own brother, let alone all the rest of the accusations. Dr. Barnett was a trusted oncologist," Rodney stated.

Kat shrugged. "Something like that would have destroyed his reputation, then his career, and I don't think he could handle that."

"Yet he admitted to helping very specific people commit suicide," Rodney pointed out. "Even if he were alive, holding the doc responsible in a criminal sense would have been pretty difficult, even if he did encourage them."

"I know, but that's already something pretty major to share with the public."

"I'm just really grateful that you got to the bottom of it, and now it'll stop," Rodney said, "but in terms of charges? ... This is pretty well a case of there not being anyone left to charge."

"Oh, not so fast," she stated, giving him a fat smile. "We're already starting a deep dive into investigating the Haven Center and the people who have been paying very significant fees to keep their family members subdued."

"Crap, that's an awful thought," he muttered, as he stared at her in shock.

"Just when you've seen enough, and you think humanity is completely depraved, something like this comes along and proves you wrong." Then she laughed. "But, unlike our Dr. Burnett, I'm not giving up on my job. I'll keep putting assholes like him behind bars."

"Or," Rodney added, "in graves."

She winced. "Thanks, I really didn't need that."

"Maybe not, but, at the end of the day, it was his choice, and he took it. So, give it a rest. You done good, kid." And, with that, he gave her a high-five and walked out of the office.

It was looking like the doctor's USB key had given them enough to shut down the clinic permanently, and, with that, she had a certain amount of satisfaction that justice was being done somewhere. She worried about all the people in those hospital beds, wondering where they would end up—prison or a hospital—and if they would ever be healthy again. As for the employees at the center, they would be out of a job, probably never to work again in that field, but not that many were on staff. And frankly, despite their claims to the contrary, Kate didn't quite believe they didn't know something shady was going on. Kate had enough on her plate right now that someone else could deal with them.

She got up and walked over to Sergeant Colby.

He nodded at her. "Nice job."

She shook her head. "Finding the truth really sucks though."

"Sure, it does, but considering what you managed to achieve"—he gave her a grin—"I'm really impressed."

She laughed. "You won't be when you see all the piles of work ahead of us. The tons of reports and headaches I'll have to deal with will be mind-boggling."

"Oh, but that's your problem," he stated, with a big grin. "Not mine."

She rolled her eyes at that. "Thanks. Don't you have to at least read my reports?"

"Technically, but I can assure you. I'll employ my best speed-reading techniques." He chuckled. "I also want you to take a few days off, before any more craziness happens."

"Then I would just come back to find this investigation still center stage."

"That's fine, but I remember talk about the *Running Mate*. You can only be a true *Running Mate* if you're out there in the water."

"It wasn't named after me."

"Maybe not, but it suits you nicely. Just remember. It takes two to tango."

She laughed. "I don't know about that."

"Whatever. Just go, take a few days if you can, and, if not, make sure you book it in for the next little bit." He added, "There will always be crazy in our world. Remember that. It's just a matter of making sure that the crazy doesn't overtake your world."

She smiled, then nodded. "In that case, I'll see you later." And, with that, she turned, walked out, and headed straight to Simon's place and the crazy kind of sanity he provided in her chaotic world. As she walked into his living room, he was waiting for her, a glass of wine in his hand.

"Is it over?" he asked.

She shrugged. "It's ongoing when it comes to the Haven Center, but ultimately it's over, yes."

"Good." He smirked.

"So, how is your nightmare psychic life?"

"It's fine. I'm still processing the fact that I was apparently getting messages from a comatose patient who was essentially being tortured, but, hey, he's not here now, and hopefully he's a little more at peace."

"God, I hope so. I can't imagine anything worse."

"I know," he murmured. "The fact that it's over is just amazing." He held out a glass of wine for her and said, "To us."

"To us," she repeated, "and hopefully to another trip or two out on the *Running Mate.*"

"Now that is music to my ears." He laughed. "Tomorrow?"

She thought about it and nodded. "Yeah, tomorrow." And together they clinked their glasses in agreement. And joy.

This concludes Book 8 of Kate Morgan:
Simon Says… Swim.

Read about Kate Morgan:
Simon Says… Die, Book 9

Simon Says... Die: Kate Morgan
(Book #9)

Detective Kate Morgan arrives at a broken-down house, supposedly the site of a suspicious death, only to receive a screaming warning from Simon *not* to enter the building. Turns out, she had been given the wrong address but does find a dead body at the corrected address.

As Kate sorts out whether she has a Black Widow on her most recent case, Simon tries to help a homeless man, who ends up in the morgue—now one of Kate's newest files because that poor man's body had been found in the broken-down house. That's nothing compared to what else she finds on the premises.

Kate's investigations into these deaths confirms the two properties have connections, including linking Simon to the haunted history of the broken-down house.

When yet another homeless man is found dead at the broken-down house, Kate struggles to sort out the different threads, before the next man is killed—and this one might not be so homeless ...

Find Book 9 here!

To find out more visit Dale Mayer's website.

https://geni.us/DMSSSDie

Sneak Peek from Simon Says... Die

First Week of December

KATE HAD FAST become quite accustomed to counterbalancing work with some free time on the *Running Mate*, where they'd been spending more and more time out on Simon's newest purchase, even if just for a couple hours here and there, plus a long weekend or two. It was a perk of the relationship that she was more than happy to enjoy.

As she walked into the bullpen, feeling content, happy, and settled somehow, the others chimed in with a chorus of greetings.

She laughed. "I made it through three whole days in a row without any witching hour calls this time."

"Yes, but even *one* day on *that* boat," Lilliana said, with an eye roll, "talk about lucky."

"Yeah, you're right about that," Kate agreed. "Talk about lucky, and I don't feel guilty about it at all."

"Good," Lilliana replied. "That's the way to do it. Besides, with a dreamboat like Simon, you should be enjoying yourself."

Having never heard her say anything remotely like that about him before, Kate just laughed.

Meanwhile Rodney looked over at her and asked, "So, are you recovered?"

"Sure, as recovered as we ever have a chance to get, with

more murder cases coming in daily. I've still got some belated reports to finalize, but it's all good."

"Great. We just got a call."

"What kind of a call?" she asked, taking off her coat. "Are we going out?"

"We sure are. Some kids were playing around in an abandoned building, and they say they found a body."

"Did any adult confirm?"

"No, they phoned us first," he replied, with a bright smile. "We're getting the public trained in some ways."

She rolled her eyes at that. "Bet the kids went back."

He laughed. "I won't bet on that because, when it comes to kids, you can never tell, except that all too frequently they're up to no good."

"Ha, good thing I don't have any."

"Oh, but you will," he presumed, with a laugh. "This thing with you and Simon? That's likely to get *hella-serious* real fast."

She stared at him in shock. "Even if it does get *hella-serious real fast*," she replied, "that has nothing to do with having kids."

He just nodded and didn't say anything.

As they got into the vehicle, she asked, "Did they say anything about the body?"

"Yeah. It was dead."

She groaned, rolled her eyes at his sick joke, and added, "I gather you're doing fine."

"I am," he said, with a nod. "Life's okay. And now we have a little wiggle room at work. It seems like some of the crime wave has eased back a bit, so … it's okay."

"Except for this one."

"Yeah, but we get these things every once in a while. It's

probably a junkie."

"Maybe," she agreed, "at least then it's likely to be a fairly open-and-shut case."

They walked up to what was once a beautiful building, at least in her day, but now she looked like a grand dame in distress. Kate stopped outside, checked with Rodney on the address.

He confirmed, "Yeah, this is the place." He frowned, as he looked around. "It's a pretty high-end area for a junkie to die in."

"I'm surprised the neighbors haven't complained about this building."

"It's probably caught up in all kinds of legal craziness, city rules, zoning issues, whatever," he noted.

Her phone rang just then. She looked down and frowned. "It's Simon."

"Go ahead and take it. I hate to disturb young love. Go on."

She glared at him.

"Take it. Take it. You'll be fussing the whole time if you don't. He probably just wants to tell you how much he misses you," he teased, with an eye roll.

She answered the phone, with a panicked screaming Simon on the other end.

"I don't know where you are or what you're up to, but don't go in that house!"

She froze, looked over at Rodney, who was already walking toward the front door. "Rodney, come back," she yelled. "Wait. Come here."

He turned, frowned, and stepped back toward her. "What's the matter?"

She held up the phone, putting Simon on Speaker. "Simon, say that again."

"Do not go into that house," he roared. "I don't know anything about it, but, all I can tell you is that, if you go into the house, the outcome will not be good."

"When you say *not good*, what do you mean?" she asked cautiously.

"Going inside that house means you'll die."

Find Book 9 here!

To find out more visit Dale Mayer's website.

https://geni.us/DMSSSDie

Author's Note

Thank you for reading Simon Says... Swim: Kate Morgan, Book 8! If you enjoyed the book, please take a moment and leave a short review.

Dear reader,

I love to hear from readers, and you can contact me at my website: www.dalemayer.com or at my Facebook author page. To be informed of new releases and special offers, sign up for my newsletter or follow me on BookBub. And if you are interested in joining Dale Mayer's Reader Group, here is the Facebook sign up page.
http://geni.us/DaleMayerFBGroup

Cheers,
Dale Mayer

About the Author

Dale Mayer is a *USA Today* best-selling author, best known for her SEALs military romances, her Psychic Visions series, and her Lovely Lethal Garden cozy series. Her contemporary romances are raw and full of passion and emotion (Broken But … Mending, Hathaway House series). Her thrillers will keep you guessing (Kate Morgan, By Death series), and her romantic comedies will keep you giggling (*It's a Dog's Life*, a stand-alone novella; and the Broken Protocols series, starring Charming Marvin, the cat).

Dale honors the stories that come to her—and some of them are crazy, break all the rules and cross multiple genres!

To go with her fiction, she also writes nonfiction in many different fields, with books available on résumé writing, companion gardening, and the US mortgage system. All her books are available in print and ebook format.

Connect with Dale Mayer Online

Dale's Website – www.dalemayer.com
Twitter – @DaleMayer
Facebook Page – geni.us/DaleMayerFBFanPage
Facebook Group – geni.us/DaleMayerFBGroup
BookBub – geni.us/DaleMayerBookbub
Instagram – geni.us/DaleMayerInstagram
Goodreads – geni.us/DaleMayerGoodreads
Newsletter – geni.us/DaleNews